NO MAN'S DAUGHTER
THE OATH OF WOE
BOOK I

T.H. ABRAM

CONTENTS

ATTRIBUTIONS

Cover Art and Design: Nada Orlic
http://erelisdesign.com/

Chapter Icon Design: Asha Akter
https://www.upwork.com/freelancers/ashaakter1

For the many orphans of the world.
Life did not give you an easy beginning,
but great things await you
if you rise and sieze them.

Know that you are loved,
and that the world needs you.

PROLOGUE

THE PROPHET OF THE LIDLESS EYE

No more dusk and no more dawn: such was the divine will of the sun.

Torches and braziers kept the large cavern lit, chasing away shadows with every pulse and flicker of their lapping flames. A small army of the faithful stood shoulder to shoulder in the tight space, sweat rolling in rivulets and further darkening their blood-orange robes, and all eyes were on him: the Prophet of Ankhatun.

The prophet stood opposite his followers before a stone slab that served as an altar, drinking in the glory of the moment. Tomorrow they would march on Qasira, the city of idolaters, worshippers of not only the Sun, but of Moon and Stars: false gods and goddesses, and shepherds of darkness.

Ever since he was a child, the prophet had taken great pains to keep himself bathed in light, reveling in the glory of day and struggling through each blackness of night, fighting back the dark with fire. Even if his mother hadn't disappeared into the cold night when he was young, he never would have trusted the dark. And certainly from the time he had received the divine mandate from Ankhatun to usher in the one who would free the world from the diurnal cycle, the prophet had been convinced of his righteousness and that the dark and its followers should be destroyed. He was a harbinger of the inevitability to come, and he had but a small part to play.

The infant on the altar in front of him was unusually quiet; he had learned that crying and mewling didn't earn him the attention he wanted. "Soon, little one," the prophet said, laying a hand on the baby's head as the boy sat on the warm stone, looking up at him with glassy eyes. "If only you knew the privilege of serving as the vessel of the one to destroy the night."

The prophet raised his muscled arms and addressed his faithful. "You are not fools," he said, his powerful voice carrying through the natural cavern further carved and dug into the canyon wall that was their refuge, "to believe in the beneficence of night! No, you are blessed of the light, of the sun and the only true god: Ankhatun! You are hierophants of his ways and heralds of his arrival, and you know the lies of those who worship the false gods of moon and stars; that any god that would hide from daylight only to shine in the darkness is no god at all."

He let the echo of his words ring and fade as the eyes of the faithful looked up at him in awe. "We shall resist the harlot moon, mother of the nightfall, and smite her foul worshippers on shafts of eternal sunlight! Tomorrow, we march on the idolaters!" he declared. "Tomorrow, we summon the eater of night, and this child will be his vessel, his doorway! To usher in the Diurnal Kingdom!" He carefully lifted the chubby baby boy under both arms and lifted him up in display. The child squirmed against his firm grip, and the prophet's followers cheered and shouted uplifting prayers and declarations of impending triumph.

"We must make our final preparations," the prophet said, setting the boy down, careful not to let him fall as he sat and swayed unsteadily. "And then, when the sun next rises, it will never again set."

His followers were ecstatic, holding their arms aloft in celebration, stirring themselves into a frenzy. The loud praise and cries of euphoric mania made the baby whimper as he held himself unsteadily upright. The prophet paid the infant no mind; he would not exist tomorrow, instead serving a greater purpose.

CHAPTER 1

GIDEON

GIDEON KNELT in a quiet corner of the barracks away from the others. The last rays of sunlight through high windows lit the big, open bay of beds and wooden trunks that had all been pushed to the edges of the room. His fellow recruits had cleared an area and were cheering as they tried to goad a pair of captured mice into racing one another across the wood floor. Their jeering and hollering buzzed in Gideon's ears as he tried to focus on the silent prayers he had learned in his time at the monastery.

Three months had passed since Gideon had left his hometown of Wintry to make the long walk to Rivenwood Monastery, where ordinary folk could enlist in the service of the Holy Order and train to become warriors in the service of the gods and their Holy Light.

Gideon had grown up on stories of old heroes wielding blades of manifested holiness, serving as executors of the gods' will, and shielding the innocent from evils while keeping the darkness at bay. Once he was old enough, all he thought and dreamt about was joining the ranks of the Holy Order, of serving the gods and becoming more than just a fisherman in a frozen village. He wanted it so bad that he was willing to give up everything and everyone he'd ever known to have a chance to prove himself worthy. So he'd bid farewell to his parents and sisters, and set off to chase his fate.

Gideon had arrived at Rivenwood Monastery with little more than the shirt on his back and a pair of travel-worn shoes, but the paladins there had seen something in him. He was naturally broad and sturdy, and a lifetime spent helping his father reel in the huge marlins of the Salient Sea had made him strong enough to be confident in starting his training.

The life of a fisherman's son had done little to prepare him for the rigors the Holy Order inflicted on its recruits, however. Long days were spent training in the sparring pits, learning to sit and ride a horse, studying the nature of the Holy Light, and learning to read. When they weren't training, the recruits were toiling in the kitchens, the latrines, or the stables; finally, at sunset, they would file into the monastery's chapel and recite their prayers and meditate on the justice and mercy of the gods.

Now, all of that was about to come to an end. Their training was complete, and tomorrow Gideon and his fellow recruits would undergo the trials to determine if they would be chosen to join the ranks of the Holy Order. Gideon's aspirations, all he'd wanted his life to be, would be decided tomorrow, and he was so nervous he could scarcely keep his hands from shaking.

As he prayed, he clenched his fists and tried to steady his breathing, but it was to no avail. As his mind wandered and the rote prayers did nothing to soothe his mind, he gave up, opened his eyes, and ran a hand through his long blond hair in exasperation.

"What's wrong, Gideon?" a voice asked behind him, and he glanced over his shoulder to see his friend Donnal walking up. "You look glum."

Gideon sighed. Donnal had proved a good friend to him over the course of their training, and he was unflappably optimistic — which was usually refreshing — but right now, the last thing Gideon wanted was encouragement.

He shook his head. "Nothing. I'm just a bit nervous for the trials tomorrow."

"What are you nervous about?" Donnal asked, and then he laughed and nudged Gideon's arm. "A strapping fisherman's son like you? You'll be a shoo-in for sure!"

"It's not the battle trial that's worrying me," Gideon said, looking out the arched window at the green monastery grounds. "I'm... afraid I won't be able to invoke the Light when they tell me to."

Donnal frowned and nodded. "Well, they say not everyone can do it. But even if we can't, you know we'll both be picked to be in the knights auxiliary — Sir Cormac basically said as much already."

"That's not enough for me," Gideon said quickly. "I don't want to be just a soldier." Restless, he pushed past his friend and started pacing nervously in the lane between rows of cots. "I've studied the texts, I've meditated, I've prayed. I've done everything they told me. But when Battlesister Gerda talks about feeling a connection to the Light, I just... don't. I feel dull inside, like a lump of clay, like I'm not meant for anything."

"Now, don't be daft," Donnal said, trying and failing to suppress a grin. "I'm sure there have been plenty of dullards who still managed to wield the Light."

Gideon frowned and sat down on the edge of his cot. He'd been feeling this way for a few weeks and had told no one, not even Donnal. He knew he should feel grateful for the blessings he'd been given. He'd grown up the son of a poor fishing family and now had the chance to become something greater by joining the Holy Order, whether he could invoke the Holy Light or not.

But he didn't care. Being a paladin was all he wanted, all he'd ever cared about. And here, on the eve of his trials, he was terrified he wouldn't be able to do it.

A droning horn call sounded from outside, and Gideon looked up at Donnal. "The call to formation?" They hadn't been expecting anything until evening prayers.

Donnal shrugged. "Let's go see what it's about." Gideon stood as the other recruits, gathered around the improvised mice racing track, scurried to put everything back where it belonged, and Donnal put his arm around Gideon's shoulder and flashed a daring grin. "Cheer up, eh, Gideon? The whole world's before us, whether we're paladins or not." He swept his hand in front of them like he was painting a beautiful vista of the future. "And it all starts tomorrow!"

Gideon forced a smile and nodded, but couldn't come close to matching his friend's enthusiasm.

The recruits filed out of the barracks, and the sun was a low orange blaze on the horizon. Gideon shivered as he and Donnal joined the throng of recruits as they headed to the chapel, and he couldn't say whether it was because of the cool evening of late spring or his persistent anxiety over the trials to come.

At the big arched doors of the chapel, beneath the twin stained glass depictions of the two founding saints of the Holy Order, Battlesister Gerda Dawnhammer stood in her weathered plate armor, waving the recruits inside the chapel. The dwarven woman was of diminutive stature compared to the human recruits, but her perpetually grim demeanor made her seem twice as tall.

"All in!" she growled, tossing her long, thick red braids behind her.

"Quite a lovely evening, eh, battlesister?" Donnal asked as he and Gideon filed past her.

The dwarven woman's pale blue eyes flashed. "Shut it, Crieg," she snapped in her rolling dwarvish burr, but Donnal just grinned as the crowd shuffled them forward, past her.

The interior of the chapel was large and high-ceilinged, and the air smelled of incense and old candle wax. At the far end, above the altar, was another mural of the saints approaching the seat of the gods to receive the gift of Holy Light. Gideon had found comfort in the quiet and contemplation of prayer since his arrival at Rivenwood, but now the iconography just reminded him of his imminent failure.

As the crowd of recruits filled in the rows of pews, Donnal nudged Gideon. "Oh, there's Teli!" he whispered, and he unceremoniously shouldered in front of a few other recruits to go sit by the reluctant third member of their little trio. Gideon felt his heart thump a little harder in his chest as he looked at the young woman sitting stoically in the pew.

Nefteli hailed from Akhum, a land far distant from West Umbria and Rivenwood Monastery, and her sun-touched skin and curtain of perfectly plaited black braids made her stand out among the fairer folk of the north. Nefteli was quiet, intense, and fiercely determined, and Gideon always felt a little breathless when she looked his way.

As Donnal settled down next to her, Nefteli graced them with a sidelong glance before returning her gaze to the front of the chapel.

"Hey, Teli," Donnal said with a grin, "are you excited about the trials tomorrow? Gideon's scared he won't be able to invoke the Light, but I told him he just worries too much."

Gideon bristled, and Nefteli turned her head to look at him, making her curtain of braids sway. "If the gods will that any of us should call upon the Light, then we will," she said calmly. "Worry has no place in it. It either will be, or it won't."

Gideon frowned, and his face flushed. "Right," he agreed, bemused. "You're right, of course."

To his surprise, Nefteli reached across Donnal and patted Gideon's knee. "You will be fine, Gideon," she said softly.

An uncomfortable heat built in his chest. "Thanks, Teli," he murmured.

Donnal cleared his throat noisily. "You know, Teli, I've been feeling awful nervous about the trials, too," he said, trying to sound piteous. "I bet a hug from a pretty girl would make me feel better...."

Nefteli rolled her eyes and gave him a dismissive wave, but as she turned her attention back to the front of the chapel, Gideon saw a subtle smile play across her lips and the hint of a blush color her proud cheeks.

"On your feet!" a booming voice called, and all the recruits leapt up and stood at attention as Sir Cormac mounted the raised dais at the front of the chapel and turned to face them. The old paladin was a titan of a man, standing head and shoulders above most others, his gleaming plate armor only adding to his bulk. His weathered face was exposed by the uplifted face guard of his steel helm, and his huge, bushy white mustache swept out grandly to either side. His temperament was about as friendly as Battlesister Gerda's, but Gideon had been nonetheless in awe of the man since their first day of training.

The recruits all stood silently for a moment in the pews, and then the shuffling of feet and the clack of the bishop's crosier sounded from the chapel entrance.

Bishop Delwyn, the aged priest who ministered the monastery and oversaw the training of new recruits, hobbled down the aisle, resting on his tall staff, the head of which was ornamented with the symbol of the Holy Order: a gold-wrought tome pierced by a hefty steel sword. A small man with stooped posture, the bishop looked frail but had a kindly, wrinkled face that belied his nervous and fretful demeanor.

As Bishop Delwyn took his place at the pulpit and looked out at the assembled recruits, Battlesister Gerda and a handful of the monastery's clerics and hospitalers came up behind, and Sir Cormac gave the order for the recruits to resume their seats.

"Young warriors," the bishop began, "tomorrow you will take the first steps on your journey to serve the Light and the will of the gods. Tomorrow, we will see who among you has the potential to be inducted into the ranks of the Church Militant and carry our banner into the far corners of the world, or join the Church Merciful, and bring the healing Light to the sick and wounded."

Bishop Delwyn paused, and his brow furrowed with concern. "But before that happens," he said gravely, "we have a very serious matter to discuss. Up until this point, you have trained in martial implements and tactics, and in the mundane healing arts of the clerics; all valuable tools of the lay members of the Holy Order.

"But what remains is to see whether any of you possess the ability to invoke the Holy Light. It is what defines the Churches' greatest warriors and healers. Only the pure of heart and righteous of purpose may call upon the Light," he explained, "but not all who are righteous are capable. Such is the nature of the Light, that the gods ordain who among the faithful may invoke its power. Sir Cormac and Hospitaler Lucas will explain further."

The old bishop stepped down from his pulpit, and the monastery's resident hospitaler stepped forward, his gold-laced white cassock painted over with a mosaic of colors by the dying sunset rays spilling through stained-glass windows. "You've all heard the clergy here speak of the Holy Light," he said, his voice smooth and even. "You've been encouraged to pray and meditate in an attempt to kindle a flicker of that Light within you, or fan one that may already reside there. Perhaps some of you have felt that flame, and perhaps others haven't."

Gideon flushed at Lucas's words and bowed his head to hide his face.

"Either way," the clean-shaven clergyman continued after a purposeful pause, "if you are to pledge your service to the Holy Order, in any role, your understanding of the Light must be more profound. Doubtless, you've heard tales of the great heroes, calling upon the Light to smite their foes or bring the wounded back from the brink of death.

"And in your time here, you've heard the clergy talk about the two bodies of the Holy Order: the Church Militant and the Church Merciful. It is the gods themselves that dictate this division, for the Holy Light can be used to mete the gods' violent justice, or it can mend the most grievous wounds and even heal otherwise incurable illnesses. But never the same at once."

He paused and looked over at the towering paladin. "Sir Cormac," he said with an inviting gesture, and the old man gave a growling cough to clear his throat.

"The Oath of Weal or Woe," he said gravely, his booming voice reverberating off the ornate architecture of the chapel interior. "The vow by which a paladin swears never to use the Light to heal, and a hospitaler never to use it to wound. Thus was the third injunction of

God-King Ulicron to the saints, that mortal kind should never corrupt that which the gods gave us."

He paused, clasping his huge, gauntleted hands behind him with a clank. "To recruits like yourselves, this might seem a strange restriction: if a paladin can invoke the Holy Light to strike down a foe on the battlefield, why should he not turn and use the same to help an ally rejoin the fight? And why, if a cleric of the Church Merciful can call on the Light to heal a dying soldier, should they not reach out to stay the hand of a killer? The gods command it, but why?" He snorted. "If it's theology you want, seek out the ecclesiasts."

A handful of scattered chuckles among the recruits was quickly stifled as Sir Cormac's squinted gaze swept across the pews, and he scowled behind his huge mustache. "I'll put it plainly to you, the only way an old soldier can: to draw upon the power of the Light to kill another being comes with a hefty price — it leaves a mark upon the soul, one never to be removed. Over time, such marks accumulate and shape that soul into something different than what it was. A paladin's soul becomes that of a warrior, a slayer; an agent of the gods and a conduit of their will, to be sure, but also a destructive force expected to snuff the life from those who choose evil and apostasy."

"Similarly," Lucas added, "a hospitaler of the church must be free of the inclination to violence, which is anathema to a healer. The instinct to nurture and care must be protected from mankind's naturally brutal ways, so they can utilize the healing powers of the Light without fearing spiritual compromise." The man bowed his head and withdrew to join the bishop and other clergy members off to the side, leaving Sir Cormac alone on the dais.

The old paladin watched the other man go, then turned back to the rows of attentive recruits. "You all understand what's been said?"

"Yes, sir!" they all cried in unison, as they'd been trained.

Sir Cormac harrumphed. "You do, eh?" He looked over and nodded at a pair of monastery guards, who withdrew to a side annex at his signal. "We'll make sure of that before you leave here this evening."

His tone was ominous, prompting Gideon to glance at Donnal, who shrugged. A moment later, the guards returned, guiding a shackled man dressed in plain sackcloth up to the apse where Sir Cormac awaited.

"Who is that?" Donnal whispered.

Gideon shook his head, a chill running down his spine as the mood among the recruits palpably shifted. "I don't know," he murmured.

Battlesister Gerda moved to stand beside Sir Cormac, her head barely level with the man's plated belt, and faced the recruits. "This man," she said, gesturing toward the prisoner, "was recently apprehended thieving from the chapel's coffers in Wendover. He was tried in the courts of the Umber King and found guilty of the crime. Wendover's sheriff was kind enough to send the man here to the monastery for justice to be administered as a demonstration."

Hushed murmurs rose from the crowd of recruits, and Donnal's eyes went wide. Gideon glanced past him at Nefteli; her face was as stoic as ever, her eyes fixed on the scene playing out before them on the dais.

Battlesister Gerda motioned, and the guards dragged a wooden chair to the middle of the dais and placed the prisoner onto the seat. The man's head had been shaved, and his features were gaunt, but he didn't look much older than Gideon himself. The guards unlocked the manacles binding the man's wrists, then tied his right arm to that of the chair with a sturdy rope.

"Now," Sir Cormac boomed, silencing the recruits, "on your feet! I'll not have you lounging about on your duffs as you witness a man lose his hand, criminal or not."

The recruits clamored to their feet, and Gideon felt his stomach twist into knots. The air was thick with tension, and the prisoner's breathing was labored as his eyes darted between Sir Cormac and Battlesister Gerda.

"Please," the man said shakily. "Please, I was only trying to provide for my boy. He was so hungry, and I couldn't find work, and—"

Sir Cormac's heavy hand closed on the man's shoulder. "You've had your chance to plead already, son," he said firmly, but not unkindly. "Don't further dishonor yourself by mewling now."

The man's mouth opened and closed twice as he stared fearfully up at the massive paladin, but he finally shut it, the muscles of his jaw tightening as he gave a small nod.

"Lucas, Sister Josephine," Sir Cormac called, and the hospitaler came forward joined by one of the chapel's clerics. "Give him a clean cloth to bite down on, will you?" the old knight asked of Sister Josephine, and the woman obliged, retrieving a white linen bandage from her satchel, folding it, and holding it up to the prisoner's mouth. He took it furtively, and then bit down on it hard.

Sir Cormac took a coiled scroll from one of the guardsmen and unfurled it, glancing over the document. Then he lifted his hard gaze back to the recruits. "Whether you fancy yourself a warrior or a healer, there's no room among the clergy of the Holy Order for the squeamish — if I see any face turn away, I'll have the whole lot of you spending the night mucking the latrine. Understood?"

"Yes, sir!" the recruits responded, but few of them looked as confident as they sounded.

"Very good."

With a wave, Sir Cormac gestured for the hospitaler and the cleric to stand off to the side as Battlesister Gerda unslung the gold-adorned warhammer at her belt and held it in both hands. Her steel boots clanked on the polished marble as she stepped over in front of the nervous young prisoner and nodded up at Sir Cormac.

The old paladin cleared his throat again and began reading off the scroll he held before him, squinting to make out the words in the low light. "Hear ye!" he announced, and everyone in the chapel listened attentively. "Cillian Carston, son of Rupert Carston, you have been found guilty of theft from the Holy Order of Saints Oronos and Thylessia and sentenced to have the offending hand severed at the wrist. Under the holy authority of Archbishop Sigismund, and by order of Umber King Galain — I, Sir Eustace Cormac, hereby charge Battlesister Gerda Dawnhammer to carry out the sentence. May the Light of the gods and the king's justice guide your soul back to righteousness," he added, looking down at the trembling young man.

Gideon couldn't quite believe he was about to witness a man have his hand severed in the apse of the monastery chapel, and he chanced a quick look around to see everyone else's expressions. Most of the other recruits had their jaws set, but a few seemed to mirror his own trepidation. Fearing the seemingly all-seeing gaze of Sir Cormac, Gideon quickly fixed his eyes forward once again as the battlesister widened her stance and hefted her hammer over one shoulder.

The dwarven woman's lips moved in a silent prayer as she entreated the gods to allow her to invoke the Holy Light, and a moment later, a warm golden glow enveloped the head of her hammer, taking the shape of a large, squared axe blade.

The prisoner bit down hard on the folded cloth and squeezed his eyes shut, his chest heaving in panicked breaths as Battlesister Gerda adjusted her grip and measured her swing to ensure a clean cut at the wrist. Sir Cormac stood stoically, replacing his gauntleted hand on the young man's shoulder, and the clerics, guards, and recruits all watched in silence as Gideon held his breath without realizing it.

The battlesister's jaw flexed as she lifted her gleaming, Light-wrought axe over her head, then brought it down with a grunt, her thick red braids swinging with the effort. The brilliant gold axe blade met no resistance as it burnt cleanly through flesh and bone and sinew, and the man's hand fell limply to the floor. A brief stream of crimson spurted from the wound, and the man's muffled howl made Gideon shiver as he struggled not to look away.

The scent of burnt flesh and singed hairs mixed unpleasantly with the lingering incense, and the man's screams died out to a pathetic whimper as he slumped in the chair. His breath came ragged through his nose, his teeth still clenched around the linen rag. The glowing axe head slowly dissipated in a shower of upward-floating golden fragments of light, and Battlesister Gerda turned away and slung her hammer on her belt, her face an emotionless mask.

Gideon heard someone behind him struggling not to retch as Sir Cormac beckoned to the awaiting Hospitaler Lucas and Sister Josephine.

"You've seen the destructive power of the Light," the huge paladin said as the hospitaler took a knee in front of the prisoner. "Now witness its mercy."

Gideon shifted to look between the rows of recruits in front of him to watch as Brother Lucas whispered prayers of his own as he laid a hand on the man's wound, stemming the rhythmic flow of blood, and a golden glow, similar but softer, emanated from the healer's hand and enveloped the severed stump.

Cillian's eyes slowly opened as the gentle Light worked on his wounded wrist. His brow knit together as the pain eased, and he tentatively glanced down at where his hand had been. The hospitaler's muttered prayers ended, the Light fading, and he withdrew his hand, revealing the healed limb, closed over with healthy, intact skin as though it had never been wounded.

"With one hand the gods mete justice, and with the other grant mercy," Sir Cormac boomed out across the pews. "Never forget that." He gave a nod to the guards, and they came and hoisted the dazed-looking man up by his arms, then escorted him back out of the chapel. Gideon watched them go, but the tension remained.

The old armored paladin glanced down at the severed hand lying amidst a small, coagulating spatter of blood on the reflective marble floor. He stooped and picked it up. "So you understand a bit better now, I think," he said. "The gods' Light is perfect, both in its vengeance and its kindness. Sadly, we are not. And thus, the separation of the two churches, to prevent our dire iniquity from polluting the grace of the Light and the gods' purpose. During your trials on the morrow, you would do well to remember these things."

His gaze swept intently over them once more as he teased one side of his mighty mustache. "Your Reverence," he said at last, "they are yours." And with that, he rejoined the other clergy as Bishop Delwyn doddered back up to the pulpit.

"Thank you, Sir Cormac," the old man said before clearing his throat noisily and feebly lifting both arms up. "Let us thank the gods for their perfect justice and mercy, and pray that our young friend will choose a better path now that he has paid for his crimes."

The recruits all knelt and bowed their heads, and the bishop led them in their nightly prayers, thanking the gods and praying for their blessings and guidance for the trials ahead. But as he knelt on the hard stone floor, Gideon's lips moved on their own, reciting the prayers absently while his mind wandered. All he could think about was how unprepared he felt for the trials, how simple being a paladin had seemed when he was just a fisherman's son, and how much more real and dangerous it felt now.

"Are you coming, Gideon?"

He looked up as he was pulled from his reverie to see Donnal and Nefteli looking back at him, and realized the bishop and clergy had left, and the other recruits were filing out of the chapel.

"Oh, right," he said, rising quickly and following them out into the cool evening, only half-present.

CHAPTER 2
SADIA

Sadia knelt in the dried-out, abandoned cistern that was her home, humming quietly to herself as she attempted to patch a tear in her little brother's trousers with an old fishbone needle. A dozen tallow candles strewn about the place gave her just enough light to work by, and the little girls she called her sisters were chatting quietly among themselves inside the makeshift tent they had set up in the corner.

The old, weathered plank door that sealed off the cistern from the world above squeaked open, and Sadia glanced up at it. A moment later, her brother Yusuf's head poked through, upside down.

"Who's hungry?" he called out with a big upside-down grin, his long dark hair hanging down and his eyes sparkling.

There was an instant clamoring from the little girls — Zara, Mirah, and Imani — and they scrambled out of the tent, giggling excitedly. Sadia smiled and set aside the trousers she'd been mending as Yusuf's head disappeared to be replaced by their other brother Reza climbing down the knotted rope ladder into the cistern, followed shortly by Yusuf, a small sack slung over his shoulder.

"Look what we have!" Reza exclaimed as he jumped off the third rung. "Yusuf found a little passageway that led to a room filled with food, and I was the only one small enough to fit in it!"

Sadia raised her eyebrows at Yusuf. "A room full of food?" she asked incredulously. "And who did the food belong to?"

Yusuf shrugged as he set down the sack and began pulling out loaves of bread and blocks of cheese.

"I have no idea," he replied, not looking at her. "It was just lying there."

Sadia sighed. "Where, exactly?"

"One of the rich houses where the princes live!" Reza answered. "There were giant rats in the basement guarding the food, but I defeated them!" he declared brazenly, pulling his beloved sling from his pocket and loading a pebble. "They leapt at me and tried to gnaw my face off, but I got them right between the eyes!" He swung the sling over his head before Sadia could stop him and sent the pebble pinging off the far wall.

"Reza!" Sadia scolded him, and the boy demurred and hid his sling away.

"It was quite the battle," Yusuf agreed with a grin as he tossed the boy a small date. "I believe you mentioned the giant rats had long, venomous fangs, too, no?"

Reza brightened, placing his hands on his hips and holding his head up high. "That's right! Huge fangs! But I defeated them all by myself. And I didn't get bitten once!" He looked up at Sadia. "The food is the reward the princes gave me for defeating them."

"Of course it is," Sadia said, but her eyes were fixed on Yusuf. "You were very brave, Reza."

"The bravest!" Reza agreed, nodding sagely.

"Come, you two. Sit down and eat," Yusuf said, passing out bread, dates, and hard cheese.

As Reza and the girls tore hungrily into the food, Sadia laid a hand on Yusuf's shoulder. "Can I speak with you, please?" she asked.

Yusuf sighed heavily but nodded. She motioned toward the far end of the cistern, away from the children. She and Yusuf walked over and stood, staring at each other.

"I thought I made it clear that I don't want you stealing from anyone," Sadia said quietly. "We're already outcasts — the last thing we need is the city guard hearing word of orphans stealing from the princes!"

"Well, what else are we supposed to do?" Yusuf said defensively, throwing his hands up. "Amir hasn't had any work for me in three days — Reza and I spent all day going around to the people who will usually toss us some crumbs, and no one had anything to spare. We had to find food somehow, didn't we?"

"There has to be another way, Yusuf," she insisted, wringing her hands. "Stealing isn't worth the risk."

"Oh?" he asked sarcastically. "And what bounty did you bring home from washing today?"

Sadia shifted uncomfortably. Each day, when Yusuf and Reza went out to look for any work, Sadia took the girls with her to go wash clothes for the merchants and wealthy families in the city. She had barely brought home enough coin to buy one small flatbread. Usually, between both their earnings, they were able to buy enough to keep them all from starving.

"I..." Sadia started, then sighed. "No more than usual, but—"

"We're starving, Sadia," Yusuf said, a little quieter. He stepped forward and took her hand. "You and I are all that's keeping them from that, but it's just not enough. We need more than we're able to earn."

Sadia felt her stomach sink. He wasn't wrong, but the thought of guardsmen catching Reza and flogging him, or worse, throwing him to the crocodiles in the river as was sometimes done to thieves, struck a deep fear in her heart.

Yusuf squeezed her hand as an array of emotions played across her face. "I promise you," he said, looking her solemnly in the eyes. "I won't let the city guard catch us. I'm far too clever for them," he added, a cocky grin lifting the corner of his lips. Then he raised his voice so the children would hear him. "And Reza is far too brave. Isn't that right, Reza?"

They looked over to see Reza, with a mouthful of cheese, leap to his feet and strike a heroic pose. She shook her head and sighed again, but couldn't keep herself from smiling.

"Fine," she conceded. "But please, be careful. And if you see a chance to make some honest money, take it. The city will eventually give us a chance, if we can only keep ourselves together. And if they don't think we're thieves," she added poignantly.

Yusuf's face fell. "This city doesn't love us, Sadia." He let go of her hand. "And it never will. If we're going to make it, it'll be on our own — no one will help us."

"Yusuf," Sadia began, but he cut her off.

"Enough of that for now. Come — let's eat before the little ones make it all disappear."

As Sadia watched, Yusuf walked back over to the children and sat down next to Reza, putting his arm around him. Reza immediately leaned into him, still chewing, and the little girls chattered happily as they portioned out food for everyone.

Sadia smiled in spite of herself and joined them.

THE NEXT DAY, Yusuf and Reza set out, and Sadia took Zara, Mirah, and Imani to go ask around for washing that needed to be done in the hopes of earning the mercy of the wealthy noble families of Qasira.

"Do you remember when we used to live in the alleys, and that one day, you and Yusuf found Mirah?" Zara asked Sadia as they walked along the dusty street toward the wealthy areas of the city. "That was the best day of my life!" she declared happily, and threw her arms around Mirah's neck, hugging her tight.

Sadia glanced over at the young girl, who was maybe about six years old. She had first met Yusuf years ago, when they were both quite young. He was an orphan like her, and they had both ended up living on the streets, scrounging to survive, sleeping on abandoned rooftops or in dilapidated buildings. Over time, they had found each of the children in their care, and slowly built their own little band of siblings.

"That was a good day," Sadia agreed with a smile, patting the girl's head.

"I remember," Mirah chimed in, wrapping her arms around Zara in return and smiling. "And it was the best day for me, too!"

"I don't remember anything," Imani said, her eyes downcast.

Sadia stopped and knelt in front of the girl.

"You were very little when Yusuf and I found you," she said softly, stroking her cheek. "You were barely walking. We found you lost near the city gates."

Imani looked up at her with tears in her eyes. "Did... did my mother leave me there?"

"Oh, no, sweetheart," Sadia said quickly, pulling her into a hug. She held the little girl's head against her chest. "I... I don't know what happened exactly, but that's alright, because we have each other, don't we? Yusuf and I will always take care of you."

"Promise?" Imani asked, her voice muffled against Sadia's dress.

"I promise."

"I wish Yusuf and Reza would find us a house," Zara said suddenly. "Then we wouldn't have to wash other people's clothes for them."

"We have a house," Sadia pointed out. "It's not like other peoples', but it's ours." They had talked long enough. She stood and beckoned the girls to follow, allowing no more talk of hopes and dreams she knew would never come true as they pressed on up the sloping hill toward the merchants' manors.

⚜

AFTER BEGGING at a few different wealthy estates, they finally managed to find an older woman who took pity on them, and allowed them to take a handful of her dressing gowns down to the little tributary nearby. The water was shallow, and the girls were able to splash around and play a little while Sadia washed.

Sadia hummed quietly to herself as she scrubbed the old woman's silky garments, trying not to think about how the simple nightgown was nicer than anything Sadia had ever owned. Other washerwomen were gathered in little cliques, tending to the needs of other households. Few of them ever spoke to Sadia, as they considered her a thief, robbing them of further business by garnering sympathy for her lowly status.

There was one woman, though, who would sometimes come over and wash beside Sadia, and she did so today. Her name was Basma, and she was a hired servant for the al-Hekhet family, which was one of the wealthiest families in the city.

"I don't know how you do it," Basma said as she scrubbed at a particularly dirty spot on one of the fine, embroidered dresses.

"Do what?" Sadia asked, glancing over at the older woman.

"Live like you do. The way those people treat you, it would break my spirit. How do you bear it?"

"I have no choice," Sadia said simply as she laid the wet garment out on a rock to dry in the sun.

Basma shook her head. "I know you're just al-Yetim, but they are too cruel, truly."

Sadia felt her neck flush at the term 'just al-Yetim', but she bit her tongue. It was Qasiran society's word for orphans: the fatherless, sons and daughters of no one, with no lineage, no history, and no family. Just al-Yetim.

"It's fine, Basma. Truly," Sadia said, forcing a smile.

Basma sighed, rinsing the pretty dress in the river, then pulling it back out and wringing it dry. "Oh, are you going to the offering of prayers and blessings the priests of Ankhat Naharia are doing tomorrow? I am, but only later in the day. My husband won't have it that I go all day and leave the little children with him for so long."

"Oh," Sadia replied, trying not to let the disappointment show on her face. "No, I'm afraid they don't allow al-Yetim inside the temple."

"Of course, I know, dear," Basma said happily. "This offering is being held in the central bazaar! There are to be blessings, and no one can stop you from going to the bazaar, so you can come! Of course, you will have to bring some offerings in order to garner the good graces of the priests, but I'm sure you'll find something, won't you? It will be wonderful!"

"I don't really have anything to offer..." Sadia said, trailing off as her heart sank.

Basma waved a hand dismissively. "Don't worry, I'm sure you'll think of something. You should go and beg for Naharia to bless you and your siblings with her protection," she minded the younger woman.

"Yes," Sadia agreed, wringing out a light cotton dress. "Yes, I will try, Basma."

"Good girl."

Sadia would have loved to ask special blessings of the priests for her little family — they needed the gods' kindness so badly, and when else would she have the opportunity to ask? But they had so little to eat, let alone offer.

As Basma finished her wash and packed up her things to return to the al-Hekhet estate, Sadia bid her goodbye and promised she would think about going. The whole rest of the day, she and her sisters were only able to get two other aristocratic women to take pity on them, and by the end of the day, a mere three silver drahm clinked quietly in the secret pocket of Sadia's dress as they walked back home. It was enough to buy a small and unsatisfying supper at best, but luckily, they had saved half of what Yusuf and Reza had brought home the day before.

When they finally arrived at the collapsed adobe house whose cistern they lived in, she found that Yusuf and Reza hadn't yet returned, so she and the little girls portioned out the remaining food and made a game of guessing what their future husbands would look like.

After a short while, the plank door squeaked open and Yusuf and Reza clambered down the ladder.

"Yusuf!" Imani cried happily, running over to him and wrapping her little arms around his waist. "What did you find today?"

Yusuf hoisted her up into the air, then sat and settled her on his knee. "Nothing today, I'm afraid, little dove. The world is not kind to the poor."

Imani's face fell, but Sadia swept up and laid a hand on each of their shoulders. "It's alright, we still have the food from yesterday. We'll be fine," she assured the little girl.

"Did you have any luck today, Sadia?" Yusuf asked, looking up at her hopefully.

Sadia frowned and looked away. "Just three houses today."

Yusuf nodded. "Tomorrow will be better," he said confidently, forcing a smile. "Come, let's eat and forget our troubles for tonight."

Sadia smiled weakly back at him, then lifted Imani off his knee and brought her over to the little circle of discarded blankets and fabrics they'd set up to sit and eat on.

As the girls started eating and Yusuf joined them, Sadia saw Reza hanging back in the darker shadows on the far wall. "Come and eat, Reza," she called to him, but he didn't move, though she could see the candlelight reflected in one eye as he looked at her. "Reza, come," she said again, more firmly, and the boy reluctantly slunk over toward her.

When he came into the light, she gasped. The right side of his face was swollen and red, starting to turn a deep blue, his eye held closed by the swelling. "Oh, Reza, what happened to you?" she cried, falling to her knees and taking his head in her hands.

"Nothing, I'm fine," he mumbled, pulling his head back.

"Who did this to you?" she demanded.

Behind her, Yusuf sighed. "He just... fell, Sadia. We were walking through a busy part of town, and he wasn't watching where he was going. Isn't that right, Reza?"

Reza nodded and tried to pull away from her, but she held him still. "Is that what happened?" she pressed, forcing him to look at her with the one eye that could. He squirmed in her grasp, and she knew it was a lie. "What really happened?" Sadia asked firmly, and when Reza still refused to answer, she looked over her shoulder at Yusuf.

The older boy held her gaze for a moment, but then he sighed and shook his head in frustration. "We tried to steal from another rich house today," he admitted. "I sent Reza inside, just like before, but... one of the servants caught him and...."

"And beat him." Sadia finished for him.

Yusuf nodded guiltily.

"Oh, Reza," she sighed, stroking his hair and pressing his head against her, her heart breaking for him. "I told you it was too danger-ous!" she said to Yusuf, unable to keep the anger from her voice.

"I know," he replied, hanging his head.

Sadia was furious, but as she realized Zara, Mirah, and Imani were all looking at her nervously, she took a deep breath. "Just... stay away from those houses. From now on, you find an honest living. I won't have you stealing anymore. It's not worth the risk," she said sternly.

"Sadia, it's not that simple," Yusuf argued. "If we don't—"

"No more stealing, Yusuf," she snapped. Then she pulled Reza closer. "Please, I'm begging you," she said more softly. "For all of us. We'll find a way."

Yusuf and Reza looked at her in silence, and she could tell neither of them was convinced.

"Let's just eat, please," Sadia said wearily, not wanting to fight further.

And they did, mostly in silence, as Sadia's frustration with Yusuf was palpable.

"You're not eating, Sadia," Zara said after a while, looking up at her with a worried expression.

"I'm... I'm saving mine," she answered. Yusuf gave her a quizzical look, and Sadia sighed. "Basma, the washerwoman who talks to me sometimes — she told me the priests are offering blessings tomorrow in the bazaar. I'm going to bring my food as an offering."

Yusuf scowled. "What? Why?"

"So that we can beg the gods' favor," Sadia replied simply. "We need it, Yusuf."

"Where have the gods ever been for us? They won't be any more kindly to you because you give them some food, Sadia."

"You don't know that."

"I do. And the priests won't waste the gods' favor on al-Yetim. They hate us — they curse us!"

"Please, Yusuf, just let me do this."

Yusuf's jaw clenched, but he said nothing.

"Fine, then," Sadia said, pushing her meager portion of food toward him. "I'm not hungry. Take it, and give some to the little ones."

Yusuf sighed, and his face softened. "If you want to go and try to get the priests' blessing, I won't try to stop you."

"Because you'll come with me?" Sadia said, and it was much more of a statement than it was a question. "We'll all go, together."

Yusuf stared at her, exasperated. "Fine. We'll all go." He ripped the last little bit of bread he had in half and handed one piece to Reza, then shoved the other in his mouth. "And we'll pray the gods can send us food since we won't be out finding work."

Sadia said nothing and simply nodded. She had no doubt that Yusuf thought she was being foolish, but neither did she have any doubt that he would go with her tomorrow. And that was enough.

CHAPTER 3

GIDEON

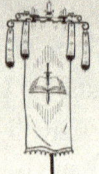

GIDEON, Donnal, and Nefteli walked along with the rest of the recruits as they made their way across the monastery grounds to the mess hall, where their evening meal awaited. Gideon found himself walking in a daze, still shaken by witnessing that man lose his hand, and even Donnal's jokes and banter failed to assuage his nervousness.

"Can you believe they did it right there in the chapel?" Donnal asked as they all sat down at the end of one of the long wooden tables. "And what do you think Sir Cormac will do with that severed hand, eh?"

Nefteli shot him a disapproving glance. "They did it to impress upon us the weight of the Oath," she said, "to make us realize the true nature of what we are being called to do, and the choice we must make if any of us can invoke the Light."

"I understand all that," Donnal said, shoving a large cut of pork into his mouth. "I just mean, they could have done it out near the monastery gates where we usually assemble." He swallowed and patted his belly as he belched. "Would have made the same impression, I think. And saved the nice shiny floor being stained with blood."

"Nothing the clergy does is hidden from the sight of the gods," Gideon muttered absently as he pushed his boiled potato cubes around, not having any appetite. "That's what Battlesister Gerda said when we started our training here. Nothing happens without the gods knowing and guiding it somehow."

"Yes, exactly," Nefteli agreed, carefully separating out her food. "You would do well to listen better, Donnal."

Donnal grinned, then leaned over the table and looked between both his friends. "So which will you choose? For the oath, I mean, the one Sir Cormac was talking about?"

Gideon looked up at his friend, surprised. He hadn't even considered the matter, so consumed with the idea of trying to invoke the Holy Light at all. His dream had always been to be a paladin, a holy warrior, but he'd never even heard about the Oath of Weal or Woe from the grey-hairs in Wintry telling their hearthside stories. He shook his head. "I... I don't even want to think about it until the trials are over."

"What about you, Teli?" Donnal asked.

Nefteli glanced up, a flicker of something in her eyes. "I... would like to be a hospitaler, if the gods permit me," she said, her voice low. "It is a noble calling. Gods know my people need all the help we can get, after the Serpent Kings...."

She trailed off and looked down at her plate, and Donnal turned his attention pointedly to Gideon. Their pretty but secretive friend had shared glimpses of her past, of her homeland, but had never betrayed much, and they'd learned not to press her after Donnal had earned himself Nefteli's considerable ire a few days into their training.

"That's very admirable," Gideon said, but Nefteli just nodded absently.

"Aren't you going to ask me?" Donnal asked after a pause, his eyes darting between them.

Nefteli sighed. "Which would you choose, Donnal?"

"Oh, me?" Donnal smiled broadly. "Why, I'm flattered you're so curious! I would choose the Oath of Woe — can you imagine what it would be like to cut a man in half with a sword made of light?" he asked, marveling at the idea. "That's a life worth living, right there."

Gideon looked at him dubiously, and Nefteli wrinkled her nose at the idea, but Donnal rolled his eyes. "Oh, don't look at me like that. You heard Sir Cormac — paladins have to have that sort of mentality, right? Violent and whatnot."

"He did not mention taking delight in it," Nefteli reminded him indignantly, and Donnal laughed.

"Don't borrow trouble, you two," he said, chuckling and shoveling more food into his mouth. "I won't be able to invoke the Light, so there's no fear of Donnal the Mighty laying waste to his enemies with the power of the gods."

Gideon cocked an eyebrow. "You seem confident of that."

"Oh yes," Donnal answered around a mouthful of food and rapped a knuckle on his head. "I've always been about as sharp as a sanded plank. The gods won't give a dullard like me the power to conjure the Holy Light."

"That is a very uncharitable way to describe yourself," Nefteli chided, frowning. "You are more clever than you think, Donnal."

"No, I'm not," he replied happily, pushing his empty plate away. "But I am loyal. And tall. And devilishly charming. And handsome!" He grinned again. "I'm sure the Holy Order can put at least some of those attributes to good use. And it'll be better than slaving away in ever-fallow fields like my father did, gods rest him."

Nefteli's stern gaze softened at that. "Well," she said, giving a small, hesitant smile, "there are many paths within the Holy Order. I am sure you will find something that suits you."

Donnal laughed. "Thank you, Teli. I'll simply be honored to share the company of two Light-wielding holy warriors such as yourselves after the trials tomorrow." He gave them both a little bow, and frowned as he saw Gideon still fretting. "Not still nervous, are you, Gid? I told you, there's nothing to it."

Gideon frowned. "I just want to pass the trials so badly, and I'm afraid... if I fail...."

"You won't," Donnal said firmly. "Look at you — big, strong, and your hair's even golden! You were born to be a paladin! Are you going to finish that, by the way?"

With a sigh, Gideon passed his plate over. He appreciated Donnal's confidence but didn't share it. The three of them lingered for a while as Donnal devoured his second plate, then rose and walked over to turn in their dishes.

"Two plates, Crieg?" one of the monks on kitchen duty asked as Donnal handed over his and Gideon's tableware. "I think that's enough to qualify you for cleanup detail." The old man smiled menacingly, showing a handful of missing teeth.

Donnal hung his head and sighed. "Yes, I suppose it does, Brother Almin." He turned to Gideon and Nefteli. "Go on and save yourselves," he muttered, clearly pained.

Gideon didn't hesitate — cleaning up after fifty recruits was never an enjoyable detail, and the monks were always quick to choose 'volunteers' randomly. There was no arguing with them, either — Sir Cormac had made sure they all learned that the day they'd arrived at the monastery.

Nefteli followed him out of the mess and out into the cool night air of West Umbria. The shadow of the mountains loomed high up to the west, but the rest of the sky was a blanket of stars, and a pleasant breeze blew down through the monastery grounds from the north.

As the two walked back towards the barracks where they were all housed, Gideon's mind was finally pulled from his troubles as he was painfully aware of Nefteli strolling easily beside him, and just her presence was enough to make him anxious for an entirely different reason. He'd realized a few days ago that once training was over, their service to the churches might take them to different corners of the earth, and as much as he would miss Donnal, the thought of never seeing Nefteli again hurt him somewhere deep in a way he didn't fully understand.

Gideon's mind raced as he tried to think of something to say to her, and feeling the awkward weight of silence as he couldn't come up with anything.

"Are you still nervous?" she asked after a bit, sounding as calm and even as ever.

Gideon felt himself blush, frustrated that he hadn't been able to think of something to say. What a useless lump he was. "What? No," he answered fearfully, then realized what she'd meant. "Oh, about the trials, you mean." She gave him a curious look and nodded. "Well... a bit, perhaps." He rubbed the back of his neck and sighed. "A little, yes."

Nefteli smiled and shook her head, then looked up at the stars. "If it is the gods' will for us to invoke their Holy Light, then we will. You are too concerned with what you want, Gideon, when you should focus on fulfilling the gods' plan for you instead."

"What?" he asked. "No, I... I just want to—"

"Yes, exactly," she interjected, "you want. Stop that. Don't think about what you want."

Gideon opened his mouth to defend himself, but shut it and clenched his teeth, embarrassed.

"Don't be angry," Nefteli said with a smirk, her eyes twinkling. "You know I am right."

Gideon frowned, but his heart softened a bit. "Fine," he admitted at last. "Yes, you're right. But am I wrong to think I could better serve the gods as a paladin than as just a regular soldier in the knights auxiliary?"

"Yes," she said simply, and he threw his arms up in frustration. "You are wrong because you cannot know what the gods have in store for you, or the path they intend you to walk."

"You have your own plans, though," he noted defensively. "You're going to go home to Akhum, right?"

Nefteli came to a halt, and her face darkened. "That is different. My people need help, and I will petition the Holy Order to send aid, whether I can serve as a hospitaler or merely a cleric. And if the gods deign not to fulfill any of my hopes, I will accept this, too."

Gideon shook his head. "You're much better than I am. I can't be that... patient." She didn't respond, but studied him with hard eyes, and he squirmed under her inquisitive gaze. "I'm sorry," he finally said, "I didn't mean to make light of... whatever's happening in your homeland. I'm sure it's important."

She sighed, but her expression softened. "Thank you. I will tell you one day."

"That would be nice," Gideon said.

"You and Donnal both," Nefteli amended with a half smile. "I can tell you both have been wondering."

Gideon nodded as the two walked on through the night towards the barracks. "Of course."

As they reached the doors of the women's barracks, Gideon was again painfully aware of the petite, beautiful girl beside him, and he had an urge to ask if she'd sit out under the stars with him a bit longer. He swallowed nervously, not wanting to say goodnight yet, but the words didn't come out.

Nefteli nodded at him. "Sleep well," she said.

Gideon smiled, trying not to show his disappointment, and bowed his head. "Goodnight, Teli."

He turned and took a step, but froze when he felt her hand touch his.

"Have faith, Gideon," she said softly, but didn't meet his gaze, "and trust the gods." She let go, turned, and quickly slipped into the women's barracks.

Gideon stood staring for a few long moments, his hand tingling where she'd touched it, and finally took an unsteady step back, shook his head clear, and made for his own barracks.

CHAPTER 4

SADIA

❦

THE NEXT MORNING, Sadia and Yusuf gathered the children and walked through the streets toward the bustling bazaar. They were silent most of the way, and Yusuf held Mirah's and Zara's hands while Sadia carried little Imani on her hip. Poor Reza had woken up with even greater swelling on his face, despite Sadia's best efforts to clean him up with a washrag before he went to sleep, but the prospect of going to the bazaar had rekindled his adventurous spirit, and he walked purposefully a little ahead of the rest of them, leading them onward.

As they entered the bazaar, they found it lively and crowded with people. It was always a busy place, but the throngs of people seemed to have tripled in size that day. All of Qasira was out, it seemed, and they had gathered in the open-air maze of the market. The city guards were present, stalking through the streets in pairs in their silver armor and stunning white hooded cloaks, their long spears glinting in the morning sunlight and blades flashing at their hips.

Reza marched proudly past the usual stalls and pavilions housing vendors and merchants, and Sadia smiled as she watched him walk.

The little boy was fearless, and she envied him that. The scent of fresh fruit, spiced vegetables, and roasted meat permeated the bazaar, and Sadia had to fight to quiet her raging stomach as they passed it all by on their way toward the center.

There, the priests had erected an ornate and lavishly decorated temporary shrine in the middle of the bazaar, and dozens of priests stood outside on raised stone platforms, offering bowls arrayed at their feet as they preached, prognosticated, prayed, and pleaded with the gods for intercession for those who gave an appropriate offering.

Sadia's heart sank as they stood along the outside edge of the huge open area and saw just how many people were flocking for blessings. Even if the gods proved to be kind, Sadia had little hope of getting a priest to actually even hear her concerns.

"We should leave," Yusuf said beside her. "There's no point."

"No," Sadia answered quickly, and started moving toward the shrine. "If there's even a chance, we should try. Come on."

With a reluctant sigh, Yusuf followed after her, the rest of the children in tow. Sadia walked around hesitantly, hoping to find a line of congregants that was shorter, but the longer she waited, the longer the lines became. Eventually, she simply picked one and stood behind a woman wearing a veil and holding a young child against her.

"Yusuf, do you have the food?" Sadia asked quietly, turning to her brother.

He held up the small cloth sack she'd entrusted to him, and she took it for safekeeping.

"Good. Thank you." She turned back around and stood quietly.

They all waited as the sun slowly climbed in the sky, and the line they were in slowly shuffled forward at a painful pace. It wasn't long before Imani wriggled out of Sadia's arms to sit in a circle with her sisters, and Reza hung his head back, staring at the empty sky and sighing loudly.

"I'm so bored I'm going to die!" Reza complained, his swollen lip slurring his words.

"Shh," Sadia hissed, giving him a warning look. "Be patient, please. This is very important for us to do."

"This is stupid," Reza grumbled. "I'm going to go see Hafuz." He dashed off before Sadia could stop him.

"I'll go get him!" Yusuf volunteered a little too eagerly, and he, too, hurried off into the crowd.

"Just... come back when you find him!" Sadia called, but both boys were already gone. She sighed and looked down at the little girls, who were sitting quietly, watching her with big eyes. "I suppose it's up to us," she told them.

"Boys are so impatient!" Zara declared, and the younger two nodded somberly.

The sun rose higher in the sky as they waited, and Sadia had to dab the sweat from her brow with her sleeve.

A sudden yelp from another nearby line of people made her jump, and she turned to see two men dragging a third before one of the priests. They held him by each arm as he trembled, yelling and rambling nonsense as he tried to wrench himself free from their grasp.

The older woman in front of Sadia sucked her teeth. "The poor thing," she muttered.

"What's wrong with him, Sadia?" Zara asked nervously. All three of the girls had huddled closer to Sadia's legs as they watched the man scream and thrash as the priest started praying over him.

"He's possessed by a spirit, dear," the older woman answered, looking down at Sadia's sisters.

"A spirit?" Zara repeated. "Like a ghost?"

"No, child," she answered gravely, "an evil spirit — an ifrit." She looked back at the possessed man piteously as she adjusted the baby in her arms. "Ifriti are evil fire spirits that roam the desert. They look for bodies to escape cold nights, and they break your mind if they get inside you."

Little Imani whimpered and started to cry, and Sadia picked her up to hold her. "No, no, don't be afraid. There are no ifriti here."

"Oh, I didn't mean to scare her," the woman said apologetically. She slid a finger beneath the chain of her necklace and lifted it to show them. "As long as you wear your protective scriptures, you...." She paused and peered closer at their bare necks. "You don't... doesn't your mother make you wear them?" she asked, sounding shocked.

Sadia bit her cheek as she stared at the little silver scroll coiled on the woman's slender necklace. Almost everyone in Qasira wore one — Basma the washerwoman had explained to her their purpose: holy words inscribed on sacred silver that served as a shield to ward away the evils of the world. They were given out at the temple in exchange for appropriate offerings, but al-Yetim weren't allowed within the temple walls, and Sadia never would have had enough to offer anyhow, as badly as she would have liked to have her siblings wear such talismans.

"We must have forgotten to wear them today," Sadia said, forcing a tight smile.

The old woman blinked. "But surely your mother wouldn't send you out without them! The world is too dangerous...." She looked back over at the man being exorcised by the priest, who was now screaming in agony. "Well... you should ask for scriptures while you're here today. I'm sure your father or mother will have something to offer, and—"

Sadia shook her head. "I'll be sure to remind her," she said more tersely than she'd intended.

The woman nodded and adjusted the delicate veil over her head. There was an awkward silence as the possessed man wrestled against the priests and screamed and spat at them. Sadia glanced down at the girls, who were still clinging to her legs, and did her best to comfort them all.

The exorcism continued in a morbid and painful display, and eventually Sadia was overwhelmed by the screaming and shouted prayers. Desperate for something to distract from the commotion, she reached out and gently touched the woman's shoulder, drawing her attention.

"Is it your child?" Sadia asked, indicating the infant in her arms.

"My grandson," she said, looking as uncomfortable as Sadia felt.

"I'm asking the priests to bless him and make him strong and wealthy so that he can provide for his family."

Sadia took a deep breath as the screaming persisted. "I hope the gods will hear your prayer," she answered politely.

The woman smiled, then cocked her head inquisitively. "And you? Your mother sent you here to...?"

"I..." Sadia began, her cheeks flushing. "Yes, she sent us to... for our brother," she finished quickly.

"His face got all big," Imani said, dried tears staining her face as she clung to Sadia's neck and looked over at the woman sadly.

"He's... disfigured," Sadia lied hastily, thinking of Reza's swollen face. "From birth. Our mother told me to ask for the priests' blessing to... fix him."

The old woman looked down at the girls at their feet, and her eyebrows crept up her forehead. "And where is your brother?"

"He wandered off," Sadia replied, squirming under the weight of the woman's gaze. "But he'll be back."

The old woman stared at her for a long moment, then nodded and turned back around, facing forward.

Time dragged on for a bit, the line crawling forward occasionally, and Sadia continually scanned the crowd behind her for Yusuf or Reza, but neither appeared. The exorcism finally concluded, and the possessed man collapsed, exhausted, and had to be carried out of the bazaar. He didn't look well, but Sadia supposed she should be grateful the priests were able to help him.

After a while, as Sadia and the girls were just a few places back in their line, the ornate, beaded curtains of the priests' lavish tent parted, and an elderly man in gilded, dark blue robes and a towering headdress exited, then shuffled up onto a stone platform nearby. A young acolyte followed him, carrying a large bowl. The elderly priest's robes were decorated with embroidery of suns, moons, and stars, and when he began to speak, his voice was strong and clear, projecting through the crowd.

"Blessed of Qasira!" he called, and the crowds all around the bazaar quieted. "Children of sun and moon, chosen of the stars! Do not despair, for the gods have not forgotten you!"

The old woman in front of them grabbed Sadia's sleeve and pulled her closer. "That's High Priest Nasir al-Moser!" she whispered. "He leads the prayers and rituals in the temple. His blessing would be more than a blessing; it would be a miracle! High priest!" she cried, waving her hand and stepping forward, but she was one of dozens of people now clamoring for the elderly priest's attention.

A group of strong young men in white garments pushed into the crowd, forming a defensive ring around the raised dais al-Moser was perched upon as he continued preaching.

"Come, bring your offerings," he called, his strong voice belying his wizened features, "and beseech the gods for their blessings!" The young acolyte beside him held the large, empty offering bowl aloft, then set it down at the high priest's feet.

Everyone around Sadia seemed to be taken by a sudden fervor, surging forward in desperation, their various offerings held aloft or even thrown toward the offering bowl. Sadia swept the girls up off the ground and gathered them around herself as they were jostled by the crowd.

"Great al-Moser! Please!" the old woman in front of them shouted, and Sadia's heart sank as more and more people shoved past her.

A hand closed around her arm and she looked up to see Yusuf, and a sense of relief washed over her. "Hey!" he barked at a man shouldering into them, "watch yourself!" He pulled Sadia and the girls back, away from the unruly throng, and Sadia saw the older boy was holding Reza by the back of his shirt in his other hand.

"I had to drag him back here," Yusuf said with a smirk once they'd extricated themselves from the crowd. "What's gotten into everyone?"

"It's the high priest," she explained, pointing at the extravagantly dressed man, "they all want—"

"Wait," Yusuf interrupted, his grip tightening on her arm, and Sadia looked up to see his brow furrow.

Following his gaze, she saw dozens of armed and armored men

entering the central area of the bazaar occupied by the priests of Ankhat Naharia. Their armor was different than that of the city guard: their hooded cloaks were a dark, bloody orange, and engraved on each bronze breastplate was an angry depiction of the sun, blazing, with a frantic pupil at its center.

"The Hierophants," the older boy muttered, taking a step back and pulling her with him.

"The what?" Reza asked, trying to peer through the crowd to see what they were talking about. The faces of the orange-robed men were set and stony, and they marched purposefully toward the high priest's tent, wickedly curved swords at their sides.

Yusuf leaned into Sadia and spoke quietly. "They're cultists. I've heard rumors about them for the last few months — they say they live out in the caves and canyons outside the city, and that they kidnap people and do horrible things to them...."

"I..." Sadia looked between the encroaching cultists and High Priest al-Moser, suddenly torn. "Should we go?"

Yusuf's jaw tightened. "I think we should—"

A booming voice suddenly thundered over the clamor, cutting Yusuf off. "O wretches of Qasira!" the voice cried, and a sudden, eerie silence fell over the crowd as all eyes turned to look at the speaker.

A tall, well-muscled man ascended the large stone platform where the priests had raised their lavish tent and were preaching from. He wore robes of dark blood-orange ornamented with bronze embroidery of a blazing eye rising over the horizon and a crown that looked like it had been twisted by hand into a frightening effigy of the sun. His garb, relative youth, and strength made him like a dark mirror of the Naharian high priest.

"The time for worship of the fell gods of moon and stars is at its end," the imposing figure said as he came to a halt at the edge of the stone dais, towering over the other priests and the crowd. His voice was like thunder, and the unnatural glowing hue of his eyes bore into those of the gathered faithful as his gaze swept over them.

The aged al-Moser looked the man up and down and answered, his own voice a little less sure than it had been moments ago. "Who would dare blaspheme our gods?"

The cultist leader sneered. "I am the prophet of the Lidless Eye, the ever-burning sun: the only true god of the cosmos." He gestured with his bare arms up at the sun, high in the sky. "And I am the harbinger of he who would drive away the night so that daylight might reign eternal."

"Bah!" the old priest scoffed, waving a hand. "I have no idea what you're talking about. You flout the laws of the gods of moon and stars and claim Ankhatun the Sun is the only god? Ha!" The old man forced a derisive laugh and coughed from the effort.

"I have heard of your cult of madmen, false prophet," he said after a moment, hoarse and looking warily up at the other man. "Take yourself and your misled followers from this holy place." The old priest had the temerity to shoo the man away with a gesture. "Flee, lest the emir have you chained to stones in the desert so that your strange god may devour you himself. I will not permit your heretical speech to be suffered by the good and faithful of Qasira."

The prophet didn't budge, his expression unreadable after the old priest's rebuke, but as the two men stood opposite each other, another surge of cultists dressed in their distinctive color entered the bazaar. These weren't armored, but each carried a single tallow candle that flickered with an oddly dark flame. Sadia stood, transfixed along with everyone around her, but she unconsciously reached out and gathered Reza and the girls closer to her as the candle-bearing cultists flooded the stone dais, and she was shocked at their number.

The prophet held up a hand, and a panicked murmur rose throughout the crowd of onlookers as the cultists surrounded the priests, their candles flickering in the midday sun. Al-Moser's acolytes shrank away, and Sadia's heart hammered in her chest.

"Sadia," Yusuf muttered through gritted teeth. "We should go."

She nodded, but remained rooted in place, unable to look away as the sense of incredible unease continued to build.

"The moon and stars will soon be dead and devoured," the prophet said, his deep voice carrying across the hushed bazaar. "Only the blazing sun will remain. No more dusk," he said, signaling to yet more cultists behind, "and no more dawn. Only the unsetting sun: Ankhatun's Lidless Eye." Another group of cultists made their way onto the dais, strong men carrying three large slabs of stone.

As the armed Hierophants gathered up the priests, a simple altar was assembled from the three hewn slabs, and then another cultist approached — a woman holding a bundle in her arms. After taking the bundle carefully from the woman, the prophet turned and placed it on the altar, holding it upright with both hands.

"Herd the ignorant cattle into their beloved tent," the large man ordered his followers over his shoulder as he began unwrapping the bundle.

The cultists obeyed without hesitation, roughly shoving al-Moser, the other priests, and their acolytes toward the entrance of the sprawling, lavish tent. Sadia saw the little bundle wriggle as the prophet unraveled it, and once the fabric came away, her stomach dropped as a very young child was revealed. He wasn't even a year old, she guessed, and he sat on the stone altar, blinking in the sunlight, staring up at the cultist leader fearfully.

"Yusuf," Sadia hissed, gripping his arm, and Yusuf took a step backward, dragging her and the children with him.

The cultist leader took his hands off the boy and lifted them up into the air, and his followers all began a slow, deep chant. "Swallower of the night!" the prophet cried, his orange-hued eyes wild and his muscled arms flexing as he held them out in supplication. "Tear the lid from the blazing eye, and let its withering gaze expurgate this world of evil and darkness!"

Yusuf tugged insistently on Sadia's sleeve, but she resisted, her eyes locked on the tiny child sitting on the altar, the corners of his mouth tugging down and his eyes glistening as he looked about fearfully at all the people around him. The sight of the poor, frightened child kept Sadia stuck in place even as Yusuf tried to pull her away, and the crowd around them churned chaotically as some people tried to mount the dais to help the priests, and others turned to flee.

"Guards!" al-Moser cried as he was shoved and pushed into the tent. "Where are the city guards?" Even as he wailed, the sound of conflict rose over the din of the crowd, and Sadia could see the emir's men pushing through the throng, spears and scimitars at the ready, and they were quickly met by the armored cultists brandishing their own weapons. The two forces met at the outer edges of the crowd, and the cultists fought to keep the central area clear for their prophet.

"Sadia!" Yusuf barked, finally succeeding in pulling her backward and away from the scene. As she was dragged back, her heart in her throat, Sadia watched the cult members finish herding the priests and acolytes into the tent.

"Conflagrate the idolaters," the prophet commanded, unperturbed by the appearance of the city guard. In unison, the candle-bearing cultists surrounding the tent stepped forward and held out their candles, allowing the dark flames to lick at the fringes of the tent's heavy canvas.

"Oh no," Sadia breathed as the deep blue, star-shot fabric caught and was engulfed by the strangely colored flames, like the smoldering orange burn of dawn as it crested the horizon. The panicked cries of those inside slowly turned into screams of pain as the fire ravenously devoured the sprawling tent. The horrible sound finally made Sadia look away, her stomach turning, and she instinctively reached out to cover her siblings' ears, even though she couldn't protect them all at once.

Yusuf led them through the teeming crowd, shoving his way through and making a path, but as they neared the edge of open space in the bazaar, Sadia turned back around, drawn by the infant on the altar. The prophet had turned and left him, approaching the burning tent as the cultists' chanting blended with the screams of the burning priests and shouting over all of it, crying out to Ankhatun and invoking the god's attention.

Sadia stopped once again, unable to move herself, as she watched the cult leader stop just in front of the pyre his followers had made of the tent. The city guard continued to clash with the armed cultists at the fringes, and the mad prophet cast his gaze up at the noon sun and bellowed, "Disgorge your eternal flame upon me, O Burning Ankhatun! Devour the idolaters, and let them fuel the fires that will scour the earth of their filth!"

Sadia sucked in a breath and held it as she watched the man plunge his arms into the inferno and hold them there, screaming as he stared into the flames lapping at his flesh. He shuddered violently, and then his screams faded, and he seemed calm. After a long moment, he withdrew his arms from the fire. They were wreathed in the dark, curling flames but somehow intact, drenched in the hissing, boiling blood of the priests burning alive within the tent.

The prophet whirled, flaming droplets of blood spraying off his fingertips as he held his arms out triumphantly. "Do you see the power of Ankhatun?" he screamed at the crowd, most of whom were attempting to run but were caught between the stampede and the fray.

Sadia finally looked back to her siblings and saw that Yusuf had pushed on, unaware that she'd stopped. He had Imani in one arm, and Reza was holding the hands of the other two girls as they tried to navigate the chaos. Yusuf glanced over his shoulder and stopped short when he saw Sadia hadn't followed. "Sadia!" he called, and waved frantically at her with his free hand, gesturing her toward them.

She looked back at the child on the altar, who was crying now, looking out at everyone around him with tears streaming down his plump cheeks as the prophet strode back over to him, his flaming, blood-soaked arms held out at his sides. Sadia didn't know what he planned to do to the child, but she was certain she couldn't let it happen without trying to stop it.

Turning back to Yusuf, she waved him away, pleading with her eyes for him to hasten the little ones as far as possible from the bazaar. Without waiting to see his reaction, Sadia turned and began weaving her way through the surging masses toward the altar. The mad prophet had begun chanting again, and the voices of his followers rose shrilly as he performed some occult ritual over the altar, drawing symbols of blood and flame that mystically hung in the air and pulsed with an energy that made the hairs on Sadia's neck stand on end.

The mystical sigils surrounded the baby, who continued sobbing as his little body was slowly lifted off the altar by some unseen force, drawn up to the center of the sinister ritual symbols the prophet frantically scrawled all around him. A man fleeing from the dais, a wild look of horror in his eyes, collided with Sadia, casting her to the ground, and she had to curl up as the crowd swarmed around her to prevent being trampled to death.

When she was finally able to scramble back to her feet, she cast her eyes up at the baby, and her heart leapt in her chest. His little body was in a state of rigor, no longer sobbing, but frozen, rigid, as the magical symbols pulsed rapidly around him. She watched in horror as his plump, healthy limbs began withering before her very eyes, and his skin took on a pallid hue.

The prophet was panting, his chest heaving, as he orchestrated the arcane ritual, his glowing eyes glazed over and his flaming arms flaring in time with the conjured sigils. A commotion rose above the deafening clangor as a small group of city guards broke through the line of cultists and rushed toward the prophet, their gore-stained scimitars held high. The prophet's head snapped around as one of the guards cried out, "Death to the heretics!" and raised his blade to strike the man down. Before his blade could fall, the prophet lashed out with an inhuman speed and wrapped his flaming hand around the man's neck, lifting him up off his feet and sending the scimitar clattering across the stone dais.

The man's scream caught in his throat as it was burned away to ash, and he fell to the ground, writhing and clawing at his destroyed neck as blood boiled up from the gaping wound and painted the sandstone dais crimson. The prophet rounded on the other guardsmen advancing on him, and Sadia took the opportunity to hoist herself up onto the dais and approach the altar.

The baby was still suspended midair as if bound in place, and she watched helplessly as his body withered before her, his chubby cheeks hollowing and his skin wrinkling and shrinking up tight against his bones. Sadia hesitated, unsure what to do or whether anything could even be done. But then the child's eyes flitted open and looked down at her, meeting her gaze, and she could see the hurt and pain reflected in them. Without thinking further, Sadia reached out and took him in both hands, then pulled him into her.

As soon as she took him, the fiery, bloody symbols hanging all around them exploded, throwing her backward through the air, and it was all she could do to keep the child clutched tightly against herself. She landed hard on her back, sucking the air from her lungs, but she wasted no time in scrambling back and checking the baby. He was so thin now, and frighteningly light in her arms, but he whimpered weakly and managed to look up at her before squeezing his eyes shut and shuddering in her arms.

A wild, violent shriek came from the center of the chaos, and Sadia looked up to see the prophet climbing back to his feet amidst the aftermath of the magical explosion, which had sent almost everyone on the dais flying and had shattered the burning tent, raining flaming canvas and timber down over the bazaar. He turned and trained his maddened, burning gaze on her and pointed. "The vessel!" he shrieked, and his followers leapt to their feet and dashed to obey the implicit command.

Sadia rose as quickly as she could and turned to run, and immediately collided with the hard steel of an armored Qasiran guardsman. He was flanked by a dozen of his comrades, and they were advancing toward the dais like a wall. The man shoved Sadia aside unceremoniously, focused on the rushing cultists and the burning chaos, and she was able to slip past, leaving them between her and the cultists now pursuing her.

She turned, clutching the baby to her chest with one hand, and with the other, she hiked up her dress and ran faster than ever before in her life.

CHAPTER 5

GIDEON

A HEAVY MIST hung over the monastery grounds, the soft yellow glow of morning sun casting ethereal shafts of light through the haze. All the monastery recruits stood at attention in formation, awaiting Battlesister Gerda as she climbed atop the elevated wooden platform to look over all of them.

Gideon struggled to slow his breathing. He and Donnal had awoken early to spar with each other and had practiced right up until the call to formation. Despite being sore and sweaty and out of breath, he felt ready for the combat trials, and was trying desperately to keep his nagging trepidation about invoking the Light tamped firmly down.

The diminutive dwarf stood looking over them, her hands clasped behind her back and her expression stern and imposing. "Well," she finally said, her rolling brogue ringing clear over the quiet grounds as the monks went about their morning duties, "today's the day, aye?"

"Yes, battlesister!" they all answered in unison. The excitement and apprehension among the gathered recruits were palpable.

The corner of her mouth lifted slightly in an uncharacteristic smirk.

"I can tell you're eager to get underway, but first, I want to offer a bit of hope to those of you who will inevitably fail to invoke the Light of the gods," she said evenly. "You can still be of great use to the Holy Order. You who aspire to be hospitalers can still serve as clerics, and failed paladins can be inducted into the knights auxiliary. Both of these lay roles compose the bulk of both churches, and there is no shame in joining their ranks. You may feel disappointed if the gods don't ordain you to access their holy gift, but understand that you are still needed.

"That being said," she continued, pacing a few steps and stopping again. "If you fail today in the trial of the Light, you will also have the option to return to your homes and pursue some other course for your life. You'll not be pressed into service to the Churches. So choose well — if you fail and decide not to dedicate your life to the Holy Order, know that you're giving up an opportunity to make a great deal of difference in the world, and on your own heads be it."

Gideon wasn't particularly inspired by her speech, but that didn't seem to be the battlesister's intent. She was a veteran warrior, he knew, and was more focused on practicalities than she was concerned with the feelings of a mob of raw recruits. It wasn't the first time he'd heard one of the cadre say something about it, but he'd never seriously considered what he would do if he couldn't summon the gods' divine light. He wasn't sure he cared what would happen to him if he failed.

A wave of quiet murmurings spread through the ranks, and Gerda lifted a hand to silence them. "In a few moments, we'll begin the trials. You'll be taken into the chapel in twos — one hoping to be a paladin and one a hospitaler. You'll understand why once you enter."

She flipped one heavy red braid behind her head, and the thick brass bead binding the end of it clanged against her armor. "When you've finished with your trial, you'll exit from the side door of the chapel and go straight to your barracks, understood?" The recruits answered together in the affirmative, and she gave a satisfied nod. "Alright, stand by for your name to be called. At ease!"

Battlesister Gerda stepped off the stage, landing heavily on the soft ground in her armor, and walked off, leaving the recruits to wait for their names to be called. Donnal and Gideon found themselves standing near the middle of the crowd of excited and nervous recruits, and Gideon found himself looking for Nefteli. He finally saw her, standing with the other junior clerics and speaking quietly with them, and he was too nervous to approach her.

Donnal nudged Gideon with an elbow and motioned toward Nefteli with his head. "Go talk to her."

"What?" Gideon asked, his heart suddenly thumping in his chest. "Why?"

"Ask her if she thinks I'm handsome," Donnal said, giving him a shove in Nefteli's direction.

Gideon felt his cheeks flush, and he got inexplicably angry. "You go ask her that if you like," he growled, returning the shove.

"It's not right if you ask a girl that yourself!" Donnal protested as he rubbed his arm. "Please, Gideon, I... I think I'm in love with her."

Gideon couldn't keep his eyes from widening at the statement, but then he scoffed. "I thought you were in love with some girl from Morningdew!"

"The girls back home are fine." Donnal waved a hand dismissively. "But Teli's special." He sighed wistfully as he looked over at the young woman. "I don't know if I could make it a day without seeing her, now that I know her."

As he stared at his friend, Gideon's hand slowly curled into a fist, and his teeth ground together. He didn't need to think about this right now. About Donnal chasing after Nefteli. The thought made him want to punch his friend in his handsome face, and the realization that he was jealous struck him with enough force that he took a step back.

Gideon shook his head, trying to clear the storm of thoughts, and Donnal finally looked over at him curiously. As he started to say something, another of the recruits walked up and clapped Donnal on the shoulder.

"What are you two lovebirds talking about, then?" James asked as he flashed a roguish smile.

Gideon forced his hand to relax and turned to look at their friend.

James was a few years younger than them — the youngest recruit currently in training at the monastery — and despite being under-sized compared to most of the others, he'd proven devoted and resilient in all of the training. The mischievous young man with curly red hair, freckled cheeks, and bright blue eyes had quickly befriended Donnal and Gideon upon their arrival, and the two had formed an unspoken agreement to look out for James during their time in training.

Gideon was surprised to see Donnal's cheeks redden a shade, and he turned his gaze to the ground as James leaned around him and waggled his eyebrows. "Ohoho, Donny boy," James crowed, "that Akhumite girl's got your eye again, has she? What was her name? Natalie?"

"Nefteli," Gideon snapped.

James shrugged dismissively and glanced back at Donnal. "Think she's interested, do you?"

Donnal glanced back up. "Why? Do you think she might be? Has she said anything about me?" He grabbed the younger man by the shoulders. "Will you go ask her for me? Gideon won't do it, he's betrayed me!"

Gideon grimaced as James shrugged Donnal off with a chuckle. "Alright, get ahold of yourself, mate. We're all heading separate ways after tomorrow anyway, like as not — what's the point in getting attached to some lass if we're never going to see each other again, eh? Focus on passing the trials so we can get on to better things."

Donnal's face fell at that. "I love her," he declared solemnly.

James threw his head back and laughed aloud. "Come now, Donny," he said, his eyes watering a little, "you're in love with a different girl every week! Wasn't it the pretty blonde you were swooning over just a few days ago?"

"Lillian?" Donnal asked, and all three looked over at the diminutive blonde, standing with her little clique, her trusted sidekick Meridith next to her. "Teli's different," Donnal said again, miserably. "And anyway, what would you know about love?" he demanded, reaching out and tussling James's mop of red hair. "You're just a little boy still. Does your mum know you ran away from home to join the Order?"

James smacked his hand away and landed a punch on his friend's shoulder. "You've only got two years on me, you dolt! And besides," he added, unable to suppress a prideful smile, "I'll have you know I had three different girls back home weep over me the day I left for the monastery. Three!"

Donnal looked down at their younger friend appreciatively. "Well, well, look at you, big man. You'll have all the girls swooning and throwing flowers when you come riding in to save the kingdom, will you? Is that the plan?"

James's grin widened. "I wouldn't complain."

Gideon felt like an outsider as the two young men joked around with one another. All he could think about was the trials, and he needed to get away so he could focus. Without saying anything, he left his friends and walked over to a quiet spot beneath a tree, making sure to stay within earshot so he could hear when his name was called.

He breathed deeply and let the tension slowly flow from his body, thinking about what Nefteli had said the previous night: not to focus on what he wanted, but on what the gods wanted. It didn't make him feel any more prepared. He sat for what felt like ages, watching others get called into the chapel before him, his hands moving idly over his prayer beads, trying to focus and failing.

Donnal's name was called, and Gideon's tall friend looked over to where he was seated under the tree and waved, then turned and went into the chapel, along with a girl whose name Gideon couldn't remember.

The sun climbed higher in the sky at an agonizing pace, and after a little while, a shadow blocked the warm sunlight on his face as someone came up and loomed over him. Gideon looked up and squinted at James's curly-headed silhouette framed against the blue sky and marching clouds.

"Feeling excited, Gid?" the younger man asked, crossing his legs as he sat beside Gideon. "Finally, eh?"

Gideon grunted but didn't respond, and James cocked his head.

"Not nervous, are you?" he asked again.

"I really wish people would stop asking me that," Gideon sighed, clenching and unclenching his fist at his side. "Yes, I'm a bit nervous, James. Aren't you?"

"What are you nervous for, then?" the ginger scoffed. "It's my scrawny little behind that should be scared, not a big, golden-haired chap like you!" He laughed and shook his head, and Gideon reluctantly grinned. A warm breeze rustled the leaves above them, and the tension in his shoulders relaxed a little.

"Listen, mate." James leaned closer, and his freckled face was serious. "I imagine Donny has given you advice, and I'm not trying to be your big brother or anything," he grinned, and Gideon cocked his eyebrow, "but I'll just remind you of one thing, alright?"

He took a breath before continuing. "You, me, and Donny — it's been us three since the beginning, right? And this whole time, we've yet even to try to invoke the Holy Light. I guess what I'm saying is, even though you're the only one in the whole world who's worried that you — of all people — might fail, it wouldn't change anything. It'll still be you, me, and Donny after these damned trials, whether we're all paladins or none of us are. Even if they send us to different ends of the earth, there's always friends to make and adventures to be had. Just... don't give up, is all I'm saying."

Gideon regarded the curly-haired ginger for a long moment. He looked even younger than he was, his blue eyes shining, his freckled cheeks rosy; at the same time, however, he spoke like an old soul, and his advice seemed to come from a wisdom beyond his years.

"Thank you, James," Gideon said finally, and he meant it.

His young friend offered an encouraging smile and nodded. Then his eyes narrowed as he looked past Gideon toward the chapel. "That Akhumite girl's looking this way," he said.

Gideon's head whipped around, and he saw Nefteli standing with another group of recruits but looking over at him, her expression unreadable.

A low whistle from James brought him back around. "I see why Donny's so over the moon for her," he said, and when Gideon felt his cheeks flush, James gawked. "Oh, don't tell me you're sweet on her, too! You and Donny both?" He sighed and looked away, his eyes still wide as he rubbed the back of his neck. "Well, that's awkward, isn't it?"

Gideon shifted and adjusted his shirt to release the uncomfortable heat building in his chest at the thought of Nefteli. "Don't suppose you've got any advice about that?" he asked dryly.

James held up his hands. "I think I'll let you two sort that out, as a matter of fact. Wouldn't be surprised if it came to blows at some point."

Gideon started to reply, but then the chapel doors crashed open, and Sir Cormac's booming voice rang out over the grounds.

"Nefteli..." he bellowed, then paused, looking down at a scroll of parchment, "Henutep! And James Byrne! Come forth — your trials await you."

"Well!" James declared, hopping to his feet and clapping his hands. "That's me. Wish me luck, Gid!" he said as he started jogging toward the chapel.

Gideon hollered after him in response, then caught a fleeting look in his direction from Nefteli before she also hurried toward the chapel. He felt the urge to call after her, too, and wish her the gods' favor, but he stopped himself, and the moment passed.

CHAPTER 6

GIDEON

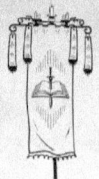

THE CROWD of recruits had thinned considerably, and he suddenly realized he'd be one of the last ones in, which only served to heighten his anxiety. As he waited for his name to be called, he turned the idea of a life serving in the knights auxiliary over and over in his head, imagining serving as a simple foot soldier. The thought left a bitter taste in his mouth, but he didn't have long to ruminate on it.

"Ballad!" Sir Cormac shouted.

Gideon leapt to his feet and quickly approached, trying to keep his pace steady despite the anxious pounding in his chest. Sir Cormac's bushy mustache twitched, his mouth set in a severe frown.

"With me," he commanded, and led the younger man inside.

The interior of the chapel was well-lit by sunlight streaming through the arched stained-glass windows and a smattering of candles and oil lamps spread about the space. As he followed after Sir Cormac, Gideon saw that all of the pews had been moved to the sides, leaving a large, open central area. Only a handful of others were present: Battlesister Dawnhammer stood in the center of the open area and watched him approach, and Hospitaler Lucas and Nefteli sat away to one side.

Gideon wondered for a brief moment why Nefteli was still in the chapel, but then he forced himself to tear his eyes away as he came to attention before the battlesister. "Gideon Ballad reporting, ma'am!" he barked out, giving her a sharp salute.

"At ease," she muttered, and he obeyed, shifting to a slightly more relaxed posture. She studied him, her face set in stone. "How are you feeling, Ballad?" she asked after a moment. "Prepared?"

He nodded firmly, trying desperately to look more confident than he felt. "Yes ma'am."

She smirked, one eyebrow raised, and shared a look with Sir Cormac. "Good." She took a step back and strode out of the open area, her steel boots clanking on the marble floor. "We've got high hopes for you, Ballad. Don't let us down." She turned on her heel to face him again, then nodded at Sir Cormac.

The old knight took up two wooden swords, the kind Gideon had been training with since the day he'd arrived, from where they leaned against one wall. One was fresh and looked hardly used, while the other was battered and stained by spots of dried blood. He tossed the fresh one to Gideon, who caught it deftly with one hand.

"Land a blow if you can, boy," Sir Cormac boomed across the space between them as he took up his huge tower shield from where it rested against a fluted column, "but at all costs, let not my blade touch your flesh, eh?" He swept the bloodstained wooden sword down in a challenge and was still, his small, dark eyes glaring out at Gideon beneath bushy white eyebrows.

Gideon's heart beat rapidly in his chest as he tightened his grip on the wooden training sword, staring across the polished marble floor at his armored opponent. Sir Cormac the Highshield was a tower of a man, his gilded armor and burnished shield reflecting the rainbow of sunlight streaming through the monastery's stained glass windows. The training sword held in his right hand looked absurdly out of place for the old paladin, who had purportedly fought and bled in countless battles during many crusades.

"You look like a spooked rabbit, boy!" Sir Cormac called, the sound echoing through the marble hall as the knight began advancing. The faceplate of his helmet was lifted and locked in place, and the old man's huge white mustache twitched as he snarled. "Show me the strength I've seen you use against the other recruits!"

Gideon took a deep breath and raised his sword, trying to steady his racing heart as he settled into the stance that Sir Cormac had taught him. Behind the old knight, he could see Battlesister Dawnhammer was watching closely, evaluating his fitness for the Holy Order. As the huge paladin's steel boots clanked across the marble floor toward him, Gideon thanked the gods he wasn't meeting him on the battlefield.

"Now," the old knight growled, "defend yourself, recruit!"

Sir Cormac launched forward with a suddenness that caught Gideon by surprise. The training sword came down in a powerful overhand swing that struck like lightning. Gideon managed to bring up his own sword to block the blow, but the impact nearly sent him to his knees and shook his bones.

"Come now, boy!" Sir Cormac jeered, striking again and again with his sword, pushing Gideon back. "You won't be bested by an old man, will you?"

Gideon grit his teeth and tried to hold his ground, but the old paladin was a battering ram, testing his defenses with a staggering relentlessness. He swung his own sword when he could, but he didn't even come close to landing a blow against the old knight's weathered plate armor.

"Have you no fire in your blood?" Sir Cormac demanded, the impact of their swords echoing in the cavernous chapel. "Are you just a meek little boy who wants pampering?"

Gideon felt a deep anger well at the taunt, and he pushed back against Sir Cormac's onslaught, letting out a cry of frustration.

"That's it, boy!" Sir Cormac laughed, still pressing forward, his training sword slamming again and again against Gideon's. "You can never be a true paladin without the passion to fight!"

Gideon parried another blow from the training sword, and then the knight's heavy tower shield swung from the other side and smashed into him, sending him skidding backward, his leather soles sliding across the smooth floor. Gideon remained on his feet, though, prompting an appreciative smirk from Sir Cormac beneath his flowing white mustache.

"Or a powerful will to live," the old man added, raising his wooden sword for another blow.

Sir Cormac came at him again, swinging his wooden blade and monstrous shield alternately. Gideon struggled to defend himself, his arms burning from the effort, and he could do little more than stave off the blows.

"Good, recruit, good!" Sir Cormac said, finally ending his assault and taking a step back, showing just a hint of labored breathing as he lifted his stained wooden sword for inspection. "No fresh blood," he mused, then looked over at Battlesister Dawnhammer. "I don't think I landed a single blow."

The dwarven woman's ginger brows lifted a touch, and she nodded, her thick, armored arms crossed over her breastplate. "Well done, Ballad."

"Thank you, battlesister," Gideon panted, trying to catch his breath as sweat dripped from his forehead.

"A fine job, boy," Sir Cormac agreed, nodding his head appreciatively. His face turned grim as he spoke again. "But we already knew you're hale and hardy. The question is: do you have the purity of heart and soul to summon the Holy Light?"

Gideon's stomach lurched. The time had come. Whatever pride he'd felt a moment before at withstanding Sir Cormac's assault vanished, and his hands shook, but not from exhaustion. The old knight strode forward and took the sword from his hands, then gave him a hard look, which Gideon thought maybe was meant to be encouraging.

"The time for your final trial has come, lad," the battlesister said, pacing slowly into the open chapel, her hands clasped behind her back, her famous golden warhammer hanging at her side. "We must know if the gods have gifted you the Holy Light or no. This is your chance to show us your true worth."

Gideon steeled himself as the dwarven woman approached him. She stalked up to the blond-haired youth and snatched the wooden sword from Sir Cormac before waving him away. The old knight stepped back, replacing his tower shield against the column and regarding Gideon gravely.

"You cannae rely on your physical strength now, recruit," Battle-sister Gerda said, circling him slowly, the wooden training sword held low. "Rather, trust in your faith. If there's any hope you can invoke the Light, it will come in a moment of desperation." She stopped and raised the sword above her head. "Defend yourself again, but this time, call on the Holy Light to block my blows!"

Gideon felt panic rising in his throat, but he nodded, raising his empty hands defensively. He didn't know what to say, or how to invoke the Light, but he started reciting silent prayers anyway, hoping against hope that perhaps the gods would hear him.

Swallowing hard, Gideon braced himself as she lunged forward, swinging the training sword downward. He raised his arms instinctively, flinching, and the training sword smacked against his forearms with a crack. He grunted in pain as she swung again, this time at his side; again the blow landed and knocked the wind from his lungs.

"Call on it, boy!" Sir Cormac shouted from the sideline. "Feel it streaming from the heavens!"

"Trust your faith and your devotion," Gerda urged him, swinging again, and Gideon just managed to deflect the blow. "Feel the Light burning within you, and let it manifest!"

Gideon felt desperate tears stinging his eyes, but he forced them back and tried to focus as he fended off more blows from the dwarven woman. He fought to remember the teachings he'd learned at the monastery, trying to summon that flicker that Hospitaler Lucas had spoken about.

"Beg the gods for their favor," Gerda cried, the wooden sword whipping through the air as she battered him, "and for the Light's mercy!" She cracked him once more, the blow smashing into his left shoulder and leaving his whole arm numb. She paused and looked him over briefly before growling, "Nothing else will spare you this beating, lad."

She flew toward him again, surprisingly quick and agile for her stout dwarven stature, and caught him along the side of his head as his numbed arm failed to block the strike.

"Invoke the Light!" the battlesister cried, swinging at him again and again, landing powerful blows all over his body. Gideon cried out, his ears ringing and his vision darkening around the edges as he was battered, but he held his ground, determined not to let her break him. "Stop sniveling and summon the Light!"

Gideon grunted as he tried to swing his bruised, near-useless arms up to block another blow, and when the splintered wooden blade met his bones, it finally snapped, one half clattering to the cold marble floor.

Battlesister Dawnhammer cast the useless hilt aside, breathing hard and glaring at him angrily. Her lip curled as she reached for the golden haft at her waist and pulled the gleaming warhammer from her belt. "You'll invoke the Light," she said, marching him down, intimidating despite her diminutive height, "or you'll die in the attempt!" And with that, she raised her warhammer over her head and brought it crashing down toward Gideon's head.

Gideon closed his eyes and forced his useless arms up to block what would surely be a fatal blow. An inexplicable memory of the day he'd left Wintry flashed through his mind, and he realized he was about to die.

All the hopes and dreams he'd had of being a paladin rushed through his mind in an instant, and he knew they were lost, that he'd failed, and the miserable, sickening thought that he was better off dead anyhow played at the back of his mind beneath the fear. He grit his teeth and waited for death to take him and end his miserable existence.

But after a few moments, no blow landed. Gideon opened one eye apprehensively and saw the battlesister holding her warhammer just an inch from his face, scowling at him still.

"Damn it all," she grumbled, then returned the heavy weapon to her side. Her demeanor softened. "It's not your fault, lad. The gods don't bless everyone." She laid a hand on his shoulder, and he winced. "You're strong and loyal. And brave. You'll make a fine warrior in the Holy Order."

Gideon swallowed thickly, shaken by the experience. "I... I can't be a paladin," he said weakly, his voice shaking, and the words stung worse than the beating she'd just given him. "I can't wield the Light."

"You can still be of use," Sir Cormac said, taking a step closer. "The Holy Order still needs good soldiers in the knights auxiliary."

"Even if you cannae wield the Light, you can still serve it," Gerda added, "and your brothers and sisters in arms. But I'm afraid the calling of a paladin is not yours." She took his hand and lifted it to inspect his injuries, making him suck in a breath against the pain. "I'm sorry for the rough treatment, lad. We had to test you in a desperate moment. But there's nothing to learn from these wounds — no failure to correct. You're just called to something else." As she spoke, she gestured to Hospitaler Lucas, who was waiting in the wings.

To his surprise, Nefteli accompanied the healer, and as Lucas approached Gideon with a compassionate smile, they both knelt beside him. "Your comrade here has proven quite adept at using the Light to heal," he said calmly, gesturing at Nefteli. Gideon's eyes flitted up to her, but he looked immediately away, too ashamed and miserable to meet her gaze.

"Recruit Henutep, if you please," the hospitaler said, and after a moment's hesitation, Nefteli reached out and placed both hands on Gideon's bruised and bloodied arms. He could tell she wanted him to look at her, but he simply couldn't.

Her touch was light, gentle, and her soft hands were cool on his hot skin. She took a deep breath, and there was a long pause as she focused, but then a shaft of warm, golden-yellow Holy Light slowly formed and and grew until it enveloped both of them, and Gideon watched the cuts and bruises on his arms gradually heal. Even as the pain ebbed away, and the feeling returned to his arms and hands, a bitterness welled in the back of his throat, and he struggled to swallow it down.

Eventually, the Light faded, leaving Gideon whole and unmarred. Even after it was done, she kept her hands on him, and as he made to pull away, her grip tightened just slightly, prompting him to finally look up at her. Nefteli's brow was furrowed, and she looked at him pleadingly, something shimmering in her dark eyes. Gideon's bile rose again as he wilted and looked back down at his feet.

Hospitaler Lucas nodded appreciatively. "Well done," he said, laying a hand on Nefteli's shoulder, and she finally released Gideon.

As he stood back up, Sir Cormac came over and clapped him roughly on the back, a sympathetic look in his dark eyes. "Be at peace, Ballad. You've the makings of a storied warrior, should you choose to serve the Order, and I hope you will."

Battlesister Dawnhammer gave a firm nod of agreement, and then gestured to the chapel doors. "Alright, back to the barracks with you, Ballad."

"Yes, battlesister," Gideon answered, unable to keep a note of misery from his voice. He glanced once again at Nefteli, whose face was still written with compassion for him, and then he turned to leave while she remained there to continue healing, invoking the Holy Light.

As Sir Cormac followed him out to call for the next of the last few recruits to be tested, Gideon fought the misery in his chest and the stinging behind his eyes. Everything had been for naught: leaving his family, the long walk to the monastery, all his training, and every last hope and dream he'd had for himself for the future. All of it was gone in a few mere moments, and deep down in the recesses of his soul, a profound anger began to stir.

CHAPTER 7

SADIA

ॐ

"WHAT ON EARTH were you thinking, Sadia?" Yusuf demanded angrily as she laid the rescued child on a clean blanket inside their cistern. Reza leaned forward beside Sadia, studying the baby intently, and the three girls huddled together in the awning of their little tent, their big eyes following Sadia and Yusuf as the two argued. Yusuf had hastened the children back, and Sadia arrived just a little afterward. The city guard engaging with the cultists had given her enough time and space to lose them as she rushed back home.

"I couldn't just leave him!" Sadia snapped back, her heart still racing as she looked down at the boy, his poor little body withered and emaciated. His hair had thinned, his cheeks sunken, and he looked frail and sickly. "They were doing something terrible to him," she said, looking up at Yusuf, and her anger faded a bit as her eyes began to water. "Look what they've done to him."

Yusuf looked down at the child and shook his head. "I see, Sadia. But I saw everything else that madman did as well. He's some kind of evil magician or something — can you imagine what he'd do to us if he finds us?"

"I—" Sadia began, but stopped. She hadn't thought of the consequences before grabbing the baby, but as Yusuf had said, she began to realize the grave danger she'd potentially put them all in. "I... what was I supposed to do?" she asked him desperately.

Yusuf opened his mouth and then stopped himself from answering.

"What's wrong with him?" Reza asked, inspecting the boy on the blanket as he shuddered, his eyes squeezed shut, and his breath shallow.

Sadia tucked the corners of the blanket together, swaddling the poor child. "I don't know, Reza," she replied, trying to keep her voice steady. "They did something awful to him."

Imani broke off from her sisters and cautiously approached the others. "What's his name?" she asked.

Sadia pulled the little girl into a hug. "I don't know, sweetheart. He's far too young to tell us."

"Maybe we can give him a name?" Zara suggested, following Imani over and pulling Mirah by the hand behind her.

"Oh," Sadia said, surprised, looking between her younger siblings. "Well, I... I don't know. I suppose we could." She sat little Imani on her knee, and lifted the bundled infant in her arms to hold him, hoping that maybe the closeness would help alleviate some of the obvious pain and discomfort he was in. "Why don't you give him a name?"

Imani nodded and stood up, taking on a very serious expression. "Yes," she agreed pensively. She put her hands on her hips and looked around the dimly lit cistern. "Hm, hm, hmm...." The other three children were all silent, watching her, and Yusuf crossed his arms and sighed.

"All I can think of is 'Blanket'!" she said finally, throwing her tiny hands up in frustration.

"We can't name him 'Blanket', Imani," Yusuf replied dryly.

"I know!" she huffed, folding her arms as frustrated tears welled in her eyes. "I just can't think of anything else!"

Sadia knelt down beside her littlest sister and wrapped an arm around her. "It's alright, Imani," she said gently. "We'll think of a name in time."

"Ibrahim," Reza declared confidently. "We should call him Ibrahim."

Yusuf gave the boy an inquisitive look. "Why Ibrahim?"

"Remember the old man who lived in the hut near the river? His name was Ibrahim." Reza shrugged. "He looks like that old man," he noted, nodding at the baby. "His skin is all pale and wrinkly, and his face looks a thousand years old!"

Sadia started to scold him for comparing the poor, sick child to an old man, but she stopped herself and took a purposeful breath. "Ibrahim is a good name. A strong name."

"Then Ibrahim is his name," Yusuf stated, putting an end to the conversation, and Sadia could tell he didn't really care. "But what on earth do you intend to do with him, Sadia? He can't stay here — the cult will doubtless be searching the city for him."

"I don't know what to do," Sadia admitted, shaking her head and looking down at the newborn as he whimpered in her arms.

"We'll keep him," Imani said, hugging Sadia and then clumsily adjusting the blanket around Ibrahim, imitating how Sadia had done it. "Just like you kept us!"

"Oh," Sadia said, looking between her and Reza, her heart heavy. "We need to take him to someone who can help him first."

"And how will you do that, with the Hierophants running around looking for him?" Yusuf demanded. "I've heard stories about them, Sadia — they're every bit as crazy as they look."

"Maybe the city guard captured them?" Sadia suggested tepidly, the memory of the mad prophet wielding dark magic already making it sound unlikely to her.

"You saw what that man did to the priests," Yusuf insisted. "The city guard is no match for him and his cult."

"Then we need to get him out of the city," Sadia said more firmly, meeting Yusuf's angry glare. "He needs a healer or... something. You didn't see what they were doing to him — you don't understand."

"I saw enough," he snapped.

"Then what do you suggest we do?" she demanded, panic and frustration welling as her brother remained staunchly obtuse.

"I'll take him and leave him at the temple at night," Yusuf answered matter-of-factly. "Let them figure out what to do with him."

"No," Sadia replied, and Yusuf's eyebrows rose in surprise.

"There's no other option," he stated flatly. "Even if the Hierophants didn't come looking for him, he doesn't look like he's going to last long in the state he's in. The priests will know what to do."

"They killed all—" she started shrilly, then looked down at Imani's big eyes glistening as she looked up at her and lowered her voice. "I don't even know if there are any priests left after what happened!"

"Surely there will be someone at the Temple of Naharia who can help him, or knows where to find someone who can. Just listen!" he said as she began to object. "You were the one who said he needed a healer, yes?"

"Yes, but—"

"Then here's what we'll do." He sighed and ran a hand through his long black hair. "I'll wait awhile and then go out and see what's happened, whether that madman was caught or if cultists are roaming the streets, and if they aren't, I'll come back to get the baby and take him to the temple."

Sadia looked down at Ibrahim, the tiny infant shuddering in his weakened state, and felt a pang of guilt as she realized she had no better ideas. She nodded slowly.

"What about me?" Reza asked, and Yusuf and Sadia looked over at him, the other three little ones all huddled close.

"You're going to stay here," Yusuf said firmly.

Reza's swollen features crumpled into a scowl. "But I can help! I'm not afraid of anyone or anything."

"Absolutely not," Yusuf interrupted. "It won't be a simple beating you'll get if you're caught, Reza," he said gravely. "I was wrong to send you to steal the food. I'm not about to make an even worse mistake and risk bringing you out where a mad cult might recognize us and get suspicious."

"But—"

"He's right, Reza," Sadia agreed. Yusuf's words scared her, and she knew the streets were no place for a brash young boy like Reza at the moment. "You need to stay here."

"It's not fair," he grumbled, and folded his arms and kicked a rock, sending it clattering across the cistern floor.

"Life isn't fair, Reza," Yusuf told him. "Besides, if one of us goes out, one of us needs to stay to protect the girls, yes?" he walked over and placed a hand on the younger boy's shoulder. "That's your job this time."

Reza rolled his eyes and pulled his shoulder away, but didn't argue further.

Yusuf shook his head and looked back at Sadia. "I'll wait till it's dark — hopefully, the dust will have settled by then, and leaving won't mean my doom." He huffed and went to lay down on his makeshift bed to wait for nightfall.

Sadia held Ibrahim and paced, and the girls played and argued together quietly in their tent. Reza sat sullenly in the corner, throwing little rocks against the wall. Hours passed, and Yusuf dozed on and off while Sadia paced and held the infant. She was annoyed that her older brother was even able to sleep, given how nervous and panicked she felt. Eventually, she sat down with the others, and Ibrahim's eyes opened slightly and looked up at her for the first time since she'd rescued him. She smiled down at him and brushed a finger against his hollowed cheek.

"Don't worry, little one," she told him, "everything will be alright. We're going to get you to someone who can help you." Ibrahim blinked and looked up at her with a vacant expression, his mouth slightly open, and she thought for a moment she could see something: a dim orange light flickering in the back of his throat, but not from the candles scattered throughout the cistern.

She blinked, and it was gone.

Her brow furrowed, and she glanced over at Yusuf, sleeping and oblivious, and then she looked back at Ibrahim, whose face scrunched up again as a new wave of discomfort seemed to wash over him.

Sadia shook her head and stood up to continue pacing, rocking Ibrahim in her arms and humming. She tried to feed him, but he kept his lips pressed tight when she brought any food to his mouth, his body curled up and quivering, so she occupied her time by reciting prayers she'd overheard and tried to memorize over the years, begging for mercy from the mother-goddess Naharia, unable to wrestle away the growing splinter of doubt that her prayers would be heard.

CHAPTER 8

SADIA

As NIGHT FELL and a thin shaft of moonlight cut through the slats in the trapdoor above them, Yusuf stirred, and Sadia went over to him. "It's time," she said, staring down at her older brother as he recovered from his nap, forcing his eyes awake and sitting up.

He yawned and got to his feet. "I hope not to be long," he said, holding his hands out for the infant. "I'll take him."

Sadia bit her lip and kept Ibrahim close. She wanted to trust Yusuf, but as she looked down at the emaciated baby clinging to her, she found herself unable to let go.

"I... I think I have to go with you," she said.

Yusuf blinked and rubbed the sleep from his eyes. "What? No, absolutely not!"

"Yes," she said more confidently, "I have to do this with you, Yusuf. I'm the one who took him." She held a blanket out to him. "Now help me wrap him to me so I can climb the ladder."

"But I—" he began, and she interrupted him.

"No, Yusuf. I'm going with you, and there's no point in arguing."

She forced her voice to be firm, keeping her nagging exhaustion at bay, and gave the blanket a little shake in his direction.

The older boy looked at her, then at the offered blanket, obviously annoyed. But he finally sighed in frustration and took the blanket from her to obey. Sadia held the frail Ibrahim carefully to her in his swaddling cloth as Yusuf wrapped the blanket in a sling around her.

"This is a bad idea," he grumbled, though a stifled yawn stole the teeth from his protest.

"Yes, yes," she sighed, gesturing at Reza, who begrudgingly left his corner to come to her. "Look after the girls while we're gone, please?" She grabbed both of the young boy's hands in hers and forced him to look at her until his one open eye finally met hers, and he nodded.

Sadia looked over at the tent, where the silhouettes of her sisters continued whispering and gesturing as Zara told some grand story to the younger two. "Girls, behave for Reza while we're gone."

They didn't respond, but there was no time to ensure their obedience. It would be better if they simply continued playing, and Sadia and Yusuf would fix any troubles that may arise once they returned.

"Let's go," Sadia prompted, carefully mounting the ladder, and Yusuf sighed and followed her.

It was dark outside, and night blanketed the abandoned alleys around their derelict home. Yusuf carefully closed the rotted wooden hatch behind them, then quickly moved ahead, leading Sadia by the hand across rubble and detritus littering the streets.

He slowed as a pool of torchlight loomed ahead of them, illuminating the broad, paved street that led to the bazaar. "Wait here," Yusuf said, stopping and turning to face her, adding weight to his words. Sadia nodded and watched as the older boy slunk off, peering carefully onto the street. Ibrahim whined from where he was carefully bound against her chest, and Sadia clutched at him instinctively.

Yusuf turned back to her and waved her on, and she moved carefully up to join him.

"Just normal people about," he said quietly. "No guard patrols or cultists that I can see."

Sadia nodded and swallowed. "The temple is that way," she said, nodding in the direction despite Yusuf knowing the city even better than she did.

He nodded. "We'll move quickly and carefully. Try to keep him quiet," he said, glancing at the baby. Sadia nodded and clutched Ibi again. "I'll walk with my arm around you and try to keep you covered."

Yusuf looked again, then stepped out into the street and gestured to her to follow, placing his arm and cloak around her shoulders.

They walked quickly through the city, trying to appear calm but urgent. It was late enough in the evening that very few people were on the streets, and this far on the outskirts, they saw no guards or — more frighteningly — the orange-robed hierophants. The moon shone bright overhead, and its light mingled with the warm glow of torches and the occasional lamps perched around Qasira.

The street they were on led them south toward the calm Tajari River, then up into the city center, where the temple sat among princely estates. Once the ornate minarets of the house of worship rose up above the rest of the city, their silver caps shining against the backdrop of stars, Yusuf's grip on Sadia tightened, and he slowed.

"What is it?" she asked urgently, but his strong arms swept her to the side of the road before she received a reply. He hushed her as they both stepped into the shadow of a stack of crates against a wall.

"Did you see the bronze?" he asked in a panicked whisper, and she shook her head. "There's a group of them, there." He pointed surreptitiously. "I caught the flash of their armor."

A roving group of men moved ahead of them in the same direction, through a spot of darkness on the street between pairs of torches, and the moonlight glinted off exposed metal. "The guards carry spears — those men aren't," Yusuf noted, sounding more sure. "Damn."

"What do we do?" Sadia asked, her heart suddenly racing. Yusuf thought for a moment, looking around. To their left was a long alley leading away from the main road.

"This way," he hissed, grabbing her hand again. "We'll see where it goes, and use the alleys to get closer." She nodded and followed him quickly into the darkness, praying they could avoid being noticed.

They crept along the side alley, and it led them into another cramped area that ran behind the adobe buildings in the direction of the temple. Moving their way carefully along, they came to the junction of another street, and Yusuf stopped again.

A bright torchlight spilled into the alleyway, wavering as it seemed to move, wobbling closer, and Yusuf pressed himself up against the shadowed alley wall.

"More Hierophants," he said, peeking around the corner. Sadia crouched low and huddled herself into the shadows behind him, then leaned and looked carefully around his leg into the street beyond.

Another group of armed and armored men strode toward them, one of them bearing a large brazier mounted at the end of a tall staff, the iron bowl smoldering with coals above their heads and spilling light across the dusty road.

Yusuf looked down toward the other end of the street and stiffened. "The city guard!" he declared in a hushed voice, keeping half his face behind the shadowed wall as he looked out with one eye.

He grasped Sadia again as the two groups moved toward each other, clearly anticipating violence.

The patrol of city guardsmen marched in disciplined lines, walking in lockstep with one another, and their captain came to an abrupt halt as the group of Hierophants neared. "Hold!" he called over his shoulder at his men, who gripped their spears but kept the weapons at their sides, pointed to the night sky, their sharpened tips glinting dangerously in the splash of torchlight.

The group of cultists slowed to a halt, their own hands on the hilts of their swords, and the two groups stood facing each other, a heavy tension between them.

"Lost without your leader?" the guard captain asked derisively, his voice carrying over the otherwise empty street. "The emir ordered that you faithless vermin not be killed on sight," he said, pointing menacingly. "But you would be wise to leave the city before any misfortune befalls you."

"A brave bark from a frightened dog," a tall man at the head of the group of Hierophants retorted. Then, the men in bronze circled carefully around the guardsmen, the staff-mounted brazier splashing light across both groups as they passed.

By flickering torchlight, Sadia watched the jaw of the guard captain harden and heard the tightening of fists on spears, and she held her breath as the orange-robed cultists passed unmolested. The guardsmen continued to face the radical group until they were a hundred paces past, then finally resumed their patrol.

"Why didn't they stop them?" Sadia hissed once the street in front of them had cleared. She looked at Yusuf but couldn't make out his expression in the darkness, and she wondered if he was as confused as she was as to why the guardsmen didn't arrest the cultists on sight.

Yusuf shook his head. "I don't know, but it doesn't matter," he said bitterly, his eyes flashing down at little Ibrahim in the darkness. "We now have two reasons to worry." He took her hand and pulled her forward, resuming their path toward the temple.

They followed the group of cultists at a great distance, moving from shadow to shadow, keeping the looming silhouette of the temple ahead until they were just outside its eaves. A single row of guardsmen lined the perimeter of the temple, their backs to the walls and their spears held out at an angle, faces set like stone masks.

When they were close, one of the guardsmen lifted his spear defensively, and Yusuf and Sadia came to an abrupt halt. "By order of the emir, none are to gain entry to the temple," he shouted.

"We need to see a priest!" Yusuf called back. "We have a child in need of healing!" Sadia lifted Ibrahim a little higher in her arms as a sort of proof.

The guardsman shook his head. "You can go to the entrance if you want to petition for help," he said sternly, pointing to their right.

Sadia held her breath, and Yusuf sighed in frustration. "Let's go," he growled. She nodded and let him lead her away down the street and around to the front.

The wide plaza before the temple entrance was decorated with standing statues of Naharia, Ankhatun, and various lesser gods of the stars. Sadia's heart fell when she saw the heavy presence of Qasiran guards standing watch, blocking the entrance.

Yusuf led her by the elbow up to the soldiers arrayed around the tall, curtain-covered opening into the temple, and the captain on duty turned at their approach. "I can't let you pass," he declared before either could speak, holding his hand up to stop them. He eyed them and their ragged clothes warily and adjusted his ornamented breastplate with his free hand.

"Please," Sadia said, gathering the bundle on her chest that concealed Ibrahim and holding it up. "My... our brother," she said, looking over her shoulder for cultists, but the streets were empty. "He's very sick, he needs healing!"

The captain shook his head. "Very few priests remain after what happened at the bazaar today," he said tersely. "They are occupied, mourning and making offerings."

"Please," Yusuf pleaded, stepping up and grabbing the captain's wrist. "We have no money to offer, but he's very unwell."

"Get back!" the captain snarled, snapping his hand away and stepping back to put space between them. He grabbed the hilt at his waist threateningly. "Go home. Nothing can be done for you here," he said, shaking his head and gesturing violently for them to leave.

Sadia stepped forward and pulled open the bundle to reveal Ibrahim's scrunched-up face and heaving, emaciated chest. "You don't understand," she said, bringing the infant close, "he's dying!"

The captain leaned over hesitantly to look at Ibrahim and recoiled at the sight. "Begone!" he yelled again, shoving Yusuf by the chest, sending him stumbling backward. "As though your rotted clothes and unwashed faces weren't proof enough of an al-Yetim's curse! Take that thing away from this holy place!"

The man stood a head taller than Yusuf and was thicker, with heavy arms, and the scowl he wore on his face brooked no argument.

Yusuf took hold of Sadia and pulled her close as he stepped warily back, keeping the guardsmen in view as they retreated toward the avenue they had come down.

"I told you this city doesn't love us," he muttered angrily beside her. Sadia felt the tightness in her chest wind up and snap, and as they hurried back down the empty street, she had to fight the panicked tears that stung behind her eyes.

CHAPTER 9

SADIA

Yusuf held out a hand for Sadia as she dismounted the ladder into their cistern, then helped to unwrap the sling around her chest as Reza came over from where he had been sitting against the wall. The girls all lay together on a blanket outside their tent, huddled close. Reza stood on tiptoe to look at the baby as Sadia fixed the swaddling cloth around the infant.

"He looks the same," Reza said, the unswollen corner of his lips tugging down.

"The temple was heavily guarded," Yusuf said, shaking his head and looking over at the three girls stirring restlessly. "They wouldn't let us in."

Reza's face scrunched up, and he looked to Sadia. "What do we do now?"

She swallowed and tried to think. "I don't know," she admitted. She sat on the ground, suddenly feeling the weight of exhaustion. Ibrahim was awake, but his eyelids were drooping heavily as he sucked at the knuckle of her thumb and whimpered. He was hot in her arms, but she didn't let that stop her from holding him tight. "Is there any food left?" she asked Yusuf, who glanced wearily at her. "In that sack we were going to give the priests?"

Yusuf nodded and went to retrieve it, and Reza sat down on his haunches in front of her. "They would have helped us if we were from a family," he said, his voice small. He was only about eight years old and sounded too tired for his age. Sadia swallowed and felt a tear run down her cheek, but she sniffed and wiped it away.

"It will be alright, Reza," she said, forcing a sad smile, though the words rang hollow.

Yusuf handed her the sack of food, and she reached in for a handful, giving some to Reza as well. She was hungry but didn't feel like eating, so she tore a piece off one of the dates, then held it up to Ibrahim, who lazily sucked at it, holding it in both bony grey fists.

"What do we do?" Sadia asked, looking to Yusuf.

The older boy swept his dark hair back. "I don't know," he admitted finally. "We should wait a few days and try at the temple again, perhaps?"

"I don't know if he has a few days, Yusuf!" she cried, her voice rising shrilly. "Look at him!" She pulled the blanket away from Ibrahim's face, and the little child shivered. The date rolled out of his feeble grasp, his eyes held shut against some terrible pain. "He's so weak, and he won't even eat! We have to take him to a healer."

"The priests are all in hiding, Sadia," Yusuf reminded her.

"Some other healer, then! The priests aren't the only ones in the city, after all." There were physicians and mystics she'd heard of, but even as she said it, she had her doubts, which Yusuf confirmed.

"You saw how the guard captain looked at us," he said, a note of anger in his voice as he straightened. "We'll get the same from anyone else. The priests taking pity on some al-Yetim was our only hope."

"Then I'll... I'll..." she floundered, not really having any idea what to do but knowing she must do something. "I'll take him somewhere else, some other city."

Yusuf frowned. "Where?" he asked incredulously.

"People talk about cities all up and down the Tajari River, don't they? One of them must have healers willing to help a sick child, even if it's an al-Yetim who brings him."

"I suppose..." he said, exasperated. "But how would you even get there? The desert is merciless to travelers, Sadia, and we don't have any way to pay for a spot on a caravan, or a ship traveling the river."

"I'll stow away," she said, the wheels turning in her mind as she planned. "If I can just get to the wharf, I'm sure I can find some way to sneak aboard a ship or a barge or... something."

"Sadia, this is...." Yusuf groaned in frustration and gave her a long look. "You would really leave us?" There was a hint of genuine hurt in his voice.

"Leave you?" She looked over at the girls all sleeping huddled close to one another, and at Reza, sitting nearby and looking at her sleepily. "No, I... we should all go, Yusuf. You said it yourself — Qasira has never loved us. Why should we stay? This could be an opportunity, granted by the gods! To escape and go someplace where we aren't hated!"

"It's not that easy," he answered, shaking his head sadly. "Whether I like it or not, Qasira is all we've ever known. You don't even know where you're going, let alone if life would be any better there."

"Maybe not. But I know we can't just let him die." She looked down at Ibrahim's wretched form. "I... I don't think I could live with myself if I didn't try to help him."

"There has to be another way," Yusuf pleaded.

Sadia's eyes brimmed with tears. "If you have any better ideas, please tell me, Yusuf. I'm willing to do anything to save him, but... we can't keep him here, and they won't let us into the temple. So what do I do?"

"Why do you care so much about him?" the older boy demanded. "You didn't know he existed yesterday!"

"Because he's like us!" Hot tears spilled over and ran down her cheeks as her hands trembled and clutched the baby tighter. "He's just like us — alone, abandoned, and worse. That man was torturing him,

Yusuf! Cursed him!" Yusuf glanced down at Ibrahim but quickly looked away. "And no one else in this whole city was going to help him!"

Sadia was furious and devastated; Ibrahim's plight forced her to admit just how alone they all were in Qasira, how destitute their chances were of surviving, let alone seeking happiness.

Yusuf held her gaze, and eventually, his shoulders slumped. "It's not fair what's happened to him," he admitted, "but we can't risk leaving behind everything we have — what little it might be. If you take those girls out into the desert, or even onto the river, to some strange city we know nothing about, what's to keep them from being taken by a slaver? Or dying of thirst, or heat, or starvation? Or to lions or hyenas or crocodiles? At least here, all we have to worry about is starvation."

"And crazy people with candles," Reza reminded him, rubbing his eyes sleepily.

"That won't last," Yusuf said with a frown. "You know I'm speaking sense, Sadia."

Sadia wiped at her eyes. She was in a difficult place: for whatever reason, she felt some connection to the baby, and a responsibility to see her decision to save him through to fruition, but she also knew Yusuf was right about trying to flee the city with the little ones. And the thought of leaving all her siblings behind broke her heart.

"Yes. You're right," she finally agreed. "I can't risk taking them. So I guess I'm going alone."

Yusuf glanced down at Reza and then at the sleeping girls. "Sadia," he began, but after a heavy pause, words failed him.

"It's fine," Sadia said, looking down at Ibrahim again. His tiny, wrinkled face turned into her, his eyelids trembling as he fought against the torture he was suffering, and she was afraid for him. "I have to go, Yusuf. If I wait too long, it might be too late."

Yusuf put his hand on her shoulder and squeezed. "I'll... I'll go instead, if you want. I'll take him... somewhere."

"No." She gave him a sad smile. "You're better at finding work and food than I am. If you go, we'll all starve while you're away."

He nodded half-heartedly, and his own angst was apparent, though he was trying hard to hide it. She could tell he wanted to argue, and that everything she said weighed heavy on his heart, so she reached up and wrapped her free arm around him, hugging him tight. "Everything will be alright. Keep them all safe while I'm gone, won't you?"

"Of course," he promised, his voice thick, and squeezed her in return.

Reza furrowed his brow. "You're going to leave us?"

"I have to," she said, kneeling down beside him and brushing the hair from the swollen side of his face. "He needs a healer, and no one else will help him."

His dark eye searched hers until he finally nodded. "You'll come back?"

"I'll come back, I promise." She pulled Reza in close, fighting the sting of unshed tears. "I'd better go, while I still can."

"No, wait till morning," Yusuf insisted. "You'll be far more suspicious at night — during the day, you'll be able to blend with the crowds. And..." he glanced over at the pile of sleeping girls. "You should say goodbye to them."

Sadia frowned; the idea of waking the children and telling them she was leaving made her stomach sick. "Alright," she replied, the lump in her throat straining her voice. She sat down beside the girls and laid Ibrahim across her lap. "I'll tell them in the morning."

Throughout the night, Sadia tried to sleep, but was never able to, nor was she able to calm the terrible sadness and fear in her heart as she looked at her little sisters and stroked their hair gently as they slept. She'd chosen each of them; they were all she had, all she cared about, and saying goodbye to them would doubtless be the most difficult thing she'd ever done.

***

When dawn broke and shafts of sunlight poured through the trapdoor, Sadia braced herself for the conversation with Zara, Mirah, and Imani. Reza had stayed awake all night, sitting with his knees up, his arms folded on top and his chin resting on his wrists as he stared blankly into space, far more somber than usual.

"Girls, wake up," Sadia called softly. Imani opened her big, dark eyes to look up at her, and Sadia's heart ached. She'd watched all four of them grow, and they were just as precious to her as if they'd shared the same blood.

"Is it morning already?" Mirah mumbled sleepily, rubbing her face as she sat up.

"It is, Mirah," Sadia replied.

"Why do you look upset, Sadia?" Zara asked, her voice worried.

Sadia forced a smile and fidgeted with a strand of her hair. "I'm not upset," she assured her. "But I have to tell you something."

"Is Ibi-heem alright?" Imani asked, sitting up and crawling over to look at the baby.

"He still needs help," Sadia explained. She swallowed hard, looming tears aching behind her eyes. "I have to take him somewhere far away, to a healer, and I can't take you with me."

"What?" Mirah asked fearfully, and she grabbed Sadia's arm. "No, don't leave!"

"I have to," she explained, and tears welled up as she spoke. "He's sick and if I don't take him, he might die."

Zara came over and knelt beside Sadia, wrapping an arm around both Mirah and Imani. She was a bit older than them, and Sadia could tell she was trying to be brave. "But you'll come back, won't you?"

"Of course I will," Sadia assured her, and touched the oldest girl's cheek. "As soon as I can. But while I'm gone, you'll have to help Yusuf, yes? All three of you."

"We will," Mirah said weepily, wiping her cheeks with her sleeve.

Sadia looked back up at Yusuf, her chest tightening. "You'll have to make sure they have enough to eat while I'm away."

"I will," he promised, and she knew she didn't need to remind him, but she couldn't stop herself.

"And if Imani has trouble going to sleep, she likes it when I sing to her. Mirah will teach you the songs we sing. Won't you, Mirah?"

The girl nodded emphatically, and Yusuf sighed. "Yes, Sadia."

Sadia hugged Mirah tight before turning to little Imani, who was staring up at her wide-eyed, holding the hem of Zara's dress. "Come here, Imani," she said softly, but the little girl recoiled at her touch.

"No!" she cried, scooting away from Sadia and clutching desperately at Zara as tears spilled down her cheeks. "No!" she said again, turning her face into her older sister's ragged dress as she wept.

"Please, Imani," Sadia coaxed, sniffling as she fought tears of her own. "I have to leave, please come hug me." But the girl just wept harder, her little body shaking with the force of her sorrow.

Yusuf came over and knelt beside them all, and Imani flung herself against him, her little fists balled up in his tunic as she sobbed. "I'll take care of her," he said hoarsely.

Sadia nodded, trying to control herself, and slowly rose to her feet. She placed a hand on Imani's back, a poor substitute for a final hug goodbye, but she didn't want to push the child. "I love you, Imani," she choked out, wiping angrily at her cheeks as soon as the tears escaped her eyes.

Reza came up to her and hugged her tightly. "I'll say prayers for you," he said, his voice muffled by her dress. "Like you taught me." She hugged him back, fiercely, and kissed his forehead as he let go.

Yusuf stood, Imani still inconsolable in his arms, and Sadia sniffed again as she struggled with one hand to reach into her secret hem-pocket to retrieve two of the three copper drahm she'd stowed there. "For food," she said, handing them to Yusuf, but he refused them.

"You'll need that for passage," he said, closing her hand around the coins with his. He held her hand a moment longer. "Come back to us, Sadia." For an instant, there was a shimmer in his own eyes.

"I will," she promised, and hugged him. Imani was still sobbing and refused to look at her, so she kissed the child's clenched fist and stepped away. Yusuf helped her make another makeshift sling, freeing her hands for the ladder, and she took one last look at her family. "I love you all," she said, the words heavy and tremulous. "And I'll be back soon."

Sadia turned and started ascending the ladder, and only then let her tears slide silently down her cheeks as she left the only people who had ever cared for her, and whom she had ever loved, behind.

CHAPTER 10

GIDEON

GIDEON STOOD at attention in the pews as he watched his fellow recruits approach the chapel altar a handful at a time to swear their oaths to the Holy Order. He stood roughly on the spot he'd failed to invoke the Light the day before, and it was yet another painful thought for him to add to the growing pile of bad memories he was rapidly accumulating.

Battlesister Gerda led the new paladins and hospitalers in the oath of service. One after the other, they stepped forward, knelt, and pledged themselves to the gods, then stood and proclaimed an oath to either Weal or Woe, as Sir Cormac had described. Only about a dozen of their entire number had been able to invoke the Light, and Gideon squirmed as he watched them, furious and ashamed and miserable.

Beside him, Donnal let out an annoyed sigh, then muttered out of the corner of his mouth. "They're making a meal out of this, aren't they, the prats?" he groused. He hadn't been able to call on the Light, either, which Gideon felt should have assuaged some of his own angst, but hadn't. As usual, Donnal didn't seem too bothered by it, and his mouth twisted in an impish grin. "Still, we'll be free soon enough. One more night as recruits, then it's out to the field!"

Gideon frowned and didn't answer, and his eyes were drawn back to the apse as the ginger-headed James took a knee before the magnificent relief covering the curved chapel wall, depicting Ulicron's pantheon locked in brutal battle against the demon lords, their golden wings spread behind them.

"Swear you, James Byrne," Battlesister Dawnhammer called out loudly from where she stood before the youth, "to serve as an agent of the gods' will, as either the executor of their vengeance, or the instrument of their mercy, and in all matters to be a shield against the evils that plague this world, from this moment until you draw your final breath?"

"Yes, I swear," James answered firmly.

"And which oath will you claim and keep?" Gerda asked, her rough voice echoing off the walls and steepled ceiling. "Weal or Woe?"

"I will keep the Oath of Woe," he answered, "and strike down evil wherever it rears its head!"

A rare smirk curled the battlesister's lips. "Rise, then, James Byrne, son of the Holy Order. Wield the Holy Light as an instrument of righteous vengeance, and never a mercy. Go forth and walk the paths of the just and righteous, and when death comes to take you, go not quietly into the void; rather ensure your enemies long remember the day of your passing."

Gideon watched somberly as their young friend strode proudly from the altar to rejoin him and Donnal in their pew.

"You look pleased with yourself," Donnal muttered down at James, keeping his eyes forward, but Gideon heard the hint of amusement in his voice.

"Don't be jealous," the ginger replied quietly as the next recruit knelt before Battlesister Gerda and began swearing her oath. "I'll use my status to make sure you've got a nice, cozy post, maybe outside my bedchamber, to guard me as I rest my holy toes."

Donnal snorted out a laugh, and the noise attracted the narrowed gaze of Sir Cormac, glaring over his bountiful white mustache from the front of the chapel, and they fell silent. The two of them, along with most of the other recruits, had stayed up late in the mess hall after the trials had concluded, feasting, cheering, telling stories and jokes. Gideon had eaten quickly and left, unable to be around the merrymaking, given his failure.

The remaining recruits slowly pledged their oaths until, finally, there was just Nefteli remaining. As she stepped forward and took a knee, Gideon forced his mind to quiet — he was miserable, but he was proud of his friend, and the moment was hers.

"Swear you, Nefteli Henutep," the battlesister began, "to serve as an agent of the gods' will, as either the executor of their vengeance, or the instrument of their mercy, and in all matters to be a shield against the evils that plague this world, from this moment until you draw your final breath?"

The Akhumite girl took a deep breath, and when she answered, her voice was thick with emotion. "I swear it," she said, then bowed her head, and Gerda gave an approving nod.

"And which oath will you claim and keep?" the dwarven woman asked for the dozenth time that afternoon. "Weal or Woe?"

"I claim the Oath of Weal," Nefteli declared, and quickly wiped an errant tear off her proud cheek where she knelt. "And I will keep it jealously."

"Rise, then, daughter of the Holy Order," the battlesister said. "Invoke the Holy Light to heal the wounds of the world, and never to inflict them. Go forth and walk the paths of the just and righteous until you meet St. Thylessia at the brink of eternity."

As Nefteli walked back and resumed her place in the pews with them, Battlesister Dawnhammer turned to face them all. "Rise!" she shouted. "Recruits! As of today, those of you who've sworn your oaths are full-fledged members of the Order. The rest of you have until tomorrow at dawn to make your decision: go back to your homes — or wherever else fortune may take you — or swear fealty as lay members of the churches. I encourage you to spend the remainder of the day in thoughtful prayer and consideration, confer with the comrades you've made here, and make your choice wisely."

The hair on the back of Gideon's neck stood on end, and he felt as though all eyes had turned to him, but a quick glance around revealed he was just strangely paranoid. He let a frustrated breath escape him, and then the battlesister barked, "Dismissed!" and all around him, the other recruits let out a chorus of cheers and flooded out of the chapel. Gideon followed his friends out, then ducked away, moving through the crowd and circling back to climb up the chapel belfry.

He was no stranger to perching in the arches of the bell tower, looking out over the grounds and beyond the monastery walls onto the rolling green hills and dense forests of West Umbria. On many nights since arriving at Rivenwood, Gideon had whiled away hours, lost in thought, his mind wandering through his proud and glorious future.

It was a different feeling, now that he'd reached the most important moment of his life and failed. The trees didn't look as green, nor the sky as blue, and Gideon couldn't conquer the incessant storm of melancholy, confusion, and bitter disappointment roiling in the back of his head. A pleasant spring wind picked up, ruffling his golden hair, but the air couldn't chase away the feeling of impending gloom that was steadily falling over his thoughts. He rested his head against the cool stone arch and looked down, watching his comrades leave the chapel, chattering excitedly as they dispersed across the grounds, laughing and embracing.

Gideon sighed and turned his gaze up toward the far western mountains. He sat there for a long time, watching the sun weave between the towering clouds on their eastward march until it was nearly kissing the mountain peaks.

"There you are!" Donnal's voice said from behind him, startling him from his miserable reverie. "Come down from your high perch, you sad sack of bones! A couple of the lads have a wager going whether James can use the Light to roast a leg of lamb they nicked from the kitchens."

Gideon stared at his friend, nonplussed.

"What?" Donnal asked casually.

Gideon just shook his head and sighed. "That fool can wield the Light, and I can't," he muttered bitterly, sinking further into himself.

"Aw, come on, Gideon," Donnal said, leaning against the stone arch opposite him. "You're not still moping about that, are you?"

"I'm not moping," he protested sullenly, his shoulders slumped.

"You're missing out on all the fun down there," his friend said, gesturing to where the recruits were milling and lounging about the grounds for the first time since their training had begun, enjoying one day of peace before they would be sent off to join their respective churches.

Gideon didn't answer, so Donnal stopped talking and simply stood there for a while, watching the sun eventually slide below the mountaintops. Little lantern lights periodically came to life, dotting the monastery walls as the groundskeepers went about lighting them.

"You know, there's talk that a lot of us will be sent to the south, to fight orcs," Donnal said after a time, glancing down at his friend. "They say the fighting there is bad. But we could all stay together — you, me, Teli, and James. I know it's not exactly what you pictured, but there's honor to be found, still, right?"

Gideon frowned. "Maybe." A dull glow out in the forest beyond the walls caught his eye. "I'm thinking maybe it would just be best to return home," he commented idly as he squinted, trying to make out what was casting the light among the dense trees.

"You'd really rather just go back to being a fisher's boy?" Donnal asked indignantly, his temper suddenly flaring. "I can't believe you're being so childish about this!"

His words fell on deaf ears as Gideon caught a glimpse of flame in the forest, high among the leafy branches, swaying gently back and forth as it appeared to be moving toward the monastery. "Donnal," he said, but his friend ignored him to continue ranting.

"Don't you think I'm disappointed, too?" Donnal demanded. Gideon watched as the pair of guardsmen posted near the gate stirred, looking and pointing out toward the lights. "You're not the only one who wanted to be a paladin, Gideon. You're just the only one letting his misery and disappointment ruin a good thing simply because it wasn't exactly what he wanted!"

Gideon finally looked back at his friend. "Donnal!"

"What?" Donnal demanded, his fists balled.

Gideon turned his head to look back out toward the fire, and Donnal followed his gaze. "I think something's wrong."

CHAPTER 11

GIDEON

G‌IDEON WATCHED the distant figure of one of the guardsmen lift something, and a moment later, a droning horn blast sounded out across the grounds.

Donnal stood up straight and squinted into the dusky light. The flame was still growing, undeniably moving closer to them, though whatever was causing it remained hidden in the trees. "That doesn't sound good," Donnal said, leaning out the window arch to peer closer.

In the courtyard below, an eerie silence had fallen as the merry-making came to a sudden halt, and the recruits were all gathering and looking toward the glow flaring up over the wall in the forest canopy.

"Ainsel! Go sound the call to formation!" Sir Cormac's booming voice shattered the brief silence, and Gideon looked down to see the old paladin stomping briskly out of the clergy quarters toward the gates. At his order, one of their fellow recruits raced toward the chapel, and Donnal and Gideon shared a look, realizing the huge bronze bell beside them was about to be tolled.

They leapt down from the arches onto the wooden stairwell and raced down as Ainsel yanked the bell rope, and Gideon's teeth vibrated in his skull as the loud, brassy clanging echoed throughout the monastery. They reached the bottom, then exited the bell tower out onto the courtyard as the alarm continued to reverberate.

All around them, the recruits scurried to obey as Battlesister Gerda stormed out of her chambers, shouting orders, and Bishop Delwyn shuffled out onto the priory steps to see what was the matter.

Together, they walked from the chapel and saw throngs of recruits streaming toward the front gates of the monastery, where they began arranging themselves in rows and columns as they'd been trained. As Gideon fell in beside Donnal, he caught sight of Nefteli a few rows in front of him. She turned her head and met his gaze for a moment in the torchlight, then turned to face forward.

"What's going on?" Donnal asked aloud of the other nearby recruits, but no one had any idea.

Battlesister Dawnhammer's heavy armor clanked as she strode in front of the formation. "At attention!" she bellowed, stopping in the center and turning to face them. "Sound off!"

One by one, the recruits started counting up from one, from the front to the back. As the count rang out, Bishop Delwyn shuffled across the Monastery grounds toward them.

As he approached, he called out to the huge paladin, who was climbing down from the battlements. "Who approaches, Sir Cormac?"

"The guards spied the Church Militant's battle standard, Your Reverence," the old paladin said, lifting his shield from where he'd leaned it against the inner wall. "And it seems they've been busy."

The recruits finally finished their count. The final number called was fifty-three, the same as always.

The battlesister turned on her iron heel to face Bishop Delwyn. "All present, Your Reverence!"

The Bishop nodded, clasping his hands together in front of his white robes. "Very good, battlesister. Have they sent a rider?"

"No sign of one yet," Sir Cormac answered, joining them in front of the formation of recruits. The dozen or so knights auxiliary assigned to guard the monastery were posted along the walls, armed and apprehensive. "But they're almost upon us." He turned and pointed over the wall, and Gideon noticed a slowly approaching light setting the forest canopy aglow.

Everyone in the monastery courtyard waited, tensed, as the sounds of trodding horses and trudging boots grew in time with the torch glow. Soon, the light became so bright that it appeared to set the leaves ablaze, and as the host came to a halt outside the gates, orange flames peeked over the walls, licking madly at the sky above.

Bishop Delwyn trundled up the stairs to the battlements, leaning on his crosier, and looked down on the visitors from above. "Who approaches Rivenwood Monastery?" he called out, his aging voice faltering. Watching intently, Gideon saw the bishop's face drain of color as he saw something beyond the walls.

"A company of warriors of the Church Militant, Your Reverence," a strong female voice answered. "I come with a few score wounded men, seeking sanctuary and care."

"A few score?" Bishop Delwyn repeated, glancing down at Sir Cormac. "What has happened to you? And why so many wounded?"

"We were sent from the Sunless Citadel to hunt witches." There was a long pause. "We found them," the woman said, and the gravity of her voice made the hairs on Gideon's nape stand up.

On the battlements, the old bishop swallowed hard and nodded, shaken by whatever he was seeing. "Open the gates!" he called, his frail voice cracking. The two monastery guards standing by cooperated to remove the brace and drag the heavy gates open.

Gideon watched, breathless, as the torchlight spilled into the monastery courtyard. The silhouette of a short, petite woman in light plate armor stood just in front of the gates, casting a looming shadow into the monastery courtyard. Dozens of men and a handful of horses and mules were arrayed behind her, and they looked the worse for wear.

On either side of the ragtag formation was a hardy ox, divested of all burden save one: each had a tall, thick post strapped to its back, jutting upward toward the forest canopy. These were the massive torches that washed the night with firelight, but as Gideon peered closer, a knot tied itself in his stomach, and he understood the fear written on Bishop Delwyn's aged face.

Fastened at the top of each post, a charred human corpse fed the flames, crackling and popping as the water boiled from their sinews and charred their bones.

The woman in front took a step forward into the monastery and lifted her face to Bishop Delwyn, the light of the flames making her gaunt features seem demonic. She wore her dark hair in a plaited braid, and her armor was blackened and bloodied. One gauntleted hand rested on a leather-bound tome slung at her waist like a weapon.

"Welcome to Rivenwood Monastery, Archoness Lorica," Bishop Delwyn said, his voice shaking.

Next to Gideon, Donnal sucked in his breath at the name, and the two looked out of the corner of their eyes at each other in amazement, left in awe that one of the seven archons stood before them.

"Thank you for your hospitality," the archoness said, taking another step forward. "My wounded need healing, and all of us are in need of food and water. We have marched all day to reach the monastery."

Bishop Delwyn nodded. "Of course, milady. We will give you everything you need. The brothers and sisters of the Church Merciful will see to your wounded. Please, allow the recruits to help your men to the chapel."

The archoness nodded, then turned and waved her soldiers forward.

"Bring your wounded into the chapel, brothers!" Sir Cormac bellowed, stepping forward to usher the wayward company inside. "Leave the horses and mules — they'll be taken care of."

Donnal looked at Gideon, his face pale in the flickering light of the blazing corpses. "Are those...?" he whispered, jerking his head toward the burning bodies.

Gideon swallowed and nodded. "They are."

They moved forward along with all the other recruits and started assisting the wounded warriors into the monastery and toward the chapel. There were many men among them with gruesome injuries: missing limbs or gaping wounds to their heads and torsos. Most were covered in crusted, brown blood, their armor dented and blackened, but their weapons were strangely clean by comparison.

Donnal rushed to the aid of one man who looked about to take his final steps, and Gideon joined him, each taking an arm over their shoulders. He was a burly, barrel-chested man, but he was weak from blood loss and could scarcely remain on his feet. They held him up and walked him toward the chapel, where they deposited him gently on the marble floor.

"Thank you, lads," the man said, leaning back against the wall and closing his eyes. His face was streaked with dirt and blood, and he looked like he hadn't slept in a week.

"What happened to you?" Donnal asked, unable to hold his tongue.

The man groaned, then looked up at them with distant eyes. "Damned coven," he said wearily. "We hunted them for a fortnight. But they were in plain sight the whole time, and caught us unawares." He paused as one of his brothers-in-arms was set down beside him, looking in an even worse state. The burly man laid a hand on his friend's sundered breastplate. "Got us good, they did."

"How'd you escape?" Donnal asked. "Did the Church send reinforcements?"

The man shook his head. "No. Archoness Lorica led the counterattack. We thought we'd lost her, but she came back out of the darkness and burned the witches' underlings to cinders." He coughed and spat a clot of bloody phlegm on the stone floor. "But not before their black magics tore the company apart, and the witches themselves escaped."

"How many fell?" Gideon asked, glancing back at the entrance to the chapel as Archoness Lorica strode in, followed by Bishop Delwyn, Battlesister Gerda, and Sir Cormac.

The burly man fixed him with a grim stare. "Most of us," was all he answered. Gideon gave a nod and then took his leave, dragging Donnal with him and moving closer to listen in on the conversation between the bishop and Archoness Lorica. They ducked into the stairwell to the belfry after walking back through the vestibule, and paused to eavesdrop.

"We've good clerics here," Sir Cormac assured the archoness, "they'll do all they can."

"My hospitalers provided as much healing as they could," the archoness said, her face gaunt as she looked around the chapel at her wounded men. "Before they themselves succumbed. But some of the wounds were... they were beyond our abilities."

Peeking around the corner, Gideon watched as she knelt beside a man curled up on a pew, holding desperately to a wound that wept blood so dark it was black in the flickering candlelight. "I'm no hospitaler," she muttered, looking up at Delwyn, Cormac, and Gerda, "but even so, some of these wounds.... They're pernicious. They refused to respond to the Holy Light."

Sir Cormac blinked and pulled at his mustache. "Impossible," he scoffed. "All wounds respond to the Light!"

"These didn't," Archoness Lorica replied firmly, shaking her head. "The witches have learned new tricks, it seems, and we paid the price for it."

"We can certainly try again," Bishop Delwyn offered, wringing his hands. "Perhaps your healers were simply too exhausted to administer aid properly."

The archoness took a deep breath, then stood as one of the monastery clerics swept up and took her place, pressing a clean white cloth to the man's wounds.

"That's a possibility," Lorica said, looking over her shoulder at her men scattered about the chapel. "We have not slept in days. My hospitalers are some of the best, but even their strength is not limitless." She looked up at Delwyn, her eyes tired, but Gideon thought he caught the faint glimmer of a pale light deep in her gaze. "Please, do what you can for them."

"Of course," Bishop Delwyn answered, nodding. "Hospitaler Lucas and his clerics are quite accomplished healers themselves. I'm sure they will do everything they can."

"Thank you," the archoness said, glancing down at the man on the pew, his eyes rolled back and his breathing shallow. "I need rest. Please, if I might be allowed to stay in the monastery...?"

"Of course," Bishop Delwyn said. "We can make up a bedchamber in the west tower for you, milady."

Archoness Lorica nodded her thanks, then strode from the chapel, leaving the wounded men groaning on the pews behind her. She cast one last look back at them, her face haunted, and then left the chapel without another word. Gideon and Donnal pressed themselves up against the shadows in the stairwell as she passed, trying to shrink from sight.

As she left, Gideon heard Bishop Delwyn clear his throat and start issuing orders. "Battlesister, send some of the recruits to help Lucas and the others see to the wounded."

"Aye, Your Reverence," Gerda replied.

"Sir Cormac, I'll entrust the monastery guard to you. See that they secure the grounds, and double the men on watch overnight — we cannot afford to assume our safety."

The old knight simply growled in agreement.

"I will prepare a chamber for our distinguished guest," Bishop Delwyn said, then he shuffled off after the archoness toward the west tower.

As Gideon and Donnal made to step out of the stairwell, Battlesister Dawnhammer rounded the corner, her arms crossed. "What do you think you're doing, lads?" she asked, glaring up at them.

"Oh, um, just, erm..." Gideon stammered, unable to come up with a suitable excuse.

"Eavesdropping," the dwarven woman said, her brow stormy. "Whatever you heard, repeat not a word of it, do you understand?" She pointed toward the doors and barked, "Now get back out there and help get the rest of the wounded in."

"Yes, battlesister," they said in unison, hurrying out into the summer evening.

As they hurried across the grounds toward the gates where a handful of wounded soldiers remained, Donnal nudged Gideon. "Did you hear that?" he asked, his voice barely above a whisper. "The witches' black magic was able to resist the Light?"

Gideon nodded, swallowing thickly, looking around to make sure they were alone. "That's what she said."

"Well, what the bloody blazes does that mean?" Donnal hissed. "That's not supposed to happen, is it?"

Gideon frowned, recalling the haunted look in the archoness' eyes. "There's something going on," he murmured, "something terrible."

"You know what that means, then," Donnal said, and Gideon could see his lips curl in a sly grin by the light of the ox-mounted pyres. "A mystery is afoot, Gideon!" his friend elaborated with a strange excitement. "Surely you can't leave now, eh?"

Gideon sighed, but nodded. "I suppose not," he agreed reluctantly.

"That's the spirit!" Donnal said, clapping him on the shoulder as they arrived at the gates. "We might even get to help, start out making a reputation for ourselves early, before even leaving the monastery!"

"Sure," Gideon replied bitterly, a grim foreboding settling over his spirit as he lifted another wounded man and helped him toward the chapel.

In the distance, a crow cried ominously in the night, and Gideon glanced up at the sky, a persistant unease weighing heavily on him.

CHAPTER 12

SADIA

Sadia carried the blanket holding Ibrahim in both arms, lower than she would normally carry a child, in the hopes that it might look more like she was carrying a bundle of fruits or vegetables rather than a baby. As Yusuf had said, the morning streets were lively as usual, although a strange hush seemed to lie like a blanket over the city as people's gazes darted nervously, and conversations were held in hushed whispers.

Groups of armed city guardsmen and cultists alike still patrolled the streets, and Sadia had so far been able to duck out of sight or otherwise make herself inconspicuous enough, hiding her face with the hood of her shawl and making haste when no cultists were in sight. She made her way down the main thoroughfare, where there were ample crowds for her to hide in, directly down the sloping hill toward the large docks that sat on the broad Tajari River.

She was careful to skirt around the bazaar where the massacre had happened the day before. As she hastened past, she wondered if the bodies of the dead had been cleared away, and if the blood that had seeped into the hewn sandstone dais could even ever be washed clean.

Her arms were beginning to tire, and the bundle containing Ibrahim was beginning to slip, so Sadia ducked into a narrow alleyway where no one was watching and paused to rearrange the blankets to a more comfortable position.

As she was tucking the last corner, Ibrahim gave a little mewling cry and his eyelids fluttered. Sadia's heartbeat quickened, and she glanced over her shoulder at the main road, hoping no one had heard him. Taking a moment to rock and comfort him in the hopes he would be quiet, she silently prayed that no roving cultists would stumble upon them.

The cries subsided after a few moments, and Sadia breathed a sigh of relief. After she was reasonably sure he was as comfortable as she could make him, she poked her head out of the alleyway to make sure no Heirophants were near, and then she set off again through the flowing crowd, hastening toward the docks, reciting in her head every prayer to merciful Naharia she'd ever learned.

As she neared the water, she saw dozens of river ships of all sizes and shapes, their colorful sails unfurled in the wind, sailing up and down the Tajari while others were moored along the wharf. Hundreds of sailors and dockworkers scurried back and forth between the ships and docks, loading and unloading goods in boxes, barrels, pots, and crates.

Sadia stood still for a moment, intimidated by how busy everyone seemed and having no idea who to talk to in order to try to beg passage. She was even less prepared to try to figure out how to stow away on one, should it come to that.

"Look at all those ships!" a young voice said beside her, and she whirled to see Reza standing next to her and looking out at the wharf, shading his eyes with his hand.

"Reza!" she gasped, and glanced quickly around as she took his arm. "What are you doing here? You should be with the others!"

He straightened and squared his shoulders before answering confidently, "I decided I need to go with you."

"No, you can't," she said, panicking. "You have to run home, quick!"

He shook his head resolutely. "Yusuf can take care of the girls. I need to protect you."

She furrowed her brow, touched by his bravery, naive though it was. "Reza, this isn't a game — the Hierophants are very dangerous!"

"So am I," he said with a mischievous grin, pulling his sling out of his trouser pocket and giving it a snap.

"Oh, Reza," Sadia groaned, reaching out and running her free hand through his hair. "Please, go back."

"No," he replied stubbornly. "I'm going with you and baby Ibrahim."

She sighed and looked down at Ibrahim's wrinkled, pained little face. She was desperate and had very little time to argue with him. "Reza," she began sternly, "you need to—"

A sudden commotion from the teeming crowd behind them interrupted her, and they both turned to see the cause. A group of cultists had strayed too close to a guard patrol, and the two groups were standing off against each other, shouting and exchanging threats, apparently more brazen during daylight.

Sadia clutched Reza to her as she watched the crowd begin to part around the two armed groups, and she had an undeniable feeling that they needed to move, quickly.

"We need to go," she hissed, and he nodded. They hurried off together down toward the wharf, and Sadia was at a loss for what to do about her brother. He was adamant and determined, and she wasn't sure she could bring herself to send him back through the city without her now that he'd already come so far. And though she hated to admit it, she felt a little calmer for some reason now that he was with her.

The wharf bazaar sprawled out from the edge of the harbor, and it was busier than even the main bazaar normally was: merchants shouting out their wares from stalls along the harbor road, doing their best to hock fish of all kinds, along with anything else that might fetch a coin or two. The noise and clamor all around grated on Sadia's nerves, which were frayed already by their harrowing flight through the city.

She looked out onto the seemingly endless line of docked ships as the two of them stood at the start of the crowded wharf, and she felt frozen, desperate to dash forward but having no idea where to start in seeking passage out of the city she'd never left. Finally, she swallowed her fear and led Reza over to a merchant ship being loaded with supplies.

"Please, let us onboard," she said breathlessly to a crew member loading cargo. "We need to leave the city."

The bare-chested man hefted a wooden crate onto his shoulder and turned away as if he hadn't heard her.

"Please," she asked another, but he ignored her as well.

She tried to ask several others, but the best responses she received were a dismissive growl or an annoyed grunt. Casting a glance back up the slope toward the bazaar, she saw the cultists and the guardsmen had begrudgingly moved past each other, and the group of orange-clad fanatics was moving down toward the harbor. They didn't have much time.

Sadia hurried down the wharf, trying to put as much distance as possible between her and the Hierophants, but too intimidated by the rough men working the dozens of merchant vessels tied off to the docks to approach most of them.

All of the ships at the wharf were large with lots of crew, and no one answered her timid request for passage, or they rebuked her angrily; the sorry state of Sadia's clothes alone spoke louder than her few measly coins. One man lifted his hand to her, but Reza stepped between them to take the blow, and they hurried away.

Tears built in Sadia's eyes as she neared the end of the wharf, and she cursed cruel Qasira. Her mind raced to decide best how to stow away on one of the large ships without Ibi giving them away as he seemed to wake and fuss so regularly.

Just as her hope started to fade, she caught sight of one more ship hiding behind a towering trade vessel. It was much smaller and looked to have been cobbled together from the remains of multiple other boats. Sadia pulled Reza along and hurried toward it, fearful their time was short.

As they neared, she saw two figures reclining on a pile of crates and sacks at the edge of the dock in front of the ship. One was a squat, black-bearded dwarf and the other was a lithe eastern man wearing a broad hat made from woven reeds. Both were taking turns sipping from a clay jar and didn't pay Sadia and Reza any attention as they approached.

"Excuse me," she said, her voice shaking. "Can you help us?"

The dwarf looked up at her and grimaced. "Away with ye!" he grumbled, and the stench of alcohol wafted from him. "I'm in no charitable mood today."

"Please," she begged, taking another step toward them. "I need to leave the city."

The dwarf waved her off dismissively. "Bugger off, lass, before I get angry."

"I can pay! I have some coin...." She reached into the secret pocket in her hem and pulled out the three copper drahm. They made her think of Yusuf and the girls, and tears welled in her eyes as she held them out, her heart thumping in her chest as she prayed someone — anyone — would take pity on them.

The dwarf looked at her and at the offering she held out to him, and the hard lines around his beady eyes softened slightly. "Alright, lass, take a breath and explain yourself," he said. He held up a hand when she tried to pass the money to him and shook his head. "No, no, I've not agreed to anything yet. Just explain."

"Please," she said. "We have to leave Qasira. Our little brother is very sick, and there are men after us. Please," she swiped at each eye as two tears escaped, "I don't know where else to go...."

The dwarf glanced over her shoulder, his stormy brows furrowing. "Men after you? What men?" he asked.

Sadia looked up to follow his gaze, catching a glimpse of orange slowly but surely moving toward them through the crowded dockyard.

She wondered if it would be wiser to lie, but she had neither the time nor ability to come up with a good one, so she dropped her voice low to tell him the truth. "The cultists," she whispered, her lip trembling.

The dwarf and the man stared at her blankly.

"The Hierophants of the Lidless Eye," she prompted after a pause.

"Oh, those mad bastards?" the dwarf asked, waving his hand. "Aye, they're a mouthy lot, but at the first sign of trouble, they scurry right back to their hidey-holes out in the desert."

"They cowards," the eastern man agreed in a strong accent, giving Sadia a reassuring nod as he lifted the clay jug to his lips. "You no fear them!"

"Lu's right, lass," the dwarf said. "You needn't fear those tail-tucking candleholders. Ha!" He chuckled and took the jug from his friend.

Sadia stared at them in surprise. "They killed all the priests in the bazaar yesterday," she said, and her words made the dwarf choke as he sipped from the jug, and he sputtered as he looked up at her wide-eyed.

"What's that now?" he asked, coughing and pounding his chest.

"The cultists killed the high priest and all of his acolytes," Sadia explained quickly, amazed anyone in the city wasn't aware of what had happened. "Now they're roaming the streets, and for some reason, the guards aren't trying to fight them." She hugged Ibrahim closer and pulled Reza into her as well. "We can't stay here," she said, "please."

"Whoa, lass," the dwarf said, holding up his hands, "we just got in — we're not leaving." He gestured to the pile of goods he and the man called Lu were sitting on. "I've got to get all this to a couple of important clients of mine."

"But it's too dangerous!" she said, desperate, feeling their chances of leaving Qasira slipping away.

Lu sucked his teeth. "She got a baby, boss!" he said, gesturing at the bundle in Sadia's arms.

"I can see that just fine," the dwarf grumbled, rolling his eyes. "You've got a lot of opinions for a bodyguard."

The other man shrugged, and as Sadia looked at him a little closer, she realized he had a short, straight sword at his hip, its scabbard crafted from a dark, crimson wood with tarnished silver and polished jadestone adornments, the hilt wrapped with bright red cord.

"I... suppose when we leave, we could take you down the river, toward the sea," the dwarf offered begrudgingly. "But I'll need a few days."

"No, please!" Sadia cried desperately, holding out her hand again with the three little coins. "We can't wait — we have to leave now!"

The dwarf sighed and stood, giving her a compassionate look. "I understand you and your kin are in a bad way, lass," he said, glancing down at Reza. "Er, what happened to your face, lad?" he asked.

Reza looked up at him, his face still swollen, but finally able to open both eyes. "A cyclops smashed me with his hammer," he said casually. "I survived, though."

"I see...." The dwarf shifted his attention back to Sadia. "Listen, lass, I've got obligations to important people in this city that I have to fulfill." He straightened out the shabby tunic he wore and drew himself up, standing just a bit smaller than Sadia herself. "I'm a Gilded Dwarf, you see, and a proud Glintstone, no less! I've a certain family reputation to uphold. I cannae turn about and leave just because of a wee bit of danger."

"Dalgrim Glintstone!" A harsh voice barked from behind Sadia. Both she and the dwarf jumped at the sound, and she turned to see a tall, dark-haired man with a gilded breastplate standing on the pier in front of a small group of city guardsmen, and her stomach lurched.

"Oh, bugger," the dwarf muttered.

CHAPTER 13

SADIA

"By writ of Emir Yasir al-Mahariq," the guard captain called loudly, his men slowly spreading out behind him and leveling their spears, "you are wanted for the crimes of larceny, piracy, and smuggling."

The dwarf ran a hand over his receding hairline before stepping past Sadia and clearing his throat to call back down the length of the jetty. "Dalgrim... what-stone?" he asked, flashing a nervous smile. "I'm, er, afraid you've got the wrong dwarf — Hamfist Gemworthy is my name."

"But you just said you're a Glintstone," Reza said skeptically from beside Sadia.

Dalgrim — presumably the dwarf's real name — glowered down at the boy, then over at his eastern friend. "Get ready to earn your pay, Lu," he growled quietly. Lu looked over at all the armored men with a disinterested expression, his legs still kicked up on one of the crates, and he took another sip from the jug.

The guard captain scoffed. "There is no mistake. You stand accused of crimes against the emirate and must answer for them. You are hereby ordered to stand down, surrender your cargo, and come with us!"

As the man bellowed across the docks, Sadia caught another flash of orange emerge from the gathering crowd. She stiffened as a group of the armored cultists seemed to materialize as if out of nowhere, their bronze breastplates gleaming dully in the sunlight. She reached over without thinking and gripped Dalgrim's arm in a panic. The Hierophants' eyes searched from beneath their dark orange hoods across the crowded wharf. Did they know what she looked like? Had they seen her rescue Ibrahim?

The dwarf ignored her clawing grasp. "Even if I was Dalgrim," he declared indignantly, "I'm certainly no thief, pirate, or smuggler!" He looked at his bodyguard and pointed to the group of city guards. "Lu, kindly disabuse these fine gentlemen of the notion that I'm a smuggler!"

The swordsman looked up at Dalgrim for a moment before casting his eyes at the captain of the guard. "He's smuggler," he slurred as he shrugged his shoulders, then he took another gulp from the clay jar.

"Why, you ungrateful, wine-soaked little—"

As Dalgrim berated Lu, Ibrahim started to fuss in Sadia's arms, giving pained little cries as he writhed in the blankets. The leader of the cultists looked over at the sound, and Sadia took a few steps back toward the dwarf's ship, grasping at Reza's wrist to drag him along. The city guardsmen took notice as the cultists advanced, and a couple of them shifted nervously, glancing at the captain.

"I told you!" she hissed at Dalgrim, tugging his sleeve. "We have to leave — now!"

The captain rounded on the approaching Heirophants, his knuckles whitening on the hilt of his gilded sword. "Halt, you heretic swine! Your presence is interfering with the execution of an edict of Emir al-Muhariq himself. Turn away and retreat like the cowardly canyon rats you are, and I won't drag you to the dungeons alongside the dwarf!"

One of the cultists took a single step forward, his jaw clenched, and fixed the guard-captain with a steely gaze as his companions arrayed themselves defensively beside him. "Your emir also decreed you should not draw arms against the faithful," he declared. "The girl stole something from us," he said, pointing at Sadia. "Let us take her, and we'll leave."

"You don't give me orders, scum!" the captain spat, ripping the scimitar at his side from its scabbard and leveling it at the cultists.

As Sadia's heart pounded, Dalgrim looked back and forth between the two armed groups. "Captain," he called out. "Can I just point out that I have absolutely nothing to do with these madmen and would very much like to be left alone? I'm sure there's some sort of... misunderstanding here?"

"There's no misunderstanding, smuggler!" the guard captain retorted, keeping his gaze on the cultists. "Stand down, now!" he ordered.

Everyone in the vicinity of the dwarf's boat stood frozen for a moment as a palpable tension built. The cultists eyed the guardsmen and Sadia alternately, while the guard captain's gaze shifted from the cultists to Dalgrim and Lu. Sadia finally took another step backward, pulling Reza along, and then chaos erupted on the wharf.

"Take the girl!" the leader of the Hierophants cried, unsheathing his wickedly curved sword and charging toward Sadia and Reza.

As he did, the guard captain started barking orders, directing most of his men to attack the cultists, while to one pair of burly soldiers he bellowed, "You two — take the dwarf and his henchman!"

The two sides clashed as a handful of guards and cultists both avoided the melee and dashed down the jetty toward Dalgrim and Sadia. "Earn your keep, Lu!" Dalgrim shouted in a panic as the men bore down on them. He kicked the easterner in the leg, and Lu finally rose unsteadily to his feet.

"He doesn't look like he's feeling too good," Reza said nervously. "What help is he going to be?"

Dalgrim turned to look down at the boy. "Let's just say I keep his drunken arse around for a reason," he answered gruffly. He glanced between Sadia and Reza and the pile of wares Lu had been resting on.

He clapped a hand on each of their shoulders. "Are you still interested in passage, lass?" Sadia nodded emphatically. "It seems I'll be leaving lovely Qasira earlier than planned. Take the babe and get aboard the *Mollysocks*," he instructed her, indicating the shallow boat bobbing in the water behind them. "Laddie, you help me get these crates back on board while Lu holds them off!"

Dalgrim threw a box up on his shoulder and jogged over to his barge as fast as his dwarven legs could carry him, Sadia and Reza in tow. He shrugged the crate off, dumping it onto the deck of the *Mollysocks*, then held Sadia's hand, helping her to step over the rail as Reza tossed a heavy, lumpy bag onto the boat as well.

As her brother and the dwarf raced back to grab more from the pile of goods on the dock, Sadia watched in trepidation as the pair of guards rushed down the jetty, followed closely by two cultists who had broken away from the main skirmish. All four of them drew to a halt as Lu moved to block their advance, unsheathing his elegant straight sword and holding it easily at his side.

The emir's men glanced at the cultists as they came up next to each other in front of Lu, and for a moment, no one seemed to know who to attack first. Lu swayed and took a clumsy sip from the jug, and then one of the guards leapt at him as the other engaged the cultists. Lu's blade flashed as he proceeded to deftly parry a series of blows as the guards attacked both him and the cultists, all three parties exchanging strikes alternately with each other. He weaved, slashed, and thrust, the clay jug sloshing in his left hand as the sword in his right glinted in the desert sunlight.

Sadia clutched Ibrahim tighter as she watched, marveling at the drunken swordsman, and the main groups of Hierophants and Qasiran royal guard clashed in the background. Finally, one of the guards managed to draw Lu into a series of maneuvers that caused him to overextend his reach, and one of them was able to strike him hard in the head with the hilt of his scimitar. Lu stumbled, and the clay jug fell from his grip to smash on the planks beneath their feet, the red liquid drenching his pants and shoes and seeping through the cracks.

"Ahya!" Lu cried, vigorously rubbing his head under the broad reed hat he wore, and Sadia's knuckles whitened on the rail of the ship as she watched one of the guardsmen take advantage of the moment and raise his scimitar high for a fatal blow.

Before the blade could fall, however, a small stone cracked the man in the forehead, drawing blood and sending him stumbling backward.

"Ha!" Reza cried, and Sadia looked over to see him standing up on the rail of the barge and holding his fist triumphantly in the air, his sling dangling from his grasp.

"Reza!" she gasped, horrified, but Dalgrim came over and grabbed her brother under the arms to lift him down onto the deck.

"Untie that rope there, lad!" Dalgrim hollered at Reza, pointing to the thick rope that moored the barge to the dock. Reza leapt on it and struggled to unbind the knots. "There's a good lad," he said, attacking a second mooring tie. "Let's get her free, and we'll be off!"

Once the little ship was unbound, Dalgrim climbed over the rail to haul one more large crate aboard before dashing over to the tiller and turning it hard toward the river. The *Mollysocks* floated free from the dock as Lu took one cultist down with a strike to the leg. "Lu!" Dalgrim shouted over his shoulder as he guided the barge onto the broad Tajari river, "come on!"

"No!" the guard-captain roared at the soldiers nearest him, "seize them!"

The guardsmen renewed their charge, but Lu managed to take another down and send a third man into the river before making a break for the barge and leaping deftly across the water to join them.

Lu and Dalgrim both took long poles from the far side of the deck and used them to quickly push the *Mollysocks* out and away from the wharf. A handful of guards and cultists both ran up to the edge of the dock but were forced to stop short as the gap to Dalgrim's boat had grown too wide to cross.

"Farewell, gentlemen!" Dalgrim laughed as he waved to them. "Give my regards to your emir!" He and Lu continued to push the barge out into open water, the dwarf red from exertion but grinning broadly.

Sadia and Reza watched the chaos on the docks grow quieter as the river carried them away, and Sadia felt the faintest bit of relief creep into her heart.

Leaving the chaos and the clamor further and further behind, the barge drifted gently on the current of the wide river, and eventually, Dalgrim brought the pole back in from the water and stepped over to take the tiller at the rear. "Lu, go unfurl the sail, and we'll let the wind take us on to Emra'adid! You two," he looked over to the siblings, "I don't suppose you've names for us to call you by?"

"I'm Sadia, and this is my little brother, Reza," Sadia said as she stroked Ibi's back, keeping him cradled against her. All the chaos hadn't seemed to affect him, and he remained curled against whatever pain gnawed at him from within, gripping her shawl in one weak fist as she held him on her shoulder. "And this is Ibrahim."

Dalgrim nodded and gave the rudder a tug, guiding them away from the shore. Then he stepped away and bowed deeply before them. "Dalgrim Glintstone, of the Gilded Dwarves, first of the sons of Dalgor, at your service," he declared with a flourish.

Sadia bowed her head politely, but Reza cocked an eyebrow. "I thought you said you were Hamfish Jam-something," he said suspiciously.

"Hamfist Gemworthy!" the dwarf answered in a huff. "And to some, I am. But here, to spite that wretched guard captain and his corrupt emir, I am indeed Dalgrim Glintstone. And this," he added, gesturing to the easterner as he climbed back down from the slightly crooked mast after releasing the sail, "is Lu Song, my loyal bodyguard."

Dalgrim cast a critical eye on the large pile of wares he had stacked on the deck, then over to his two young passengers. "Well, it seems fate has forced our paths together after all. Ah," he cleared his throat noisily and held out an open palm to Sadia.

"Oh," she said, realizing he wanted the payment she'd promised earlier. She retrieved the coins and placed the paltry sum in his palm.

Dalgrim studied them for a moment and seemed to struggle with the decision before closing his meaty fist around them and shoving them in a pouch. "That'll be sufficient to get you to Emra'adid," he said gruffly as he walked back toward the tiller. "Passage includes three squares a day and a spot to lie down on the deck to sleep. Now, why don't you—"

"Uh, boss?" Lu asked, and they all turned to see him staring back at Qasira, his round hat tilted back on his head. Sadia followed his gaze, and her heart sank as she saw a ship pulling away from the wharf. The gentle wind caught its sail as it unfurled, revealing the distinctive emblem of the Qasiran Emirate: a desert palm against a blazing sun on a brilliant blue field.

"Bugger!" Dalgrim cursed as he stepped back from the tiller to the stern rail. "That'll be the royal guard after us." He gripped the edge of the deck as he peered across the water. "Quick vessel, by the look of her. Quicker than my faithful *Mollysocks*, at any rate."

Sadia held Ibrahim close as she stepped up beside the dwarf, her whole body tense as she watched the other vessel set after them, as though she could will the little barge they were on to move faster. "But surely there's a way we can escape them...."

The dwarf gave a hefty chuckle. "Oh aye, lass — my trusty *Mollysocks* has a few tricks up her sleeve," he explained, patting the railing of the ship fondly. He turned to her and pointed. "You take your brothers and hunker down there by the bow, and hold onto the rail tight!" He looked up at Lu, who had retrieved another jug of wine and was taking a long swig, leaning casually against the mast. "Get on up to that rigging, Lu, and take in the sail, quick!"

"I just put it down!" the man complained, but Dalgrim snatched the jug and glowered at him, and with a sigh, Lu did as he was told.

The dwarf disappeared into the freestanding cabin toward the front of the barge, through a curtain of hanging beads. A cacophony of clattering and crashing came out of the cabin, mixed with Dalgrim's cursing, as he was apparently searching the little room for something.

After a moment, he emerged, holding a small glass phial triumphantly aloft. "Here we are!" he declared confidently, strutting back toward the stern.

"What is that?" Reza asked curiously as he and Sadia sunk down next to the low wall of the deck as he had advised them.

"A gift from Tandaharian pirates, lad," the dwarf chuckled as he uncorked the phial and held it off the back of the barge. He paused and looked back to Lu, who was pulling on ropes to furl the sail. "Are you about done, you useless layabout?"

Lu shot a dark look over at his employer as he hauled the sail all the way up, then swung down and landed a little unsteadily on his feet. "Sail up," he muttered, throwing the loose rope down to the deck in a pile, "sail down!" He wagged a finger at the dwarf. "You crazy!"

Dalgrim rolled his eyes. "Just come over here and take the tiller!" he barked. The easterner obliged, recovering the discarded wine jug from the deck as he did, and joined the dwarf as the latter swirled the violet liquid within the phial. "Hold on tight now!" he called loudly, and Lu held the tiller steady as Dalgrim lifted the glass globe again, pouring its contents out over the water behind them, a faint purple trail lingering in the air before quickly dissipating.

The dwarf stoppered the phial and stowed it in a pocket before dropping quickly to the deck and grasping the barge's rail in a white knuckle grip. Sadia tightened her own grip, then peered up at Dalgrim's bearded face as a moment passed and nothing happened. The dwarf lifted his head carefully to look over the rail and then Sadia heard the water begin to churn and bubble noisily behind the *Mollysocks*, and suddenly the barge lurched forward.

Sadia was thrown against the rail as they picked up speed, and she scrambled to hold on to her brothers as Ibi awoke with a frightened wail and started to cry. She hugged the boy close and peered back, her hair whipping in her eyes as she did, and saw that they had created a frothing wake and left a swirling purple miasma in the water behind them.

"What... what did you do?!" Sadia exclaimed breathlessly as she turned to look up at Dalgrim. The dwarf grinned from ear to ear as Sadia wrestled with her hair in the wind.

"Ha! It worked!" he laughed, his braided black beard and hair blown back as the clumsy barge cut through the river like an arrow slicing the air. Lu's hat flew off his head, the strap around his neck the only thing stopping it from flying off into the river behind them. Dalgrim reached out to take the tiller back from the easterner. "Don't worry," he called cheerily over the whipping wind, "It only lasts a few minutes! But it'll give us a healthy head start on the fools!"

Lu leaned against the rail and hoisted his clay jug, seemingly unperturbed by the sudden, magical burst of speed. Sadia, Ibi, and Reza watched the city of Qasira grow smaller and smaller behind them until the *Mollysocks* finally slowed back down to a leisurely pace. The emir's ship was no longer visible in the distance, and it seemed they'd actually finally gotten away.

The dwarf looked up at the sky, a bank of fluffy white clouds marching toward them from the distant desert mountains to the west. "Ah, it's good to be back on the broad Tajari, eh, Lu?" He cast a glance back toward the receding Qasira, then took a long pull on a small metal flask retrieved from his breast pocket and grinned, revealing the gap in his teeth.

"Why are they both so thirsty?" Reza asked quietly at her side, and Sadia frowned.

"They must work very hard," she answered through her teeth, not wanting to explain to him that, in her desperation, she'd led them aboard a ship manned by criminals and drunks. At least they seemed harmless enough.

"Well, settle in, children!" Dalgrim said, nodding toward the pile of his belongings on the deck. "There's fruit and dried meat in one of those crates if you're hungry, and otherwise, get some rest — we're a few days from the next city on the river." He took another swig from the flask and adjusted the tiller as the *Mollysocks* rode the gentle current toward the sea.

As Reza pounced on the crates in search of the promised food, Sadia stood and looked back toward the ever-dwindling Qasira, feeling as though half her heart remained in the city with Yusuf and her little sisters.

CHAPTER 14

GIDEON

"Recruit!" a harried voice called from behind Gideon. He turned and saw Sister Josephine kneeling over a wounded man as he lay on the cold marble, pressing a sullied cloth to the man's abdomen. "Come here and help me hold him down!"

Gideon obeyed, jogging over and going to his knees to help. He had just finished watching over the walls with the guards, and before retiring to the barracks for some rest, he'd come to the chapel to offer any aid he could. Sister Josephine's pretty, angular features looked haggard as she worked on the wound, and her eyes were weary from her long labor.

"Hold his shoulders," she said, nodding toward the man on the floor. He was writhing and groaning, a worrisome, pale hue to his cheeks.

"What happened to him?" Gideon asked, putting his hands on the man's shoulders as instructed.

Sister Josephine answered without taking her eyes from the wound. "Some kind of curse, I think. I've had a poultice on it for hours, but the wound is... growing." Gideon glanced up at her and saw sweat beading on her brow. "It's as though whatever wounded him is still wounding him."

Gideon wasn't sure what that meant exactly, but his blood ran cold at the sound of it. He clenched his jaw as he watched the dressing slowly turn a dark, bitter crimson, and he had to use all his weight to try and keep the man still beneath him. The cleric sucked her teeth and pulled the soiled cloth away, a new one at the ready. Gideon froze at the sight of the raw injury beneath.

It looked as he imagined a sword-cut might, a long gash across his abdomen. Blood seeped thickly from whatever was damaged inside him and oozed out, mixed with the pungent herbal poultice and other humors. But what sucked the air from Gideon's breath was that the wound was moving. It pulled itself open from the edges, refusing all efforts to close it, as though something was tugging at it, trying to rip the flesh further.

The man let out a pained moan as the bandage came away, and Gideon saw his eyelids flicker as he looked around like he was in the throes of some delirious dream. "No," he groaned, "no!"

"Keep ahold of him," the clergywoman said again, putting a hand on the man's brow. "He's dangerously feverish."

"No!" he screamed, his eyes shooting wide open and darting around frantically. "No, I can't!"

Gideon's head swam as he struggled to hold the man writhing beneath him, and he was unable to tear his eyes from the horrific, mystical wound that was killing him.

"I need a hospitaler, please!" Sister Josephine shouted over her shoulder as she hurried to apply another dressing, seemingly in vain.

Gideon looked up from the wound to the man's face and found him staring right back at him. "They're coming," he whispered, his eyes wide and terrified, his hands clenching Gideon's wrists. "They're coming."

"What?" Gideon glanced up at the cleric, but she was looking over her shoulder for help, not paying attention to them. Gideon looked back down at the wounded man, and saw his eyes were clear, focused. "Who's coming?"

"The Sisters," he rasped, his voice dry and cracked. "They're coming for me. They'll take me!"

Gideon's mouth hung open as he stared into the man's eyes before a clatter of footsteps roused him, and Hospitaler Lucas arrived and knelt beside them.

"What do you need, sister?" he asked, and Gideon looked up to see Nefteli accompanying him, her drab uniform spattered with dried gore.

"There's some kind of lingering magic here," she said, her hands red and wet. "I've never seen anything like this. He's in need of the healing Light."

The hospitaler frowned and glanced at the wound, then nodded grimly. "I'll do what I can," he said, folding his sleeves back. "Nefteli, just as before, yes?" he instructed, and the girl nodded. Together, they held their hands out over the violent wound.

Gideon looked back down at the dying man, but his brief moment of lucidity had passed; his eyes were once again shut, and he writhed against the pain. As Nefteli closed her eyes and mouthed a silent prayer, Lucas lifted up his leather-bound tome and rapidly flipped to a marked page.

He raised his free hand in supplication and began an invocation of the Light. "This humble servant implores the gods for their Holy Light, the purgative Light, the Light which smote the darkness," he muttered, reading from the tome, "abandon not this faithful warrior."

"May the gods watch over him," Nefteli recited, giving the ritual response.

"Grant unto him healing," Lucas continued, "that he may fight again to bring the burning flame of justice to our enemies."

Nefteli responded again. "And fulfill his purpose in the Light of holy faith."

"As St. Oronos burned the heretics of the Gnostic Arcanum, let—"

The words of the prayer were drowned out by a sudden loud, animalistic yowl from the wounded man, and Gideon had to redouble his efforts to keep him pinned down. As he did, he looked down at where Sister Josephine was still trying valiantly to stem the constant flow of blood and bile, but the hospitaler's invocation seemed to make the wound worse somehow, as though it was fighting against his very prayer.

The edges of the wound split further, and blood and pus welled forth anew, soaking through the cleric's cloth. She bit her lip and pushed down, but the wound seemed to have a life of its own, and it resisted her efforts.

"Why isn't it working?" Gideon asked, overcome for a moment by terror as he remembered the archoness's words the previous night. He looked up at Nefteli, who had opened her eyes, her brow furrowed as she stared down at the pitiful man. Lucas continued reading from the holy tome, seemingly unperturbed.

"Keep him still!" Sister Josephine shouted to Gideon over the man's howling, ceaseless in her work.

Gideon looked back down at the wound, and his stomach roiled as he saw the flesh had split open further, almost all the way up to the man's breastbone. "Please!" Josephine begged as a panic seemed to seize her. She looked desperately up at the hospitaler, whose eyes had closed in concentration as his voice rose above the clamor.

Nefteli continued providing the antiphons, and after a moment, a mystical wind rose up in the chapel as the two hospitalers channeled Holy Light from the heavens. Gideon had never seen the Light used in such a dire moment, and the two of them were able to call down a brilliant golden pillar of Light, centered on the man's wound.

Gideon was awe-struck as he watched glimmering rays pierce through the vaulted chapel ceiling like a ray of sun at dawn peeking over the horizon, bathing the wounded man in warmth.

But the reaction wasn't one of healing. The wound began to writhe and pulsate, as though in time with a heartbeat, and Gideon saw something moving inside of it. His blood ran cold as he watched the torn flesh leap and jerk, tearing itself wider and wider apart like the mouth of some awful monster struggling to wrench itself open.

"What's happening?" Sister Josephine asked, looking up at the hospitaler, then down at the wound, her eyes wide and brimming with fear.

Hospitaler Lucas tore his eyes from the tome at the panicked sound of her voice, and when he saw what was happening, the prayer died on his lips, and the column of Light faded.

As she sensed the warmth of the Light retreating, Nefteli's eyes opened, and she looked down and gasped, sitting back in shock.

Gideon couldn't tear his eyes away from the terrible sight as he struggled in vain to force strength into his enfeebled arms to restrain the man, who was attempting to sit upright, his hands clawing at the wound, screaming and trying desperately to keep himself whole.

The lump within the wound swelled and grew, and then it exploded outward, bursting through the man's rib cage with a horrendous chorus of splintering bone and tearing flesh. The man's flailing arms threw Gideon off, sending him to his back beside Nefteli. His hand clutched at hers, and he scrambled them both backward.

The wounded man sat up and looked down at the wound ripping itself deeper into him, and he screamed, pain and a profound sadness mingled in a shrill, sobbing screech as he watched his chest cave inward, his ribs collapsing like shattered branches, and his flesh tearing and ripping apart.

Blood sprayed into the air as a horrific transformation took place, and his body contorted and twisted into a monstrous perversion of a man, standing on all four limbs like an animal, bones torn from the flesh, every humor seeping from perforated organs and flowing across the polished marble floor of the chapel.

Gideon scuttled backward on the floor, dragging Nefteli with him as he stared in horror at what had become of the man.

"What in blazes is going on over there?" Sir Cormac bellowed, his heavy armor clanking as he jogged toward the scene.

A wet, otherworldly shriek echoed off the walls of the chapel as a feral-looking head ripped through the shredded flesh of the man's abdomen, and huge yellow eyes blinked away the gore and viscera.

Gideon found himself unable to move, unable to do anything but watch as the unholy transformation occurred. He was dimly aware of Nefteli's hand clutching at his arm, and both of them remained frozen in shock and terror.

The creature that had twisted itself into existence from the soldier's body shifted its unnatural eyes, its gaze settling on Hospitaler Lucas as the healer slowly backed away. It was only then that Gideon realized the wounded man's head, hanging grotesquely from the underside of what had become the monster's sinuous body, was still screaming, his eyes darting around wildly. Somehow, he was still alive.

His frantic gaze finally met Gideon's, confusion and abject terror graved upon his face. Then the monster reached down and pulled and twisted the man's head off of its body. Gideon recoiled at the sickening sound of tearing flesh and snapping ligaments, and he felt Nefteli shudder beside him.

The booming voice of Sir Cormac rang throughout the cathedral as the huge old knight broke into a run. "Stand back!" came the cry as he charged the abomination, pulling his long zweihander from the scabbard on his back. The monster regarded him with a hissing shriek and hurled the poor man's severed head at the surging paladin. Sir Cormac deflected it deftly, sending it careening off his blade to skitter wetly across the marble floor and roll to a halt between Gideon's legs.

The head stared up at him, and Gideon was unable to look away from the man's now lifeless eyes, hooded and unseeing.

He only looked up when he heard a sickening crunching sound as Sir Cormac brought his sword down with a heavy overhead swing that split the monster's torso clean through, sending it crashing to the ground in a mist of blood and bile.

Gideon's breath caught in his throat as he watched the terrible creature scramble back up and swing its cloven halves around like a fleshy whip, attacking the old paladin from the side.

Sir Cormac grunted in surprise as he swung his sword around to block the blow, but the creature was far stronger than it looked, and the force of its claw-like shattered bones sent the old knight stumbling.

"Sacred Light!" Sister Josephine screamed as she fell backward and clawed the floor to drag herself away, her white robes spattered with blood.

"Run, you fools!" Sir Cormac shouted as the monstrosity pounced on him, the flat of his blade held out in both hands as a brace to keep the thing at bay. As the unholy creature's shattered, formerly human limbs battered the old knight, his eyes lighted on Gideon and Nefteli.

"Get everyone out of the chapel!" the paladin shouted at them, and his words finally broke Gideon from his stupor.

He scrambled back and away from the severed head, and Nefteli leapt deftly to her feet and helped to pull him up beside her. Gideon steadied himself against a nearby fluted column as his legs shook beneath him, his eyes locked on Sir Cormac's struggle with the monster.

Nefteli dashed over and began helping one of the other wounded soldiers up to his feet, lifting his arm over her shoulders to support the weight he couldn't bear. She started for the chapel doors but paused when she glanced over her shoulder and saw Gideon frozen there.

"Gideon!" she cried, beckoning him and pointing toward other casualties in need of evacuation from the chapel.

Gideon tore his eyes from the grotesque melee at the sound of her voice, but his attention was immediately returned to Sir Cormac as the gory flesh-beast let out a gurgling cry as it assailed the big paladin.

"We have to help him!" Gideon called back to her without looking. He cast around for something to use as a weapon as Nefteli grunted in frustration and turned, helping guide the man she was supporting to the chapel entrance.

Sister Josephine hauled herself up off the floor and grabbed his arm. "We have to flee!" she pleaded with him, clutching the prayer beads around her neck with her other hand and taking a faltering step backward, tugging on his wrist.

Gideon swallowed, his mouth dry as he struggled to overcome the fear clawing along his spine. "I'm not leaving him," he insisted, and he pulled free of her grasp and seized one of the tall candelabras lining the walls of the chapel. Hefting it in both hands like a spear, Gideon turned back toward Sir Cormac as Sister Josephine shook her head fearfully and continued her reluctant retreat toward the chapel doors. Tightening his grip on the glorified candle stand, Gideon only hesitated for a moment before charging toward the fray.

The mustachioed old knight roared and threw the beast off him, and it slammed into the stone wall of the chapel, its limbs flailing. Sir Cormac used the opportunity to right himself, and Gideon helped the massively armored paladin climb back to his feet, only to receive a powerful shove to the chest from the old man.

"Go, boy!" he growled, "get the rest of the wounded out!" He turned back toward the monster, which had splayed its deformed, broken limbs out like a spider.

A chill raised the hairs on Gideon's arms as he watched it skitter backward and climb halfway up the chapel wall, using the shattered bones poking like claws from its flesh. It crawled across the arched, stained glass window in the apse of the chapel, the dawning sun shining through and casting its hideous shadow across Gideon and Sir Cormac. Another guttural, piercing shriek reverberated off the chapel walls and ceiling, and the thing launched itself from the wall at the paladin.

Sir Cormac strode forward to meet it as Gideon took a step backward, and then another, torn on what to do. He wanted to help the paladin but felt more afraid than he ever had been before in his life. Looking around at the dozens of wounded men and the clergy trying to gather and guide them out of the chapel, he finally swallowed his pride and shame both. He dashed over to one of the archoness's injured men, laid the long candelabra on the floor, and helped him to his feet.

The wounded man groaned and leaned heavily on him, and the two started shambling toward the door of the chapel. "What's happening?" the man asked, his voice slurred with pain and exhaustion.

"I don't know," Gideon answered truthfully, glancing over his shoulder at Sir Cormac, whose arcing zweihander glinted in the colorful shafts of sunlight through the stained glass as it hacked bits off the profane creature, "but we have to get out of here."

As they joined the throng of clergy helping the wounded make their way to the chapel doors, Gideon looked around and saw that many of the wounded men were too badly hurt to move on their own. They were either being carried out or still lay where they had been placed when brought in, their limbs broken, or their insides exposed and stinking, and he knew that the monster would make quick work of them should it break past Sir Cormac.

The old paladin was an unstoppable force, however, and his sword was a blur of motion as he hacked chunks of flesh from the monster, but none of his powerful blows stopped the strange, bone-crunching undulation of the fleshy extremities which it flailed wildly about, battering the knight's plate armor.

Sir Cormac ducked under one swing from the abomination, then answered with a mighty blow of his own, but the monster's jagged, jutting ribs closed over the blade like a mouth, trapping it and using it to drag the knight in close.

Gideon's heart pounded in his chest as he turned away, desperate to get his soldier out of the chapel and rush back to help Sir Cormac, but the crowd of people looking to escape was pressed close in the vestibule, slowing him to a halt. He came up beside Nefteli, who fixed him with a look he couldn't quite decipher.

Someone at the front of the throng began to push the big doors open, and Gideon looked up to see a figure waiting just outside.

Archoness Lorica stood squarely, blocking the way out, flanked by her small cadre of paladins who had remained uninjured.

"What's happened?" she asked, her voice loud and unwavering.

"It's a... an unspeakable evil, my lady!" one of the monks answered, struggling even to get the words out, "some wicked creature has gained access to the chapel." The monk shifted the weight of the man he was escorting and took a small step forward. "We're trying to get the wounded out!"

The archoness didn't move. She looked to one of the wounded men, supported by two clerics. "Explain, Burgess," she commanded.

The soldier coughed, his voice weak. "It was Domhnall, milady, he... the witches' magics did something, and now he's...." The man's voice trailed off as he craned his neck to look back, past Gideon, to the combat still being waged in the chapel. Archoness Lorica followed his gaze, her eyes narrowing.

Suddenly, the soldier Gideon was helping doubled over and let out a single, sharp cry. The man let his weight fully rest on the young recruit, who struggled to keep him upright as he started grasping his chest and howling in pain.

"Holy Light!" a nearby cleric exclaimed in horror, looking down at the commotion. "It's happening to another one!"

Gideon glanced up and saw the archoness's eyes widen as she realized what was happening, but before she could speak, the man he was supporting suddenly crumpled to the ground, his body writhing and convulsing as his torso began to pulse, the ribs crackling, just like the first man.

The cleric took hold of Gideon and dragged him back as everyone recoiled from the scene and turned to flee the chapel.

As the throng made to push out past the archoness, she took a step back with one foot and held out her hand. "Halt!" she called, and her voice was like a thunderclap as her eyes flashed and a wave of righteous authority rolled off her like a tide, stopping the pressing crowd in their tracks.

Gideon felt the pressure of her divine power like a heavy hand pushing him back, and the hairs on the back of his neck stood on end as the air itself seemed to resonate around them. Everyone stopped, and only the abomination's feral shrieks and the singing of Sir Cormac's blade from within the chapel persisted through the sudden silence.

Gideon glanced over at Nefteli and saw the tension held in her brow as they all waited fearfully before the archoness's might.

Lorica's men stood resolute beside her, the hand of each subtly resting on his weapon's hilt as their hard eyes searched those of the waylaid clergy.

"Sergeant Findlay," the archoness finally said, glancing to the man at her right, "see the clergy out of the chapel. We will deal with our brothers ourselves." The sergeant nodded and stepped past Archoness Lorica to start ushering the clergy and the handful of recruits outside while the rest of her cadre took up their wounded brothers to bring them back inside.

The cleric holding Gideon by the shirt started pulling on him to follow, and Nefteli reluctantly handed off the wounded man to one of the cadre and took a hesitant step toward the doors.

The archoness strode through the crowd of terrified clergy as they were herded out by Sergeant Findlay, her eyes locked on the battle still being waged across the chapel.

Gideon's breath caught in his throat as he watched her. Despite her diminutive stature, her steps were so long and sure that she almost seemed to glide across the polished stone floor, and her gaze never wavered from the creature as she pulled her gilded tome from her belt like she was drawing a blade.

As he and Nefteli were urged out of the chapel by the archoness's men, Gideon looked back at Sir Cormac, who let out a hoarse cry as he hacked his sword through the monster's left side. It swung its flexuous, fleshy body around, the sword blow seemingly meaningless as its relentless assault on the old knight continued.

Gideon's heart sank as he was pushed toward the chapel doors; Sir Cormac was mighty, but he was breathing hard and slowing, and Gideon clenched his jaw as he watched the creature redouble its assault. He stopped before reaching the doors and turned and cried, "Sir Cormac needs help!" None of the soldiers moved to help the old man, though; three were dragging their wounded comrades back in, and another two remained at the archoness's side, awaiting her command.

Sergeant Findlay gave him a rough shove. "Get out!" the man

barked, and Gideon stumbled back, but couldn't look away from the old knight whose sword swings grew more wearied blow by blow.

"Gideon, come," Nefteli urged, reaching out and taking his hand. He glanced down and met her amber eyes, and she squeezed his hand and nodded. She started guiding him away, but he stopped to look back one last time.

The faces of the archoness's cadre were grim and battle-weathered, and Gideon had a horrible feeling they didn't care at all what happened to Sir Cormac. In a moment, he knew he had no choice.

Turning quickly back to Nefteli, he took her hand in both of his, and she looked up at him, her gentle brow furrowed in confusion. He held her gaze for a heartbeat, and just as her eyes widened in understanding, he let go and dashed back into the chapel.

CHAPTER 15

GIDEON

GIDEON WAS YOUNG, strong, and spry, and he quickly ducked under Sergeant Findlay's outstretched arms as he was hauling closed the doors, and raced passed them all, even the archoness, toward the flailing creature and embattled old knight.

All around him, the remaining wounded moaned and writhed in pain and fear as they looked around for help. Gideon wondered if it was only a matter of time before the same twisted fate befell them all, and he could only surmise what that would mean for him, given his choice to remain.

"Stop him!" one of the archoness's men called, but Gideon was already past them all, scooping up the discarded candelabra stand as he went.

Sir Cormac grunted and swore as he was slammed against the far wall by the monster, his sword knocked from his grip. The paladin went heavily to one knee as the beast advanced on him, but Gideon charged, thrusting the candelabra forward, driving the branched, wax-coated end toward the creature's center.

The beast turned in time to catch the attack on one of its jutting ribs, but that didn't stop Gideon, who let out a cry both furious and terrified as he pulled the candelabra back and swung it like a club, battering the thing in its unnatural face.

The creature shrieked and reeled, flailing its fleshy limbs out as it stumbled away from the paladin, and Gideon followed, beating it back again and again. His blows didn't seem to hurt it, but its sickeningly sinuous body gave way easily under the weight of the long candelabra.

As he kept the monster at bay, his arms numb from the impact of his blows, he heard Sir Cormac groan as he fetched his sword from the ground and climbed back to his feet. "By the Light," he growled, holding his sword aloft with both hands and glaring at the creature, "I shall give you a proper death and end this foul transformation!"

In that moment, the paladin's massive blade burst into a holy golden glow, and Sir Cormac swung his blade down, cleaving clean through the beast's torso, which fell in two pieces to the floor, sizzling and smoking from the heat of the Holy Light. Gideon stumbled back in surprise, dropping the battered candelabra. The monster's head whipped around wildly, and it lunged toward him in its death throes with its huge, dripping maw, but he managed to leap back out of the way.

Sir Cormac brought his sword down again, splitting the thing's head open, and a geyser of blood and gore sprayed outward, coating the two of them. The monster finally seemed to die, its limbs flopping limply to the floor as roiling black blood seeped from its cloven head.

Gideon panted heavily, looking around at the carnage, then back at the old knight. Sir Cormac was bent over with his hands on his knees, taking deep, labored breaths, the Light slowly fading from his heavy blade. He looked up at the young man and nodded once. "Good work, Ballad," he said, but then muttered a curse as he looked past him toward the vestibule.

Gideon turned and saw the archoness standing over the other man he had helped, who was currently undergoing the dark transformation where he lay on the floor. Her cadre were arrayed around the man, muttering prayers, and her hefty tome was open in her left hand, while her right hand was held aloft. Her eyes were closed, and the air hummed around her as she channeled the power of the Holy Light.

Gideon jumped as Sir Cormac's heavy, gauntleted hand clapped his shoulder, his wary eyes fixed on the scene playing out before them.

"Please, help me, milady!" the man on the ground shrieked, his body convulsing violently as the change took him.

The archoness opened her eyes, and they smoldered like golden embers. "By the justice of St. Oronos," she intoned, and her voice was a reverent, omnipresent whisper that Gideon heard as clearly as if she was standing beside him, "and the mercy of St. Thylessia, I will cleanse you of this unholy corruption."

As she said the words, a white light flashed in her palm, and Gideon had to shield his eyes as the radiant brilliance illuminated every corner of the chapel. When he was finally able to look back, he saw the shimmering white effigy of an elegantly curved saber held in her hand, made purely of Holy Light.

The man at her feet reached a feeble hand up in supplication as his bones began to audibly snap beneath his flesh, only for the burning hot tip of the immaterial blade to pass effortlessly through his palm. The sound of his screams and the hissing, popping, and burning of the Light purging him echoed off the marble walls and made Gideon's skin crawl.

The archoness pressed the blade deeper into the man, and his flesh was burned away as it went. The other soldiers stood around him, heads bowed, as he looked desperately among them all for mercy. Gideon couldn't tear his eyes away from the awful sight of the man's chest melting and collapsing into ash. His screams echoed as he burned alive and finally died.

The archoness held the holy blade sheathed inside the man's body until every inch of him was consumed by sacred fire, and only an oily black mark and an empty, smoking breastplate were left where he'd lain.

Gideon looked up from the gruesome scene at the archoness, who held the glowing saber at her side. Her eyes closed for a moment, and she took a deep breath. Then, as one, she and her cadre moved on to the next of her injured soldiers who lay nearby. The man was in a bad state, his wounds festering, his flesh sickly and pale, but he had not yet begun to turn as the other two had.

As the archoness's men formed another circle around their wounded comrade, Sir Cormac stepped forward. "Milady!" he called out hoarsely, "what are you doing?"

The archoness glanced up from her tome, her golden eyes hard. "What must be done," she replied.

"That man isn't corrupted yet!" the old knight protested, taking a step toward her. "He might yet be saved!"

Gideon thought back to how Hospitaler Lucas's prayers had failed to heal the wounds of the first man who'd turned, and his stomach twisted at the thought of what would happen next.

"The Holy Light cannot heal this evil," she answered, her voice so calm yet so loud and piercing that it left Gideon's ears ringing. "But it can destroy it."

"But—" Sir Cormac began, and one of the archoness's men, the one she'd called Sergeant Findlay, turned his head and fixed the old paladin with hard eyes.

"Enough," he barked across the distance between them. "It's not our place to question the archoness."

Sir Cormac's jaw tightened, and a storm of emotions was written on his face as he stood there, seemingly torn between his fealty to the Holy Order and his duty to his fellow soldiers.

Lorica turned her head to regard the two interlopers. "I will not leave my men to suffer such a horrible fate, sir knight," she said, her voice softening a touch.

Sir Cormac opened his mouth to speak, but was cut off by a terrible moan from the dying man on the floor, and the telltale sound of snapping bones and rending flesh sounded dully from within him.

The big paladin relented, returning his huge sword to the scabbard on his back. "Yes, milady," he answered wearily.

As the wounded soldier's gurgling screams clawed at the ears of all present, the archoness closed her eyes, hiding their otherworldly gleam for a moment, then returned to her unenviable duty. She placed her glowing saber on the man's chest, and holy fire was kindled in his insides, burning and melting his body to nothingness in a matter of painful moments that felt to Gideon like hours.

Afterward, only another grizzly black stain remained of the man.

The others of the archoness's wounded men started panicking and clamoring as they saw their comrade annihilated by their own commander. They were all in bad shape, but a few managed to get to their feet and stumble toward the chapel doors, apparently hoping to escape.

"Stop them," Archoness Lorica commanded, her quiet voice booming over the commotion, and her cadre leapt to block the doors and seize the men who were fleeing.

Gideon's heart beat faster as he watched the men try to resist, but they were quickly subdued and dragged back to the center of the chapel.

"Please!" one of the men cried, tears streaming down his face. "I don't want to die!"

Archoness Lorica looked down at him, her face an emotionless mask. "You've already been killed," she said softly. "But I'll save your soul from an endless torment."

The man sobbed and wrestled weakly against the firm grips holding him. "Please! I want to go home! Please, don't do this!"

The archoness recited a prayer for mercy, then drove her saber into the man's chest, and he was consumed by the Light just as the others had been. His screams hollowed Gideon's mind as he looked around the chapel at the dozens of wounded still remaining. Would any of them be spared by the archoness and her men?

Gideon looked up at Sir Cormac, desperate for the paladin to give him something to do to help stop the men from being killed. The old man's face was a stony mask, but the subtle twitch of his mustache revealed the conflicted emotions storming behind his steely eyes.

"What can we do, sir?" Gideon asked quietly, afraid to be overheard.

Sir Cormac started, and his jaw finally relaxed as he breathed heavily out of his nose and looked askance at Gideon. "Stand fast, Ballad," he said, his voice low and strained, "the archoness has made her decision."

"But, Sir Cormac," Gideon whispered back, "you're right — they haven't changed yet. We don't even know if they will! There must be some way to save them!"

Sir Cormac shook his head. "Even if there was, we cannot stand against the archoness. It would be a heresy." A bitter resignation soured the old knight's face as he watched the archoness's men usher the next of the wounded toward death upon their commander's burning saber.

Gideon clenched his fist and turned back to the slaughter. He couldn't bear the thought of letting this happen, of doing nothing, when it felt so wrong. He looked around at the wounded men, and his stomach turned as he saw some weeping in fear while others simply watched in stunned silence, as though they'd already accepted their fates.

The screaming, the weeping, and the sizzling; the smell of melted flesh and the wild-eyed last moments of the men brought before the archoness finally proved too much for Gideon, and he took a step forward, driven by some deep instinct to protect. Instantly, the crushing force of Sir Cormac's heavy gauntlet closed on his shoulder, locking him in place.

"I said, stand fast," the fierce old paladin growled, keeping his eyes fixed on the archoness. "A soldier's business isn't always pleasant, boy." Gideon looked up at him, wincing from the knight's painful grasp. "Never forget that."

Unable to free himself from Sir Cormac's iron grip, Gideon looked on miserably as the archoness continued her grim work.

CHAPTER 16

SADIA

"And then, Hofnir threw his mighty hammer, striking the frost giant king in his great, frozen noggin, and felled him on the spot, finally bringing an end to the Great Boreal War," Dalgrim recounted to Reza as the boy sat cross-legged, staring up at the dwarf with rapt attention. Sadia stood nearby, leaning against the rail of the ship and watching as the calm river rippled in the wake of the *Mollysocks*.

"That's how he became known as Hofnir Hammer-Flight, and he went down in dwarven history as a great hero of the Gilded Dwarves, who reigned as King of the Auric Bastions for many decades thereafter. That was, ah, until a terrible case of frost giant foot fungus that he'd contracted during the war finally proved too much for the noble old king." The dwarf sighed, looking out contemplatively across the river. "Aye, he was little more than a rimy pile of warts by the time he passed."

Reza was completely enchanted by the tale, and Dalgrim had seemed to enjoy having someone so eager to hear him talk. After a few days of regaling the irrepressibly curious boy, however, the dwarf's enthusiasm was waning.

"What happened next?" Reza demanded eagerly.

Dalgrim scratched his beard. "Uh, next? What do you mean?"

"After the Great Boreal War!" the boy explained. "What then?"

"Ach, laddie, are you expecting to hear the entire Annals of the Dwarven Kingdoms?"

Reza blinked. "Yes."

"Well, forget about it, you've talked me out, lad — I'm parched!" He reached for a wineskin atop the pile of goods they'd dumped onto the deck of the *Mollysocks* and uncorked it to take a long swig. "Why don't you go ask Lu for another game of dice, eh?"

"Lu won't play with me anymore," Reza said glumly. "He says I win too much."

Dalgrim glanced sidelong at the boy. "Is that so? Well, why don't you go ask him to tell you some stories, then? He hails from the distant land of Xibang, you know, far across the Barrier Sea. I'm sure he'd tell you a bit about it."

Reza climbed to his feet without a word and marched off toward the prow, where Lu was cooking some fish he'd caught from the river.

Dalgrim heaved a long, tired sigh. "Hofnir's frozen fingertips," he grumbled, glancing up at the sky, "that brother of yours has quite the appetite for stories, eh?"

"He's always been very curious," Sadia explained, and the dwarf waved his hand.

"Nothing wrong with it," he admitted. "So it was just the three of you in Qasira, then?" he asked, looking over to Ibrahim, who was resting quietly in her arms.

Sadia shook her head. "We have another brother and three sisters," she answered softly. "We had to leave them behind."

"Ah," the dwarf said, nodding sympathetically. "I'm sorry." He cleared his throat noisily and nodded at the baby. "You mentioned the wee one is sick, yes? Do you know what ails him?"

Sadia shook her head. "All I know is that he needs a healer, desper-

ately. The priests of Ankhat Naharia were all killed when the Hierophants attacked, and... and they probably wouldn't have helped him
anyway," she sighed, finally admitting to herself that Yusuf had been
right. "There's little love for the fatherless in Qasira."

"Hmm," Dalgrim said, eyeing her shrewdly, his lips pursed. "Well,
there's few better places than Emra'adid to find all sorts of holy men
and healers," he assured her. "We should be able to help him once we
reach the port city."

Sadia gave him a grateful smile, then turned back to watch Reza as
he sat next to Lu, listening intently to something the man was saying as
he roasted the fish he'd caught. "Thank you," she said after a moment.
"For your help. I wasn't sure what would happen when we tried to
escape the city, but... you and Lu really saved us."

Dalgrim huffed and took another swig from the wineskin. "What
kind of a dwarf would I be to turn away three orphans, eh?" He glanced
nervously at her before looking away, almost as though he was ashamed
that he had been about to do just that before the Qasiran guards had
arrived looking for him.

They were quiet for a time, Dalgrim idly guiding the tiller of his
little barge and Sadia losing herself in the swirling waters sliding past
its hull. She finally looked up as she heard Reza and Lu coming back to
the stern.

"Hot, hot, hot!" Lu hissed as he hurried over, holding a roasted filet
of river fish on a thin cloth. He set it down beside her and pulled his
hands quickly away, giving them a shake and blowing on his fingers.
"Hot," he warned her, then went over to Dalgrim and reached for the
wineskin.

The dwarf looked him up and down, holding the container out of
Lu's reach. "Where's mine?" he growled.

"Next to fire," the easterner said, gesturing back toward the clay
basin at the bow where the crackling fire was dying out. Dalgrim gave
his bodyguard a bemused look, then shoved the wineskin against the
man's chest. He stalked off, glowering and muttering to himself.

Sadia looked down at the cooked fish as Lu placed a hand on the tiller and looked at her. "Reza tell me about the bad man," he said in his thick accent, "who hurt the baby. I tell him, you no worry — if bad men come, I protect." He held her gaze firmly, and she was surprised by the fervent tone of his voice.

Thrown off her guard, she struggled for a moment to respond, and before she could, Dalgrim stomped back over. "What bad men?" he asked around a mouthful of fish.

"One who hurt baby," Lu repeated.

Dalgrim looked confused. "Who hurt the baby?"

"One of the Hierophants," Sadia explained reluctantly, afraid to give too many details. "He was a very dangerous man."

"Ach, those damned madmen," the dwarf growled, lowering himself with a grunt onto the deck beside Reza. "Bunch of witless evil-doers, you ask me! The kind what will follow any brash idiot who can convince them he's otherwise, then talk them into committing atrocities while calling them mercies."

"Evildoers?" Lu asked, tipping his hat up and furrowing his brow.

Dalgrim took a slender fish bone and picked at his teeth with it. "Aye, Lu, evildoers — bad men, villains, wicked folk."

"Evildoers," the other man repeated slowly, then nodded.

"What do you know about them, Master Glintstone?" Sadia asked.

"Them what?"

"The Hierophants."

"Oh," the dwarf said, leaning back against the low wall at the edge of the deck. "Well, I've occasionally heard them rant and rave on street corners about the end of the world — they seem obsessed with it. But I haven't paid them much mind, myself. They're a bunch of fanatics and zealots and madmen, but there's no real telling what they're on about."

Sadia shifted uncomfortably. "Have you ever seen any of them do magic?"

Dalgrim frowned and gave a shrug. "Well, I can't say I've never seen them do anything strange or suspicious," he conceded. "But whether that was magic, I've no idea. Why do you ask?"

"Because the giant boss cultist threw fireballs all over!" Reza exclaimed, jumping to his feet and punching the air as a demonstration. "And he made one of the guards explode and his guts splattered everywhere and there was blood all over the ground and—"

"Reza!" Sadia scolded.

"What? It's true!" he said, dropping his fists and looking up at her defiantly.

"That's not exactly what happened," she insisted, "and it's not nice to talk about things like that."

"He asked," her brother moped, and he plopped back down on the deck.

Sadia took a deep breath and looked back at Dalgrim. "One of the cultists, the one who called himself a prophet, painted symbols in the air around Ibrahim with fire, and I think it may have... cursed him, or... or something."

The dwarf leapt up at the word. "Cursed?" he cried, eyes bulging as he stalked up to Sadia and bent over to peer at Ibrahim with a cocked eyebrow. "What kind of curse, eh? A hex? A malediction? A magic spell? A word of woe?"

"I... I don't know!" Sadia said, taken aback by his reaction.

"It can't spread, can it?" He gasped, and his eyes went wide. "Mountainhammer's might! You've not cursed my poor *Mollysocks* by bringing him aboard, have you?" he exclaimed, reaching out a fat finger and poking at Ibrahim.

"Please!" Sadia gasped, pulling Ibrahim away from him as the infant whimpered. "Please, stop."

Dalgrim blinked and straightened. "Ach, apologies, lass," he muttered, running a hand through his beard as he calmed. "But curses are nothing to mess about with!" He stepped back and eyed the child for a moment, fiddling with a heavy golden bead wound into his beard. "Madam Jalila might be the one to go to for something like this," he mused.

"Who?" Reza asked.

"Madam Jalila," the dwarf repeated. "A woman of great status and renown in Emra'adid — the next city along the Tajari. She runs an emporium and deals in all kinds of goods and trinkets. But she also trades in knowledge and secrets," he added, looking up at Sadia. "She knows more than just about anyone I've ever met, and she's exactly the kind to ask about some occult ritual used on your wee brother there."

Sadia's spirits began to lift at that, but then she remembered just how destitute they were. "I... we don't have much money...." Her words hung in the air as Dalgrim looked away and Lu was preoccupied by something on the bottom of his boot, but Sadia thought she caught a furtive glance pass between them.

"Never mind, lass, never mind," Dalgrim said hastily, waving her off. "Emra'adid is a city rife with opportunity for those with an eye for it! And er..." he rubbed the back of his neck. "I suppose a night or two at a caravanserai once we reach the city could be included in your fare aboard the *Mollysocks*," he added after another moment of uncomfortable silence. "That'll give you enough time to find some sort of employ."

Sadia sighed, nodding gratefully. She reached over to ruffle Reza's hair and smiled at him reassuringly as he gazed sadly at little Ibrahim, who seemed to have found some respite in his fever and fallen into an exhausted sleep in Sadia's lap. Reza turned back to look up at the dwarf.

"What's a caravanserai?" he asked.

"It's an inn for traveling merchants. The proprietress of the Gentle Djinni has a soft spot for me," Dalgrim added with a wink. "We'll get to Emra'adid and rest our weary heads. I've a good deal of wares that I need to sell there, now that we've been forced on from Qasira."

He held up the metal flask to Lu, who reached for it with a grateful nod as he sat down by the tiller, taking a sip before handing it back to Dalgrim, who also took a drink. "And you know, lass," he said, wiping his lips on the back of his hand, "most folk tend to look kindly on orphans such as yourselves. I know Qasira has a bug in their bum about family and lineage, and important as that may be, not every city in the Nahridi will treat you as harsh as they did in Qasira."

Sadia nodded slowly, hesitant to believe that but hopeful nonetheless.

"Even the madam," Dalgrim continued, "shrewd as she is, isn't heartless. She'll likely take pity on you three. And honestly, you might have a way of paying her you'd never have imagined," he said thoughtfully.

Sadia's brow furrowed. "What's that?"

"Well, as I say, the madam trades in all manner of goods, but there's one above all others she desires, and can never get enough of — a good puzzle to solve. And whatever happened to your wee one seems a mystery indeed." He lifted his flask back to his lips and took a deep draught.

Sadia regarded him for a long moment, holding Ibrahim close as the water lapped gently against the *Mollysocks* and a warm breeze blew over them, filling the barge's sail and sending them onward. She thought about Dalgrim's words, and the unknown fate that awaited them all in Emra'adid.

CHAPTER 17

SADIA

"Ah, the Jewel of the Tatanqa!" Dalgrim exclaimed fondly, standing at the tiller as he looked on the city rising up around the river to meet them. "The most glorious city in the whole Nahridi Desert."

Sadia looked up, gazing wide-eyed as the spires of Emra'adid loomed above them and the broad Tajari River finally opened into a wide delta. The waterway that had carried them from Qasira was dwarfed by the dozens of channels that wove around islands and spits of sand to converge upon the mighty port city of Emra'adid. Hundreds of barges and skiffs like their own floated up and down the waterways, sails, oars, and the current itself propelling them all around the city.

"It's so pretty," Sadia said, amazed at the turquoise stone and tarnished silver adorning the towering spires and high walls.

The *Mollysocks* had entered the labyrinth of river channels leading into the port, and they glided past great carracks and barges filled with exotic goods and passengers as they approached the towering sandstone walls.

"Aye, it's a wondrous city indeed," the dwarf replied, tapping his broad nose as Sadia tore her gaze from the dazzling architecture to look at him. "The river runs through the city, then empties into Tatanqa Bay, and thenceforth out to the Salient Sea. Every bit of wealth that passes from south to north and back is funneled through here, and you can be sure a healthy chunk of it stays," he chuckled, his eyes gleaming.

Lu peered from under the brim of his woven reed hat ahead at the waterway in front of them, then up to the tall walls and spires beyond, nodding appreciatively.

Sadia looked back and saw Reza standing at the rail on the opposite side of the boat, Ibi held against his chest as he looked wide-eyed at the massive city around them, pointing things out to the baby and talking to him excitedly. It made her smile, and she stood up from her spot in the corner to walk over and join them.

"It's beautiful, isn't it, Reza?" she asked, coming up beside him. She rubbed Ibi's back as Reza held him, and he squirmed beneath her hand. He looked flushed but more awake.

Reza looked up at her. "Yes," he answered, turning back to the city. "I wish the others had come with us."

Sadia frowned, thinking of Yusuf and the girls, and she hoped fervently that they were all safe. "Me too," she whispered, and she was quiet for a long moment. "But we'll go back to them soon, Reza. And if we can find a bit of work, maybe we'll be able to bring some coin back with us to make life a little easier."

Reza nodded.

"Here." She took Ibi and held him in one arm, then she reached out to brush a lock of hair out of Reza's face. "The swelling's gone down," she observed, inspecting the damage that had been done to his face.

"I'm fine," he insisted, but she knew better. She sighed, and hugged him with her free arm.

"It'll be alright," she whispered.

"Make way!" Dalgrim bellowed from behind them, and they turned to see him waving aggressively at a larger ship that was gliding through the river alongside them. "You're in my damn way, you!" the dwarf hollered. Sadia looked up the imposing walls of the ship, but didn't see who the dwarf was addressing.

A moment later, a man with olive skin and a short, dark beard appeared at the railing, peering down at them. "Salutations, little vessel!" he called out to them with a grin, bringing the long stem of a tobacco pipe to his lips. "Where might you be traveling today?" He wore a tunic of green silk embroidered with fine golden thread.

"To the other side of your fat arse!" Dalgrim growled in reply, jabbing a thick finger angrily at the larger vessel. "I've important goods to deliver, so get out of my way!"

The man's grin grew broader, and he looked over his shoulder to share something in a foreign tongue with someone behind him on the ship. "And just what is it you're transporting, dwarf?" he asked, turning his attention back down to Dalgrim, and Lu stepped up behind his boss. "That pathetic excuse for a boat couldn't carry more than a few loaves of bread."

"Don't you talk about my *Mollysocks* that way!" Dalgrim bellowed, shaking his fist angrily. Sadia noted a bemused smirk on Lu's face as he stood behind the dwarf. "And my wares are my business!" he added. "Now, out of my damn way!"

"The river belongs to everyone," the man said, spreading his arms magnanimously. He leaned against the ship's railing, and his eyes narrowed. "Perhaps if you were a little friendlier, dwarf, you'd find people more inclined to accommodate you."

"Maybe if you weren't piloting that hideous sea cow, gentle folk like myself could go freely about the river as intended!" Dalgrim retorted, red-faced and furious.

The man chuckled. "Very well, then." He blew a smoke ring out over the water between their two vessels. "The *Emerald Manta* shall stay her course. Have a lovely day, dwarf." He stepped away from the railing and was gone.

"Bah!" the dwarf grumbled. "Lu, take the tiller, will you?" he asked, turning to look back at the easterner, who shrugged and took his place.

The dwarf hopped off the platform by the tiller and made his way over to the side of the barge near the *Emerald Manta*. He mumbled to himself as he looked back at the stern of the large ship, then at the rigging and the sail above. Sadia was perplexed. She watched curiously as Dalgrim nodded and hummed, stroking his beard, and then he reached into one of the pouches on his belt and produced the phial of purple liquid he had used to escape Qasira.

"A wee drop remains," she heard him murmur with satisfaction. He looked over his shoulder at Lu with a devious grin. "Just enough, I'd wager." Lu cocked an eyebrow, then seemed to understand and sighed, shaking his head.

"What are you doing?" Sadia asked nervously, wasting no time grabbing Reza and holding both her brothers a little tighter.

Dalgrim looked at her with a gleam in his eye. He nodded at the glass tube in his hand. "Oh, don't worry lass — it's not for us this time." He gave her a wink that failed in every way to reassure her, and she gathered her brothers close and hunkered them all down onto the deck.

"Oh, my fair *Mollysocks*," the dwarf called out loudly as he sauntered along the railing, holding the nearly-empty phial in hand, "what to do when a giant sea-heifer" — he shouted the words up at the deck of the *Emerald Manta* — "refuses to let you pass?" Dalgrim held the phial aloft and took careful aim toward the back of the other ship. "There's but one way," he answered himself, and then he tossed the tiny glass phial across the water.

It sailed through the air and shattered on the hull of the *Emerald Manta*, near her stern end, sending a spray of glass shards and a few solitary drops of violet liquid into the peaceful river beneath the ship.

A few drops was all it took, however, as a moment later the water began to boil and froth, and then the ship lurched forward, its stern kicking out to one side. Sadia's heart seized in her chest as she watched the *Emerald Manta* loom over them as it careered ahead, the bow rising out of the water as the vessel veered sideways.

Dalgrim cackled gleefully and jogged over to Lu at the tiller. "Get ready to pull her hard to starboard!" he said, grabbing on tight as the

Mollysocks slid into the larger vessel's wake, gliding just behind the vessel's aft end as it hurtled forward downriver.

The *Emerald Manta* splashed down a moment later, sending a huge wave crashing over other smaller ships sailing along the river. Sadia clutched her brothers tight as their barge rode the waves left by the larger vessel. Ibrahim wailed in terror as the boat rocked, but Reza had an excited grin on his face, and his eyes were as big as saucers.

Sadia watched, her stomach still in knots, as the *Emerald Manta* cut headlong through the river traffic, upturning and sinking a few of the smaller boats as it careened wildly from side to side. She could hear the crew shouting and calling as they fought valiantly to regain control of the ship, but to no avail. A huge river galleon was headed upstream, propelled by banks of oars, and the *Emerald Manta* was on a course to collide with it.

Sadia looked over at Dalgrim in a panic and saw that his smile had faded, his hands gripping the railing hard. "Oh, dear," he murmured, realizing what was about to happen.

Lu wrestled with the tiller as the *Mollysocks* slid across the river, away from the chaos. As Sadia turned back, she watched the *Manta* slam into the side of the river galleon in an explosion of timber, and both ships rocked violently, masts and rigging tangling in a cacophony. A great wave crashed across the river from the collision, and Sadia held her brothers close as the dwarf's barge rode the swell toward the safety of the far bank.

They sailed past the stricken galleon as it struggled to stay afloat with its keel cracked, and the oarsmen began abandoning their posts as the river slowly started to claim both sinking ships. Dalgrim whistled low and shook his head as they sailed easily away.

"Well," he said, stroking his beard thoughtfully as he surveyed the chaos on the other side of the river. "That didn't go exactly how I had intended, but you can't argue with the results, eh?"

The rest of them stood in silent shock for a moment before Sadia recovered enough to respond. "What's wrong with you?" she cried, and at the same moment, Lu exclaimed, "You crazy! You crazy dwarf!"

"Bah!" Dalgrim growled, waving them off and taking the tiller. "Those bastards got what they deserved. They should've listened when I asked them politely to get out of my way!" He leaned into the tiller and steered the *Mollysocks* hard off the main river and down a small channel flowing between the crowded buildings of the city. "Still, though, best to beat a hasty retreat, before they can falsely accuse me of having a hand in it," he added.

Sadia was still in a state of shock, her mind struggling to believe what had just happened. "You're a madman," she breathed, inspecting the dwarf for any sign of remorse or concern over what he'd just done. "Surely the city guard will be after us here, too, now!"

Dalgrim shook his head. "They'll not find us," he said. "Not where we're going. We needed to lie low for a while anyhow."

"I don't think that counts as lying low," Reza said, unable to tear his eyes from the havoc unfolding behind them.

"Well, no," the dwarf agreed, "but I know of a secret little jetty where we can hide the *Mollysocks*, and after a night or two at the Gentle Djinni, all that mess back there will be a thing of the past, you'll see."

Sadia sighed heavily. She couldn't help but wonder just what kind of trouble she'd invited into her life by boarding the ramshackle *Mollysocks* back in Qasira.

CHAPTER 18

GIDEON

"GIDEON," a soft voice called to him, and then something touched his hand, and Gideon woke with a start. He leapt to his feet and cracked his head against the hanging branch above him. He cried out and rubbed his head where he'd struck it as the pain wrenched him fully awake.

"Everything is alright," Nefteli's voice said, and when she touched his arm again, he didn't recoil.

Gideon blinked against the morning sunlight streaming through the leaves overhead as the pain in his head slowly ebbed away. He realized his friend was standing beside him, her almond eyes brimming with concern.

"Are you alright?" she asked, keeping her hand on his arm. "I have been looking for you since...." She glanced past him back toward the chapel. "Gideon, what happened?"

He shook his head to clear the lingering fog of sleep, and the brief glimmer of hope that the previous evening had been a nightmare faded with it. Gideon was surprised he'd actually fallen asleep — after the massacre in the chapel, Sir Cormac had instructed him to return to the barracks, but he'd slipped away and wandered the grounds instead, unable to stop his hands from shaking or his mind replaying the painful scene over and over. Eventually, he'd fallen to his knees behind a large oak near the monastery wall, praying and grasping for any peace or assurance he could find from the gods.

"The archoness," he said, finally lifting his head and sweeping his long hair out of his face, "she... she killed her own men. All of them. All the wounded we tried to help." The screams and acrid smell of melting flesh and blood filled his senses as he spoke, and the sudden clarity forced a hitching breath. "Couldn't you hear it?"

Nefteli's face hardened. "After the archoness's men closed the chapel doors, the clergy ordered all the recruits back to the barracks," she explained, clearly frustrated. "We saw flashes of light through the windows, but did not know what was happening."

Gideon nodded, swallowing hard. "The archoness used the Light to destroy the corruption in them. But...." He paused, glancing up at the girl's inquisitive eyes. "But they hadn't started changing yet, Teli," he said, dropping his voice. "Like the one you and Lucas were trying to heal. She killed them as men, and many of them begged for mercy, but none received it." He looked away from her, unable to keep the rancor from his face. "We could have saved them," he insisted. "At least, we should have tried. But the archoness wouldn't hear it, not even from Sir Cormac."

Nefteli nodded. "I see. Battlesister Dawnhammer gave us a brief explanation when we were finally released from the barracks." She searched his eyes for a moment before taking a deep breath. "It seems that the archoness had no choice, Gideon," she began, prompting an exasperated sigh from him, but she persisted. "You saw what happened to that man. The Light would not heal him." A subtle quiver in her voice caught him off-guard as he realized she was actually afraid.

"I saw," he admitted wearily, leaning back against the rough, flaking bark of the oak. "But you didn't see the men beg for their lives. It was brutal, Teli. Nothing good or holy happened last night."

She sighed, and her hand squeezed his. "Why did you go back?" she asked, almost angrily. "They ordered us to leave, why did you not obey?"

"To help Sir Cormac," he answered indignantly. "I'm not sure I really did help much, but I couldn't just leave him. The archoness and her men would have left him to fight that monster on his own. What else could I do?"

"You should have obeyed!" Nefteli cried, her eyes flashing. "It was too soon for you to see that, for any of us to have seen what happened!"

Gideon blinked, not understanding. She was gripping his hand in hers like a vice to the point that it was a little painful, and when he adjusted his fingers, she realized and quickly released him. "What does that mean?" he demanded, subtly trying to work the cramp out of his hand.

Nefteli turned away and placed a hand on her brow. "When they made us watch that man lose his hand," she said after a moment, looking back at him, "it was difficult, yes?"

Gideon hesitated, then nodded.

"Why do you think they did not make us watch them execute someone instead?" She held his gaze poignantly. "Because we were not ready for it. It was too soon for us to see something like that. They showed us something hard for new recruits to see, but nothing for the likes of Sir Cormac and Battlesister Dawnhammer."

He frowned. "I don't understand your point, Teli."

"My point is that you have no place to say that what you saw in the chapel was not right," she said, her voice sharp, "or that the archoness did anything unjust."

"You can't be serious!" Gideon scoffed. "How could you possibly think that?"

Nefteli took a deep breath and seemed to force the tension from her shoulders. "Gideon, you are strong. Strong of mind, of will. The gods gave you that strength when they made you."

"What does this—" he started, but she ignored him and continued.

"That strength is not the one you want, though." Nefteli folded her arms, her brow furrowed. "You want a strength they chose not to give you. And here you are again, questioning their will because what you saw was difficult."

Gideon felt his neck flush at her words. He was taken aback and had no idea how to respond.

Her expression softened a touch. "Where is your faith, Gideon? Your dedication to the gods' will and not your own?"

"I don't...." He let out a frustrated sigh and looked away, feeling chastened. But as embarrassed as he felt, he couldn't bring himself to say she was entirely wrong. "What do you want from me, Teli?" he asked at last.

"I want you to remember what drew you to the monastery in the first place," she said quietly. "What drew all of us. Sir Cormac and the battlesister both see greatness in you, even after you failed the trials — even Donnal knows you have great things before you. And I..." she glanced at him and then quickly away again. "We all see it, Gideon. But the greatest strength any of us has is our faith."

The monastery bell suddenly peeled, making Gideon flinch. They both looked around the big oak to see the recruits and clergy all streaming toward the chapel.

"We should go," Nefteli said from beside him. "But please — think about what I have said. Trust in the gods and the Holy Order, Gideon." She gave him a sad smile, then started back across the grounds. Gideon ran a hand through his hair in exasperation and stared after her for a moment before following.

Battlesister Gerda stood atop the chapel steps, her arms folded behind her as she watched the remaining recruits and clergy gather. Gideon caught sight of Bishop Delwyn and Sir Cormac standing inside the Cathedral vestibule behind her, speaking quietly between themselves. No rank and file were formed; everyone simply gathered in a throng in front of the chapel, looking up expectantly at the grim-faced dwarven woman.

Once the last stragglers arrived, the battlesister stepped forward, but as she was about to speak, Sir Cormac's voice carried out from behind her. "Damn it, man, it's too soon!" Gerda paused and looked over her shoulder to where the old knight was gesturing aggressively in an apparent argument with the flustered bishop.

"Battlesister," Delwyn called to her, his aged voice carrying easily in the still morning air. "Could you please...?" he asked, gesturing for her to join him and Sir Cormac.

Gerda turned back to the gathered crowd. "Alright, stand fast," she growled, then turned and stalked to join the two men in the vestibule, her heavy armor clanking as she crossed the stone.

A few moments passed, and Gideon caught snippets of the conversations around him, people whispering fearfully about what had happened in the chapel. Some of them eyed him sidelong, and he felt his ears burning. Seeming to sense his unease, Nefteli cast withering glances at a few nosy recruits, and they wilted and looked away, leaving Gideon alone.

Someone nudged his shoulder, and he turned to see James' freckled face studying him intently. "Hey, Gid," he said hesitantly, and nodded toward the chapel. "I heard you were inside till the end. You alright?"

Gideon opened his mouth but hesitated.

James nodded. "No worries, mate. You don't have to tell me anything, yeah? Just wanted to check on you." He sighed and gestured at the monastery walls. "Donnal and I were posted up on the walls when it all happened," he explained. "Heard the screams, saw the flashes. Can't imagine it was good."

Gideon's throat tightened, and he gave a curt nod. He looked over James's mop of ginger locks, then back the other way, scrutinizing the crowd. "Where is Donnal, anyhow?" he asked, prompting a gleeful grin from the redhead.

"As soon as we got off the walls, he went and started pestering all the clergy, trying to figure out what had happened. They were all too stunned and horrified to give him anything, though. Finally, Battlesister Gerda caught wind of it and sent him to dig a new latrine. He's still out there," he added with a devious chuckle.

Gideon rolled his eyes. "Why does that not surprise me?"

James snorted, then coughed and fell silent at a disapproving glance from Nefteli.

A moment later, Battlesister Gerda returned from the vestibule, her face as hard and unreadable as ever, and she said nothing as the two men came up beside her at the top of the steps. Sir Cormac's expression was stormy, and the bishop's hands fidgeted on his crosier as he stood between the two warriors, looking somehow smaller than even the dwarven woman.

Gideon's eyes roved across the chapel facade, from the stained glass window depicting the ascension of Saint Thylessia to that of Saint Oronos, his spear held aloft as the sun's rays illuminated it as though it was infused with the Holy Light. Where once the sight had comforted and inspired him, however, he now felt a deep unease at the thought of the gods who had allowed such a slaughter to happen in their own chapel. Nefteli's words played in the back of his mind, and he took a breath, trying to still his thoughts.

He glanced at her and saw she was staring forward at Gerda, her chin high and shoulders squared, as unflappable and resolute as ever. Gideon felt ashamed of himself as he stood beside her. She was exactly the kind of woman the Holy Order wanted, and he realized suddenly how he must look in comparison, the hopelessness and defeat evident in him down to his posture.

Finally, after a moment of tense silence, Delwyn cleared his throat and stepped forward. "My children," he called, his voice quavering, "a most... disturbing discovery has been made." He paused, as though unsure what to say next, or whether he should say it, and Sir Cormac stepped forward to stand beside him, glaring at the crowd.

"You all heard about what happened last night in the chapel," the paladin called gruffly. "The archoness, through her holy wisdom, discovered that our wounded comrades had been cursed by the witches in their battle the day previous, and their wounds corrupted." Delwyn looked at him uncomfortably, and some of the clergy exchanged nervous glances with one another. "To prevent those curses from taking hold, the archoness spared them a fate worse than death."

Gideon grit his teeth and bristled at the charitable description of the slaughter, but Nefteli's hand closed around his arm in warning, and he took a deep breath and bit his tongue.

Sir Cormac's gaze swept over the crowd. "This witch's hex—" he spat in disgust into the bushes beside the chapel "— is an abomination to creation itself. The healing Light was unable to mend those men's wounds, or prevent their ghastly transformation."

Hushed whispers rose within the crowd as the rumors that had spread through the barracks in the intervening hours were confirmed.

The old knight's face hardened. "It is a terrible thing," he said, his voice low. "And in response to this new... development, the archoness is mounting an urgent mission to finish off the coven before they can escape to sow their havoc elsewhere. She needs volunteers to rebuild her numbers," he finished gravely.

Another round of murmuring broke out, quickly rising as both excitement and trepidation seized the fifty-odd recruits who had just endured their trials. For them, the slaughter in the chapel was just a story, and they had no way of understanding the dire implications of what Sir Cormac had just said.

Gideon tensed at the thought of going to hunt those very witches who had a means of defying the Light of the gods. It seemed to him like madness, but there was an undercurrent of fear at the thought of such a thing escaping into the wider world, of having to live knowing that they were out there, free to curse or kill whoever they pleased.

Bishop Delwyn raised a hand for quiet, and the whispering died down. "The prospects of dark magics," he said fretfully, struggling to raise his aged voice, "that somehow withstand the healing power of the Holy Light are... truly terrible." He paused, taking a deep breath. "But we must stand fast against the darkness. Such is our calling, our vocation."

The bishop's voice trailed off as his attention was drawn to something behind the crowd, and Gideon looked back to see the archoness striding toward them, flanked by her cadre, from the rooms Delwyn had granted them in the west tower. The stooped old man cleared his throat and continued speaking, but everyone gathered in the crowd quickly started looking away from him to watch the archoness's approach.

She and her men stalked purposefully past the throng of clergy and recruits and ascended the chapel stairs, unconcerned with the bishop's droning address.

"Steel yourselves in the brilliance of the Light," Delwyn said, clutching his crosier tight as his own eyes were locked on the archoness. "Reject the darkness and withstand its horrors. Neither fear its malice. Nor that... that of man..." he finished lamely.

"Have you chosen new soldiers for me, Your Reverence? " the archoness asked, and her voice had lost the frightening resonance it had carried throughout the night; she sounded more like a normal woman. Peering closer, Gideon saw a great weariness written in her features, and she leaned slightly on the man beside her, Sergeant Findlay.

"No, milady," Delwyn said, wringing his hands. "I was just about to announce a prayer vigil. We must petition the gods to—"

"There's no time for that," the archoness said, cutting him off with a sharp gesture. "I need soldiers. I will not allow the coven to survive another day." She swept her tired gaze over the crowd, then looked to Gerda. "Which are your best, battlesister?"

Gerda stepped forward. "These are green recruits, milady. They have yet to be tested in battle."

"Desperate times," Lorica answered bitterly. "I require no fewer than twenty able bodies who are strong of arm and spirit. I leave the selection to you."

"The bishop wants to let the recruits volunteer," Sir Cormac growled.

"Oh," Bishop Delwyn cleared his throat, his gaze flitting nervously to the archoness. "Well, yes, we... well, given the... terrors of last night," he said, glancing back into the chapel, which still bore the marks of tragedy, "I don't think it would be in the service of justice to choose for these young folk which of them must go to their... to go with you." He swallowed thickly and added, "Let the bravest among them volunteer."

The archoness closed her eyes and drew a breath. "I don't need your bravest, bishop." Her eyes reopened, and they had regained their soft but unmistakable golden glow. "I need your best. I need the most capable, the most violent, and the most disciplined. I will take those who follow orders unquestioningly, and the swiftest to execute. We have no time to waste."

Delwyn's hands shook on his crosier as he beheld her, and he took a step backward as though afraid. "I... well, milady, I...."

"Archoness," Battlesister Gerda said, stepping past the bishop. "These young soldiers are barely trained. Only a handful even passed the trials and swore their oaths. They're ill-prepared to march against a coven the likes of which we're dealing with." She gestured at the towering old paladin behind her. "Sir Cormac and I will join you."

The knight nodded and teased one end of his mustache. "We're no strangers to the battle," he offered gruffly.

"Yes," the archoness agreed, "you will join me. But I see only four hands between you. I need more. More bodies, more weapons." She drew herself up and stepped away from Sergeant Findlay, standing fully under her own strength. "As we've learned, healers are of no use in this fight. Show me only those who swore the Oath of Woe." Even without the divine resonance in her voice, she was undeniable.

The battlesister and the old knight looked at each other, and Gideon saw the resignation settle over their faces. Gerda nodded and turned to the gathered crowd. "Alright, form up!" she cried, and the trainees all leapt instinctively to obey.

CHAPTER 19

GIDEON

"Recruits over here!" Sir Cormac cried, his voice bellowing out over the peaceful monastery grounds. "Clergy, there!" He and Battlesister Gerda coordinated and quickly had rows and columns formed from the two groups facing the chapel, ready to be sorted.

At the front of the formations, Sir Cormac bent down to confer quietly with the dwarven woman as their gazes swept the rank and file.

"If you swore the Oath of Weal," she called, "fall out and join the clergy."

Gideon glanced at Nefteli beside him, and she met his gaze sidelong for a heartbeat before stepping back and jogging away as the battlesister had commanded. Three other recruits followed her.

"Those of you who swore the Oath of Woe, fall out in front of the formation," Gerda directed, indicating the space just in front of the chapel.

On Gideon's other side, James obeyed without hesitation, and he was joined by the remaining recruits who had passed their trials. He watched his friend go, and the jealousy he felt was undercut by a fear of the young lad marching to face the coven.

Archoness Lorica paced down the line of young men and women who'd sworn the Oath of Woe, looking them up and down as though she could measure their merit with her golden-hued eyes. "Eight of them?" she asked, glancing back at Gerda once she'd reached the end of the row. "That's it?"

Gideon was shocked to see the battlesister's fair cheeks color as she frowned and nodded.

"Piteous," the archoness murmured, then shook her head. "I need more bodies than this. Healers will be useless against this gods-forsaken coven, but I could find a purpose for those who failed the trials. I need might and brawn."

Gideon's stomach turned. Sir Cormac and Battlesister Gerda exchanged glances again, and then the battlesister nodded slowly. "We've got a few who were unable to manifest the Light, but they'll be capable warriors."

The archoness nodded, and Sir Cormac turned to face the formations. "Ballad!" he shouted, "Crieg! Covington! Fall out!"

Gideon's ears rang as he jogged down the line of other recruits, and the old paladin called out a handful of other names. His feet moved of their own accord as he realized that he was about to be chosen to accompany the archoness and her cadre. His mind raced, but all he could think of was how he didn't want to turn into one of those monstrosities, and he was ashamed of how afraid he felt.

When he reached the front, he took his place beside the other chosen recruits and glanced subtly down the line at them, trying to get a sense of how they felt. All of them were grimly focused — even the affable James — but none of them looked terrified like he felt. He could only hope that he didn't look it.

The archoness stood in front of them, appraising them with her unnerving gaze, and her eyes lingered on Gideon.

"Crieg!" Sir Cormac bellowed again, and there was no sound of movement from the formation behind them. The knight grumbled and stalked over to Gideon. "Ballad, where's your idiot friend?"

"Ach, I put him on latrine detail," Gerda remembered with a sigh.

Sir Cormac looked down at Gideon. "Run and get him, boy, hurry!" Gideon obeyed and dashed off around the barracks building to the latrine pits behind. He found Donnal sloppily digging up waste, a filthy apron around his middle. He was grumbling and complaining to himself as he worked, and turned and leaned on his shovel handle when Gideon approached.

"Gideon!" he said, his face lighting up, "I heard there were monsters in the chapel! Did you see them? What were they like? How did you and Sir Cormac defeat them?"

Gideon came to a sudden halt as a wall of stench hit him, and he turned his head away, ignoring his friend's questions. "Come on, Donnal, we have to go," he said, trying in vain to clear the air around him with his hand.

Donnal scowled. "Battlesister Gerda told me I wasn't allowed to leave before I filled in one pit and dug a new one."

"She and Sir Cormac just sent me to get you," Gideon replied impatiently. "The archoness is waiting on us."

"The archoness?" Donnal gawked at him. "Us? What does she—"

"We have to go, Donnal!" he pressed, and his friend hastily threw his shovel aside, cast off his soiled apron, and jogged after Gideon back toward the formation.

"I don't understand, Gideon," he said, breathing hard as they ran. "What would the archoness want with us?"

"They're recruiting men to go fight the witches," Gideon replied, glancing over his shoulder at his taller friend.

Donnal skidded to a halt and stared at Gideon in shock, his face paling. "We're... We're going with the archoness to hunt witches?"

"Yes, now hurry," Gideon said urgently, and turned to start running again back to the chapel.

"But... but we both failed the trials! What good are we going to be against witches?"

Gideon stopped again and rounded on his friend. "I don't know anything more than you, Donnal!" he said, throwing up his hands. "But they're not exactly giving us a choice. Now, come on."

Donnal nodded and they hurried back to the chapel, where they rejoined the group at the front, the other recruits staring at them curiously.

"There he is," the battlesister said, folding her arms over her chest. "These are the best from this training rotation, archoness," she said, nodding her chin at the line of recruits. "Everyone we plan on recommending for further training as paladins, or to join the ranks of the knights auxiliary."

"Very well," the archoness said. She paced slowly before the row of young men and women before her, looking less than impressed. "You have been chosen to participate in a desperate push to exterminate the coven who wounded my men, resulting in the tragedy in the chapel last night."

Her eyes met each of their gazes in turn. "Gird yourselves, young warriors — these witches are unlike any enemies the Church Militant has ever faced. But we will strike before they can flee, and we will overwhelm them. The gods favor us, the Light bolsters us, and we will emerge victorious."

Gideon ground his teeth, struggling to understand what he was hearing, how quickly his situation had changed, given it had been less than a day since he'd failed his trials and planned to go back home to Wintry.

The archoness turned to Bishop Delwyn. "Does the monastery keep enough horses to outfit them all?" she asked, gesturing at the line of recruits.

The old man cleared his throat and tugged at his clerical robe. The violence that had erupted inside the chapel had clearly put the old clergyman out of his preferred purview, and all the unexpected goings-on apparently had him flustered. "Yes, archoness, I... we keep a full stable. The horses are for the clerics who venture out to minister to the sick and afflicted, but we can certainly—"

"They're no warhorses," Sir Cormac interrupted, "but a few of them are doughty enough to carry an armored rider a good way."

Archoness Lorica nodded and looked down at Gerda. "How soon can you have them ready to march, battlesister?"

"I'll have them ready right away, milady," the dwarven woman answered. The archoness nodded and withdrew along with her cadre, returning to the west tower.

"As for the rest of you," Sir Cormac called loudly, rounding on the formation. "Head to the stables and help the monks ready a horse for each rider." He glanced back at Bishop Delwyn, who gave a shaky nod.

As he was speaking, Hospitaler Lucas took a few backward steps toward the stables. "Follow me," he called to the recruits still in formation.

"You lot head to the armory," Battlesister Gerda said to those of them who had been chosen, and gestured toward the converted shed that housed all the arms and armor they'd used in training.

As Gideon and the others marched toward the armory, he glanced over among the other group headed to the stables, but couldn't see Nefteli in the crowd. Everything was changing so quickly, and he realized very suddenly how real the situation was. Even if he and Donnal and James returned alive, they, along with Nefteli, would all be summarily whisked away to some distant corner of the earth to fight for the Holy Order, likely never to see each other again.

He swallowed hard and shook the thoughts from his head as he followed Donnal into the cramped armory. The recruits all lined the far wall and waited awhile before Sir Cormac entered with the armorer, Brother Percival. The grizzled old monk grunted when he saw the volunteers and got to work immediately, pulling worn and weathered arms from where they hung on the wall and handing one to each of them.

Gideon stepped up, and Brother Percival handed him a worn, flanged mace and a wooden round shield. He looked over the dented and scraped armaments that had been given to him; it was a far cry from the shining broadsword he had once dreamt of wielding, but he said nothing and took his place against the wall again.

"James," Donnal muttered, looking down at the tiny steel buckler shield he'd been given, "trade me yours, will you?"

Gideon looked up to see the scrawny ginger hefting a long kite shield and a notched short sword. He scoffed and shook his head. "Not a chance, Donny,"

"I'm twice your size, you little runt!" Donnal hissed. "And I can't use the Light!" He gave James a miserable look, and the redhead sighed.

"Alright, you big ninny," the boy finally relented, sliding the kite shield off his arm and passing it over.

"Good man, James! Good man!" Donnal declared, grinning as he traded the younger man his small buckler shield.

"No trouble," James replied with a laugh. "Just be sure to stand behind me when danger's afoot, yeah? Wouldn't want you soiling your trousers, now, would we?"

"I'd prefer not to," Donnal grumbled, and James laughed aloud.

"Ballad!" Sir Cormac called, beckoning all three of them over to the other side of the armory, and he handed them each a breastplate and mismatched pairs of greaves and gauntlets. As Gideon loosed the straps of the body armor to slip it on, he caught a strong scent coming from it, and the cries of burning men rang again in his ears. His heartbeat thudded in his neck as he turned the breastplate over and saw the black marks inside: burnt leather and tarnished steel from the heat of burning flesh.

"These..." he stuttered, shocked, "these are from the archoness's men." He looked wide-eyed up at Sir Cormac. "They wore these when... when they were... they died in these!"

The knight glared down at him. "They'll turn a blade as well as any other armor, boy — the only thing that makes them any different is their story. Now put them on." Gideon's stomach churned as he slipped the breastplate over his head, and Donnal helped him secure the side straps. He shuddered at the thought of wearing the breastplate of a man he'd watched die, but he grit his teeth and did his best to ignore the acrid scent.

Donnal took the armor handed to him without question or complaint, but he stared down at it with a thoughtful frown. "These belonged to the men who died last night?" he asked, and the old knight nodded. "But if it didn't save them, why even bother wearing it?"

"You can fight in your knickers if you prefer," Sir Cormac rumbled darkly, fixing him with a glowering gaze.

Donnal swallowed and slipped the armor on without further complaint.

While they were securing the last straps and taking up their arms, Battlesister Gerda entered and appraised them, then turned to her comrade. "I told Lucas just to saddle a few of the monastery's sturdiest — the gelding and the dapple grey," she said, folding her arms. "The archoness' fallen detachment has enough horses remaining to seat everyone else."

"Is there anything from those poor bastards we're not taking?" Gideon muttered, and Donnal chuckled, oblivious to the bitterness of his friend's words.

"Good enough," Sir Cormac answered with a nod. "You lot remember how to sit a horse?" he asked as the recruits finished securing their arms and armor.

Donnal glanced uncertainly at Gideon. Riding had been a brief part of their training at the monastery; some had taken to it better than others. Donnal had famously struggled to maintain the saddle at anything faster than a trot. "It's been a while, sir," he said, his voice rising in pitch, "but I'll do my best."

"Let's go," Gerda growled, and Sir Cormac followed her out of the armory.

Gideon was the first to step outside, and he squinted against the bright morning light. As the others filed out, he heard James clap Donnal on the shoulder. "You'll be fine, mate," he said encouragingly. "You did great once you stopped falling off. Just don't get bucked this time, yeah?"

Donnal glared at him, then looked apprehensively past Gideon to the courtyard where the archoness and her cadre were gathered. All six of them were mounted, and their steeds' fine tack was adorned with polished golden metalwork that gleamed in the sunlight. He hadn't realized their splendor upon the detachment's arrival the previous night, and he realized how ridiculous the recruits all looked by comparison in their battered, ill-fitting armor.

Another horse stood riderless, off to one side, a jet black stallion whose muscles rippled under his shiny coat as he snorted and stomped: Dauntless, Sir Cormac's mighty steed. His saddle was simpler than the others', but the huge warhorse dwarfed every other steed on the monastery grounds.

"Those are much finer than the ones we learned to ride on," Donnal said, gawking at the riders atop their fine mounts.

Battlesister Dawnhammer overheard him. "Aye," she said with a solemn nod as she strode beside them, keeping pace despite her dwarven stature. "You humans and yer fancy warhorses," she grunted. "I'd rather have a hardy battle-yak any day."

"Come," Sir Cormac bellowed, and he and Battlesister Gerda led the way to the stables, where Gideon saw the rest of the recruits busy securing tack and saddles to the remaining horses of the archoness's fallen knights.

Gideon and the other volunteered recruits entered the stables after the old knight and waited as the horses were readied. He caught sight of Nefteli saddling a chestnut mare, and he watched her as she worked. Her face was stoic as ever, but Gideon knew her well enough to recognize the tension in her shoulders, the subtle frown tugging at the corners of her full lips.

The young woman finished cinching the saddle strap tight, then stepped away from the horse and turned. Their eyes met for a moment before they both looked away, and Gideon shifted uncomfortably in his borrowed armor as Sir Cormac started pairing off recruits and horses.

"Ballad! Crieg!" he called, gesturing to the two horses at the end of the stables. "That one's yours," he said to Gideon, pointing at the chestnut brown mare, "and Crieg, take that one," he said to Donnal, pointing at the dark grey gelding standing beside her. "Take them to the gate and wait there."

As they led their horses outside, Gideon could feel Donnal's nervousness as he side-eyed the saddle on the gelding's back.

As they clopped across the monastery yard, Nefteli caught up to them, a saddle blanket tucked under her arm. "I... I forgot to put this on the gelding," she said, unable to look either of them in the eye.

"Oh," Donnal said, smiling as she approached. "Here, I'll help you." They worked together in awkward silence to slide the blanket under the saddle.

"So..." Gideon started, and he faltered, trying to figure out what to say. The young woman looked up at him, waiting.

"I hope," he finally managed, "they wait to send you all to the citadel. Til we come back, I mean," he added quickly. "If we do come back."

Nefteli's flawless brow furrowed, and he could tell she was about to scold him for being so morose when Donnal carefully skirted around the gelding to join them and spoke up. "I'd certainly feel better if you were coming with us, Teli," he admitted, forcing a cheerful tone.

"Yes, I..." Nefteli bit her lip and glanced up at both of them. "I would feel better, too," she said softly, and looked away again.

A look of confusion and concern passed over Donnal's face, as though he didn't know the words to put to his feelings in the moment. Then he chuckled.

"Ah, well," he said, placing a hand on each of their shoulders. "We'll be back together in no time, right?" His smile faltered briefly, but he held it. "You'll be as strong as Lucas in no time," he said to Nefteli. "And Gideon and I will be fine — James the Magnificent will see to that!" he added as the redhead passed them, leading his horse toward the gates.

James looked over as he heard his name mentioned. "Eh, what's that?" he asked.

Donnal gave him a dismissive wave, and James shrugged and moved on. Nefteli's brow was still creased with worry.

"The greatest strength we have is our faith, right?" Gideon asked quietly.

The Akhumite girl glanced up at hearing him repeat her own words, and she nodded resolutely.

"Get moving, you two!" Battlesister Gerda called from the monastery entrance as the guards dragged the heavy gates open.

"Listen," Nefteli said quickly, her voice low as she stepped closer to them. "Be careful, both of you, yes? Watch out for each other." She looked between them, her expression hard. "I know you do not trust the archoness," she added, her gaze lingering on Gideon. "But you must listen to her — she will keep you alive."

Gideon opened his mouth to respond, but she placed a hand against his borrowed breastplate. "Please, Gideon," she said, her amber eyes searching his blue ones. "Please. If you can not trust her, trust the gods. They will protect you."

Sir Cormac's voice boomed over the monastery yard. "Riders! Form up!"

Nefteli pulled her hand away and looked up at each of them in turn.

"Teli," Gideon began, but Donnal stepped forward quickly, interrupting him and sweeping Nefteli up into a powerful hug, lifting the girl off her feet.

"Oh!" she exclaimed softly, then chuckled and returned the young man's hug, squeezing her arms around him and closing her eyes until the moment passed.

"Stay safe, Teli," Donnal said, the words muffled on her shoulder. When he released her, he quickly turned and wiped surreptitiously at his eye before grabbing the saddle horn and swinging himself clumsily up onto the gelding's back.

Nefteli and Gideon watched him awkwardly attempt to settle in the saddle before the young woman turned back to him with an expectant look.

Gideon felt a tightness in his chest. He swallowed, and his heart beat hard. He wanted to say something, but yet again, he couldn't find the words.

"Ballad! Crieg!" Sir Cormac's voice thundered across the grounds. "Move your arses!"

Gideon sighed, and Nefteli stepped back as he climbed into his saddle. She stared up at both of them for a long moment as they turned their horses, her lips parted as though she was about to speak. But she closed her mouth, shook her head, and simply watched as they moved over to the assembled riders, Donnal waving sadly back at her in farewell.

A wave of emotions washed over Gideon as they joined the other riders in line. He was leaving his training behind without passing the trials and swearing his vows. He was going to fight evil witches despite having no connection to the Light. Nefteli and the others were moving on, and he didn't know when or if he would see her again. And he was wearing the armor of a dead man.

They fell in line behind the archoness, and her cadre regarded them silently, their faces masks of distaste for the green recruits. Sir Cormac climbed deftly up onto his black stallion with a grace that defied his massive size.

"Where's your mount, battlesister?" Donnal asked of Gerda, looking around for the fabled battle-yak as the dwarven woman remained the last unmounted of the company.

"I'll ride with Sir Cormac," she said, grunting as the two of them clasped gauntleted hands and the big paladin swung her up into the saddle in front of him. "Dwarven legs weren't meant for such unwieldy beasts."

Donnal shrugged in disappointment, and the archoness spun her elegant white palfrey to face the assembled riders.

"All of you, listen well!" she called, her voice having regained the powerful, divine resonance Gideon remembered from the chapel, and it sent a chill down his spine. "The witches of this coven will rot the West Umbrals with their corruption if left unchecked."

Her penetrative gaze swept over those gathered around her. "But we are champions of the gods, charged with a sacred duty under the auspices of Holy Light. We will smite these wretches in the name of justice and virtue, and they will rue their wickedness with their final, dying gasps!"

Without waiting for a response, the archoness wheeled her horse around and raced out of the gate, beginning the hunt for the coven.

As her cadre followed, Sir Cormac's burly mount reared as he pointed after the archoness and looked around at the eager and fearful recruits. "Onward, men!" he roared, and it was perhaps the first time he'd ever addressed any of them as anything other than 'boy'. "Onward to glory!"

Gideon urged the mare beneath him forward with his heels, then turned and looked back one last time at the monastery, his home away from home over the last few months, and at Nefteli, standing stoically as she watched him and Donnal leave without her. He pondered what she'd said, and as he leaned forward in the saddle, his hair whipping behind him as the company thundered down the road, he resolved to follow her advice. After what he'd seen, he wasn't sure if he could trust the archoness — or even the gods themselves.

But he knew he could trust Nefteli.

CHAPTER 20

SADIA

Reza reached out for Sadia's hand and helped her step up onto the sodden boards of Suleiman's Berth, an unimpressive little dock sequestered away from the main river on an irrigation channel that slithered its way beneath and between the buildings of the city. Sadia stepped gingerly off the *Mollysocks* and adjusted Ibi on her hip as she looked up from the little pier.

The towering adobe buildings surrounding the channel blocked out most of the setting sunlight, and it seemed the denizens of this dark and dank section of the city relied almost entirely on the flickering oil lamps dotted along the damp, algae-covered walls to provide illumination. The only sounds in the channel were the gentle lapping of the river against the pier, the rustle of the reeds on the embankment, and the slow drip of accumulated humidity down the adobe and sandstone walls.

"Here we are," Dalgrim announced in a gruff voice as he handed Lu the mooring rope and hopped off the boat himself with a wet thud. "Suley's place is just at the end there," the dwarf said, waving toward the far end of the little canal, where the dim glow of lanternlight shone between the reeds in front of a little shack that had seen better days.

"Who?" Sadia asked, finding herself impatient with the dwarf's peculiar personality after what he'd done on the river.

"Suleiman the Fat," Dalgrim explained. "Old friend of mine — leastways, I think that's how we left it. I may also owe him a few drahm. But everyone's always happy to see the ol' *Mollysocks* slip into port," he hurried to reassure her. "Suley will take care of us, have no fear!" He gestured for them to follow and trudged his way along the slippery, uneven boards of the pier, leaving Lu to secure the ship.

The eastern man watched his employer go with a sour expression, then went about tying off the *Mollysocks* while complaining in his native tongue.

Sadia and Reza watched Dalgrim forge ahead. "Come along, children," he called over his shoulder without looking back. Reza looked up at Sadia, and she nodded, taking a breath and following after the dwarf, who was already nearing the little hut at the other end. Dalgrim pushed through the hanging beads that served as a door and disappeared inside, his silhouette illuminated by the warm glow within.

Reza marched into the dilapidated building after him, shoving the curtain aside without a second thought, and Sadia followed more carefully, holding Ibi tight against her.

When she entered, her first impression of the place was the cloying aroma of incense that made her head spin for a moment. She glanced around in surprise at the decor; extravagant cushions were arranged in one corner around a small tea table, shelves filled with all manner of goods were tastefully arranged on two adjacent walls, and a magnificently woven rug of intricate patterns was arrayed across the floor, somehow defying the wet that seemed to permeate the riverside wharf. It was a far different environment than she would have thought from the exterior.

At the far end of the room, Dalgrim was already arguing with the proprietor: a tall man with a long, drooping black mustache that fell to his massive belly. He wore a decorated turban that scraped the ceiling of the shack, and his muscular arms were crossed, displaying huge gold bracelets on both wrists that glimmered in the light of the oil lanterns hanging from the low rafters. His robes were fine and rich — contrasting with Dalgrim's worn and weathered garments — with gold and silver trim and jewels adorning the front. If not for the fact that his cozy little house was hidden in a drainage canal beneath Emra'adid, Sadia might have thought he was some kind of sultan.

"Madam Jalila, eh?" the huge man boomed in response to something Dalgrim had said. His voice was low and thick, and his accent sounded lyrical as it rolled from his tongue. "You owe her far more than mere dues, master dwarf." His smile was huge and showed the pearly white of his teeth as he reached up and scratched at his shaven, dimpled chin.

Sadia didn't catch the rest of their conversation as her attention was caught by a low growl that came from the shadows next to the tea table. She looked nervously that way, but saw nothing until a massive hound stirred and rose slowly to its feet from among the plush cushions. Ibi stirred at the noise and let out a whimper, and Sadia stood petrified in place as the beast approached, sure that at any moment it would pounce, but instead, the great creature plopped himself down on the floor and laid his head heavily on one of Sadia's sandaled feet.

"Sadia?" Reza asked nervously, staring down at the sleepy hound with the same trepidation she felt.

"Get out of here, you little rats!" the big man's voice came booming from across the room. "Or I'll sic Dandan on you!"

Sadia was torn between her fear of both dog and man and couldn't bring herself to move, but then Dalgrim glanced over his shoulder at the children and waved his hand.

"Bah, they're with me, Suley, if you can believe it," he grumbled, and the other man's thick black eyebrows crept up his forehead. "I'm giving 'em a ride out of the desert, and they'll be no trouble. The pup's fine, lassie," he added, "a gentle beast — he'll not harm you."

Sadia still wasn't convinced; the only dogs she'd ever seen before had been wild, starving pack animals that stalked the Qasiran alley-ways, and the size of the beast alone filled her with dread.

"The dwarf speaks truth," the big man said, his demeanor soften-ing. "Even when I tell him to attack, he never listens. Ha!" his laughter made the shelves of delicate trinkets clink and chatter.

Dandan let out a huge, gaping yawn that exposed a row of glisten-ing, sharp teeth, then rolled over onto his back and closed his eyes once again, and a rumbling snore filled the tiny room. Reza swallowed hard and slowly went to his knees, reaching out to scratch the great hound's soft belly, his fingers sinking into the thick grey fur, and he chuckled a bit as the dog twitched happily in its sleep. He looked up at Sadia with an irrepressible grin. "He's a friendly dog," he said, and although it seemed true, Sadia stepped back as she forced a little smile and hugged Ibrahim tighter.

"So, Glintstone," Suleiman said, turning back to the dwarf and teasing one side of his long mustache as Reza vigorously rubbed Dandan's belly, laughing, "what brings you back to Emra'adid finally?"

"Well, I had buyers in Qasira, but there was some nasty business — something about a cult causing trouble," the dwarf explained. "I figured Jalila might appreciate some of what I had for the merchant princes."

"Hmm," Suley murmured, stroking his chin, "a cult, you say?"

"Aye, those Lidless Eye maniacs," Dalgrim replied, glancing at Sadia and Reza. "Those three are refugees of a sort, I suppose."

Suleiman furrowed his brow. "That's the first I've heard anything happening in Qasira," he mused, and Dalgrim perked up.

"You don't say?" the dwarf clapped his hands and rubbed them together with a grin. "I'll bet Jalila would pay a pretty sum for that bit of news."

"Perhaps," the man said with a shrug, reaching for a long hookah pipe that rested on one of the many cluttered shelves. "And speaking of payments," he said, releasing two gouts of smoke from his nostrils, "I assume you haven't forgotten your debts to me, eh, dwarf?"

Dalgrim cleared his throat and tugged at his beard. "Aye, about that," he grumbled, rubbing the back of his neck. "I need to pay a little visit to Madam Jalila's before I can grease that sweaty palm of yours, Suley." He held up his hands quickly to defend against whatever outburst the shopkeep would unleash at such news, but none came.

Suleiman shrugged his enormous shoulders and nodded slowly. "Go to the wise madam, then," he said and pulled aside a window drape next to him to peer out at the dwarf's moored barge. "I'll hold onto the *Mollysocks* as collateral, as usual."

"Aye, I suppose that'll have to do," Dalgrim growled in displeasure.

The curtain in the doorway behind Sadia was drawn back, and she turned to see Lu enter. He grinned as he saw Reza sitting cross-legged on the floor with the giant dog's head in his lap. Dandan looked up as the easterner entered and leapt to his feet and pounced happily on the man.

"Hello, doggy!" Lu laughed, taking the dog's head in his hands. "Are you hungry?" He pulled a few spare scraps of dried meat from one of his belt pouches and tossed it on the floor where Dandan promptly devoured it, then licked Lu's hand in thanks.

"Alright," Dalgrim said with a heavy sigh, pushing himself off from where he was leaning against the shopkeeper's counter, "it's high time we go secure some soft bedding after our long journey." He fished a pair of dull silver coins from his pocket and let them clatter onto the countertop before Suleiman. "I'll have the rest after I see Jalila, Suley. Oh, and, ah..." Dalgrim turned and made for the door, "if the city guard come snooping around, it's not the *Mollysocks* that's moored out there, aye?"

"What?" Suleiman asked, but the dwarf was already pushing through the bead curtain.

"Come along, children!" Dalgrim called to them from outside. Sadia gave an apologetic look to Suleiman as the big man scooped up the measly coin, and Reza and Lu each gave Dandan a final pat on his massive head before they all followed the dwarf out into Emra'adid.

High above, a deep orange light from the setting sun was just visible in a narrow cleft between the buildings crowding the canal.

They followed the damp jetty along the waterway up winding, curving stairs cut into the adobe buildings toward the higher tiers of the city.

"Where are we going?" Reza asked as he took the steps easily by twos.

"To a... palace... of luxury!" Dalgrim panted, pausing and resting his hands on his knees. "We'll spend the night in proper beds at the Gentle Djinni," he explained, "and head to Madam Jalila's in the morning."

Reza looked at Sadia, his eyes alight with excitement at the idea of sleeping in an actual bed. For the likes of them, the best bed they'd ever had was a discarded blanket laid across the cool, stony floor in their cistern.

"Will they let us in?" Sadia asked, looking down at her tattered, faded blue dress and feeling self-conscious.

"Oh aye, lass," Dalgrim nodded confidently. "The owner is an old friend of mine, and with enough coin to turn her head, she'll have a room for even the most dastardly and wanted criminals and fugitives in all the Great Nahridi!"

Sadia wasn't sure if she should be comforted by his words, but the dwarf continued on up the hewn stairs before she could inquire further, huffing and puffing as he struggled up each set of steps, muttering curses on his short legs until they finally came out of the canals.

The streets in the upper city were a stark contrast to the dark, wet, dingy world of the canal. They were lined with beautiful fountains of cool water, and the air was thick with the scent of spices, cooked meats, and dishes from the stalls at every street corner. People of all colors, races, and manners of dress passed them as they made their way to whatever destination was at the end of the busy thoroughfare.

Sadia glanced at Reza and smiled as she saw him marveling at everything they saw. "It's amazing," he whispered, his head swiveling from side to side to take in all the sights, his nose in the air as he savored all the fragrant scents of the exotic cuisine being sold by street vendors.

"It is," she whispered back. The buildings were mostly made of adobe, like in Qasira, but some were also constructed from huge blocks of smooth stone or had intricately detailed reliefs carved into their edifices so that every building was a work of art. Wrought copper adornments covered in verdigris were a common accoutrement for almost everything. It was beautiful, exotic, and far beyond anything she had ever known or imagined.

Dalgrim marched ahead of the children and Lu, and they did their best to keep pace through the busy crowds milling as the sun sank toward the distant dunes. Finally, the dwarf stopped short and gestured up to a huge building, rising up over the square in which they stood. "This is the place," he said. "The Gentle Djinni!"

Sadia gazed up at the beautiful facade; its adobe walls were clean and decorated with turquoise and wood trim. Wide, open-air balconies looked out over the street from the second story, and the doors and windows were covered by awnings of pretty patterned cloth. A raucous din carried out into the street from within the place, and as they entered, they were met by the thick, heady scents of smoke, alcohol, and meat.

Dalgrim shouldered his way past the throngs of people inside, weaving through the tables of people feasting and drinking, toward a crowded bar at the back of the place. Sadia kept a firm grip on Reza as she followed.

The dwarf strode up to the bar where a large, full-figured woman was cleaning dishes with a rag. She had dusky, tanned skin and black hair streaked with silver, bound into a huge braid that draped over one shoulder, and her soft cheeks paled when she saw him approaching.

"Roya, you beautiful beast!" Dalgrim called warmly, throwing his arms wide as he approached.

"Dalgrim Glintstone," the woman replied evenly, quickly regaining her composure. "I didn't expect to see you walk in my doors again, after the last time." She set the dish and rag aside and crossed her arms over her ample bosom as she stared down at him, her expression unreadable. "What kind of trouble do you bring to my house now, you old drunk?"

Dalgrim laughed uproariously, as if he'd been told a great joke, and slapped a hand on the bar top. "No trouble, you delicate desert flower." Roya flushed and shifted uncomfortably. "I am but a weary traveler seeking succor after a long journey, and I've just enough coin in my pockets to pay handsomely for the renowned luxuries of the Gentle Djinni." He leaned a little closer and waggled his eyebrows. "My old bones could use a decent rest, and my lips could use a drink. What do you say?"

Roya looked the dwarf up and down, considering. "The last time you came through my doors, Dalgrim, you had a half dozen of the city watch on your heels," she said with a frown, apparently unswayed by the dwarf's charm. "How can I be sure you won't cause any trouble this time?"

"Dwarves know no trouble, but only opportunity," the dwarf answered smoothly. "But aye," he added, "I promise to keep the ruckus to a minimum this time. But, er... having said that," he glanced around conspiratorially, "if anyone comes looking for retribution for a little... accident... on the river a while ago, you haven't seen me, agreed?"

Roya frowned. "Back to our old arrangement? Just like that?"

Dalgrim let out a nervous chuckle but maintained his smile. "Just looking for a bit of kindness, Roya," he said, and the woman's nostrils flared indignantly. "If not for me, then for the children here," he added quickly, grabbing Sadia and Reza and pulling them forward. "Orphans from Qasira — gave them a ride on the *Mollysocks*, and they need a place to stay."

The big woman glared angrily at Dalgrim for a moment before finally tearing her eyes from him and looking at Sadia and Reza. Her expression softened, and she unfolded her arms reluctantly. "I won't turn you or your friends away, Dalgrim," she said with a sigh. "Rooms, then?"

The dwarf's grin broadened further behind his thick black beard. "You're a treasure to be sure, Roya!" he declared, slipping a small pile of coins across the bar to her. "Make it a pair of rooms and a meal as well, if you please."

Roya looked from Dalgrim to the pile of coins and finally scooped up the payment and secreted it away. "Some things never change," she muttered to herself, then turned and barked at her attendants behind the bar, sending a pair of boys scampering off with orders to prepare rooms for the travelers. She turned her attention back to the dwarf with an even expression, her dark eyes reflecting the lanternlight. "A drink while you wait, I suppose?" she asked.

Dalgrim clapped his hands together and rubbed them vigorously. "A drink, aye! And one for my loyal—" he turned to look at Lu and interrupted himself as he saw the man walking away, back toward the entrance. "Lu!" he called, "where are you going?"

The easterner turned around and glared angrily at Dalgrim. "I go now," he said simply, jabbing a finger toward the door. "I go find new boss!"

"Oh, well, I haven't heard that before," the dwarf said, rolling his eyes.

"You crazy! Get me killed!" Lu shot back.

Dalgrim waved a hand. "I haven't yet, have I?" he asked incredulously, "and I pay you well... er, usually, least ways. Stay! Drink with me!" He slapped the counter again with a meaty palm and waved the eastern man over to him, then nodded at Roya, and she reached for a glass to pour him a drink.

Lu muttered something in his own language, but then turned around and came back to the counter, sitting on the stool next to the dwarf with a defeated sigh. "One drink," he said, holding a finger up. "You owe me. Then I go."

"Aye, of course, of course!" Dalgrim exclaimed as Roya finished pouring. The dwarf picked up his glass and gave Lu a hearty slap on the back that earned him a dangerous glare, but the easterner took the offered drink. Dalgrim lifted his own cup and clinked it against Lu's. "To your health, my loyal bodyguard!"

Lu scowled, but drank.

CHAPTER 21

SADIA

"But none as fair as she!" Dalgrim and Lu sang together, hoisting their drinks up in the air, "'twas the tale of Bearded Mary!" They both burst into raucous laughter, falling over each other and emptying their cups.

Sadia watched them, bemused. They had been at it all evening, drinking, telling raunchy stories, and singing bawdy songs. The pair were an odd match, to be sure, and it seemed their bond resided almost wholly in liquor.

She turned to Reza, who sat beside her, valiantly trying to clean his fourth plate of food that Roya had brought him. Dalgrim had paid for their meals, and Sadia had never seen Reza's eyes so large as when the caravanserai owner had brought the first course to their table. The food was rich and delicious, like nothing Sadia had ever had before. There was rice mixed with saffron and cinnamon and seasoned with roasted nuts and vegetables, a meat pie that steamed when they cut into it, and morsels of fried dough that were tangy and sweet. Life in the Qasiran cisterns had never brought such a feast their way before.

Even Ibi had taken an interest in the food, which he had seldom done so far, and although he had only nibbled, she could tell that it had done something for him, and his frail body looked a little less peaked.

Reza groaned, rubbing his belly with his free hand and flopping his head back on the plush cushions as he pushed his plate away. "I can't eat any more!" he moaned, then yawned. Sadia ruffled his hair and was surprised when he immediately let out a snore. She chuckled, the most amazing sense of relief and contentment blooming in her chest as she realized, almost reluctantly, that she felt strangely safe here, despite everything that had happened. But then her mind was instantly pulled to Yusuf and the girls, and her heart ached violently at the idea of them splitting a stale piece of flatbread or a handful of rice while she was filling her belly.

She looked over at Dalgrim and Lu in the dim, smoky light — they were already onto their next round and showed no signs of stopping.

Roya appeared at the small table where she'd situated them and smiled as she looked down on Reza and Ibi, who had both fallen asleep. "Aw, perhaps it's time you turn in for the night, yes? Let me help you get him upstairs," she said, lifting Reza in strong arms. He was still dozing, and Sadia followed after the big woman, glancing over her shoulder at the dwarf and the easterner, still very much absorbed in some drinking game with half a dozen others, before following Roya up the winding stone steps to their rooms on the second floor.

"Dalgrim paid for your stay for two nights," Roya told her as she opened a door and carried Reza inside. She laid the boy down on a pile of soft, plush cushions arrayed in a corner of the little room, then turned to Sadia. "How on earth did you fall in with the likes of Dalgrim Glintstone?" she asked after a moment, as though having lost an argument with herself.

Sadia laid Ibi down next to Reza and smoothed his brow. "We had to leave Qasira," she answered after a moment, struggling to choose how much to share. "Dalgrim was the only one willing to take on three orphans."

"I've never known the man to be one for charity," Roya sighed, shaking her head. "I suppose he must have a soft spot in there somewhere, then. Do you have anyone in Emra'adid you can stay with?" she asked.

Sadia shook her head. "No, we... we're all each other has, really," she said after a moment, watching Reza and Ibi sleep, blissfully ignorant, finally somewhere safe and with food in their bellies. "Ibrahim, the little one, is very... unwell," she said, choosing her words carefully. "I couldn't find any help in Qasira for him. They don't help people like us," Sadia explained. "I'm just trying to find someone who can help him."

Roya looked heart-stricken as she listened. "Oh, my dear," she said, "I'm so sorry. Emra'adid has no shortage of healers," she offered after a moment. "Priestesses, shamans, apothecaries... surely you will find someone who can help him. And in the meantime, if you need a safe place to stay, you are welcome here. If you like, you can come downstairs tomorrow, and I'll find work for you. There are always dishes and laundry that need doing, and I can pay you a fair wage."

Sadia was shocked by the offer and was at a loss for words. "I don't know what to say," she finally managed, and the woman waved a hand and smiled warmly.

"I never had any children of my own," Roya said sadly, "but I always wanted to. My mother — she passed long ago, before I left Maramasa to come here — but she always told her daughters that it was a joy for any house to have children within its walls. So you are most welcome here."

The stress of their flight from Qasira, of rescuing Ibrahim and leaving the rest of her little family behind, welled behind Sadia's eyes, and two tears escaped as she blinked.

"Oh," Roya exclaimed sympathetically, bustling over and wrapping Sadia up in a strong hug. "Fret not, my dear. Emra'adid is not Qasira. You will find many here who will spare you the kindness you've been denied for so long."

Sadia hugged the woman back, and even though Roya was a stranger to her, she felt such a kind and supportive strength in the embrace that she never wanted to let go. "Thank you," she whispered, and the woman stroked her head affectionately.

"You will be safe here," the older woman said, holding her out at arm's length and smiling reassuringly.

Sadia's eyes still brimmed with tears as she nodded her thanks. "I suppose I'm truly blessed to have met Dalgrim, aren't I?" she asked, wiping at her eyes with the sleeve of her dress.

Roya chuckled. "No one would call Dalgrim a blessing, I think," she said, "but I've known the man for a long time." She paused, her gaze lingering on a spot on the wall as though it were a hundred yards away. Then she suddenly returned to herself. "There's some good left in him yet, it seems," she said, then made for the door. "Sleep well, dear; tomorrow, the sun will shine a little brighter on you."

Sadia smiled as the door closed behind Roya and turned back to the bed. She slid a pillow beneath Reza's head and caressed Ibi's hollow cheek; then she took a moment to recite her prayers, begging for mercy and health for her chosen brothers and sisters.

CHAPTER 22

GIDEON

THE ARCHONESS HAD NOT SLOWED her pace as she led the ragtag company of green recruits in search of the coven. As the sun passed its zenith and started arcing down toward the mountains, Gideon began to feel sore in the saddle. Donnal, however, was faring much worse.

His friend was struggling to stay upright, and he winced and complained every time the gelding moved faster than a gentle walk. Gideon glanced behind him at James, who rode just a few yards behind, and the redhead rolled his eyes and smirked. Over the course of the march, Donnal had slowly fallen back toward the tail end of the formation, and both James and Gideon had stayed with him, trying to offer encouragement.

Truthfully, he was glad to hang back with Donnal; the other recruits kept eyeing him curiously, and he could tell they wanted to ask about what had happened in the chapel, to hear it from someone who'd been present. None of them had, though, and he was thankful.

"All halt!" a cry came from the head of the column of riders, and it was echoed by others down to the end.

"Oh, blessed day!" Donnal groaned as he tugged the reins and brought his gelding to a stop. Gideon watched as all the riders ahead dismounted, and he looked to James, who shrugged and slid out of his saddle.

Gideon swung his leg over and landed on the road beside his mare. "What's going on?" he wondered aloud as everyone ahead started leading their horses off the road and into the trees.

"I don't know," James sighed, stretching his limbs before grabbing the reins of his own mount and following. "Can't hear anything back here."

Gideon helped Donnal dismount and caught him as his legs threatened to give way, and then the two of them led their horses after the others. Just a hundred paces or so off the road, Gideon heard the faint trickling of running water, and as he guided his mare past a stand of trees, he saw the rest of the company watering their horses at a stream down a shallow embankment.

"Crieg!" Sir Cormac's voice boomed as he held a large, lumpy brown sack aloft. "Come and pass these out."

Donnal grumbled and passed his gelding's bridle to Gideon before moving quickly to the big paladin, his legs unsteady. "Yes, sir!"

Gideon and James brought their horses up to the stream, and the animals drank greedily.

"Not very exciting yet, is it?" James asked from the other side of his mount, his freckled face barely visible over the saddle.

Gideon scoffed. "I'm not sure we should be hoping for excitement in this situation, James."

"Ah, come on," James protested. "We're finally out of the monastery! We've been waiting for months, and all I've got so far is two sore cheeks!"

Gideon sighed but didn't respond. It wasn't long before Donnal came down the line, handing out bread and smoked meat. He handed James two dried strips of venison and Gideon half a loaf of stale bread. "We'll have to split those between us," he said, turning the empty bag over and shaking out crumbs. "This is all there was left."

The three of them joined a handful of other recruits sitting in a rough circle on the ground while they ate. Gideon sat down, and his mare, tethered by her reins to his belt, lowered her head and started chewing on the grass beside him. As Gideon tore the bread into three chunks, he caught the two young women who'd been volunteered side-eyeing Donnal.

The one named Meredith tucked a stray lock of dark hair behind her ear, then scooped up a piece of bark and tossed it at Donnal to get his attention. "How many times have you fallen off that big beautiful gelding today, then, Donnal?"

"None at all, if you can believe it!" Donnal answered proudly, drawing himself up with a smug smile.

The other girl, Lillian, gave a sarcastic clap. "Well, well, looks like they'll make a rider out of you after all."

Donnal preened. "As my da always said — there's no problem a Crieg's not stubborn enough to solve."

James laughed and reached over to pat his arm. "Don't think we're not proud of you, mate," he said, "but maybe save the showboating til after you've survived a battle on horseback, eh?"

Donnal scowled, but Meredith's brows drew together. "You think they'll actually let us fight? The archoness and her men don't really seem to want us here."

"We're fresh recruits," Lillian noted. Her blond hair was bound in a fancy sequence of braids, keeping it tight to her head, and she looked ever-so-slightly down her button nose at the others around her. "Surely they don't actually expect us to fight."

"Oh, we'll fight," Gideon said, surprising himself with his ardor. All eyes in the circle turned to him, and he felt his cheeks flush. He lowered his voice and continued tearing his bread into smaller and smaller pieces without purpose. "They'll make us," he mumbled.

"How do you know?" Lillian asked, frowning. "We're untested, the battlesister said it herself."

"He was in the chapel," James said sharply, fixing the girl with a stare.

"Right," Donnal added. "He knows what happened in there."

Lillian blinked, looking taken aback at the rebuke.

Gideon felt the stares of the others, and he shifted uncomfortably.

"What did happen in there, exactly?" Meredith asked, and everyone seemed to lean a little closer, unable to keep their curiosity in check any longer.

Gideon sighed and looked around the circle. They were all looking at him expectantly, and he swallowed the sudden lump in his throat.

"Well," he began, looking past them to make sure none of their officers were within earshot. He told them what had happened, and what he'd witnessed, keeping the details sparse. A part of him wanted to explain how horrific it had been, how ruthless the archoness actually was, but if Nefteli were there, he knew she wouldn't approve, so he kept his personal commentary on the incident to himself.

"Gods above," Donnal breathed, looking from Gideon to the others. "Is that what we're going to go fight?" he asked nervously. "Invincible flesh monsters?"

"They weren't invincible once Sir Cormac called on the Holy Light," Gideon said, shaking his head.

James frowned and scratched his chin. "I guess that's why they wanted all of us," he said, "all of us who swore the Oath of Woe, I mean."

The recruits who'd passed the trials all looked at one another. In the little circle they'd formed, only Gideon and Donnal had failed.

"So what are you two going to do, then?" Lillian asked them, looking unimpressed.

Gideon clenched his jaw and stood. "Whatever Sir Cormac tells us to," he answered, dusting off the seat of his trousers.

The blonde girl opened her mouth to say something, but stopped herself as Battlesister Dawnhammer came clanking up to them.

"All of you who swore the Oath of Woe," she growled at them, "come with me." She turned and stalked away, heading further upstream.

James and the other paladins-in-training rose and followed the dwarven woman, and Gideon and Donnal were left watching them go.

"Ballad!" Sir Cormac called, and Gideon whipped his head around to look over at the big man. "Come. Bring that mare with you."

Gideon grabbed the horse's lead and started over without hesitating. Donnal lifted his arms as he passed, then let them fall in frustration as he was left alone, glancing apprehensively at his grey gelding.

"Yes, sir?" Gideon asked as he joined the paladin.

Sir Cormac looked down at him over his huge mustache. "When next we ride, the archoness wants a new bannerman," he explained, and nodded over at the tall banner bearing the sword-and-tome emblem of the Church Militant. It swayed gently, suspended from a thick, heavy pole mounted to one of the cadre's horses. "I told her you were the man for the job."

Gideon frowned. "Oh," he said, his pulse quickening as he glanced over at the archoness and two of her men quietly conferring downstream. "Yes, sir."

If Sir Cormac noticed his hesitation, he didn't acknowledge it. "Come," he said, "we'll outfit that mare of yours with the equipment you need." He turned and beckoned him after.

The old knight showed him how to affix a thick leather strap with an iron cup at the end to his saddle. He explained how to rest the banner pole in the iron cup and how to hold it properly, both as he rode and when dismounted. Gideon absorbed the information as best he could, intent on making Sir Cormac proud.

Despite all his misgivings about what the archoness had done, being outside of the monastery, having been given a task, made Gideon feel purposeful. It wasn't what he had planned his life to be, but somehow, in that moment, things felt alright.

As Sir Cormac observed him practicing with the banner, a series of brilliant bursts of light flashed from upstream, where the battlesister had led the other recruits. Gideon glanced back at the old paladin, whose mustache twitched.

"They're practicing, same as you," he said calmly.

Gideon nodded and slid deftly from the saddle, bringing the banner down with him and then standing at attention and presenting the tall, heavy battle standard with a subtle flourish, as he'd been taught.

"Well done, Ballad," Sir Cormac said approvingly. "Now, once we—"

The unmistakable sound of hoofbeats slowly grew from the other side of the creek, and after a moment, two of the archoness's cadre appeared.

"The scouts are back," Sir Cormac muttered, then glanced at Gideon. "Stand fast, Ballad." He stalked over to join the archoness as the riders splashed through the stream and came up beside her.

Gideon moved to the far side of his mare, trying to look inconspicuous as the men began relaying their report, but he was well within earshot and couldn't help but overhear.

"No signs of the witches' thralls in the hamlet, milady," one of them said after dismounting. "But we did sight a number of their twisted abominations, as in the chapel."

"Villagers wounded in the fray with the coven, most likely," Sergeant Findlay murmured, and the archoness nodded.

"Were you able to discern which way the coven fled?" she asked.

The other scout, a tall, lean man with dark skin, nodded and pointed west. "We were able to identify traces of rank magic headed into the hills," he explained. "Only something very powerful could have left that kind of mark on the land."

The archoness seemed unperturbed. She regarded the scouts coolly, her hands folded neatly atop her palfrey's withers.

"We must cleanse the hamlet first," she said firmly, looking out into the forest, "then pursue the coven. Their lair will not be far." She looked back down at her cadre and Sir Cormac. "I want as few casualties among the recruits as possible. Each of you take two or three of them, split them as evenly as you can between those who passed their trials and those who didn't."

"Yes, milady," Sir Cormac replied. "Gerda is giving them a quick lesson as we speak."

"Much is being asked of them — to ride to battle so soon after their trials," the archoness admitted, a note of softness in her voice. "But such is the nature of our business." She turned her head and looked directly at Gideon, who immediately looked away in a panic and started fussing nervously with the standard.

"You've chosen my new bannerman, I see," he heard her say.

Sir Cormac grunted in the affirmative. "Recruit Ballad," he informed her. "He's as stout and hardy as they come, and I think he'll be courageous in battle, though not foolhardy."

"Good temperament for a soldier," Sergeant Findlay observed.

Archoness Lorica said nothing, and Gideon tried his best not to squirm as he sensed her scrutiny. After a long moment, she spoke again, and her voice was strong and commanding. "Gather the recruits. We've tarried long enough."

As her men obeyed, Gideon watched out of the corner of his eye as she wheeled her steed around and urged it back up the hill toward the road.

"What's going on?" Donnal whispered beside him, and Gideon jumped at his friend's sudden appearance. He was hunched over, hiding behind Gideon's mare, and looked up at the gently swaying banner with a cocked eyebrow. "And what are you doing with that?"

Gideon sighed as Sir Cormac and the battlesister called the recruits together, and he tugged on the mare's lead. "I'm the archoness's bannerman now, apparently."

Donnal grinned and stood, giving him a congratulatory slap on the shoulder. "Nice, mate!"

"I suppose," he answered with a shrug. Donnal dashed away to grab his gelding, and they joined the rest of the company forming up on the road.

"Are you a master paladin now, then, James?" Donnal asked as they came up beside the scrawny ginger.

James scoffed. "Hardly," he said, shaking his head, then leaned toward them conspiratorially. "Battlesister Dawnhammer was teaching us a trick, though," he whispered. "She said it will help us channel the Light better."

Sir Cormac started barking orders from the head of the column of riders, calling out names to form smaller groups.

Donnal's name was called, and he led his steed forward. "Well, whatever it is, it'd better work," he said, then gave a lazy salute as he left them.

After a short time organizing the groups, Gideon found himself at the head of the formation beside the archoness. The blonde girl, Lillian, had been assigned to the archoness as well, and the rest of the recruits were split among the other officers.

Archoness Lorica looked out across her assembled troops from her perch in the saddle, sitting straight with an aura of calm power about her. "The hamlet ahead served as the battlefield upon which we confronted the coven," she called out, her voice carrying easily through the clearing around the road. "They've fled, but left in their wake horrible abominations of dead flesh and bone. These unholy creatures must be crushed under the hammer of the Holy Light."

She urged her stunning white palfrey forward, sauntering down the line and regarding each rider in turn. "Those of you who've sworn your oath — go forth in faith, and with a dire thirst for vengeance! Many innocent lives were lost in the fight against the coven, some of whom were twisted into the very creatures we must now destroy, who we must lay to rest, that their souls may be freed to join the gods.

"The rest of you," she continued, speaking to those of them who'd failed the trials, "bring your martial training to bear with violent intent!" She reached the rear and wheeled her horse around. "We will ride them down like a storm, relentless until the last is felled, or none of us remain to draw breath!"

Her cadre drew their weapons and raised them up, roaring in support. The recruits followed their example and added their voices to the cry. Gideon caught Sir Cormac looking at him and gesturing with his hand in a lifting motion, and he understood.

Gideon took the banner in both hands, lifting it from its rest and thrusting it up into the air. Another cry rang out, fiercer this time, and the archoness unslung her heavy, gilded tome and recited a sacred prayer. A golden light glowed from within its pages, and a moment later, every weapon held aloft was enveloped in a brilliant light infused with holiness. Even the sharp iron tip of the banner burned radiant as the gods blessed it.

"Ride now!" the archoness cried, returning her holy book to her belt. She urged her horse forward and it broke into a trot and then a swift canter as she flew down the column back to the fore. "And may the gods guide our hand!"

With that, she spurred her mount into a gallop and thundered down the road, leaving the dust swirling in her wake. The mare beneath Gideon whinnied as she passed, and he dug his heels into her flanks and hurried to give chase, holding the banner of the Church Militant high above his head.

CHAPTER 23

GIDEON

THE HAMLET WAS IN RUINS.

Stone walls in various states of collapse, thatched roofs fallen in and blackened — if not burnt away entirely — and an oppressive silence were all that remained of the place.

The smell of the massacre hit Gideon like a wall before they even reached the hamlet, the scent of blood and decay, of the flesh of dead things in the afternoon heat. A stagnant air clung to everything, and Gideon had to force himself not to cover his mouth and nose against the stench.

His right arm was already tiring from holding the battle standard steady as he struggled to keep up with the archoness. Lorica surged like a bolt of lightning as she led them, and her palfrey's hooves churned the road as they raced along. She was a sight to behold, and the simple force of her will inspired something in Gideon, a sense of awe that overpowered his previous opinion of her, even if just in that moment.

Gideon felt his mare's hooves slipping and skidding beneath him as she tried to keep pace, and he spurred her on with both heels. Beside him, Lillian was bent over the saddle, her expression grim and determined as the three of them led the furious charge.

As they bore down on the hamlet, passing abandoned crops and the charred remains of a windmill, the archoness slowed and brought her mount down to a trot. The other groups flanked out around them, circling the hamlet to close in from all sides. Gideon was amazed by the silent concert in which the officers worked, coordinating their movements in near-perfect synchronization.

The archoness pulled at the reins and came to a halt at the edge of the village. Gideon came alongside her, his eyes darting around wildly in search of any sign of the abominations the scouts had sighted, but he saw none. The burnt husks of houses provided plenty of places for the lurking witch-beasts to hide, and they stood as a testament to the violence that had destroyed the place.

"I don't see anything," Lillian breathed, her voice low.

The archoness remained still and silent, her expression stern as she scanned the little town before them.

A chill ran down Gideon's spine, and his heart began to race as the quiet set in. The mare's flanks quivered beneath him, her ears twitching as she tossed her head nervously.

"Follow," Archoness Lorica ordered, urging her horse forward, "and be on your guard." The two recruits followed, and Gideon's grip on the banner tightened.

The eerie silence magnified the crunch of their horses' hooves on the rubble-strewn ground, and the tension hanging over the place was palpable, like a taut rope poised to snap. The three of them moved slowly, cautiously, their eyes roaming every dark doorway and shadowed corner for any sign of movement.

"What happened here?" Gideon asked aloud without meaning to, awestruck by the destruction the hamlet had sustained. Dried blood that had turned a dark brown under the sun stained what remained of walls, thatched rooves, and sheaves of wheat lining the road. Further ahead he could see a large pile of dried sticks, vines, and brambles in the middle of the hamlet that seemed strangely out of place.

The archoness rode close to one of the half-collapsed walls and reined in her palfrey. "The battle here was dire," she answered in a murmur, her eyes roving purposefully over the wreckage. "We managed to expose the witches, and..." she ran one gauntleted finger through a bloodstain on the wall, sending flakes of dried gore floating to the ground, "and they didn't refrain from unleashing their true power."

Further down the main road that ran through the hamlet, one of her cadre and the recruits assigned to him appeared from a side street. He signaled to the archoness, and she responded with a single, slow nod.

Gideon swallowed, trying not to imagine the fight, or what had happened to the villagers who lived there.

He glanced over at Lillian, who frowned and asked, "The witches hid among the people here, milady?"

"Yes," the archoness replied, her voice cold, "they appeared to be three harmless old women — a sage, a seamstress, and a washerwoman." A bitter revulsion crossed her face. "A ruse to hide their vile meddling. Three they seemed, and yet...." The look on her face changed to one of confusion and trepidation. "Perhaps one hiding as three. I can't yet be certain whether—"

She was cut off as a cry rose from ahead of them. "Look out!" one of the recruits yelled, and Gideon looked up to see one of the ropey abominations appear over the other side of a damaged roof, its flesh greyed and rotted, covered in weeping sores and pustules. The human head of the person the thing had once been was hanging off its back, but unlike the soldier in the chapel, the poor soul mercifully seemed fully dead and unmoving.

The thing screeched and leapt toward the other group, and Gideon's mare shied as the recruits scrambled to react. Weapons were drawn, and the cadre started shouting orders, but the abomination moved with a terrifying speed and pounced on him before any of them could react, driving him from the saddle.

The archoness held her hand out to one side, and her holy blade of Light materialized in her open palm just as Sir Cormac's group rounded another corner farther down.

"With me!" Archoness Lorica cried, spurring her steed forward.

Gideon yanked hard on the reins and dug his heels into the mare's flanks. With a snort, she took off after the archoness, the white and gold banner snapping above him as it cut through the air.

Ahead, the recruits were hacking down from horseback at the creature, their gleaming weapons burning and slicing through its fleshy, putrid limbs. The thing shrieked and flailed against the man on the ground, and Gideon could see the shattered bones in its extremities tearing through his chain and leather armor, splashing crimson across the flanks of the recruit's circling mounts.

The archoness rode up and leapt deftly from the saddle into the fray, her ethereal saber dancing in golden flashes, burning through the twisted body of the creature attacking her soldier.

Gideon's horse reared up as she neighed and bucked, her eyes rolling and her teeth gnashing, and he toppled backward to the ground, landing in a heap and instantly scrambling back to his feet, the banner still clutched tight in his hands. The mare danced away from the melee, terrified, and Gideon let her go, charging instead to rejoin the archoness.

Lillian flew past him on her dapple grey but skidded to a halt as another twisted monstrosity slithered out into the street and reared up before her. It lashed out with three sinuous arms punctured by jagged, shattered bones, and the recruit threw her arms up with a frightened scream.

The glimmer of gold coalesced before her in an instant, forming a shimmering barrier between her and the surging creature. Its limbs collided with the wall of Light, and it shattered in a burst that forced Gideon to cover his eyes. When he looked back, he saw the abomination had rebounded from the power of the deflection and staggered backward.

Before it could recover, the golden effigy of a huge shield crashed into it, shattering and exploding with divine might. The monster was sent flying backward into a nearby house, leaving bloody streaks where its limbs had burst against the stone. Gideon and Lillian both looked down the byway where the golden shield had come from and saw Sir Cormac standing tall, his sword resting on one shoulder and the massive tower shield in his other hand glowing red hot and slowly dimming after having projected the shield of Light.

"Forward!" he roared, and the recruits with him advanced as more inhuman shrieks rose from the ruins and rubble around them.

Lillian spurred her mount forward, and Gideon turned back to the archoness. The first creature lay in pieces at her feet, the severed segments of its body smoking and hissing from the Light's purification. She looked down at her man as he lay on the ground, clutching desperately at the tattered remains of his throat in a vain attempt to stem the flow of blood.

Gideon rushed up alongside her while the two mounted recruits looked nervously down on the wounded man.

"Can we do anything, milady?" one of them asked, and Archoness Lorica's expression grew grave.

"No," she said firmly, and Gideon could see the pain and pity in her eyes. She lifted the burning golden blade in her hand and pressed it into the man's chest, and he convulsed violently, staring up in fear at his commander, the gurgling at his throat intensifying and spraying blood into the air as he tried to scream.

Gideon's knuckles turned white on the banner pole, and he finally had to look away as the man was burned to cinders at their feet. More unearthly screaming carried seemingly from all directions, along with the shouted orders of the officers as they tried to coordinate the attack.

The archoness stood still, staring at the black stain on the weathered road that had been her soldier. Gideon glanced up at the other two recruits, still mounted and unsure what to do.

"Milady?" he finally said, and Lorica stirred, as if coming awake.

Tearing her eyes from the charred remains, she turned gracefully on her heel and stalked forward toward the sounds of battle. "Press on!"

she barked over her shoulder, and Gideon and the others rushed to follow.

Archoness Lorica led them through the hamlet, flying from one group to the next, smiting the witch-monsters wherever they appeared. All throughout the ruined place, monstrosities crept out from wrecked homes and shops like cockroaches, quickly to be met by the archoness's dispassionate violence. She was a storm of righteous fury, her holy blade burning through corrupted flush, calling down pillars of purgative Light and cleansing the unholy perversions of humanity with a passion that awed Gideon.

Along the streets were more piles of brambles, inexplicably placed and scattered as though they had fallen, but Gideon had little time to wonder about them.

Upon reaching the edge of the hamlet, they came upon one of the other embattled groups. The paladin leading them threw up a golden shield to repel the assaulting monster, and Archoness Lorica dashed forward, slicing her ethereal blade through the air and sending an arc of Light at the creature. It split apart at the middle where the Light seared through it, and fell in a flailing heap to the ground.

The rear half of the creature's torso continued to scuttle forward, and Lorica advanced to finish it. Before she could, however, Donnal leapt out from behind the golden shield, his dented, Light-wreathed shortsword held over his head, and threw himself in a fury into the thing as it tried to lash out again. He brought the sword down with a grunt, then chopped at it repeatedly, sending charred pieces flying as he hacked it to stillness.

He stood over the smoking corpse, breathing hard, and turned to look at the archoness. She returned the gaze, her expression flat, then turned to the two recruits still mounted beside Gideon.

"You two," she called, pointing along the row of ruined homes at the edge of the village, "ride along the perimeter and tell everyone you see to start pushing toward the center. Go!"

The two recruits shared a nervous glance, but spurred their horses onward as directed. As the archoness turned to press back into the hamlet, Gideon followed, and Donnal ran up beside him.

"How's this, Gid?" he asked excitedly, his hands shaking and cheeks flushed. "A real battle!"

Gideon nodded and spared his friend a nervous smile, but his arms ached with the weight of the banner, and his stomach churned from the scent of death that hung all around them. They followed the archoness as the slaughter continued, and Gideon was astounded at how many of the fleshy abominations there were — the whole hamlet must have fallen to the witches' curse.

Before long, the warriors of the Church Militant had closed in on the hamlet square, fighting as they went, and finally, the hissing shrieks of the creatures had died out as the last of the twisted things fell to Battlesister Gerda's gleaming hammer.

Gideon was breathing hard just from having kept pace with the archoness, the acrid scent of incinerated flesh burning his nostrils. He felt a little self-conscious as he looked around at the others, most of whom were spattered by black blood, having actually partaken in the melee. He, meanwhile, had merely held their lady's banner aloft and tried not to die.

All those gathered in the square turned their attention to Archoness Lorica. She stood at the center, her golden blade burning brightly in one hand, her sacred tome held aloft in the other, and waited for a long moment, her keen gaze searching the dark corners of collapsed buildings all around. Finally, she straightened.

"I want an accounting of any dead or wounded at once," she ordered, and the blade of manifested Light blinked away in her hand. "We lost Hughes — who else?"

"One of my recruits fell," Sergeant Findlay reported, taking a step forward. "He was overcome on the outskirts."

"The brunette lass as well," Gerda added, her face hard and streaked with a line of gore.

Across the square from Gideon, Lillian sucked in a breath. "Meredith," she said miserably, her face draining of color.

The archoness stared at the group for a long moment, then nodded. "I see. Gather up the bodies and—"

"Wait, do you hear that?" Donnal asked suddenly, craning his neck to listen. Everyone fell silent for a moment, and then a pained grunt and a faint cry sounded from somewhere beyond the square. Donnal dashed off immediately, cutting down a side road in search of the noise.

CHAPTER 24

GIDEON

"Hold fast, Crieg!" Sir Cormac barked, but Donnal was already gone. The old knight growled in frustration. "Get after him, Ballad!" he ordered, and Gideon obeyed.

He chased his wayward friend through the rubble-strewn gaps between the houses and buildings, the heft of the banner slowing him down and making it awkward to navigate the tight spaces. Finally, he saw Donnal stop in a dead end ahead and go to one knee.

Gideon caught up, and his heart sank as he saw their young, red-headed friend lying on the ground beneath the half-charred remains of one of the witch-twisted creatures. James looked up at them with frightened eyes, his chest fluttering with rapid, hitching breaths. A large, splintered bone had shattered through his small buckler shield and driven all the way through him, the jagged end sticking out of his back.

James lifted one arm weakly and Donnal took his hand fast in his own. "I think I'm... a goner, Donny," he wheezed. His face was even paler than usual, and even his freckles seemed to have lost their color.

"No, don't say that, mate," Donnal pleaded, squeezing his friend's hand. "Just hold on, alright? We'll get you back to the archoness, and she'll fix you up, you'll see." He looked up at Gideon with a desperate expression. All three of them knew there was no help to be given.

Gideon swallowed hard and carefully stepped around to James' other side to rest the banner against the wall. Then he took a knee beside their friend.

"It's no good," James said softly, leaning his head back against the brick. "I can feel it inside already." He closed his eyes and screwed his face up in pain. "The curse, whatever." His eyes opened and he looked up meaningfully between the two of them. "Help me get this thing out of me, will you?"

Gideon glanced at Donnal. "Are you sure?"

"Yes," the youth answered firmly. "It feels alive inside me. I can feel it crawling and twisting in me. I want it out." He pulled out of Donnal's grip and placed both hands on the large, shattered bone sticking from his chest. "Help me, please," he begged.

Donnal looked up at Gideon. "Hold him steady?"

Gideon nodded and put a firm hand on James' shoulder. The youth whimpered pitifully and nodded.

"Alright, mate, on three."

On the count, Donnal yanked hard on the exposed end, and James howled through gritted teeth, his legs kicking under the monster's corpse as the bone pulled free. A rush of blood poured out from both ends of the wound, and Gideon panicked and covered it with his hands, trying to stem the flow.

James wrestled weakly beneath him, crying out and grabbing Gideon's shoulder against the pain. Donnal cast the limb that the bone was attached to aside, then shoved the twisted corpse off of James.

Somewhere behind them, Sir Cormac was calling out for them and cursing in frustration as he tried to find where they'd gone. Gideon turned his head to call out to the paladin, but James' grip on him tightened.

"Wait," he gasped, then coughed violently, the gaping wound in his chest making a sickening sucking noise with each shallow breath. Donnal scrambled back over and took James' hand again.

"I don't know what to do," Gideon said, his voice shaking as he struggled to keep his hands over the wound as blood seeped through his fingers in time with the wracking coughs.

Donnal's mouth opened, but he couldn't find anything to say. James shook his head and fought to speak. "They'll burn me... one way... or another," he managed, moving one hand to where Gideon held his wound. "I'd rather they do it once I'm dead." He shifted his gaze to Gideon, and his eyes were distant, unfocused. "Just let it go, mate, please."

"James, no," Gideon insisted, "I... I can't just let you die." A sharp pain grew behind his eyes and he ground his teeth against the unbidden tears.

James' head lolled back and he slumped further down the wall as the tension in his body started to slacken. "It's already done," he said as Sir Cormac bellowed angrily for them in the background.

"We're here!" Gideon cried over his shoulder, unwilling to simply sit and watch his friend die. Surely Sir Cormac would be able to do something for his recruit, Gideon was sure of it.

"You two were... good friends," James whispered, his eyes closed. The deathly pallor touched even his lips, and the flow of blood through Gideon's fingers from the wound beneath slowed. His breaths were rapid and shallow, and his grip on each of them loosened. "Tell... my mum...." His voice failed him, and he took a few last twitching breaths, then he was still.

"We will, James," Donnal said, tears sliding silently down his rough cheeks.

"There you are!" Sir Cormac growled from behind them, startling Gideon. "Why in blazes didn't you...?" Gideon looked back at him and finally took his hands from James' wound. "Oh," the old paladin said, the hard lines of his face softening.

Gideon blinked and looked back down at James. His sight was blurry, but he refused to cry in front of Sir Cormac, even as Donnal's unabashed tears mingled silently with their friend's blood pooling on the ground beneath them.

Sir Cormac looked from James to the lifeless creature that had killed him and gave a solemn nod of understanding. He remained still for a long moment, the silence punctuated by a forlorn wind blowing between the buildings, before he stepped forward to rest a hand on the shoulder of each Donnal and Gideon and bowed his head. "May this brave warrior's soul traverse the void on hasted wings," he prayed, reciting a dirge they had learned at the monastery, and the two recruits joined him in finishing it. "May he join the gods at eternity's edge and be granted a deserved rest, cloaked in the glory of noble death."

They remained silent a moment longer before Sir Cormac straightened. "The others are preparing a pyre for any remains," he said heavily. "We must take him there before the curse seizes him."

He stooped to lift James in his arms, but Donnal's hand shot out and caught the old paladin's steel gauntlet, stopping him. "I'll carry him," he said, and his voice was firm despite his still-flowing tears. Sir Cormac hesitated, his brows deeply furrowed, then nodded and stepped back.

"Very well," he said. "Ballad, gather his arms. I'll take this thing," he added with a growl, stooping to pick up the remains of the witch-twisted monster. Gideon gathered up James' sword, its blade now bereft of Holy Light, and his shattered shield, and Donnal lifted the redhead's lax body reverently in his arms.

They followed the paladin back through the crumbling buildings, retracing their steps to rejoin the others. Gideon followed Donnal, carrying his and James' arms along with the heavy banner, feeling numb inside. When they arrived, they saw the strange piles of brambles that had been spread throughout the hamlet had been gathered into two huge mounds in the center of the square.

Battlesister Gerda was directing the recruits as they tossed whatever remained of the vanquished monsters onto one pyre, while the fallen of their company were laid to rest on the other. Gideon accompanied Donnal as he carried James to the latter, and helped lay him in a space between the others who had fallen. As Donnal worked to arrange James in a peaceful position, Sir Cormac shrugged the monster corpse he carried off onto the other pile of sticks and nettles and walked over to join them.

"Lay his weapon with him, Ballad," he instructed quietly as he looked down at the slain young recruit. "He held it to the end, and it would not do that he should leave this world without it." Gideon nodded, still in a daze, and stepped carefully onto the unlit pyre to return the stained and dented blade. His eyes were drawn to James' face, and he could hardly believe there was no life in him. Aside from the deathly pallor, he looked as though he could jump up at any moment and laugh at the haunted looks on his friends' faces. But as Gideon closed the young man's cold, lifeless hand around the hilt of his sword, he understood he'd never hear that laugh again.

He backed away and returned to Donnal's side. The other survivors were slowly gathering around, and as the archoness approached the pyre, Gideon heard a wet crack and saw out of the corner of his eye as James' leg twitched. The witches' curse was taking root. He looked over at Sir Cormac, whose lips twisted into a scowl beneath his mighty mustache.

Archoness Lorica seemed to be aware of the need for urgency, as she took her holy book in hand and led them once more in the dirge for the fallen. She entreated the gods for mercy for the dead, and a flickering golden flame was kindled in the heart of the pyre, slowly spreading throughout and licking up at their dead comrades.

Gideon and Donnal stood close together, watching as James was consumed in the blaze. Lillian stood off to the side, and she was shaking and fighting back tears as she watched the flames take Meredith, too. The archoness went over to ignite the other pile of bramble and branches, and as the flames caught, she and her cadre moved away, no doubt to plan their next move.

Donnal swayed unsteadily as they stood before the pyre and fell to one knee, and Gideon laid a hand on his shoulder. Leaning on the banner, he knelt beside his friend, whose brow was beaded with a heavy sweat.

"I... I killed him," Donnal said, his breath quickened by panic.

Gideon's brows knit together. "What? Killed who?"

"James," Donnal managed shakily. His eyes never moved from the dark shape of James' body as the flames devoured it.

"What are you talking about, Donnal?" Gideon asked hesitantly.

"I made him... swap shields with me, remember?" He took a few gasping breaths and swayed where he knelt. "I made him take the smaller one. The one that shattered when... when...." He bowed his head and his broad shoulders started shaking violently as he wept. "It was my fault. The kite shield wouldn't have broken, and he'd still be here if I hadn't...." He trailed off as he sobbed into his hands.

Gideon stared at him, unsure what to say. He tightened his grip on Donnal's shoulder, and his gaze was drawn back to the pyre. Gideon himself still wasn't sure what to make of James' death. Their witty young friend was the one who had passed the trials, who would go on to become a paladin — how had he perished when they survived?

His mind raced with doubts and regrets as he knelt, doing what he could to comfort Donnal while watching as James was taken away on an ashen wind, along with Meredith and the two others whose names he'd never even known.

CHAPTER 25

SADIA

Sadia sat up, her heart racing.

At first, she had no idea why she had awoken. Everything was dark; the Gentle Djinni had finally calmed, and the silence that had likewise fallen across the rest of the city was thick and still. Only Dalgrim's drunken snores from the next room broke the blanket of quiet that night had brought. She couldn't say exactly why, but she had awoken from a dream, and it was with a stark feeling of dread.

Sadia rose silently from her cushion bed, careful not to wake her brothers, and padded out onto the balcony. Emra'adid slept beneath her, dark and still. Her breath caught in her throat, and she held it for a moment before letting out a shaky sigh. The moon had risen to its zenith, and Naharia bathed the world in her cool glow.

Sadia couldn't remember what her dream had been about. Whispering, she seemed to recall. Awful words spoken by a voice that shook the earth, words she couldn't recall but left her shivering in the temperate night.

She put a hand over her heart, willing it to calm, then whispered a quick prayer to ward away the evil that had awoken her. After a few more minutes, she crept back inside, pulling the curtains to the balcony closed behind her. Reza let out a little snore as he twitched in his sleep, and Sadia returned to the bed, lying back down carefully next to Ibi. His brow was hot, but dry.

She laid a hand gently on top of him and closed her eyes.

"Supplications mount upon the hating flame...."

Sadia's eyes fluttered open. She had just been on the brink of falling back to sleep when the whisper came, barely audible, thrumming in an impossibly deep voice. She felt Ibi take a shuddering breath beneath her hand and she looked down at him as a little whimper escaped his lips. In the moonlight that spilled in through the balcony, she could see little tears streaming from the corners of Ibrahim's eyes as he squeezed them tight, his lip trembling.

Sadia reached out to him, but froze as the voice spoke again in a slow, violent whisper. "Dread charge the sundry; might eternal, suffering." The voice was almost more of a tremor than a sound. It resonated from somewhere near Ibrahim, but not from his lips, and it pulsed in the air around them. Had the voice spoken any louder, she was sure she'd have been suffocated merely by the sound.

Tears sprang to Sadia's own eyes as a primal fear gripped her, and for a split second, she couldn't will herself to move. But then she came back to herself and took Ibrahim in both hands to lift him. As soon as she touched him, though, he stiffened and another whisper thrummed from around him. "Pyre thyself..." it said, the words burning in her mind. "Devour thyself... ware the wandering, distant star."

Sadia lifted him up, and he remained in rigor, like a plank in her arms. "Ibi!" she cried, jostling him, trying to rouse him. "Ibrahim!"

Beside her, Reza stirred and looked up wildly, and a moment later,

Ibrahim relaxed; his eyes opened, and he started wailing in pain and fear.

"Oh, Ibi..." Sadia said through sobbing breaths, clutching him tight and instinctively grabbing Reza and pulling him close to her as well.

There was a commotion from the hall outside their room, and the door burst open. A shirtless Lu Song entered, his blade held at the ready and glinting in the lantern light spilling in from the hall.

"Whass wrong?" he shouted, looking around as though for an intruder. "Evildoers?"

Dalgrim stumbled in behind him, dressed in a flowing nightgown and nightcap. Both were still obviously very drunk.

"Whasss it? Wasssit?" the dwarf asked, slurring, holding his meaty fists in front of him defensively. Then he stopped and frowned when he saw the children all clinging to each other on the cushion bed.

"There was someone," Sadia gasped, struggling to calm herself and soothe Ibrahim.

"Where?" Lu demanded again, turning one way, then the other, ready to fend off an attacker.

Sadia shook her head. "No, it's not here, it was... a voice, from...." She looked down at Ibrahim's swaddling cloth, then at the piled cushions, and realized she didn't know where it had come from or how to explain.

Lu and Dalgrim both looked confused.

"He just woke up," she tried to explain. "He... there was a voice...."

Dalgrim sighed, and Lu clumsily sheathed his sword. "Alright, a bad dream, was it?" the dwarf asked, taking off his nightcap and scratching his balding head. "Ah, now, now." He shuffled into the room and over to the pile of cushions where the children were all huddled. "The Jimble Djinni is a good place! Very safe," he assured them, waving his hand and barely catching himself as the motion made him sway.

"It wasn't a dream," she insisted, but Dalgrim shook his head, his eyelids drooping as he took a blanket from one of the cushions and started draping it over them.

"There, there," he muttered, "just go back asleep. All will be better by the morn." He patted Reza's head and turned unsteadily to leave.

"Wait!" Sadia said. "Please don't go. I think we're in danger." She looked up at both men, unsure what to do, but feeling somehow safer with them in the room, drunk and useless as they might be.

Lu looked down at Dalgrim and shrugged, and the dwarf huffed. "Ach, alright!" he groaned, stumbling toward the door. "Just let me go get a pillow and... I'll...." Before he could reach the hallway, he stumbled and fell against the wall, then slumped onto the floor. A snore escaped him almost immediately and the children looked from the dwarf to Lu in disbelief. The easterner shrugged.

"He drink too much," he said, then stepped over Dalgrim to shut the door. "Everything alright," he added, mustering a smile as he laid himself down on the floor. "We stay."

"Thank you, Lu," Sadia said, still cradling her brothers. He only nodded before yawning, rolling over, and promptly falling asleep.

Sadia lay back down and felt Ibi snuggling against her side. He had finally stopped crying, and his frail little hands clutched at her. Reza lay close beside them, and tried to ask what had happened, but Sadia shushed him and told him to sleep.

She did not close her eyes again that night.

CHAPTER 26

SADIA

As DAWN BROKE, Sadia continued to fight the exhaustion tugging at her eyelids and kept Ibi and Reza hugged tight, even though the older boy occasionally struggled uncomfortably. She breathed a sigh of relief as the rising sun poured through the windows of their room, chasing away the shadows she'd watched all night with a deep trepidation. She could hardly remember a time when she'd felt so tired, but she simply refused to fall asleep.

At first, she tried to convince herself it had been a nightmare after all, a natural consequence of the terror and exhaustion the flight from Qasira had caused her. But the voice... it had been real, undeniably so — more real than anything else she'd ever heard. It had seeped into the back of her mind and wouldn't leave her be, even though the words themselves were difficult to recall.

The most distressing thought was whether it was really a curse, as she'd originally believed, or something more sinister. Did a curse speak?

Sadia thought back to the strange ritual she'd rescued him from, of the dark, fiery magics invoked by the prophet, and in the sleepless, early hours of morning, a memory had struck her.

The possessed man in the bazaar. The old woman's warning of ifriti invading a person's body.

A violent chill took her at the thought. Had the prophet summoned an ifrit to possess Ibrahim? Did the malevolent voice she had heard belong to a wayward fire spirit?

If so, she had no idea what that meant for the infant, but Sadia cursed herself for not seeing it sooner, and she was utterly convinced that there could be no more delay.

The city of Emra'adid woke, the noises and clatter from outside their windows filling the caravanserai, but Dalgrim and Lu remained fast asleep on the floor. Their snoring had been oddly comforting throughout Sadia's long night. Ibrahim had slept fitfully since his episode, and she had not heard the voice again, though its strange and horrible words had played through her mind a hundred times in the dark and quiet.

As Sadia prepared herself to get up and rouse the others, a soft knock came at the door, and a moment later, it opened up. The door bumped into Dalgrim's hip, making him snort, and Roya's head poked through the gap. "Good morning, my — oh, what's going on here?" she asked, interrupting herself as she saw the two men curled up on the floor.

Her entrance startled both of them awake. Lu's arm had fallen over Dalgrim as the two had slept, and as they woke and realized how unintentionally close they'd gotten, both men scrambled away from each other, climbing unsteadily to their feet.

"What are you two doing in here?" the older woman demanded, but Dalgrim could only groan in response, pressing his fingers to his temples.

"Reza had a nightmare last night," Sadia said quickly, too afraid to attempt to explain what had actually happened.

"No I didn't!" Reza declared defiantly, but she shot him a look, and he folded his arms and glared at her.

"Dalgrim and Lu came in to make sure we were alright," she continued, "and stayed so we would feel safe."

"Well," Roya huffed, her eyes narrowed suspiciously at the dwarf and Lu, "it seems to me they got the best of it, snoozing away while you three look exhausted! Come, then — I already have a hot meal ready for you all downstairs. The two of you," she pointed at Lu and Dalgrim, "go make yourselves decent before you come down, and do something about those reeking breaths of yours!"

Then she swept past them, taking Reza's hand, and ushered the three children out of their room. "Come now," she said, her voice sweet and soft. "You'll all feel better with a little breakfast in your bellies. I always make fresh chai."

The children followed Roya down into the main room of the Gentle Djinni. Already, it was filled with guests sitting at the little tables, sipping tea and quietly conversing as attendants bustled from the kitchens with platters of savory-smelling food.

The proprietress led them to a small table in a secluded corner where their breakfast waited, steaming hot on the table.

"Are you sure everything is alright, dear?" Roya asked Sadia quietly, her brow knit as though she could sense the angst Sadia was trying so hard to hide.

Sadia nodded quickly, forcing a smile. "Yes, I'm sure. Just a bit tired, is all."

Roya glanced once more at the boys and then gave her a sympathetic look. "Of course," she said. "Go ahead and eat. And drink your tea — it will warm your spirits!" She turned and disappeared back into her kitchens.

Sadia broke off a little piece of some kind of fried dumpling and brought it to her mouth. It was sweet and hearty, so she took another piece and put it to Ibrahim's lips, but he grimaced and turned his head away, moaning quietly. Reza ate as though the feast from the previous night had never reached his belly, but Sadia couldn't bring herself to eat very much if Ibrahim wouldn't. She looked down at Ibi and remembered the voice and the child's wailing cries, and the fear washed over her again, erasing what little remained of her appetite.

As she struggled to calm herself, she caught Dalgrim and Lu stumbling down the stairs, dressed but disheveled, still obviously hurting from their night of heavy drinking. The two strode unsteadily over to where the children sat and flopped down on the plush cushions opposite them.

"Good morning," Sadia greeted them softly, and Dalgrim sucked his teeth.

"Ach, not so loud, lass!" he groaned, holding his head in both hands as he sat with his legs spread out in front of him. "My poor head is still full of demons after last night."

"Dalgrim..." Sadia started, but he waved her off.

"Whatever you're going to say, let it wait," he muttered. "I need something to calm the thunder 'twixt my ears."

"Me too," Lu groaned, waving for a serving boy who brought them a carafe of spiced tea and two empty glasses. "You pay," he said to Dalgrim.

"Bah," Dalgrim scoffed but tossed the boy a copper coin anyway.

"Can you please take us to Madame Jalila's now?" Sadia asked as the two men chugged from their cups.

The dwarf groaned, leaning back into the cushions and closing his eyes. "Lu and I have to get all the goods off the *Mollysocks* first, maybe take 'em to the bazaar and see if we can find anyone who'll pay more for it than the madam herself will." He grasped around blindly on the table for a dumpling and crammed it into his mouth, crumbs littering his thick, black beard and mustache. "We'll go see Jalila this evening."

"Please," Sadia said, and the tremor in her voice prompted Dalgrim to open one eye and peek out at her in surprise. "Please, I need to take Ibi to her right away," she begged, and her lip trembled, tears threatening to spill from her eyes.

Dalgrim sat up and instantly winced. "No, no — it's alright, lass," he said through gritted teeth, rubbing his brow with one hand. "Don't cry, now." He squinted at her, and even in his sorry state, she saw a touch of compassion in his eyes as he looked between her and Ibrahim. "The wee one's not doing so well, eh?" he asked gently.

Sadia shook her head and the tears did fall, then. "I thought he was a bit better yesterday, but last night, he... There's something very wrong with him," she finished, holding Ibi close as Reza sat up to wipe at her tears with his sleeve. "I don't think the cultists cursed him after all, I think they... I think they summoned an ifrit inside him!"

Dalgrim cocked a bushy black eyebrow. "An ifrit?" he asked. "An evil demon-spirit-thingy, aye?" Sadia nodded. "I thought you said he was cursed."

"Well, I thought so, yes, but...." She bit her lip. "I've been thinking back to what happened in the bazaar, and I think it makes more sense that they put an evil spirit in him with magic. Because when I rescued Ibi, that madman — the one that called himself a prophet — conjured flames all around him," she explained. "And then last night, I...." She swallowed hard and paused.

"What happened last night?" the dwarf prompted, furrowing his brow, struggling to remember. "Someone had a nightmare, was it?"

Reza sat up suddenly and pointed indignantly down at Ibi as Sadia cradled him. "He did!" he declared. "Not me!" And he sat back against the cushions, folding his arms, his face scrunched up in defiance.

Roya swept back out of the kitchens carrying a large platter stacked with more food and drink. "Finally come down to join us?" she asked dryly, seeing Dalgrim and Lu. "I don't suppose you — oh, what's wrong, my dear?" she asked, noticing Sadia's distress. She looked sternly down at Dalgrim and rapped his bald patch with a knuckle. "What did you say to make the poor girl distraught?" she demanded, setting the platter down on the table.

"Ach!" the dwarf exclaimed in surprise, raising his arms to fend off any further blows. "It's the wee one, Roya, not me! He's... a bit sick, you see. I told the lass we'll take him to Madam Jalila as soon as possible."

Roya's scowl softened and her brow knit together. "Jalila?" she muttered, then sat beside Sadia. "Let me see him," she said, and Sadia carefully handed Ibrahim over.

The proprietress pulled back the blanket covering him and laid her hand gently on Ibi's forehead, then his chest. "He's hot," she said, "and pale. And so, so thin." She cradled the child in her arms as she shot a look back at Dalgrim. "He needs to go to a healer, not to that old snake."

"Aw, come now," Dalgrim replied, hesitantly reaching for some of the food Roya had brought. "That's a bit harsh, don't you think?" Just as his fingers took up a small bowl of steaming soup, Roya's arm flashed across the table, and she rapped the back of the dwarf's hand, making him curse and abandon the soup as he pulled his hand back and shook it, looking fearfully at her.

"Jalila is a charlatan!" Roya snapped. "She's a criminal and dangerous, Dalgrim. Children shouldn't be anywhere near a person like that."

"Calling Jalila a criminal is a bit hypocritical of you, now, Roya," the dwarf observed, arching his brow, and the woman bristled at the insult.

"We're nothing alike," she answered firmly. Roya turned to Sadia as she passed the child back. "My dear, there are many churches and temples in Emra'adid, religions from all across the world. Take your brother to one of them, and do not let this foolish old dwarf lead you astray. There is even a part of the city with many Qasirans, and they have a small temple of Ankhat Naharia if you would prefer it."

"No!" Saida answered quickly, more shrilly than she intended. "No, not them."

Roya's eyes widened a bit at the response, but she simply nodded. "Then I would beg you to take him to the Temple of Vaharabajra — there they have water from a famous river in my homeland, known for its healing powers. They know me very well, and will see to your little one if you tell them I sent you." She tapped a finger on her chin. "You'll need to bring an offering. Give me a moment." She stood and hurried back to the kitchens.

Dalgrim waited until she was gone to finally grab some food off the platter without fear of being smacked.

"Do you think Roya's right about the temple she mentioned?" Sadia asked quietly after a moment. "Can they help Ibrahim?"

The dwarf grunted. "If you believe in that sort of thing, perhaps." He swallowed a mouthful before continuing. "I've heard folk say the jadhari — their priests — have been able to cure illnesses and whatnot, but you never can tell with people."

"You don't believe in the gods?" Reza asked skeptically.

Dalgrim fixed him with a bemused look. "Which gods, lad? The gods of sun and moon and stars in Qasira? Or the gods of the rivers and mountains and monsoons in Maramasa? Or perhaps the Holy Light-wielding pantheon they worship in West Umbria, eh?"

"I don't know," Reza said, frowning and looking to Sadia.

"Dwarves believe in the stone of the mountain, the steel of a good axe, and the bite of a proper stout. Ha!" he barked, and immediately winced and held his head again.

"I believe in Naharia," Reza replied fiercely. "I say my prayers every night."

Lu took an interest in the conversation for the first time, and looked at Reza and asked, "Who Naharia?"

"She's the goddess of the moon," the boy explained. "She looks out for us al-Yetim."

"Al... wha?" Lu asked uncertainly.

"It means 'the fatherless'," Sadia answered absently, her mind elsewhere. "Orphans." She sat up as she saw Roya returning with a small basket filled with fruits and bread and other things.

"Here," she said, thrusting the basket at Dalgrim, "take this to the jadhari at the temple as an offering."

"Thank you, Roya," Sadia said as she stood and beckoned to Reza. Dalgrim foisted the basket onto Lu, who took it while grabbing a few handfuls of dumplings to shove into his pockets.

"Do you remember your way to the temple?" Roya asked Dalgrim.

"Aye, I remember," the dwarf grumbled, and downed the last of his chai tea. "How could I forget?"

Roya stared down at the dwarf with a pained expression for a long moment before turning to Sadia and laying a hand on her arm. "Tell them I sent you — they will take good care of him."

"Thank you," Sadia repeated, her heart swelling with gratitude and hope, and she clutched Ibrahim tight as she followed Dalgrim out into the bazaar.

CHAPTER 27

SADIA

Both the dwarf and Lu staggered out into the sunlight, their legs still not quite their own. Emra'adid was bustling with activity, merchants hawking their wares, and musicians and acrobats performing for alms. Dalgrim led them down toward the river, grumbling and shielding his eyes from the bright morning sun as he stalked along.

Glancing over from under his broad reed hat, Lu nudged Dalgrim as the dwarf cursed the harsh light. "You should wear a hat," the man suggested after shoving another dumpling into his mouth, and he tapped his woven brim.

Dalgrim glared at the man, but then his attention was drawn to a group of tall baskets sitting beside a merchant's stall. The dwarf surreptitiously sidled over and took the lid off one of them, revealing a pile of oranges, then hurried on down the street, holding the basket lid under his arm.

Once they were out of view of the fruit stand, Dalgrim looked at the basket lid and then put it on top of his head, mimicking Lu's reed hat.

"Look pretty good!" Lu said approvingly, and the dwarf seemed pleased with himself. Sadia rolled her eyes, and they moved on.

Dalgrim's good mood was short-lived, and his grumpy misanthropy returned, but Sadia was glad he had agreed to accompany them, as he seemed to know the streets of Emra'adid well. He led them through a number of distinct areas of the city, each seemingly occupied primarily by a particular culture.

One quarter was filled with people much darker than Sadia or Reza, many of whom dressed in bright reds, greens, and yellows. Another reminded her a bit of Qasira, but the people spoke a different tongue, and the men's turbans were brightly colored and wrapped differently, and the women's dresses were spun from a light and airy material. Sadia found herself wishing she could afford something to replace her own worn and tattered garments, but she quickly turned her mind to the task at hand.

As they neared the river, they were surrounded by the sounds and smells of the fish market, and then they crossed a narrow bridge over the Tajari. On the other side was the largest marketplace yet, filled with vendors from all over the world, selling everything imaginable, and some things unimaginable. The air was filled with exotic spices, strange perfumes, and hundreds of voices.

"Where do all these people come from?" Reza asked excitedly, his head on a swivel as they passed through the market.

"All over, lad," Dalgrim said. "Some have sailed across the Salient Sea, and some have traveled overland from the east and west. They don't call it the Jewel of the Tatanqa for nothing — a man could live and die never leaving Emra'adid, and he'd not have missed anything the world had to offer."

Sadia had no trouble believing that, and she had to keep pulling Reza along as he was continually distracted by the sights and sounds around them. She kept Ibrahim tucked close and comforted him when he whimpered. Eventually, they left the market and arrived at the Temple of Vaharabajra, nestled among verdant gardens.

A large fountain decorated the front of the temple, and two great statues, one of a man wearing an ornate crown and the other of a woman surrounded by a wreath of lush flowers, rose up on either side. The woman's head was bowed, her palms held outward, her flowing dress cascading all the way down to her feet.

"That's Vamudri," Dalgrim said, nodding to the statue of a woman. "Roya's goddess." He then gestured to the other. "And that's Raja Gama, the king who founded the first dynasty of Maramasa, where Roya's from."

Sadia looked up at the imposing statues, and then at Dalgrim.

"What?" the dwarf asked as he saw her staring inquisitively at him. "You looked curious."

"I just wonder how you know so much about Roya's religion," she said, and was surprised when the dwarf's pale cheeks reddened beneath his wiry black beard.

"Well, I just, you know, I've..." he sputtered, fidgeting with the basket lid he wore as a hat, "I've just known her for a long time, and folk talk about those sorts of things, don't they?" He snorted and grabbed the offering basket from Lu before shoving it at Reza. "You two go on, take your brother in there and get him all healed and made well. Lu and I need to go see about hiring a cart and a few strong lads to unload the *Mollysocks* and get my wares sold."

"You're not coming with us?" Sadia asked nervously, glancing at the tall, arched doorway leading into the temple, incense wafting from within.

"Just tell them Roya sent you," Dalgrim called, walking back the way they'd come. "We'll meet you back here when the sun's highest!" Lu followed him, giving the children a little wave as he munched on another dumpling.

Sadia sighed as she watched them go. "Come on," she said, and she pulled Reza up the steps to enter the Temple of Vaharabajra.

They were met by a large foyer lined with tapestries depicting scenes from a jungle with a wide river flowing through it. On the opposite wall, a pair of tall wooden doors stood open, leading into a great domed chamber filled with people and lit with scores of candles and oil lamps. Incense filled the room with a strong fragrance, and the sound of a low, droning hum echoed through the space, punctuated occasionally by the tinkling of bells.

Reza held the basket in both arms and shifted uncomfortably. "Where do I put this thing?" he whispered.

"Hush," Sadia told him as a thin man with a thick beard approached them. He wore a plain robe with a blue sash.

"Good day," he greeted them in a lilting accent similar to Roya's. "Are you seeking shelter or healing?"

"We were told to come here and ask for help for our little brother," Sadia explained, nodding down at Ibrahim. "Roya, from the Gentle Djinni, sent us here."

The man nodded sagely. "Then you are most welcome. She sent with you an offering?" he asked, and Reza held the basket up to him.

"This is very good," the man said, looking through the foodstuffs. "This will be pleasing to the gods. Come," he said, taking the basket and leading them to a small chamber on the left. It was sparsely decorated and filled with cushions. There were several people inside, some praying, others lying or sitting in a state of deep meditation. "Wait here," the man said, "I will ask the jadhari to come and see you." He laid the basket of food on the floor next to them and then disappeared back into the main room.

Reza slumped onto the cushions. "I'm bored," he complained, but Sadia ignored him. She sat on the floor and gently laid Ibrahim on her lap to cradle him, and she felt him tremble in her arms.

"After they fix him, will we go straight back to Qasira?" Reza asked. "I miss Yusuf and Mirah and Imani and Zara."

Sadia sighed. "I do, too, Reza. We'll go back as soon as we can," she promised, even though she knew that the cultists of the Lidless Eye would make that very difficult, and she had no idea how to make it happen.

Reza sat for a few more minutes, fidgeting and restless, before he got up and walked toward the door.

"Reza!" Sadia hissed, but he didn't stop.

"I'm going to explore," he said, "I'll be back!"

Sadia got to her feet and started after him, but the man from before appeared in the chamber doorway, helping to support a much older man whose eyes were dim and drooping. He was thin and frail-looking, and his white beard reached down to his waist.

"Sit, child," the younger man said, leading the elder over to where Sadia stood. He guided him onto a cushion and the older man closed his eyes and sat silently. "You may tell the jadhari your troubles."

Sadia glanced at Reza as he disappeared outside, but bit her cheek and knelt. "Please, my little brother is very sick," she began, "and the healers in Qasira would not help him. I don't know what's wrong with him, but I think... I think someone put an evil spirit inside him, and it's hurting him. Roya says you have a special river and the water has healing powers, and I—"

The jadhari held up a hand to stop her, his unseeing eyes roving the ceiling. "Peace," he said softly, his voice hoarse and raspy. "Tell me about your brother."

"His name is Ibrahim," Sadia explained. "He's not really my brother... well, he is now, but I rescued him from a madman who was performing some ritual on him. I don't know what they were trying to do, but... there was fire, and Ibrahim was crying and in pain."

"I see," the jadhari rasped, "and you think an evil spirit has entered him?"

Sadia nodded, but then realized the jadhari couldn't see her. "Yes," she said, sniffling. "Please, can you help him?"

The jadhari took a deep breath and moved his head around, as though listening closely for something. "May I hold him?" he asked.

"Of course," Sadia said, and the old man took the withered child in his arms and held him to his chest.

"Shh," he soothed as Ibi whimpered and wriggled. "I can hear his heart. It's weak, and it flutters. He is in pain," the jadhari confirmed.

"There is a fiery heat in his soul, an evil presence. You were wise to bring him here."

Sadia watched with glistening eyes as the old man held the child and hummed something. "Go prepare the offerings for the jadhar, please, Pradeep," he said to his assistant after a time.

"Of course," the other man said, bowing, and left.

"We will call upon Vamudri to visit the child and bring to him her healing touch," the jadhari explained to Sadia. "We must make offerings to beckon her." He rocked Ibi gently in his frail arms. "In addition, we will bathe the boy in water from the Dira — a sacred river in Maramasa. Its waters have been healing the sick for centuries." He smiled, his unseeing eyes wandering the walls as he shared with Sadia. "I was one of the first to come to Emra'adid from our homeland, and with us, we brought a jug of water from the Dira. It has never emptied," he said, and Sadia was in awe.

The man named Pradeep finally returned and spoke quietly to the jadhari. "Everything is prepared."

"Thank you, Pradeep," the old man said, handing the child back to Sadia. "The ritual must be completed at the altar to Vamudri," he explained, struggling to stand. His assistant helped him up and then led him into the next room.

Sadia followed, cradling Ibi and wondering if these foreign gods really would save him. In the next room, Pradeep had laid out a small plate of food, incense, flowers, candles, and a cup of water around a small idol of a woman with a flower garland in her hair, a smaller version of the statue outside.

"Sit, child," the jadhari instructed, and Pradeep helped him kneel. "You may hold the child while we invite the goddess."

Sadia did as she was told and watched with wide, hopeful eyes as the jadhari raised his hands and began to chant something in his native tongue.

He sang the strange song for a long time, intermittently picking up the items at the altar and offering them to the statue. Pradeep lit the candles and incense, and a soft glow and sweet scent filled the room.

After a while, Sadia looked down and found Ibrahim's brow smoothed, his breathing calm. He was sleeping, not the torturous sleep he had endured since the cultist's ritual, but a peaceful sleep.

As the chanting continued, the jadhari reached out to lay his hands on the child and closed his eyes. He began to speak, but this time it was in their common tongue.

"Great goddess, mother of all," he intoned. "Vamudri, the Blossom Vine. Bring your healing touch to this poor boy. Drive out the evil dwelling in him, and wash away his pain and anguish. Send your gentle spirit to fill him and heal his wounded soul."

A breeze came up, swirling through the room, and the incense burned more brightly. Ibrahim began to writhe in Sadia's lap, and she clutched him tight and prayed with all her heart to Naharia and Vamudri both to save the little boy.

The jadhari reached out and laid a shaky, ancient hand on Ibrahim's chest, and Sadia instantly felt him stiffen. At the same time, the swirling current in the sanctuary suddenly stilled, and the jadhari's hooded grey eyes widened. His mouth fell open. The incense flickered, and darkness fell over the large, domed room.

Pradeep shifted nervously and touched the older man's arm, but he received no response as the jadhari continued to stare at Ibrahim.

Sadia tensed as an uncanny feeling gripped her, and she adjusted her hold on her brother, hoping to relax him. He remained rigid, however, and as she watched, his eyes slowly opened and looked into the jadhari's. A dull, smoldering light rose from somewhere inside Ibrahim, spilling from his eyes, nostrils, and mouth as if a blazing ember resided in the back of his throat. The unnatural glow cast a dark orange light onto the jadhari's face, and a look of horror was written on the old man's expression.

"Foreswear the onslaught night; tendrils bitter coiling...."

The same voice from the previous night — impossible, bone-shaking, and mind-shattering — spoke around them, truer and more real than any human voice she'd ever heard. Sadia sat in shock as a panic broke out among the other people gathered around different shrines in the temple. Pradeep's mouth hung agape as he stared at the boy, and he struggled to pull the old jadhari back.

The candlelight flared and the incense sticks all burnt in an instant into ash and smoke. Ibrahim's eyes were fixed on the jadhari as his little belly began to flutter, and his entire body grew hot in Sadia's arms.

"What's happening?" she whispered, tears streaming unbidden down her face as she held him in spite of the heat rolling off him in waves, but she refused to let go even though the fire inside him felt as though it was about to consume them both.

Finally, Pradeep wrenched the old man's hand off of Ibrahim, and the two of them tumbled back onto the floor. The child in Sadia's arms jerked, and all at once, the fire went out of his eyes, the strange glow fading, and he was wailing in his weak, tiny voice, clutching her desperately and sobbing.

"What happened?" Sadia begged, looking up at Pradeep, but he looked at her aghast. The old jadhari looked up at them both from a crumpled heap on the floor, his unseeing eyes seeming to pierce them both as his limbs quivered in fear.

"You must leave!" Pradeep shouted, climbing to his feet and grabbing Sadia roughly by the arm. All around them, other worshipers and supplicants were staring and murmuring fearfully. "You and your demon brother! Get out!"

Sadia pleaded with the man as he dragged her toward the temple doors, but he refused to listen, and the old jadhari's blind eyes followed them, but he did nothing more to help.

"No, please!" Sadia begged. "He's just a baby! He's just a little boy! You have to help him!"

"You have brought a great evil into the house of the gods and risked driving them away," Pradeep growled, pushing her out into the sunlight. "Leave! I will not warn you again!"

"Please!" Sadia cried again. "You can't just leave him like this!"

Pradeep glared at her, then drew the great wooden doors of the temple closed.

Sadia stood, shaking, staring at the doors and holding Ibrahim close as he wept. She was too afraid to look at him. She remained there, feeling unable even to move, or decide what to do, for what seemed like ages before she finally forced herself to turn and leave the Temple of Vaharabajra.

She walked back down the steps and sat on the stone rim of the fountain, the sound of the water rushing and spouting around her. Ibrahim's tears died down, and he looked up at her with his wide, innocent eyes, once again normal, and she quickly looked away.

"It's alright," she said, her voice quavering. "You'll be alright." Her words felt hollow, but she had no idea what else to say. If the gods couldn't help him.... She dared not finish the thought. Her whole body was tingling and numb, and unbidden thoughts warred in her mind.

"Reza?" she asked aloud without thinking, remembering he had run off. She looked around, but there were only a handful of people milling in the courtyard of the temple looking askance at her, with Reza nowhere to be seen.

Sadia reluctantly stood and made her way back out to the street to search for her brother. She kept Ibrahim held against her, but she wished she could put him down or pass him on to someone else to worry about, and she hated herself for it.

CHAPTER 28

GIDEON

THE THROATY CAW of a crow woke Gideon while it was still dark. He rolled over on the itchy saddle blanket beneath him and rubbed at his eyes as his tired mind wavered in a place between sleep and waking. The flapping of wings woke him fully, and he shifted again to look up at the silhouettes of the crumbled walls all around.

The light from the twin pyres still glowed as the watch maintained a mundane fire, feeding it with timber and thatch from the village houses. As Gideon blinked away the sleep, a sudden movement caught his eye.

A small black shape that blotted out the stars behind it hopped forward into the firelight, and the crow's wings fluttered again, its head twitching as it looked around. The firelight reflected a dark, foreboding crimson off its wet feathers, and Gideon sat up, feeling his hair rise at the back of his neck. The crow cocked its head and seemed to look down at him with one eye, and he could see its beak was chipped and jagged and weeping blood.

Gideon rubbed his eyes again, and when he looked back up, the crow was gone. He stared at the spot where it had been for a moment before looking over to the smoldering remains of the pyre, where the huge form of Sir Cormac sat, stoking the embers. Beside him, Battlesister Dawnhammer worked a worn rag into the intricate ornamentation wrought into her hammer.

Glancing back briefly at the darkness, Gideon realized he didn't want to try to sleep again, so he got up and moved carefully through the other sleeping recruits to join the watch by the fire. The battlesister and the paladin looked up at him as he approached, their faces hard.

"You need sleep, Ballad," Sir Cormac muttered softly, but he rolled a large log over with his steel boot, and Gideon took it as an invitation to sit.

"I know, sir," he said quietly. "I just... I don't think I can sleep right now." He stared into the embers of the fire as a silence stretched out between them. He looked up to see the two older warriors staring at him.

"I'm sorry for your loss, lad," the dwarven woman said after a moment, her brow furrowed.

Gideon nodded and folded his arms against the cool breeze at his back, leaning into the heat from the flames.

"Crieg took it hard, eh?" Sir Cormac asked, resting his hands on his plated knees. "Byrne was quite the character," he added, a genuine smirk crossing his dried lips, and Gerda snorted in agreement. Gideon imagined James' sarcastic reply to that, and a brief smile tugged at the corner of his mouth before his friend's absence echoed painfully in his chest.

Taking a deep breath, he looked up at the older man and nodded again. "He'll be missed." A pregnant pause followed. "Donnal blames himself," Gideon finally murmured.

The old paladin grunted thoughtfully, and Gideon looked into the fire.

"That's not the road to go down," Battlesister Dawnhammer said bluntly as she continued cleaning her golden hammer. "The life of a soldier will acquaint you well with death, and you cannae bear the weight of guilt for each man you lose."

"She's right." Sir Cormac clapped a heavy hand on Gideon's shoulder. "All of you young recruits fought well and bravely today, there's no doubt about that. Most of us lived, and we thank the gods for that." He tilted his head and sighed. "Some fell, and we mourned them. They'll be remembered, though," he said tightly, "and what guilt there may be lies with the coven."

Gideon nodded, ruminating on the words. "They all did fight well," he agreed quietly. "But I just carried the lady's banner — I didn't even strike a blow."

Sir Cormac frowned, his mustache drooping. "You were appointed her bannerman," he growled. "You did exactly as you were supposed to do."

Gideon grimaced as he stared into the fire. They sat for some time, and Gideon found himself comforted by the easy silence between his two officers. The battlesister handed some portioned rations to each of them without a word, and Sir Cormac kept the fire alive, grunting occasionally for no immediately apparent reason and keeping his eyes fixed on the wall of night surrounding them on all sides.

After a while, Gideon's curiosity got the better of him, and he cleared his throat to ask a question. "I heard the scouts talking, before we charged the hamlet," he said, and both of them turned their attention toward him. "They said something about tracking the witches into the woods." He stopped talking, feeling their gaze like a weight on his shoulders.

"Yes," Sir Cormac agreed, looking back out into the darkness. "It leads up into the hills, a place where witches are wont to make their lairs."

"By dawn, the archoness and her paladins should be rested enough to make the final push," the battlesister said, and looked pointedly at Gideon. "There's not long left to sleep, if you want it, Ballad." She nodded with her chin back toward his empty saddle blanket.

"Does an archoness actually need rest?" he asked with a nervous chuckle, having no desire to return to his nightmares.

"Invoking the Holy Light of the gods is no wee thing," Gerda said, tossing him another square of hardtack. "All of them need to recover from the exertion of it, especially these fresh recruits."

Gideon took the hard bread gratefully, but hesitated before breaking it apart. His stomach rumbled noisily, but her words made him think of the others, and so he surreptitiously moved it to a pocket. "Shouldn't you both be sleeping, then?" he asked.

The big paladin and the diminutive dwarven woman exchanged a look. "Gerda—" Sir Cormac began before stopping himself, "er, Battlesister Dawnhammer and I belong to a somewhat different school of thought than many in the Church." He smoothed his bushy white mustache absently.

Gideon cocked his head, curious, and Battlesister Dawnhammer elaborated. "You should know this, even if you cannae wield the Light yourself," she said, leaning forward and keeping her voice low. "among the paladins you'll serve under, lad, most believe that the Light of the gods defines us and our purpose. That everything they do must be shaped by it, must use it in some way."

"Is that not so?" Gideon asked cautiously.

"No," Sir Cormac said. "The Light of the gods is a tool — a powerful one, to be sure — but just one of many the gods gave mortalkind." He drew his shoulders back, the different plates of his armor shifting and clinking against each other. "Tempered steel is another, as is a strong arm, and a clever mind. Some within our order lean too heavily on the gift of the Light, which will drain a man's strength quicker even than bringing arms to bear."

Battlesister Dawnhammer sucked her teeth and shook her head, her thick red braids swaying. "Pompous fools, mostly. Cormac and I have seen many fall because they were weak of body, and relied on the power of the Light instead of their gods-given strength."

"There is merit to both schools of thought," the old knight said, holding up a hand. "But it's a poor soldier who relies too heavily on any one weapon."

Gideon nodded, surprised to hear the two officers speaking so bluntly to him. They had been tough and demanding instructors in training, and he wasn't used to partaking in such an informal conversation with them.

"The sun's not touched the horizon yet," Sir Cormac mused, looking eastward. "Go get a bit more sleep while you can, Ballad. That's an order."

Gideon frowned and stood. "Yes, sir," he answered, then reluctantly returned to his empty spot on the ground. Donnal was snoring softly nearby, and he was relieved his friend, at least, could rest. He lay down and tried to find a comfortable position on the hard ground, but his eyes were repeatedly drawn to the spot on the wall where the strange crow had appeared, though it never returned. He tossed restlessly until the sun's rays finally ignited the underside of the clouds above.

Sir Cormac rose from his log seat and moved among the recruits, rousing them with his rumbling voice, and Gideon pulled up his saddle blanket from the ground. As he beat the dirt and dust from it, Donnal sat up and stretched noisily. He looked over at Gideon, and the corner of his lips twitched into the shadow of a grin before his face fell and his shoulders slumped.

"Morning, Gid," he murmured as he hauled himself to his feet.

Birds chirped happily from the surrounding treeline, ignorant of the slaughter that had ruined the hamlet and the heavy sorrow carried by the survivors. Battlesister Gerda started giving orders, readying them all for the next leg of the journey, and as they moved over to re-saddle their horses, Gideon pulled the square of hardtack from his pocket and handed it to Donnal.

"Here," he said, hoping some food would lift his friend's spirits. "I don't have the stomach for it." Donnal looked down at it and hesitated. "Take it," Gideon insisted.

Donnal accepted it reluctantly. "Thanks, mate," he said, lifting his head to meet Gideon's gaze gratefully. Then his eyes were drawn to something behind Gideon. "Hold this for me, will you?" he asked, pressing his saddle blanket into his friend's arms before moving past him.

Gideon took the blanket and turned and watched Donnal walk up to Lillian. The blonde girl's eyes were puffy, and her face drawn. She looked up warily as Donnal stopped in front of her, then held out the hardtack to her. She blinked in surprise, but took it and murmured her thanks. Donnal nodded and walked back over to Gideon, his steps a little lighter.

"That was good of you," Gideon said, handing the saddle blanket back over.

Donnal shrugged. "I've still got you, and you've got me," he replied as they walked over to their horses. "Meredith was her only friend." He paused and swallowed thickly as they reached their mounts. "I figured she could do with a good turn."

Gideon smiled sadly. "You're a good man, Donnal," he said. "I hope you know that."

They worked together to get the horses saddled back up, and soon, the last embers of the fires were snuffed, and the company was mounted up and ready to ride. This time, there was no rousing speech from the archoness, who sat her brilliant white palfrey proudly, her soft features marked by an unmistakable intensity. Instead, a grim mood had taken them all, and they followed their lady into the woods in silence.

Gideon kept a firm grip on the banner as he rode beside her, and as soon as they passed the treeline, he was plagued by a nagging feeling that they were being watched.

CHAPTER 29

GIDEON

THE RAGTAG COMPANY followed after the archoness as she and her scouts guided them through the forest in the late afternoon. They'd been tracking signs of the coven's retreat since dawn, and Gideon had ridden beside the archoness the entire time, banner held high. Two paladins from her cadre ranged ahead, scouting the way through the wooded hills.

As the sun sank toward the mountains, shafts of warm light pierced the canopy above, painting the forest with a golden hue. It would have been quite beautiful, Gideon mused, had the circumstances of their journey not been so grim.

He looked back over his shoulder as they rode and saw Donnal toward the rear, looking a little more comfortable in the saddle. He held his gelding's reins in one hand, and with the other, he guided James' horse by its lead, insisting that he be the one to care for it. Lillian rode quietly on his other side, her eyes unfocused as she stared down at her horse's withers.

Gideon sighed and turned back around in his saddle. This wasn't the grand adventure he'd imagined awaiting him when he left home for the monastery. James' death had been so dark, so inglorious, and nothing like the noble deaths of heroes in the stories. The pallor of death on his friend's face haunted Gideon, and he wondered if he would ever be able to close his eyes again without seeing him like that.

Gideon clenched his jaw and looked up at the sound of hoofbeats approaching ahead. The two scouts raced back through the trees and pulled up in front of the archoness.

"There's a mist ahead, milady," one of them reported. "A long wall of it that stretches as far as we could see."

Archoness Lorica narrowed her eyes and looked up through the leafy treetops at the spots of clear blue sky above them. "Lead on," she commanded.

The scouts turned their mounts around, and the archoness steered her white horse after them. The rest of the company followed, and the thunder of hoofbeats shattered the afternoon calm. Eventually, the trees ahead thinned out, and the birdsong that had kept them company since leaving the hamlet quieted as they came upon the mist the scouts had reported.

As they'd said, a thick wall of fog suddenly loomed from between the trees, rising high up into the canopy. It was so dense that they couldn't see beyond it, and it rolled and churned as though alive.

The archoness pulled her mount to a stop, and the company followed suit, staring at the mist apprehensively. Sir Cormac urged his huge warhorse closer to the roiling wall of fog, and Dauntless remained calm beneath him while the other horses stamped and snorted nervously. Battlesister Gerda, who sat in front of the big paladin, leaned forward and dragged her hefty gauntlet through the wall, leaving a swirling gap behind which quickly closed over.

The dwarven woman glanced up at Sir Cormac behind her, and he nodded and wheeled Dauntless around to address the archoness. "Allow us to scout ahead, milady," he requested respectfully, and the big warhorse stamped a single hoof as if in agreement.

"As you wish," the archoness answered after a moment, her eyes fixed on the mist. "Be careful."

Sir Cormac inclined his head to her and turned back to the fog. "Forward," he said, and he nudged Dauntless into motion. The great horse stepped into the wall of mist, and it pressed close over them as they entered, swallowing them and closing back up behind them, muffling the sound of Dauntless's heavy gait until it faded entirely.

Gideon's mare shifted uncomfortably beneath him, and he adjusted his grip on the banner as his palms started to sweat. Another horse whinnied nervously as it came up beside him, and Gideon turned to see Donnal staring intently at the fog.

"What do you reckon, Gideon?" he asked quietly, glancing at the archoness, who was conferring with Sergeant Findlay a little way off. "This has got to be where the witches are hiding, right?"

Gideon looked back up at the unnatural wall of mist. "It certainly feels like it."

Donnal swallowed and nodded, his jaw set. "We've got to kill them," he said, and the sudden conviction in his voice drew Gideon's attention. "To avenge James."

Gideon studied his friend's face. He knew Donnal didn't fully understand what he was saying — the witches had killed dozens upon dozens of veteran paladins and warriors, the wretched curse they'd wrought turning men against their own brothers in death. The idea that either of them could actually stand against such a foe was preposterous on its face.

And yet, Donnal meant it, heart and soul, and it was obvious the words were spoken as an oath. He envied that kind of bravery, reckless as it was.

Gideon dried his palms on his trouser leg, his heart beating uncomfortably quickly. "For James," he agreed, trying to echo his friend's courage.

"And for Meredith," Lillian's voice said from behind them.

They both turned to look back at her as she maneuvered her horse closer, her face gaunt.

"Right," Donnal agreed grimly. He looked back to the mist and sighed. "I don't have any idea what awaits us, but I'll swear to this," he said, his voice low and the muscles in his jaw flexing. "I will not leave this place alive unless these damned witches are dead."

Gideon's chest tightened. He didn't know if it was fear, or shame, or something else, but he could feel his friend's resolve, and it made him want to vomit. He felt as though he should say something to Donnal, something brave and inspiring, but when he opened his mouth, nothing came out.

"I'll swear to that, too," Lillian said fiercely, and her horse shifted nervously as her hands tightened on the reins.

"Me, too," Gideon finally managed quietly.

The three of them stared into the wall of fog. It swirled and pulsed unceasingly, and Gideon could feel an ominous presence within it, as though it was awaiting them.

The horses shifted, their hooves crunching softly in the fallen leaves and acorns as they waited. Archoness Lorica sat with her hands folded patiently on the pommel of her saddle, her expression unreadable. Sir Cormac and Battlesister Gerda had been in the fog longer than Gideon had expected, and he wondered how long they would wait before following.

He wasn't alone in that thought, apparently, as Sergeant Findlay squirmed impatiently in his saddle. "We should go in after them," he said, his voice tight with concern.

"Have patience, sergeant," Lorica said evenly, not looking at the man. "Sir Cormac and the battlesister are more than capable of taking care of themselves."

Findlay frowned. "But, milady, we can't risk—"

Furious, heavy hoofbeats sounded suddenly from beyond the fog, and a moment later, a golden glow burned through the churning mist. Dauntless burst through the wall, sending the fog cascading off him and his riders in molten waves.

Battlesister Dawnhammer held her warhammer out in front of her like a torch as it burned with an imbuement of Holy Light. Both she and Sir Cormac looked wild-eyed around at the rest of the company as Dauntless reared and snorted.

"Is it them?" the old paladin asked, his hand reaching for the huge sword on his back.

The battlesister's shrewd blue eyes flew across their faces before she finally relaxed and lowered her hammer. "I think it's them, Cormac."

Gideon glanced at Donnal, and his friend's expression mirrored his own confusion.

The archoness urged her horse forward. "What do you have to report?"

"The witches certainly lie beyond," Sir Cormac said as he gestured behind, his breathing labored. "But this damnable fog, it's...."

"It's bewitched," the fiery dwarven woman finished. "We traversed the mist a number of times, only to find ourselves back out here, instead of within. But each time, you lot weren't...." She grimaced. "Well, you weren't yourselves."

"Battlesister Dawnhammer had the idea to use the Holy Light to force a true path," Sir Cormac explained. "We finally made it to the other side, and there's no doubt your witches are hiding within."

"What do you mean we weren't ourselves?" Findlay asked, his expression stern.

Sir Cormac's sweeping mustache twitched. "A foul machination, a mockery." He didn't elaborate further.

"And what did you find on the other side precisely?" the archoness asked.

"The forest on the other side is dead," Battlesister Dawnhammer said grimly. "Twisted, cold, and black. We saw no signs of life, or the witches themselves, but their presence pervades every inch."

"A great, dead tree sits atop a rising hill, in the center of it all," Sir Cormac added. "I'll wager the coven makes its nest there."

Lorica's lips tightened, and she seemed to consider for a moment. "Let us not tarry a moment longer, then," she said, retrieving her holy book from her belt. Once again, she prayed and invoked the gods to bless the armaments of those assembled, and her eyes burned golden.

Gideon watched the tip of the banner and the flanged head of his mace gleam as the Light enveloped them. He thought bitterly to how little the blessing had done for poor James, but swallowed his angst down as the rest of the company gathered closer around the archoness.

"The coven's great evil ends this day," she declared, closing her tome and returning it to her belt. She held a hand aloft, and a golden flame sprang from her palm, casting a soft yellow glow across the ground around them.

The archoness's eyes were still bright gold as she turned them to the fog bank. "The witches will not escape me again. Forward — and may the grace of the gods see us victorious!"

Her palfrey started forward, and she rode straight into the wall of mist as Gideon put heel to flank to catch up to her.

The fog barrier loomed menacingly as he approached, the banner ornaments glowing warmly above him, and the mist recoiled and receded in a small radius around him as the Holy Light advanced. Even despite its warming glow, Gideon felt his stomach flip in a moment of fear as he passed through. Darkness quickly pressed in around him until all he could see was the horse's trotting white haunches ahead and the shimmering wake of Holy Light as they pushed farther. After a few tense moments, the swirling fog slowly cleared until he could see again.

A warm afternoon sun shining through leafy treetops had watched the company enter the mist, but a barren landscape met them on the other side. Gideon gawked at the dead forest all around: rotted leaves and dried, thorny brambles blanketed the ground, twisted black trees with bare branches stretched up towards a sky shrouded in sickly pale clouds. The forest itself was silent but for the sound of horses' hooves stirring the desiccated leaves, and an immediate sense of dread settled over the company, held at bay only by the lingering warmth of the archoness's blessing.

Before them, towering over the surrounding hills, stood a huge, gnarled tree, blackened and dead like everything else. Several crooked branches dipped beneath the ceiling of mist and were themselves larger than most trees, stretching hundreds of yards from the trunk and looming over the rolling hills all around.

The rest of the company made it through the mist, and Sir Cormac harrumphed as Dauntless brought him and the battlesister up alongside the archoness. "These witches of yours must be powerful indeed to hide something like this," he said.

"They are," Lorica agreed. "I'll be very curious to learn why they were hiding in the hamlet among normal folk," she mused as Sergeant Findlay joined them.

"It reeks of dark magic," the sergeant grumbled. "They've drained every ounce of life from this place."

"There," Archoness Lorica said, staring at the base of the massive trunk. Gideon followed her line of sight and saw that a large hollow had split the blackened wood, its shadow seeming to stare menacingly back out at them. "We ride for the hollow," she finished, then spurred her nimble mount forward.

CHAPTER 30

GIDEON

GIDEON and the rest of the company followed after the archoness, moving through the dead forest at a guarded pace, the gleaming iron bits on the banner high above them and on each of their weapons keeping the oppressive gloom at bay. Gideon's gaze swept across the rotted forest floor, and the stench of death and decay grew more powerful the closer they moved to the tree.

A sudden rustling drew his attention to the right, where something was moving through the detritus toward them. Gideon thought for a moment he might be seeing things, a slithering among the leaves, and then something exploded from the forest floor in a shower of dead vegetation. He turned in his saddle and watched in horror as scattered brambles leapt from the ground and coalesced into a solid mass, the individual vines forming together into a long, winding serpent of dead plant matter. It sailed through the air, its thorns churning, toward one of the riders behind.

The thing wound itself around him and constricted, dragging him off his horse. He cried out in pain and terror as the brambles writhed around his arms and legs, dragging him down beneath the dried leaves and earth until his panicked screams faded.

Gideon pulled back on the reins, slowing his frightened mare, but it was already too late to help. The dead forest seemed to come alive around them as more shapes snaked through the rotted leaves toward them, and some of the smaller skeletal trees twitched and shuddered in a way that made Gideon sick.

His mare bucked and danced away as another of the bramble snakes tunneled its way toward him, and all Gideon could do was try not to fall off as the thing sprang toward him. He desperately fought the wild horse beneath him, forced to hold the banner in place to keep it from falling to the ground, leaving him to watch the thing's thorny maw fly toward him, unable to look away.

A pillar of Light streaked down out of the mist, piercing through the middle of the squirming mass of brambles and igniting it, and it was driven to the ground, thrashing as its vines uncoiled and turned to ash.

Gideon turned to stare wide-eyed at the archoness, her holy book in hand and her eyes burning bright. "Ride!" she ordered, and Gideon steeled himself, gripping the banner of the Church Militant tighter in his hand as the small company charged forward.

His heart hammered against his ribs as the archoness led the charge up to the base of the tree, pushing a harried pace. All around them, more brambles were converging on them, crawling and slithering along the ground toward them as the soldiers hacked and slashed at the animated plants, their Light-blessed armaments burning through the desiccated brush. Further out, deep in the barren hills all around them, Gideon watched as dead bushes and vines were sewn together by some wicked power, forming huge, lumbering constructs of wicker in the shapes of ogres or giants.

A bramble snake suddenly coiled around another rider to Gideon's left, and the man's cry was cut short as it constricted and crushed the life from him. Gideon swallowed hard but did not stop or slow his mount.

One of the giant wicker constructs shook the ground beneath them as it rushed toward the company of riders, shattering a number of skeletal black trees as it lunged and swung a massive limb at the archoness. She spurred her horse past it, slashing at it with her blade of manifested Holy Light, and as the giant slowly turned to follow, her blessed weapon tore it open, the brambles within igniting and turning the thing into a lumbering bonfire.

Gideon's mare whinnied fearfully as she swerved to avoid the flames, and he adjusted his cramped grip on the banner as he urged his mount onward, galloping after the archoness. He looked over his shoulder and saw the rest of the company following while the rear-guard fought off more leaping brambles.

The hollow of the tree rose like a cavernous shadow before them, much larger than it had looked from the edge of the dead forest. It was easily wide enough for several men to stand abreast, and it spanned half a dozen yards up the hollowed trunk. A set of roughly hewn stairs led up to it from the ground.

They thundered up the hill toward the tree, the golden Light which adorned their weapons seeming to wane as they approached. Gideon caught up with the archoness, trying to ignore the occasional strangled cry from behind, when a sudden movement ahead drew his eye.

Layers of withered vines laced the hulking trunk like decrepit cobwebs, and as Gideon watched, they suddenly shuddered into motion. Slithering across the dead wood and creeping across the gaping hollow, they formed a wall of thorns and nettles, barring entry.

As they neared the massive tree trunk, the bramble wall grew higher, thicker, and more impenetrable. Gideon pulled up beside the archoness as she dismounted, and he followed suit as her cadre gathered around her. "We must break through!" she commanded, her voice ringing through the air as she surveyed the animate forest surging after them from further down the hill.

Sir Cormac and the battlesister had circled around to bring up the rear, and as Dauntless charged toward the tree, the old paladin swung his huge, glowing sword and lopped an arm off one of the towering wicker monsters. The stump burned as the thing teetered and swung its other arm at the pair of riders. Sir Cormac lifted his heavy shield to block the blow, and as the sound reverberated through the mist, his mighty warhorse smashed its armored flank into the monster's wicker chest, knocking it backward.

Another golem charged in pursuit of the riders, and as Dauntless bore down on it, Battlesister Gerda stood and leapt from the saddle toward the profane creation. Her golden hammer flared, and as she flew through the air, she brought the weapon down upon the monster's thorny head. Holy Light burned through the brambles, and the construct exploded as it was driven to the ground under the weight of the armored dwarf.

Dauntless galloped up to the base of the tree, and Sir Cormac slid smoothly out of the saddle, landing beside the archoness. "We'll not get the horses through there," he barked, quickly surveying the bramble lattice across the hollow. "They'll have to flee."

As the animated horde closed on the recruits gathered around the tree, the old knight quickly turned where he stood and whistled through his teeth at the huge black warhorse, waving a hand downhill on the far side of massive trunk, where the dead forest had yet to come alive. Dauntless snorted and started moving away as the old paladin went quickly among the remaining horses, shouting and slapping hinds to get them to follow the mighty stallion.

As Sir Cormac turned back and hurried to join the others, Battlesister Dawnhammer started shouting orders, forming the paladins and recruits into an organized defensive line around the hollow.

Gideon and Donnal moved to fall in, but the stout dwarven woman held out a hand to stop them. "You two get that barrier down!" she barked before turning and hefting her warhammer. Sir Cormac joined her, one hand hefting his huge, glowing two-hander, the other lifting his tower shield and holding it out in front of him like a wall.

"Come on!" Donnal shouted to Gideon, and they both ran up to the bramble barrier, their weapons drawn and gleaming. Gideon raised his mace and brought it down with all his strength against the wall of thorns and vines, the Light coursing through it. The glowing weapon slammed into the barricade, and the brambles withered and turned to ash beneath its blow.

As soon as one section had crumbled, however, the reanimated briar knit itself back together, thicker and more tightly bound. He looked over to see Donnal hacking at the wall with as little success, and both redoubled their efforts, but to no avail.

The rest of the company had splayed out in an arc around them like a shield against the towering wicker monstrosities closing in from all sides. The paladins and recruits worked together, steel and blinding Light cutting through twisted branch and vine as holy fire consumed the remnants.

Sir Cormac's greatsword arced in golden waves as the battle-sister's warhammer whistled through the air with each powerful blow. The pages of the archoness's gilded tome fluttered as she called down more pillars of purgative Light from the heavens that tore through the misty ceiling above and crushed the charging behemoths to shattered husks.

Gideon and Donnal continued hacking uselessly at the wall of woven thickets, but they were quickly tiring with no progress to show for their efforts. Gideon lowered his mace and took a step back, heaving to catch his breath, but Donnal continued wailing relentlessly against the barrier.

"What are you two doing?" Lillian demanded as she suddenly appeared beside him. She glared at him and pointed her sword at the tree. "We have to get through there, now!"

"We're trying!" Gideon called back over the din of battle unfolding all around. "It's not working!"

"Get out of the way!" she shouted at Donnal as she strode forward and planted her feet before the barrier. Donnal glanced at her, saw the intensity in her eyes, and reluctantly stepped away as the girl placed both hands on the bramble wall and screwed her face up in concentration.

A moment passed, and nothing happened. Gideon looked over his shoulder at the others as they hacked and slashed the animated brambles. Each lumbering construct that was felled was replaced by another that magically knit itself together from the wreckage.

"Lillian," Donnal said nervously, his eyes locked on the fray.

She didn't respond, and Gideon moved over to her. "Lillian," he said louder, and still she didn't reply. Her palms were flat against the woven barrier, and her eyes were wide and unfocused. The color had drained from her face, and she seemed petrified. "Lillian!" Gideon called over the cacophony, taking her shoulder and shaking.

"No!" she suddenly screamed, her voice high and wavering. "No, please!" She yanked her hands away and stumbled backward, falling to the ground and staring up at the tree with a look of abject horror.

"Lillian, what—" Gideon began to ask, but Donnal cut him off.

"It doesn't matter," his friend cried, "we have to get through it! Come on!" Donnal raised his sword and brought it down with all his might against the thicket, but it had no more effect than before.

Gideon swallowed hard and looked back again. Behind him, the teeming throng of living wicker was slowly overwhelming his comrades, pushing them back and hedging them in against the thicket of woven, regenerating vines that blocked their way into the tree.

On his left, one of the other recruits was overwhelmed by a number of the smaller bramble snakes as they converged and coiled around him, their thorns and splinters rending his flesh and sending a mist of crimson into the air. He fell dead before he could even cry out. Sir Cormac leapt to fill the gap as the witches' minions bore down on them, and Gideon's heart sank as he looked back at Donnal.

"This is hopeless!" he shouted over the cacophony of violence. "There's too many!"

"We have to try!" Donnal shouted back, his sword blazing with golden Light as he brought it down on the bramble wall again, the vines shriveling and withering away, only for new ones to continue replacing them.

Gideon raised his mace to strike at the wall again, but he paused as the air around them was suddenly sapped of what little warmth remained in the corrupted area around the tree. Gideon watched as a thin frost quickly crusted his breastplate, though the dim gleam of Holy Light infusing the flanges of his mace held the rime at bay. He turned to see all of the witch-constructs shudder to a halt in a wall around the company, standing shoulder to twisted shoulder and looming over them.

The soldiers who remained all regrouped, tightening their defensive formation, and there was a long, tense moment where nothing happened. Sir Cormac eventually lowered his tower shield and hefted his huge sword over his shoulder with a harrumph. "Well, I don't like this at all," he mused gruffly.

The area around the tree was completely still. The only thing that seemed to be moving was the bramble barrier, and Gideon watched hopelessly as it grew higher, taller, thicker.

"Why did they stop?" Battlesister Dawnhammer wondered aloud, stepping up beside the big knight and staring up at the motionless wicker beasts.

Almost as in answer, a chorus of voices suddenly rose from somewhere beyond the wall of brambles, startling Gideon and Donnal both. The voices of a dozen women all rose in a haunting chant, singing some ancient song in a language Gideon had never heard before.

The surviving members of the company stood still, the sudden tension thicker than the mist itself, and listened as the voices seemed to slither through the air, coiling around them and lapping at their ears. Gideon shuddered at the sensation of the alien words penetrating his mind.

The chant suddenly stopped, and the most complete silence he'd ever experienced hung over the desecrated forest. Then, the voices rose again from the hollow.

"What do the pretty golden warriors want with us, do you think?" Multiple feminine voices asked the question, while others rose immediately in answer. "They've come to burn us, like they burned our poor pets in the hamlet."

Sir Cormac sneered at the sound of the voices and turned back to the frozen wicker beasts, eyeing them distrustfully.

"We'll not let them!" another chorus of voices exclaimed, and then all of the many voices spoke in a discordant cacophony. "Come forth and face the Sisters Seidh," they declared in unison.

The wall of thorny vines covering the hollow slithered apart, creating a small gap just large enough for a person to fit through. Gideon felt a cold shiver run through his body as he stared at the dark opening.

All eyes went to the archoness as she stood before the hollow, seemingly transfixed, her eyes wide and staring. Gideon looked over at Sir Cormac, who was watching her intently over his shoulder, his huge sword held once again out in front of him against the unmoving wicker army.

Lorica trembled where she stood, and her lips moved silently in what Gideon assumed were silent prayers. To see her so shaken disturbed him, and made him even more fearful than he'd already been.

Sergeant Findlay took a step backward, coming alongside the archoness. "Milady?" he asked quietly, but received no response. The unnerving chorus of voices resumed its chant, the dissonant murmur swirling all around the hedged-in soldiers as they waited for the archoness to command them. Lorica continued to mouth her prayers for a moment longer, her eyes squeezed shut and brow furrowed.

Her prayer stopped short, and she opened her eyes. "You're wrong!" she cried, her voice quavering and raw, drawing looks of confusion from all others around her. "I will burn you with the Light!" she screamed, and with that, she took half a dozen swift steps, passing through the opening in the wall of brambles.

Immediately, the wicker monstrosities behind them shuddered back to life, just as the thicket wall covering the gaping maw in the tree sewed itself shut again, closing them off after the archoness had strode through.

"No!" Sergeant Findlay bellowed as he and another paladin charged the bramble wall. Their swords flashed and blazed as they hacked and slashed at the dense barrier, and it slowly began to crumble and wilt away.

All around them, the wicker constructs closed in, and Gideon took a step back from the wall, gripping the battle standard of the Church Militant tight in one hand and his worn mace in the other, forcing his feet to stay firmly planted as the things closed in on him.

"Get that wall down!" Sir Cormac roared at Sergeant Findlay as he and Battlesister Gerda charged the line of animated creations. "The rest of you, stand firm!"

Gideon swallowed hard as he turned to face the wall of brambles, watching as the remaining recruits rushed to stand shoulder to shoulder with Sir Cormac and Battlesister Dawnhammer. The old knight hacked at the surging giants with his huge sword as the battlesister raised her golden warhammer to the sky, and all at once, a bolt of brilliant Light streaked down from the heavens, striking one of the big wicker golems in a blinding flash.

The whole of the hilltop was illuminated for a moment, and Gideon recoiled as he looked down the slope. Every yard of the hillside was writhing, coming alive with the witches' vile magic. He was awestruck and horrified as he watched the dead forest thrash and crawl with thousands of reanimated brambles, all headed directly for them.

Donnal suddenly grabbed him by the shoulder. "Come on!" he shouted, pulling Gideon back toward Sergeant Findlay. Gideon looked back at the horde and felt a chill run down his spine as Sir Cormac and the battlesister led the remaining recruits in a desperate defense.

Lillian was still on the ground, looking suddenly lost and terrified. As Donnal launched himself against the wall of vines alongside the sergeant and the other paladin, Gideon stooped to try to rally the girl.

He grabbed her by the arm and pulled her to her feet. She stared at him with wide, frightened eyes, and Gideon could tell at once she was in no shape to fight. "Help them with the wall!" he called, pointing back at the tree.

She went rigid in his grip. "No!" she shrieked. "No, we can't go in there!"

Gideon tried to shove her toward Donnal, but she fought against him with a surprising strength. She dug her feet in and grabbed his arms, her nails digging through his shirt.

"We can't go in there," she insisted, flashes of Light from the battle reflected in her wide, glassy eyes. "If we go in there, we won't come out!"

Gideon paused for a moment, the fear in her voice infecting his own mind. Then a cry came from behind them, and he turned to watch one of the wicker golems bring both arms down and crush one of their fellow recruits into the ground. Wicker and bone alike shattered and splintered, and the golem shuddered as it lifted itself back up, the ends of its branched, thorny arms dripping crimson. Its headless shoulders squared up to Gideon and Lillian, and it took a step toward them, further crushing the body of the dead recruit beneath it.

"Just go!" Gideon barked as he gave Lillian another shove toward the wall, and he turned to face the approaching construct. The others were all beset, and Gideon knew that if he let the thing breach their defensive line, the end would swiftly follow.

As he stared up at the hulking golem, all the martial training he'd undergone seemed to abandon him, and he felt like he had no idea what he was doing, and no business being in that place. But as he glanced over at Sir Cormac locked in valiant combat, his resolve was bolstered. His eyes wandered up to the banner above him and he realized it was essentially a long spear with a sharp, glowing point — as ready for battle as any other weapon on the field. So he slung his mace, took the banner in both hands, and charged.

The golem towered over him, slow but menacing, and Gideon didn't give himself a moment to think or cower. He rushed straight toward his foe, the banner's gleaming steel ornament leveled like the razor head of an arrow. It reared back to swing a huge, bloodied arm at him as he neared, and a rush of frigid air blasted his face as he barely evaded the blow.

Gideon planted his feet and thrust the banner upward with all his strength, biting deep. The tangles of withered vines and roots burned away as Holy Light pierced the golem's chest and ignited a fire deep within. Unperturbed, the massive construct raised both arms into the air, poised to smash. Gideon yanked on the banner, but it caught on something in the tangled mess, and in that wasted moment, the golem's knotted limbs started coming down on him.

He froze, unable to look away from the gnarled, blood-soaked stumps, his fear overwhelming any other instinct he had. As he watched his death descend on him, a golden hammer flew through the air and smashed into the wicker giant in a ringing explosion that blasted a hole in its chest. The golem faltered as the banner pulled free, slowly toppling where it stood.

"Fall back!" Battlesister Dawnhammer cried as she grabbed him by the collar and threw him toward the tree. "Get to the hollow!"

Gideon stumbled back, clinging to the battle standard, as she hastened to retrieve her fallen hammer. He finally managed to collect his wits and look back at the witches' tree, where Sir Cormac stood before the bramble barrier, his huge golden blade lodged through the interwoven vines, holding a jagged gash open through which the others were hastily escaping.

"Inside, Ballad!" the paladin bellowed at him. "Move!"

Gideon sprinted for the tree as the horde of wicker monsters closed on them. The battlesister was right behind him, raining fiery bolts of Light down on the closest pursuers, and Gideon could only hope the others had made it safely inside. He threw himself through the gash in the barrier as Sir Cormac waved him through, the skin on his arms and neck burning as he passed through the thorny vines, and he scrambled to his feet once he reached the other side, clutching the banner pole tight.

Battlesister Dawnhammer followed after him, and Sir Cormac brought up the rear, smashing his broad shoulders through the gap just as the wicker army crashed into it. The bramble wall slithered back together the moment he pulled his blade from it, and through the tiny gaps in the weave, Gideon watched as the golems outside once again shuddered to a halt, standing frozen in an impenetrable cordon.

He exchanged a wary look with Donnal as they fought to catch their breath in the small, cramped space. The dim glow from the Holy Light still gracing their weapons was all that illuminated the dark hollow. His tall friend still held Lillian by the arms, as though he'd had to drag her through. She was trembling, and her face was streaked with tears.

Sir Cormac breathed heavily as he surveyed the woven barrier and held his sword aloft to illuminate the hollow. After a moment, he glanced down at Battlesister Gerda and tugged at his big mustache. "Well," he breathed, "further in, then, eh?"

"Aye," the dwarven woman agreed, her freckled face set grimly. She shouldered her way through the few remaining recruits to head deeper into the hollow. "Findlay and the other cadre pressed on already, it seems," she called back to Sir Cormac.

"Let's make haste to join them," the old paladin answered loudly, waving Gideon and the others on ahead of him.

"Please," Lillian said, pulling herself from Donnal's grasp, her lip trembling as she looked up at the knight. "We can't stay here, we can't! The witches, they'll—"

"Shut your mouth, girl," Battlesister Dawnhammer growled from ahead, "before you disgrace the oath you swore."

Lillian's eyes darted to Sir Cormac, but she found no sympathy there, either. She lowered her gaze and nodded, and Gideon could see the fresh tears welling in her eyes.

The battlesister glared at the girl and threw her heavy red braids over her shoulders. "Steel yourselves and follow me," she ordered, and plodded forward.

Gideon followed after Donnal as Sir Cormac brought up the rear, the disembodied voices deeper within continuing their eerie chant, and though his mind might have been playing a trick on him, it seemed as though the Holy Light at the end of his banner flickered.

CHAPTER 31

SADIA

SADIA WANDERED the streets around the Temple of Vaharabajra in a state of shock as she searched for Reza. Ibrahim clung tightly to her, and her heart broke as she thought about the look of sheer horror on the jadhari's face and the words spoken by the being had manifested. She remembered the man who had been possessed at the bazaar, but even his violent outburst hadn't scared her the way Ibrahim's episodes did. The fear was indescribable, and she was numb as she moved through the crowds, calling weakly for Reza.

After searching the area around the temple until the sun was high in the sky, she remembered through the haze in her mind that Dalgrim had told her they'd meet back at the statues of Vamudri and Raja Gama, so she made her way back to the verdant garden near the temple.

When she arrived, Dalgrim and Lu were already standing there waiting.

"Alright, lassie," the dwarf said as he saw her approaching. "Were Roya's gods able to heal your wee one?"

"No, they weren't," Sadia said, and her lip trembled as she looked at the ground. "They tried, but...." She couldn't bring herself to tell them the rest, and she couldn't look at the boy in her arms.

"What is it?" the dwarf asked with a sigh.

Sadia closed her eyes, her shoulders slumped. "Can you please take us to Jalila's now?" she whispered.

"Aye," Dalgrim replied after a moment, his brow furrowing. "We just need to go unload the *Mollysocks* and hock her wares, and then—"

"Please," Sadia pressed, desperate. "I can't wait any longer."

The dwarf nodded and laid a hand on her shoulder. "I'll take you, but just like everyone else in Emra'adid, Madam Jalila requires a... stipend, let's say, for her services. So we need to take what I've got on the *Mollysocks* as payment in order even to see her. We just need to find a few stout lads to help us drag the cart up from Suleiman's."

"I thought that's what you left to look for earlier," Sadia said, confused.

Dalgrim rubbed his bald head and shrugged. "Eh, no. Lu and I got a bit... distracted."

"He like shiny things," Lu informed her, and Sadia cocked her eyebrow. "Look!" the easterner declared, reaching into one of the dwarf's pockets and pulling out a tangle of delicate jewelry.

"Give me that!" Dalgrim growled, wrestling the glimmering mess back from Lu. "I bought those at a discount to sell for a profit, thank you kindly!"

"Bought?" Lu scoffed, and he looked back at Sadia. "He stole!" He reached smoothly into another pocket as Dalgrim fought to replace the first handful he'd produced, revealing another bundle of valuables.

Sadia groaned. "You were wanted by the Qasiran guard, then you made that ship on the Tajari sink, and now you're stealing?" She looked at him, her patience spent. "Do you want to spend your life in a dungeon?"

"Lu stole from them, too!" Dalgrim sputtered, glowering at his bodyguard.

Lu gave Sadia a sheepish smile and shrugged. "He's bad influence," he said simply. "I only take one orange! And only 'cause he no pay me for three weeks!" He held up the last three fingers of his hand for emphasis.

Dalgrim rolled his eyes. "Ach, come on, let's go get the goods," he muttered. "You'll get your damned wages after, alright?" He took a step and then paused, looking at Sadia, then behind her. "Where's the other one?" he asked gruffly.

"I don't know," she admitted, and she was suddenly shocked at herself for how casual she sounded. "He ran off and I can't find him." Ibrahim and the spirit inside him were destroying her, sapping her of the will to fight anymore. She felt hollow, like a different, worse person.

As if on cue, Reza rounded the corner into the temple gardens and marched purposefully toward them.

"Reza!" Sadia exclaimed in relief. "Where have you been?"

"I found a pregnant lady," he declared simply, jerking his thumb over one shoulder.

A young woman not much older than Sadia followed behind him, heavy with child. She was pretty, with long, curly black hair that tumbled down her shoulders. Her dress was simple but elegant, and perfectly white with blue trim, and Sadia instantly felt self-conscious in her drab, faded dress.

"Hello," the woman said with a smile and a nervous wave.

Sadia, Dalgrim, and Lu all looked at the woman, and then at each other. "Hello," Sadia said before looking down at Reza. "I'm sorry if my brother bothered you," she began, but the woman shook her head and waved her hands.

"Oh no, no! Not at all," she insisted in an accent Sadia couldn't place. "He told me that his friends were looking for able-bodied men, and it just so happens my husband is seeking work." She looked expectantly between Dalgrim and Lu.

"I suppose we are, aye," the dwarf said slowly, looking at the woman appraisingly. "We're in need of a few strong men to transport goods to the bazaar."

The woman waved her hand. "My husband can do all the work you need himself. He's very strong," she assured them.

"And where is he?" Dalgrim asked, looking around.

"He went down to the docks to look for work while I was at the Temple of Hyphaestia," she replied, gesturing back to another temple across from that of Vaharabajra.

"Ah," Dalgrim grunted. "You're Thrakian, then, eh?"

The woman nodded happily. "My name is Mariam. My husband is Heidroksimos."

"And you say he can do the job all on his own?" the dwarf asked, looking unconvinced. Mariam nodded again. "Well, what will he charge me?"

"Actually, Reza here told me that you have a ship, and that you're taking passengers," she said, and Dalgrim glared down at the boy, who shuffled his feet and smiled nervously. "We're looking for passage out of Emra'adid."

"It seems there's been a misunderstanding, I'm afraid," the dwarf answered, his gaze lingering on Reza. "We've just got into the city, and I've no plans on leaving yet."

"We have coin," Mariam said, unfazed. "We'll be happy to pay you, and as I said, my husband is willing to work for you, as well. And I can cook," she added with a confident grin. "If you've never had a Thrakian woman prepare you a meal, you don't know what you've been missing!"

Dalgrim gave a polite chuckle. "That is very tempting, madam, but I really don't—"

"I'll pay you thirty gold drachmae," the woman interrupted, and the dwarf's eyes bugged out.

"Thirty... drachmae!" he declared, sputtering over the words. "Gold drachmae!" His bushy brows sunk low as he looked the woman up and down shrewdly. "And, er... just how did coin like that make its way to your purse, madam?"

"Worry yourself not about this," Mariam answered casually. "I can promise you payment, just as I have said, before we leave."

Dalgrim's lips slowly lifted into a gleeful grin. "Very well, then!" he declared, rubbing his thick hands together. "Very well, indeed. How about you take me to your husband, and we'll have a nice long chat, eh?"

Mariam's eyes sparkled. "Wonderful."

"But what about Madam Jalila?" Sadia asked, and Dalgrim scoffed.

"For thirty gold drachmae, I'd dump every last wretched bauble in the *Mollysocks'* cabin into the Tajari!" he laughed as he straightened his robes. "Who needs Jalila?"

"I do!" Sadia cried angrily, drawing all eyes to her.

An awkward silence lingered for a moment before Mariam spoke up. "I do not mean to encroach," she said softly. "If you have previous business, you should conclude it." She glanced over at the bundled-up child in Sadia's arms. "Reza told me your brother isn't well?"

"He's not," Sadia replied. She swiped impatiently at an errant lock of hair to tuck it behind her ear. The weariness and the fear were playing on her nerves, and she didn't appreciate being dismissed. "I've been looking for someone to help him, but no one has been able to yet. Dalgrim has a friend who he says can help, and I need him to take me there."

Mariam nodded. "Then he must do so," she agreed, looking at the dwarf. "We can meet later, then."

"No," the dwarf sighed, waving a hand. "I told the lass I'd take her to Jalila's, and I will — but if we're going there, I might as well bring everything aboard the *Mollysocks* to her, eh?" He looked to Sadia, but his optimism quickly wilted at the hard gaze he received. "Alright," he said with a nervous chuckle, "well, let's go gather this husband of yours."

"Very well," Mariam acquiesced, looking hesitantly at Sadia. "He's at the docks, and he won't be difficult to find."

"Let's be off, then," the dwarf proclaimed, and gestured for the group to follow as he set off out of the temple garden back toward the Tajari River.

As they walked, Reza tugged on Sadia's tunic. "So... Roya's gods couldn't fix him?" he asked, rising on his tip-toes to look at Ibrahim.

"No," she answered sharply.

"Oh." Reza looked up at her with sad eyes. He reached out and ran a hand through the infant's thin hair. "He'll be okay, though?" he asked, but Sadia didn't answer.

She wished she could tell him everything would be alright, but she couldn't. Her mind wandered as they walked, thinking about the Hierophants of the Lidless Eye, and how the priests in the Temple of Vaharabajra had reacted to Ibrahim's affliction. His plight was far more dire than she'd even imagined back in Qasira, and a guilty part of her wished she'd followed Yusuf's advice and stayed with her family, despite what that would have meant for Ibi.

Before long, the party arrived back at the bridge spanning the broad Tajari, and Dalgrim stopped short to look up at Mariam.

"Whereabouts did you say your husband went?" he asked.

Mariam looked left and right down the length of the river, at all the variously sized ships lining the piers. "He shouldn't be too hard to find," she mused, her gaze searching all along the waterfront.

They all looked around, even though Mariam was the only one who knew what the man looked like.

"There's triremes, there," Dalgrim said, pointing downriver to a pair of multi-level ships. "That's your folk, isn't it?"

"Yes," Mariam answered slowly, following his gaze before turning around to look upriver. "He'll be this way, then." She headed off through the crowds, and the rest followed her.

"Er, wouldn't he seek out your countrymen?" Dalgrim asked, struggling to keep up on his short legs.

Mariam didn't answer, but stopped periodically to stand up on tip-toe to look over the crowd, holding Lu's shoulder for support.

"Oh, there he is!" she finally said happily, pointing at a wide, square-sailed barge bobbing gently against the pier, dockworkers busy unloading her.

They all turned to follow her gaze, and Dalgrim gasped. "Braided beard of my ancestors!" he exclaimed upon seeing the man she was pointing at.

He was massive, the largest man Sadia had ever seen, standing half again as tall as any other man around him. He had a thick black beard and swarthy skin. Bare-chested and glistening with sweat from the work, he was as broad as two men standing abreast and had a thickly muscled build. He was loading cargo into the hold of one of the large ships, hauling the heavy chests and barrels on his shoulders like they weighed nothing.

"You never mentioned your husband was a giant," Dalgrim hissed as Mariam stepped past them.

She smiled. "Oh, Heidroksimos isn't really a giant," she said cheerily. "He's...." Her smile flickered, and the words caught in her throat before she continued. "He's only... a half-giant," she finished, and Sadia looked at the man again, wondering how much larger a full giant could possibly be.

Mariam waved, and the enormous man spotted her and immediately dropped the chest he was carrying onto the deck of the ship with a crash. He made his way down the gangway toward his wife as his fellow workers cursed him and gathered up his discarded responsibility. The pier quaked under the gigantic man's footfalls, but as he arrived to Mariam, he knelt to hug her gently and plant his lips on her cheek. Sadia's eyes widened at the sight of the deep, pale scars covering his bronze arms and chest.

Mariam spoke to her husband in their native tongue, gesturing at Dalgrim and Lu, and he nodded. Then he stood to his full, towering height, his stony shoulders squared, and placed a hand on his chest. "Heidroksimos," he said, and even the gravel of his voice sent little reverberations through the dock planks under Sadia's feet.

"Forgive my husband," Mariam said, holding his massive hand in both of hers, "he is a man of few words, but he has agreed to work for you today, and wishes to discuss leaving Emra'adid afterward."

Sadia could almost see the lump in Dalgrim's throat as he stood in the shadow of the giant, looking up at him with trepidation. "Aye... er, yes," he said, and the giant man's eyes narrowed as the dwarf's voice shook slightly. "That would be, er, splendid, thank you."

"Wonderful," Mariam said happily, and the group set off toward Suleiman's wharf, drawing the attention of other passersby as the crowds parted before the huge Thrakian.

CHAPTER 32

SADIA

"Whoa, big man, whoa!" Dalgrim cried as Heidroksimos stepped onto the *Mollysocks*, making the ramshackle old barge list dangerously beneath him. "Slowly, lad! Gently, like."

The half-giant looked down at the dwarf with an unamused expression and stepped aboard with his other foot, and the ship bobbed precariously in the water. Sadia stood beside Mariam on the moldy wharf, watching the men as they started to pull the goods from the cabin.

"Glimmerdeep's toothy maw," Dalgrim swore, gripping the railing to keep from falling. "Just, come here and start carrying those boxes over to Lu there," he said, pantomiming to the foreign giant what to do.

As the two women stood waiting, Mariam reached out and squeezed Sadia's shoulder. "I didn't ask your name," she said softly.

"Sadia," she answered, and the pregnant woman smiled.

"Beautiful!" She smiled. "And the little one?"

"Ibrahim."

"Ibrahim," Mariam repeated the foreign name slowly. "How old is he?"

Sadia blinked, "I don't know," she admitted, a humorless laugh escaping her lips. The baby in her arms terrified her, and the guilt from that terror rent her heart. "I-I don't even know," she repeated, wiping her sleeve across her eyes.

Mariam nodded and took Sadia's hand in her own, and the stinging pain behind her eyes finally gave, and she wept as the other woman tried to comfort her. Sadia proceeded to tell her through hitching breaths and falling tears about her life as an orphan in Qasira, finding the other lost children and choosing them as her own siblings, and how difficult and beautiful it had all been. Then she explained how she'd rescued Ibrahim, leaving Yusuf and the girls behind as they'd escaped Qasira, being thrown out of the Temple of Vaharabajra, and that Madam Jalila seemed to be her last remaining hope.

"You poor, sweet girl," Mariam said as Sadia finally ran out of words. She pulled her into an embrace and held her tightly. "I am sorry you are in such a position. But fear not — my Heidroksimos will help your dwarf friend get his goods to this Madam Jalila so that she can help little Ibrahim."

Over the woman's shoulder, Sadia saw Dalgrim look over at them and roll his eyes, but she was too lost in gratitude for Mariam to pay him any heed.

Eventually, Mariam released her and she took a step back, wiping her eyes.

"Thank you," Sadia sniffled, and Mariam smiled.

"Everything will be alright," she replied, "just have faith."

The dwarf shouted from the boat, drawing their attention.

"Look out, lad!" Dalgrim cried, pulling Reza back by the collar. A moment later, a huge, oblong object fell out of the cabin and clanged onto the deck with a hollow, metallic ring, sending the diminutive *Mollysocks* bouncing in the water. Dalgrim stopped it rolling with a booted foot. "Almost crushed you, it did!" he noted, patting Reza's shoulder as the boy stared down at the thing with a puzzled expression.

"What is it?" he asked, and dropped to his knees to look into an opening on one end.

"No, lad!" the dwarf shouted again, yanking Reza away from the vase-shaped object and lifting him by the shirt to move him further away. "Don't... don't even touch it, it's... valuable," he said, shooing Reza away and stooping and straining as he attempted to lift whatever it was back up onto one end. "Just go grab that last crate of textiles," he huffed, a vein in his forehead bulging.

Heidroksimos watched the dwarf for a moment, then bent down and picked the long iron jar up with one hand, setting it upright inside the cabin, seemingly without effort.

"Well done," Dalgrim said, his hands on his knees and his breath ragged. He stood and wiped his brow. "Alright, let's get the last of it loaded up and we'll be off." He gestured at the old, half-rotted cart Suleiman had let him dig out from behind the man's wharf-side shack, and Lu and Reza carried the final cargo off the *Mollysocks* and piled it on top of the rest.

As Dalgrim stepped shakily back off his barge, Heidroksimos took the handles of the cart in his oversized hands and lifted it easily, setting off back up the steep, narrow climb to the main street.

"Where did you say you and your husband are from?" Sadia asked quietly as she and Mariam fell in line behind the rest of the party. The woman was so beautiful, so elegant in the way she carried herself, in her soft but assured speech, and Sadia couldn't help wanting to know more about her.

"We are from Thrakia," Mariam answered as the cart trundled up the steps ahead of them. "You know it?" Sadia shook her head. "It is a little group of islands north of Emra'adid, in the middle of the sea."

"Do you miss it there?" Sadia asked, thinking about her own home and family.

Mariam shrugged. "The islands are very beautiful, and my father owns an expansive estate in the great city of Ithakos, but...." Her brow furrowed, and a frown passed over her delicate lips. "Much was asked of Heidroksimos there. He was no longer treated well, and so I decided to rescue him."

The cart came to an abrupt halt and Sadia looked up to see Heidroksimos grunt and squat, then lift the entire cart up onto his massive shoulders, a shower of loose ornaments and valuables tumbling off the back as the giant hefted it.

"You rescued... him?" she asked skeptically, and Mariam chuckled.

"My husband was... very famous in Thrakia, but also very miserable," she explained as Dalgrim cursed and scrambled to collect the valuables showering the stairs as Heidroksimos stalked up the steep steps three at a time. "It broke my heart to see him so." She sighed, and her dark eyes shimmered in the sunlight as she stared lovingly up at her husband. "I will go as far as he needs us to go, for him to find peace."

Sadia stared at Mariam for a long moment before realizing it. She had never heard anyone talk that way, but it resonated with her deeply. "That's beautiful," she said, and Mariam smiled.

They made their way back up the stairs and onto the main road. The sun slowly fell toward the horizon, and the streets were as lively as ever. Heidroksimos set the cart back down, and Reza immediately clambered up on top of it as the huge man started hauling it down the street, following Dalgrim. Sadia and Mariam continued to talk as they wound their way toward Madam Jalila's, and Sadia was enthralled by her. The washerwomen in Qasira had always chatted just as she was now with Mariam, but Sadia had never been a part of it, always shunned and looked down upon by the others, all of whom had families.

The thought of her sisters brought a pang to her chest. She missed them terribly, and as Ibrahim squirmed in her arms, she felt a subtle resentment building in her heart, alongside the terrible fear of the spirit hiding inside the tiny boy. She didn't regret saving him, or even giving up her family to try to seek a cure for him, but that resolve had started to wane for the first time. Adjusting him on her shoulder, Sadia forced the thoughts from her mind, blaming them on her sleeplessness.

CHAPTER 33

GIDEON

GIDEON TRUDGED through the dark passage, an uneasy feeling settling in the pit of his stomach. The hollow had narrowed almost immediately into a tunnel carved into the rotted wood walls and ceiling, and sodden wood eventually gave way to dangling roots and crumbling earth. The walls closed in on them even further as they went, and eventually, Gideon lowered the standard, holding it in both hands like a spear.

Donnal was ahead of him, using his sword to chop away at the dangling roots and vines, while Sir Cormac grunted behind as he stooped, struggling to force his massive, armored frame through the tight passage.

"There's light ahead!" the battlesister called from the front, her voice muffled by the stifling closeness of the earthen walls and barely audible over the witches' incessant chanting.

Peering past Donnal, Gideon saw a faint gleam glancing off the walls further on, illuminating the passage just a little. Battlesister Dawnhammer forged onward, and the rest followed, eager to escape the cramped passage.

Gideon squinted as they neared the source of the light, and it quickly became so bright that he needed to shield his eyes. He stumbled on, and suddenly, the uneven, hewed ground beneath him changed, and he skidded to a halt on loose gravel over hard stone. A heavy wind buffeted against him, and Gideon had to grip the battle standard tighter to keep it from being whisked from his grasp.

The bright light faded without warning or cause, and his eyes stung as they adjusted. Once they did and he was able to look around, it took him a painful moment to comprehend what he was seeing.

He stood on a precipice jutting from the side of a mountain, overlooking a dark, forested valley. It was dark, and the only light came from storm clouds churning angrily overhead as lightning traced through them and illuminated darting flocks of... something... within.

Gideon turned to look at the others and realized they weren't there. He stood alone on the precipice; all of his companions had suddenly vanished. He turned back the way they had come and could see the blackened roots and vines of the huge tree couched in the slope of the mountain above him, but the path they had taken into the hollow was gone.

"Donnal!" he called out, dashing to where the passage had been that they'd just exited, but there was only solid earth and rock. "Sir Cormac!" he called, his eyes wild as he cast around, trying to understand what was happening. He was alone in some strange place, and the drone of the witches chanting still suffused the air around him, even over the rushing wind, thrumming in his mind more than his ears.

Gideon's heart hammered in his chest as he looked all around, and he stumbled to catch himself as his foot slid, nearly taking him off the edge of the precipice. He stared down into the valley as he righted himself and saw the grasping fingers of more dead, black trees. They swayed back and forth, but not with the wind. Each moved independently, articulating in twitching, grasping movements, as if they were reaching up for him.

He stumbled back from the ledge and gripped the battle standard tight as the wind violently lashed against the banner above him. Taking a careful step back toward the disappeared passage, he froze as he caught something out of the corner of his eye. Scattered bursts of lightning illuminated the heavy clouds, and the things swarming within were pulsing and darting like a flock of skylarks. As he stood staring, the flock changed direction and surged directly toward him.

He could hear them now, over the rushing wind and the chanting, and as they approached, he saw them more clearly: crows with ragged black feathers wet with blood, gore flowing from their eyeless sockets, beaks chipped and cracked and wickedly curved. They swarmed toward him, shrieking, and the cry of each was like the cry of a hundred.

Filled with dread, Gideon pressed himself up against the rocky slope that had replaced the tunnel, and then suddenly, he fell backward, landing hard on his rear end as the wall behind him somehow vanished, revealing the passage that had led him to this terrible place. He scrambled to his feet and fled, back through the tunnel of earth and rotted wood, shouldering through the corridor, desperate to flee the pursuing crows.

Gideon stumbled out of the tunnel, falling to the ground and rolling as he did. He jumped back to his feet, expecting immediately to have to defend himself from the living bramble creatures, but instead, as he looked up, he found himself on the same precipice, and the bloody flock wheeled in the sky, focusing on him once again.

He screamed and stumbled back toward the passage, but stopped when he heard a cry rise from the left, and he looked over to see two of the archoness's cadre running toward him in a sprint along the rocky slope. "Retreat!" one of them screamed. "Flee!" Both had lost their weapons and were running for their lives, stumbling along the incline as fast as they could.

Gideon's eyes widened as he watched the swarm of half-molted crows descend upon the men, spraying crimson droplets with every frantic flap of their wings. One of the men stopped and turned, holding his shield aloft and invoking the Holy Light, but nothing happened, and the bloody flock overwhelmed the two men, their broken, jagged beaks ripping into the soft, fleshy spots between their armored plates. Their screams curdled Gideon's blood as he watched them fall, rolling down the slope and leaving a trail of gore in their wake as the crows followed them, relentless.

Gideon dashed to the edge of the precipice and watched them fall, but then a dozen crows wheeled and darted toward him, screaming and crying, their hollow sockets somehow trained on him. He turned and ran again, the banner whipping overhead, and scrambled and slipped as he rushed back to the passage with the crows in close pursuit. He cursed his own cowardice as he ran, but ran nonetheless.

Pushing back through the passage, he emerged once again onto the clifftop. The bloody crows were nowhere to be seen, and neither had they followed him through the passage. Instead, Lillian stood at the edge of the precipice, her back to him, and someone was with her: Meredith.

The girl who had died the day before stood beside Lillian in plain clothing, her hand resting gently on the blond girl's shoulder as she whispered into her ear. She looked just as she had in life, and Gideon had no idea what to make of it as he came to a halt, doubled over and panting. A jagged spear of lightning crawled across the underbellies of the clouds, and he saw Meredith's eyes flit over to meet his in the bright flash, and a wicked grin lifted the corner of her lips.

Gideon straightened and took a hesitant step toward the pair. He wasn't sure exactly what he was seeing, or whether it was even real. "Lillian?" he called over the wind.

She started at the sound of his voice and glanced back over her shoulder. Her eyes were sad, and clean lines cut through the dirt on her cheeks where many tears had run. She looked away from him, hanging her head and staring down into the valley.

Gideon walked slowly forward, Meredith's eyes following him as she continued whispering in Lillian's ear. "Lillian," he said again once he was just a few paces behind her, on the other side from the dead girl. "Have you seen any of the others?"

Tears welled in Lillian's eyes as she stared down at the twitching, grasping black branches below. "It's too late, Gideon," she said, almost too softly for him to hear. "The Sisters Seidh, they... they are not what the archoness thinks."

"What do you mean?" Gideon pressed, unnerved by Meredith's malevolent, unblinking gaze.

"I told them we shouldn't go into the hollow," Lillian moaned, and two heavy tears rolled down her cheeks before falling into the valley. "Meredith's right about everything."

Gideon swallowed and tried hard not to look at the dead girl. "Lillian," he said evenly, "Meredith died in the hamlet, remember?"

She didn't look at him, but brought her hands up to her face and sobbed. "I wasn't with her," she wailed, weeping in earnest. "I should have stayed with her, begged them to let us stay together!"

Her chest shuddered as she sobbed into her hands. Meredith's lips moved tirelessly, but she never took her eyes off Gideon. "Lillian, listen to me," he said urgently. "This isn't real. Whatever you're hearing, it's not real." He reached out and touched her shoulder in an attempt to pull her away from the cliff's edge.

"No!" She whirled around, drawing her blade in the same motion and holding it out defensively, her tear-streaked face twisted in anger. Gideon leapt back and held the banner in front of himself defensively. "I failed my oath!" she screamed, and took a sobbing breath. Meredith stepped closer to Lillian, laying a hand on each of the girl's shoulders, keeping her whispering lips close to her ear. "I've failed everyone!"

"Lillian," Gideon tried again, raising a placative hand. "Come with me. If we can find the archoness, she—"

Her sobs turned into a bitter laugh. "The archoness has killed us all," she spat. "I tried to tell you, Gideon, but you wouldn't listen!" The lines in her face changed to sorrow again briefly before returning to a manic rage. "You wouldn't listen!"

Gideon shook his head, as much in confusion as in denial. Meredith's appearance must be the witches' doing, he surmised, or else some wicked manifestation of the terrible place in which they were trapped.

"She had no right to bring us here!" Lillian continued, her blade shaking as her body quivered. "We weren't ready for this...." Meredith whispered rapidly into her ear, and Lillian nodded through her tears. "There was never any hope, was there?"

"There's always hope," Gideon answered reflexively, repeating what they'd heard a hundred times at the monastery. "The Holy Light shines brightest in the dark."

"There is no Light here," she said sadly, slowly lowering her sword. "It doesn't reach this place." Gideon glanced up at the tip of the banner and realized for the first time that the blessing from Archoness Lorica had faded, and it was plain, dull steel once again.

Lillian nodded again as she listened to Meredith's whispers. "I see," she said. "I understand. I must." She looked up at Gideon with red-rimmed, sad eyes. "You should follow me, Gideon," she said as Meredith lowered her hands and stepped away, still grinning wickedly and staring at him. "For failing James."

Her words surprised him, and as he struggled to respond, Lillian took a step backward and tumbled over the cliff's edge before he could react. He ran forward to peer over the edge, and watched her fall. He looked away instinctively just before she hit the ground, and when he was able to look back, he watched half a dozen of the grasping black trees reaching for her with flailing, clawing branches.

In shock at Lillian's sudden absence, Gideon stared for a long moment before he caught Meredith out of the corner of his eye standing beside him. He spun around and backed away from the specter, and in another flash of lightning, her face changed. Nefteli stood before him, her brow creased with worry, a single tear sliding down her cheek. "Gideon... where is Donnal?" she asked fearfully.

Gideon was lightheaded as he stumbled away, and she took slow steps toward him, backing him up toward the tunnel behind.

"I told you to look out for him, remember?" her voice was accusatory and wounded, and it broke his heart.

"I... I don't...."

She shook her head sadly. "This is all your fault, Gideon. Donnal,

Lillian, Meredith, James... if you had not failed your trials, you could have saved them."

He was nearly at the mouth of the tunnel, and he wanted nothing more than to run and hide from her. "No," he said softly. "This isn't real. You didn't come with us."

"You understand that I will die, too, yes?" she asked, her breath hitching and more tears spilling over her elegant cheeks. "Someday, I will be called to battle to heal, and I will not return." As she spoke, wounds tore open magically across her body, and bright red spots seeped through her clothing before his eyes.

He reached out instinctively toward her, even as he continued walking backward. "No, Teli...."

"You could save me if you had not failed to call on the Holy Light." A thin red line drew itself across her slender neck, and a sheet of blood spilled out as she spoke.

"Stop!" he begged, blinking away tears that welled at the sight of her dying in front of him.

He was at the mouth of the tunnel, and as she fell into him, he stumbled backward into the passageway and through a curtain of blackness that swallowed him up.

CHAPTER 34

GIDEON

❦

GIDEON FELL through the darkness and landed hard on his back, the banner clattering out of his grip and across the rough stone ground. He groaned and sat up, looking for Nefteli, but she was gone, and under the frantic lightning tracing the sky, there was no sign of her blood on his armor or clothing.

He looked up, bleary-eyed, and saw a big figure standing at the edge of the precipice. Blinking his eyesight clear, he saw it was Sir Cormac, and he scrambled to his feet, terrified that what had happened to Lillian might befall the old paladin, too.

"Sir Cormac!" Gideon called, and the big man whirled around at his voice. He lifted his huge sword and held it aloft, the long, unerring blade pointed directly at Gideon's chest.

"Halt!" Sir Cormac ordered, though Gideon had already skidded to a stop at the sight of the man's readied blade. "Be you the real Ballad or a deceit?"

"Wh... what?" Gideon asked, unable to steady his voice.

Sir Cormac strode forward, his sword still leveled at Gideon's chest.

"You appear as a man," he said, his tone serious, "but the crones have sent imitations before."

Gideon felt a cold chill run down his back as the knight approached, and he swallowed hard. "I... I am Gideon — er, Ballad, sir," he managed, forcing some semblance of composure. "What's happening, Sir Cormac?" he asked, glancing up at the storming skies, then back at the passageway that seemed only ever to lead back to this place. "I don't understand what's happening...."

The huge paladin swept his sword aside and used his free hand to close on Gideon's shoulder in a crushing grip, then brought him close, inspecting his eyes carefully. After a moment, he released him, and Gideon winced and tried to work the pain from his shoulder.

Sir Cormac's eyes narrowed and he snarled. "The witches' malefic trickery," he growled, turning back to look at the dark world in which they found themselves; an ugly, twisted mirror of their own. "But also more than that." He looked back to Gideon, his expression still harsh. "Have you seen any of the others? Gerda? The archoness?"

Gideon swallowed hard. "I saw two of her cadre, and...." He shuddered. "And Lillian. They didn't...." Gideon grit his teeth and looked away, and the knight's face hardened in understanding. "Where is everyone else, sir?" he asked, struggling to keep his voice steady. "We were all together, and then... it was just me. And the tunnel just led back here, here but different." He knew he sounded either insane or foolish, and very likely both.

Sir Cormac was unperturbed, though. "The witches have trapped us in a twisted place," he said, his voice grave. "An endless circle of their perversions of nature." His armored hand closed into a fist as he gazed out across the vale. "It seems that even if we stand and face their darkest machinations, they will only return us to this place, over and over, until we succumb to madness and despair. We've been here over a day already, I think, though this endless storm makes it difficult to say."

"A day?" Gideon asked, trying not to look out into the writhing, lightning-lit valley. "Sir, we just came through the hollow."

Sir Cormac cocked a bushy white eyebrow and grunted. "It's

different for you, then. Damned black magic," he cursed. "Well, however long it's been, time is certainly not on our side. I wager our only way out is to find the coven somewhere in this labyrinth and put them to the sword."

"But how?" Gideon asked, a cold panic gripping him. "Each time I've gone through that tunnel, I come back out in the same place, just to see some terrible new thing!"

Sir Cormac sighed. He held a gauntleted hand palm-up and furrowed his brow as he stared at it. "The Holy Light will not reach this place, it seems. It does not heed my call."

The metal finger plates clanked together as he closed his fist, and he looked back at Gideon. "But remember what we talked about at the hamlet — a paladin is not merely a conduit for the Light. The gods crafted each of us by hand and gifted us strength, and we have fostered that strength, have we not?"

Gideon nodded even though the question sounded rhetorical, and Sir Cormac walked over and once again placed a hand on his shoulder, but this time a palpable warmth and strength seemed to pass between them. "Take heart, Ballad, and succumb not to fear, for we have a pure and noble purpose." He stooped, bringing his face closer to Gideon's. "Hold fast to faith — use the strength given you rightly, and justice will win out, in the end. Trust in that."

"Yes, sir," Gideon said as he fought down the panic in his chest. The veteran paladin's unwavering courage and determination were inspiring, and he resolved to follow his advice.

Sir Cormac gave him a firm nod and opened his mouth to speak again, but he was cut off by a voice from behind.

"Sir Cormus?" it asked hesitantly. Gideon glanced past the paladin and saw a figure approaching from along the slope. He had to look again, though, because the figure appeared to be... himself.

He, Gideon, stood further along the precipice, having appeared as if out of thin air, clutching the battle standard in one hand and looking confused.

Only, it wasn't quite right.

The emblem on the banner wasn't the Church Militant's sword and open tome, but a spilled chalice with the head of an infant peeking out wickedly from within the cup. The way it rippled in the wind was strange; it flowed of its own accord, with no concern for the rushing gale.

The man holding it wasn't right either. His hands had been transposed, the left switched with the right, the thumbs on the wrong sides, and his complexion betrayed a sickly pallor. The face was confused and frightened, but mischievous, as though he held a terrifying secret he could hardly stand to keep.

"Sir Cormant?" he asked again, taking a fumbling step toward them. Sir Cormac whirled, standing between Gideon and whatever it was that was approaching them. "Where are the brothers?" he cried, stumbling as though he'd just learned to walk. "We must find the arches! To save us!"

"Another foul deceit!" the paladin declared, brandishing his blade. He threw a glance back at Gideon. "I'll take care of this. You must go," he said, nodding toward the passage behind. "Go, find the archoness!"

"Yes!" the doppelganger shouted, his voice laced with a primal fear that disturbed something deep inside Gideon. "Find the larches!" He dropped to his knees, weeping, tossing the banner aside in a fit and pulling at his pale blond hair, ripping it from his scalp. He shrieked in horror as he looked down at the bloody bits of scalp that had come loose and then up at Sir Cormac. "Honor me, third! Noble, holy Bird Cormorant!" He wailed again before descending into the most unnerving laugh Gideon had ever heard.

Sir Cormac's jaw set sternly beneath his mighty mustache. "Go, Ballad," he said again, and lowered the faceplate of his iron helm.

Gideon reluctantly obeyed the paladin's order, stepping backward toward the passageway as the witch-wrought version of himself screamed again in despair, casting his uneven eyes up toward the swirling black sky. As Sir Cormac approached him, sword ready to cleave, it gazed up at him as if at a god, then pulled a wicked, curved dagger from behind its back, the blade wreathed in an unholy green glow. "Praise him! Praise the Holy Bird Cormorant!" it howled, and then lunged forward, trying to drive the blade into the paladin's chest, but Sir Cormac swung his sword in a wide arc, slashing through the man's torso and cleaving him in two.

Gideon recoiled as he saw his uncanny effigy fall and the upper half flail frantically, trying to stab at the paladin's armored boots as he gushed smoking, putrid ooze from his wounds. "Go!" Sir Cormac bellowed at him, waving him away, and Gideon turned and raced back through the passageway, into the hollow of the tree.

Once again, he pushed through the pressing, clinging roots, and he steeled himself, swearing a silent oath not to let the old paladin down. After having seen all he had, he felt he understood a bit better the zeal and fervor of the archoness and her cadre to hunt these witches and put an end to their villainy.

As he stumbled out onto the same, damnable precipice, he stopped short as he saw a handful of soldiers, their corpses held aloft by grasping brambles like puppets, their blood still wet and shining in the bursts of lightning above. His jaw clenched, and he turned from them and glanced around for any sign of the archoness, but saw none.

There was no time to waste, nor to mourn, so Gideon turned and dashed back to the tunnel, reciting a silent prayer for his fallen comrades. The archoness had to be somewhere in the mystical labyrinth, and he would find her, even if he had to wrestle his way through that same passage a hundred times. He was determined, but as he mounted a desperate push, charging through the tunnel again and again, arriving on the same precipice each time, the fire Sir Cormac had rekindled in him flickered.

Sometimes when he emerged, there was another corpse of one of his fellow soldiers, or some new terror, and other times there was nothing. Each time, the discordant chorus grew a little louder, beginning to overpower his own thoughts, making it difficult to focus, and the constant repetition of the passage was wearing him thin. He couldn't keep going forever.

CHAPTER 35

SADIA

❧

THE SUN WAS low in the sky by the time Dalgrim had stopped in a little square lined by stalls, and he turned to look up at the looming facade of a building magnificently decorated in a riot of colors and carved figures and shapes. "Alright," the dwarf announced, dusting his hands off and nodding. "Here we are."

Heidroksimos let the cart drop unceremoniously and went to his wife's side as Lu lifted Reza down from the pile of goods.

"Madam Jalila is a woman of good taste," Dalgrim said, turning to them with a glower. "She's a collector and purveyor of fine, delicate bits and bobs, and as such, I cannae afford to have a giant wrecking through the place." He glanced up at Heidroksimos, who regarded him blankly, and then the dwarf's gaze fell on Reza. "Nor a wee rascal with a penchant for wandering off."

"Aw," Reza groaned, and the dwarf scowled at him.

"Stay here and guard the cart," Dalgrim ordered, and he pointed at Sadia as Mariam translated quietly to her husband. "Come along, lass," the dwarf said. "You, too, Lu — the madam took a shine to you last time, remember?"

Lu looked as if he didn't remember at all, but he checked his breath against his hand and then straightened his loose linen shirt and followed after Sadia as Dalgrim shoved through the ornate doors.

A wave of cool, scented air rolled out over the three as they entered. They walked past a long line of people waiting to purchase their wares, and the dwarf nodded to the doorman as he made his way to the counter where a thin, severe-looking man was weighing coins on a small balance. His sharp eyebrows rose imperiously when he saw the dwarf.

"Ah," the man sneered, looking down his arched nose. "Glintstone. I'd heard a dwarf was recently hanged in the Tandahar for thievery. I was hoping it was you," he said with a frown.

"Happy to disappoint you, Cyrus," Dalgrim answered unfazed. "Go let the madam know I'd like to see her."

Cyrus scoffed. "Why on earth would I do that?"

"Because I've got a whole cart full of goods outside she'll find quite interesting," Dalgrim replied through gritted teeth, tapping the counter impatiently.

Cyrus's dark, beady eyes roamed over Dalgrim and Lu, and a wide smile split his lips as his gaze landed on Sadia and Ibrahim. "Hello, my dear," the man said in a silky tone, bringing his long face closer to her across the counter. His skin was oiled, and his face clean-shaven save for a thick, gold-banded braid that jutted from his chin.

Sadia blinked at him and clutched Ibrahim tighter. "Hello," she said uncertainly, and looked away under the uncomfortable weight of his gaze.

"Oh, my," Cyrus gasped as the bundle wrapped around Ibrahim shifted, and his dark eyes glittered with a disturbing interest. "So young to be a mother...." The words slithered from between his thin lips and made Sadia shiver. "What is the little one's name, my—"

His words were cut off as Dalgrim's meaty hand reached over and clamped around Cyrus's chin-beard, pulling his head back over to face the dwarf. "Maybe you didn't hear me," Dalgrim said, his eyes boring into Cyrus's. "I said, let Jalila know I've come calling."

"You retain your famous dwarven charm, I see," Cyrus replied tersely, his narrow beard still held captive in Dalgrim's fist. "I happened to hear about a commotion on the Tajari yesterday. They say a decrepit raft piloted by a fat little dwarf ran a merchant ship into the riverbank, sinking it and half a dozen other smaller ships in the process. You wouldn't happen to know anything about that, would you?"

Dalgrim's thick eyebrows sunk lower than Sadia had ever seen, and his grip on Cyrus's beard tightened. "Well, I've heard the crocodiles around here have a taste for skinny, creepy little bastards like yourself," the dwarf snarled. "Isn't that right, Lu?" Lu tipped his hat back to look pointedly at the man, and grinned.

Cyrus's dark eyes flared and his mouth opened, but a woman's voice called out from above them, and they all looked up to a balcony Sadia hadn't even noticed was there. "Dalgrim!" the woman announced happily, leaning over the railing and looking down at them. "I'd heard the *Mollysocks* had been spotted, but I didn't believe it. It's been years!" She was flanked by two muscular men wearing molded leather armor and stoic expressions.

The dwarf released Cyrus's chin beard, and the man straightened, rubbing his jaw.

"Jalila," the dwarf said, smiling genuinely as he stepped back from the counter and bowed. "You're a sight for old eyes! You've only grown more beautiful since the last time."

"And you've grown only more charming," the woman laughed. She was of middling age, her lustrous black hair streaked with silver and her olive skin weathered by the sun. "Have you come to pay your debts or to try to make new ones?"

Dalgrim spread his hands magnanimously. "Must a man choose only one?"

Madam Jalila grinned and shook her head, then gestured for them to join her. Dalgrim waited until she'd turned back from the balcony to scowl at Cyrus before leading Lu and Sadia to a staircase hidden behind a jumble of shelves. It led them up to the balcony where the surprisingly tall Madam Jalila stood waiting, flanked by her imposing guards. She wore a striking red dress that trailed behind her, and one crimson fingernail rested against her chin as she watched them approach.

"I trust you don't come to my house empty-handed," she said, and neither her tone nor expression were easy to read.

Dalgrim stopped mid-stride. "Heh, of course not!" he declared, shifting and tugging at the collar of his robe. "I've a whole cart of precious goods just out front, awaiting your perusal — rare totems from Imwa, spices from Sharquf, fabulous Maramasan textiles, and more," he assured her.

"Wonderful," she said with a smile that failed to reach her eyes. "And how much of it is counterfeit?"

Dalgrim sputtered in surprise, but before he could provide an answer, Lu smiled happily and said, "Only half!" as though it was good news, and earned an elbow to the hip from Dalgrim.

Madam Jalila shook her head and sighed, but this time, the smile that played across her lips seemed genuine. "I had hoped you might have reformed in your absence," she said, and she gave Sadia a cursory once-over before turning her attention to Lu.

"Why, Lu Song," she said, her eyes flashing, and the man froze in place. "Our dear dwarf has deprived me of your company for far too long." She held out a hand to him, and Lu blushed before taking it and planting a kiss on the back of her fingers.

"I am honored," the man said, enunciating the words carefully as his cheeks flushed.

"The honor is all mine, my dear," she replied, her gaze lingering on him before she finally turned to one of her guards. "Take Cyrus and evaluate the goods our fine guests have brought," she told him quietly. The man nodded and swept past the visitors, heading downstairs. "Shall we adjourn to the lounge?"

"Of course," Dalgrim said, forcing a smile and gesturing for her to lead. Madam Jalila inclined her head, then turned gracefully and started down a long hallway. Dalgrim smacked Lu as they followed, and Lu smacked him back indignantly.

"I must admit, Emra'adid has been a bit duller over the last few years without Dalgrim Glintstone causing havoc in its streets," she said over her shoulder as she led them down the lavishly decorated hall.

"I'll take that as a compliment," the dwarf answered, and Jalila chuckled.

"And who is your lovely friend?" the woman asked, glancing at Sadia.

"Er, this is Sadia, she's—"

"My name is Sadia al-Yetim, madam," she answered firmly, and Dalgrim blinked at her.

"Al-Yetim," Jalila noted. "Very interesting." She stopped at an intricately carved door, and her guard pushed it open, holding it for the rest of the group as they passed into a spacious lounge, decorated in an ostentatious style with colorful pillows and carpets, and intricately woven drapes hanging over a bank of windows on one side.

"It's beautiful," Sadia offered, feeling out of place in the wealthy accommodations, and Jalila gave a small nod.

"Please, everyone, make yourselves comfortable," she said, gesturing around the room as the guard pulled the door closed.

Sadia took a seat on one of the huge cushions beside Dalgrim and Lu as Madam Jalila clapped her hands once and a pair of serving men stepped away from the wall and approached, bearing tea trays.

"While we wait for Cyrus's evaluation," the madam said, taking a tiny cup of tea from the offered tray, "do tell me where the winds took you, my dear dwarf. Were they fell or fair?"

Dalgrim grinned and launched into a tale of his adventures leading up until the day Sadia had met him. Lu interjected occasionally, too, and Sadia soon learned that the two of them had been sailing together for years, all up and down the Tajari River, out into the Salient Sea, and beyond. As the dwarf told their stories, the men poured tea, and they all ate from an assortment of delicate foods offered by the servants.

As interesting as the dwarf's stories were, Sadia only half-listened, her attention split between the conversation and the frail, restless child in her arms. She tried to feed Ibrahim a bit of the food from her plate while Dalgrim told a tall tale about fighting a man-tiger in a distant, mist-shrouded land, but the toddler wouldn't even part his lips to taste.

"But why have you returned now, after all this time?" Madam Jalila asked after the pair had concluded their elaborate — and somewhat unbelievable — tale.

"I'm afraid the fates have decided my return, not I," Dalgrim said heavily. "I was aiming to do trade in Qasira, but there was apparently a bit of trouble with a cult or some such nonsense."

"Qasira," Jalila mused. "I've heard rumors that a mysterious cult appeared as if out of nowhere and committed atrocities of some account." Her dark eyes slid over to Sadia. "Given your surname, I gather you come from the emirates. Am I right in assuming you are a refugee from the beleaguered city?"

Sadia felt her neck flush as she was suddenly expected to speak, and she took a breath before answering. "I was there when those cultists attacked the priests of Ankhat Naharia. They killed them all," she said, her eyes focused on the beautifully chiseled patterns carved along the edges of the table between them as she remembered what she'd witnessed. "They burned them alive and..." she hesitated, thinking of Ibi on the altar, crying and looking around fearfully.

"Go on, please," Jalila prodded gently.

Sadia cleared her throat. "They did something..." she said, and she glanced down at Ibrahim's withered face before looking away again. "Their leader — he called himself a prophet — he tried to do something to... to my brother. Ibrahim."

"He is unwell," Jalila guessed, pulling Sadia from her thoughts.

She nodded. "I think he's dying," she said, surprising herself, and the admission caused tears to well in her tired eyes.

"I see." The elegant lines of the older woman's face softened. "And Dalgrim told you that I may be able to help?"

"Yes," Sadia whispered.

"Then perhaps the fates have not been entirely cruel," the woman answered, reaching a hand out. "Come here, let me see him."

As Sadia rose and went to kneel beside her, she was relieved to be able to give Ibrahim to someone else, if only for a few moments. As soon as she let him go, though, she felt like something was missing. Her arm was tired from carrying him, but in his absence, she felt cold and empty. He was just beside her, but it felt wrong to see someone else holding him.

"Oh my," the woman gasped softly, her fingers touching the child's feverish, dry skin. "Tell me again what happened to him."

"There was a ritual in the bazaar, and I think the cultists summoned an ifrit inside him," Sadia explained, the words coming out more quickly than she intended. "The man who wanted to hurt him conjured fire, and—"

"An ifrit?" Madam Jalila interjected, her eyes wide. "What on earth makes you think that?"

Sadia squirmed under her penetrative gaze. "I... an old woman told me they roam the desert outside the city, and the cult leader drew circles of fire in the air all around him, and then Ibrahim changed. He looked healthy and well one moment, and the next...." She looked down at the withered baby.

"I see," the madam said, her dark eyes narrowed thoughtfully. "I suppose it could be. Ifriti are beings of chaos," the woman explained as her fingers probed gently at Ibrahim's chest and belly, running over his bony, emaciated form, "and once they occupy a body alongside that person's soul, it requires very rigorous and difficult effort to expel them.

"Although," she added wryly, "where a Qasiran sees an ifrit, a West Umbrian will see a demon; and a Maramasan, a Rakshasa."

Dalgrim snorted and nodded in agreement from his seat on the cushion.

Sadia didn't understand half the words the woman had said, but she didn't care. "Please, Madam Jalila," she whispered, her heart pounding in her chest. "Do you know how to get rid of it?"

"No," Jalila answered, and Sadia's heart sank. "To exorcise an ifrit, you need a healer."

"I took him to a healer!" Sadia cried miserably. "Roya sent me to the Temple of Vaharabajra, but when the jadhari tried to heal Ibrahim, the ifrit spoke, and frightened the old man so badly that they kicked us out!"

"It spoke?" the woman exclaimed, her face drawn, and Dalgrim sat up.

"What's this now?" he asked as Lu looked worriedly at Ibrahim. "Ye didnae mention that, lass!"

"What did it say?" Jalila demanded, ignoring Dalgrim's interruption.

Sadia shuddered as she recalled the strange words that had thrummed around Ibrahim. "I don't remember exactly," she said, closing her eyes and clenching her jaw. "Burning... sacrifices... punishing someone, I think." She hoped never to hear the voice again, and was glad she couldn't remember the words precisely.

When she opened her eyes, Madam Jalila was staring at her intently, an odd smile playing on her lips. "Fascinating," she breathed, her eyes sparkling as she turned them back to Ibrahim. She began muttering to herself thoughtfully. "Conjured magical fire and a disembodied voice from within a withered child...."

"Can't you do anything to help him?" Sadia asked desperately, and Jalila blinked as though coming out of a trance.

"I don't know, my dear," she said softly, and reached a hand up to run a finger down the side of Ibrahim's face. "But I am very curious about this little boy." Sadia looked nervously to Dalgrim and Lu as Jalila stared intently at Ibrahim for a long moment before sighing. "You demonstrate your savvy by bringing me such a peculiar little puzzle, Dalgrim," she said, looking at the dwarf. "If this proves as interesting as I think, I will cut your debt in half."

Dalgrim took a deep breath and then smiled. "An intellect like yours is hard to challenge, no doubt, madam."

Sadia looked between them and couldn't help but bristle at the way they were talking about Ibrahim. "He's not a puzzle!" she said angrily. "He's just a baby, and he needs help."

Madam Jalila looked up at her and waved a hand. "Calm yourself, girl. I meant no disrespect. I simply cannot make a judgment or commitment until I can learn more about this child and the true nature of what has possessed him."

Sadia opened her mouth, but a knock came at the door, and Cyrus appeared, seeming almost to slither through the crack. "The evaluation of the dwarf's pilfered goods," he said, holding a folded parchment aloft.

"Pilfered?" Dalgrim growled, adjusting himself on his cushions to glower back at the man as Jalila gestured him forward.

"What did you find, Cyrus?" she asked as he handed her the report and stood beside her, his eyes never leaving Dalgrim.

"As expected," the man replied, wearing a perpetual sneer. "The textiles are genuine, but the rest is... suspect."

"Suspect?" Dalgrim cried again, his cheeks flushing beneath his thick black beard. "Jalila, you know you have to add at least half again onto whatever number this idiot gave you!"

"Are you questioning my integrity, dwarf?" Cyrus snapped.

"Gentlemen, please," the madam interjected, looking from one man to the other, and both of them quieted. "That will be all, Cyrus," she said curtly.

The perfumed man shifted and pointed with a limp wrist at the paper in Jalila's hand. "Er, please, look at what I wrote there at the—"

"Cyrus!" the madam said again, and her tone was final.

Cyrus bowed and withdrew, his expression stony. "Of course, Jalila."

He and Dalgrim sneered at each other as Cyrus passed.

"Aye, do as your sister says, you pants-pissing diddy," the dwarf jeered under his breath, and Lu snickered.

Cyrus stopped and turned to the dwarf, but Madam Jalila cleared her throat purposefully, and the man continued to slink out as the guard opened the door for him.

Once he was gone, the woman sighed. "I wish you and Cyrus would learn to get along, Dalgrim, dear."

"That brother of yours is a real piece of work, Jalila," Dalgrim growled. "Keeping him around doesn't do your reputation any favors."

"My brother can be... difficult," she acquiesced, sounding reluctant to admit it. "But we don't choose our family, do we?"

She looked up at Sadia, who swallowed and nodded despite the fact that she had, indeed, chosen her family. Few would understand that, though.

Madam Jalila soothed Ibrahim as he fussed in the crook of her arm, and with her free hand, she flicked open the folded parchment Cyrus had brought her and perused it. "My brother recommends I pay you no more than fifty silver drahm for the goods you've brought me," she said.

"Ach, Jalila," Dalgrim complained, "I paid no less than a hundred, not to mention trekked it halfway across the world to reach your door! Surely you'll not—"

"Yes, yes," the madam said impatiently, tossing the parchment aside. "I'll make sure you leave here quite comfortable, Dalgrim. When have I not?" The dwarf relaxed a little, still looking a bit suspicious. "For now, however," Jalila continued, staring down at Ibrahim intently, "I wish to conduct some experiments on the boy to ferret out what truly ails him."

"Experiments?" Sadia asked nervously.

Madam Jalila snapped the fingers of her free hand, and the servants stepped forward once more. "Fetch me the little black trunk from my bedchambers," she ordered them, and the men headed for the door as Jalila turned her attention to Sadia. "Fear not, my lovely — I only wish to help you find how best to help your brother."

Sadia wasn't convinced, but she didn't want to jeopardize the madam's decision to help them. She was already beside herself with what had happened with the jadhari, and so she swallowed her concerns and stood meekly by, steeling herself for what might come.

A few moments later, the two serving men returned with a small, rectangular black trunk and set it on the floor beside the madam. She delivered Ibrahim back into Sadia's arms and bent over, unlatching the trunk and opening it.

Dalgrim and Lu both leaned over to peer at what the madam was doing as she pulled out a number of instruments, phials, bundles of dried herbs, and a few small boxes. One of the objects was a thin, flat metal rod with a handle, which she handed to Lu.

"What's this — spoon?" Lu asked, and Jalila laughed.

"No, my dear. That is a dowsing rod," she explained.

"A... what?" Lu asked, holding it awkwardly.

"It is a tool that diviners use to seek out the presence of magic. I'll have you assist me with that in a moment."

Lu looked the object over and shrugged, and Jalila handed an ornate, lidded metal basket to Dalgrim, who shuddered and groaned. "I'm going to need something a bit stiffer than tea if you're going where I think you are, Jalila," he grumbled.

The woman smiled sweetly and pointedly ignored the request. "That is a sacred censer, dear," she explained. "Kindly light the coals, please".

Dalgrim scowled and did as she asked, cursing as he fumbled awkwardly with a candle to heat the coals within the censer.

"What is all this?" Sadia brought herself to ask.

"This," Madam Jalila explained as she removed another handful of things from the trunk, "is the sum total of everything I know about spiritual communication and rituals of binding."

"Binding?" Sadia repeated, and Jalila glanced up.

"If an ifrit or any other evil spirit has occupied the child's body, you cannot simply drive it out. It would kill him," the woman explained, and Sadia's stomach lurched. "A proper exorcism requires an expert trained in such matters and of a holy and righteous disposition." She gave the girl a meaningful look. "I am not one such. Instead, these tools will help us narrow down a long list of possibilities of what ails him. Lay the boy down here, on the table," she instructed.

Sadia hesitated a moment as Madam Jalila arranged her implements, then did as she was bade. "Will it hurt him?" she asked.

"It will not injure him," the woman answered carefully. She picked up one of the glass phials and pulled the blanket away from Ibrahim, exposing the boy's emaciated chest, the bones visible beneath his pallid skin, and carefully placed a drop of a thick, oily liquid on his belly. Using an immaculately white cloth, she gently rubbed the substance into his skin, then sprinkled a fragrant powder over him as well. Ibi sneezed as the little resultant cloud dissipated.

"First, we'll see if there is indeed a magical nature to his affliction," the madam explained, gesturing to Lu and instructing him to hold the rod out and slowly bring it closer to the boy. He did as he was instructed and held the rod in the general direction of Ibrahim, then slowly lowered it. As it came closer, the rod started visibly quavering, and when he was a few inches away, Lu had to use his other hand to hold it still.

"Ah!" Lu shouted as the metal rod leapt from his hand and clattered across the wooden floor. "Did you see that?" he asked, slapping Dalgrim's shoulder. "It move by itself!"

"There's no doubt of the magical nature of his affliction," Jalila said as the dwarf slapped him back. "I didn't expect anything else, really, after the girl's description of what happened in the Temple of Vaharabajra. Still," she sighed and looked at Sadia. "The next part may prove... difficult for you. I will try to summon the entity within him, that we may question it."

Sadia's eyes went wide. "If it will help him... do it," she said, trying to keep her voice steady, and Jalila raised an eyebrow.

"A wise choice," the madam acknowledged with a nod before turning to pick up the lighted censer. She took a bundle of dried herbs and placed them inside the container, and after a moment, plumes of incense poured from the little holes in the top. A warm, spiced aroma filled the room, making Sadia's head swim.

Jalila picked up a small knife, and Sadia recoiled, her heart pounding in her chest, but the woman calmly reached out and cut her own palm with it, then held the wound over a ceramic bowl, allowing a few crimson drops to drip into it.

"Blood magic," Dalgrim whispered, his voice heavy.

"This is a very old ritual to summon spiritual entities," she said, shooting Dalgrim a look. "It's not as nefarious as it may seem." She wrapped her hand with a clean cloth, then retrieved a single vellum page from the trunk and laid it out on the table beside Ibrahim. "Now, all of you, remain silent."

She turned back to Ibrahim and began chanting softly, reading from the vellum. As she did, her finger dipped into the blood and she used it to paint some kind of arcane symbol on Ibirahim's gaunt chest. Her words seemed unintelligible, but they had a haunting rhythm.

Sadia fought to keep herself still as Ibrahim's belly started moving faster, his nostrils flaring as he breathed hard and his eyes squeezing tight like he was in pain.

"Speak, you who have invaded this boy," Jalila commanded. There was a silence as Dalgrim shifted uncomfortably, and Sadia clenched her fists to stop herself from reaching out for the child.

Finally, the madam received a response, and Sadia's fingers went cold as the same, deep, malevolent voice thrummed throughout the room. "Ware thyself... the lust behind the Light," it said, rattling the various objects Jalila had laid out on the table. The guards at the door tensed, each reaching for the hilt of the sword at his hip.

The woman sat back in surprise, her eyes locked on Ibrahim as he squirmed and shuddered. "Is... is that the voice you heard? At the temple?" she asked Sadia without looking at her.

"Yes," Sadia breathed, bracing herself as the horrible voice rose again from somewhere around Ibrahim.

"Charge the dread... make way, ye chattel — unfettered pale," It grew louder as it spoke, and Sadia had to reach out to steady herself as the very walls and floor quaked at the power of it. "Gird thyself... against the cold beyond the stars."

As the final word faded and the room stopped shaking, a dangerous silence fell like a blanket over the room. The heady aroma of the censer was overwhelmed by another, foul smell of sulfur and melting flesh, and Lu retched as the odor washed over them. The guards rushed forward, but Madam Jalila stood and held out her hand to stop them. She was shaking, staring down at Ibrahim as the child stiffened and his mouth slowly opened, as if his lips were being pulled apart by an invisible force.

"Sacred sands," Jalila whispered, and there were tears in the woman's eyes as she stared into Ibi's open mouth.

Terrified, Sadia leaned over to see what it was she saw, and she stifled a miserable cry as she beheld it: a burning, searching eye blazed from within the child's mouth, its pupil a ragged, angry slit that looked like it contained the night sky. It was huge, as if it belonged to a giant, and far too large even to fit where it was. It was impossible, indescribable, and Sadia's heart pounded in her chest and her vision began to darken at the edges as she stared in shock at Ibrahim.

"Who... who are you?" Madam Jalila asked, and her voice had lost all of its strength and command.

The smoldering eyeball flitted briefly to Jalila, but there was no response for a long moment. The madam grabbed the censer off the table and started adding different herbs to it when a sudden sound came from Ibrahim. It was faint at first, a droning blast from far, far away, but then it echoed, louder, closer, and echoed again, and again, and finally the sound exploded through the room, the sheer power of it knocking all four of them back away from Ibrahim.

The thick wooden planks in the ceiling above the boy were crushed upward, buckling and splintering. A shower of wood fragments and dust rained down on them, and various objects in the room were launched toward the walls, skittering and clattering across the floor.

Sadia's ears rang, and she felt a warm, wet trickle down the left side of her neck as she scrambled to her knees. Lu had landed on Dalgrim, and the dwarf was cursing and sputtering, trying to disentangle himself as Lu sat on him, dazed, his reed hat tipped up and his eyes wide.

"Ibi!" Sadia shouted, her voice muffled in her own ears, and her heart seized as she saw him sitting upright, the burning eye still blazing from within his mouth.

Jalila crawled back over to the table and knelt at the edge, her hands on Ibrahim's face. "Who are you?" she screamed, her eyes wild as she stared into the relentless gaze peering back at her. The echo from beyond the blast faded, and in its place rose a chorus of tortured screams, of thousands of men and women wailing in pain. The sound made Sadia sick in her stomach.

Jalila's guards picked themselves up and rushed over, swords drawn, and the bronze blades shone dully as they were leveled at Ibrahim.

"Stop this!" Sadia cried, crawling across the floor toward Jalila. She grabbed the woman's red sleeve and shook her. "Please, make this stop!" she begged, too afraid to look at Ibrahim.

Madam Jalila seemed not to have heard her. "Tell me your name!" she shouted again, and then she recoiled as the thunderous voice spoke again.

"Supplications mount upon the hating flame...."

Sadia shook the woman as hard as she could, finally drawing her attention. "Please," she cried, squeezing her arms. "It's killing him!" Sadia finally risked a look back to Ibrahim, whose tiny body was in rigor, the unholy manifestation within seizing him, and she could see the fluttering of his little heart in the soft flesh just below his breast-bone. "Please," she said again, losing her composure and weeping desperately.

Madam Jalila furrowed her brow and slowly nodded, and then she waved her guards away and quickly began preparing different phials, herbal bundles, and instruments. "Dalgrim!" she barked, and as the dwarf hesitantly trundled over, she held the censer back out to him, having filled it with a third batch of different herbs. "Wave this over the child. Girl, hold out your hands."

Sadia obeyed, and Jalila poured two oils from different phials into her open palms. "Start rubbing them into his chest." The madam herself took a smooth stone medallion in the shape of an open hand from her trunk and held it aloft, closing her eyes and whispering inaudibly.

Sadia steeled herself to apply the oils to Ibrahim and tried not to look at the impossible eye glaring out angrily from his gaping mouth. As she touched Ibrahim's chest, his flesh burned her, but she clenched her jaw and quickly worked the oils in, disrupting the blood sigil the madam had painted on him.

"What's happening to him?!" she cried as her brother's tiny chest swelled and contracted rapidly.

"He's fighting," Jalila said, scooting closer to the boy on her knees. "He's fighting for his soul." Sadia looked at Ibrahim's eyes for the first time and saw that he was looking at her, tears falling down his cheeks. "Hold your brother's hand, child," Jalila instructed her, lifting the hand-shaped medallion aloft. "He needs your strength."

Sadia took his hand, and his fingers smoldered against her palm like dying coals, but she held it nonetheless, her eyes locked on his as the madam flipped the vellum page over and began chanting a different magical spell. As she spoke the foreign words, lines carved into the palm of the medallion began to glow, casting a warm emerald light throughout the room.

Ibi's body convulsed as whatever magic Jalila was invoking seemed to be having an effect. Sadia held her little brother's hand tightly in her own, and the burning heat slowly receded as he blinked, his eyes locked on hers as tears streamed down his cheeks. "It's alright, Ibi," she assured him, stroking the back of his hand with her thumb. "Everything is going to be alright, I promise."

The burning eye within him glared balefully at them, but as the burning heat in Ibrahim's flesh gradually cooled, the eye slowly receded, disappearing into the inexplicable shadow within the boy's mouth, until it had faded completely from sight. Ibi swayed and fell backward on the table, and Sadia scooped him up in her arms and pressed him close as he started wailing and crying uncontrollably.

CHAPTER 36

GIDEON

CHARGING through the passage so many times had begun to cause Gideon's pace to flag, as though his boots were weighted with iron. As he wrestled to force himself on, he suddenly realized he'd been in the tunnel longer than usual. He wasn't sure if his mind was playing tricks on him, or the witches were torturing him with some new ruse.

He didn't know, and he didn't care. If he was being led into some trap, it was a chance he was willing to take. Anything to get out of the cycle of madness they had charged unwittingly into.

A few long moments passed, and the passage was definitely longer than before, and it took twists and turns it never had. He pressed on, his legs burning, his arms aching from carrying the battle standard and hacking away at the roots and thorns of the passage, but he pushed forward.

Then, without warning, the passage emptied him out onto the precipice yet again. As he stepped out into the open air, he froze. Something was in the valley before him that hadn't been there before. It stood among the dead, grasping trees, rising high into the sky like a tower.

But it was moving.

At first, Gideon's mind conjured the word 'giant'. He quickly realized, however, that word wasn't enough; it wasn't a giant, but a titan. Larger than any tower or spire, the height of a mountain, though it was shaped somewhat like a man, with distinguishable arms and legs among the blackened, smoldering dross that seemed to coat its body. Smoke and shadow in equal measure roiled angrily from its flesh in waves.

The spikes of a wicked crown upon its head scraped the underbellies of the clouds, cutting a trail through the storm as the titan moved. It lifted one foot and took a long, protracted step that eventually crashed back down into the mass of writhing black trees, sending an explosive wave through the valley in its wake.

Gideon trembled as he beheld it, its face a stoic mask of deep-cut features in the angry embers of its flesh. As it lifted its other foot to take another arcing step over hills and forests, its whole body seethed, heat and smoke pulsing from its flesh, and a blast of sound like the low droning of a warhorn exploded from somewhere within it. The sound made Gideon recoil, and he dropped the battle standard to the ground to cover his ears.

A moment after the terrible sound faded, another rose in its place. Gideon didn't know what it was at first, but he pulled his hands away from his ears, and his stomach dropped as he heard the sound of screaming.

Hundreds, maybe thousands of voices rose, shrieking in pain and terror, and as Gideon peered more closely at the titan, he saw them: charred, ashen bodies melted and grafted into the titan's flesh. He could barely make them out as they struggled and writhed and screamed as the seething heat consumed them but would not let them die, and they were unable to escape the hellish torment that had gripped them.

Gideon was paralyzed, horrified by what he saw, and the idea that the thing might turn and see him was almost too much to bear. But then something else caught his attention.

In his terror at seeing the titan, Gideon hadn't realized that he wasn't alone on the precipice. At the edge, overlooking the valley, there was a tall chair wrought from black, rotted brambles, twisting and curling around each other to form a heinous throne. He couldn't see who sat upon it, but beside the throne was a hunched figure in a tattered cloak, the hood pulled up over its head, a frail, wizened hand holding a gnarled staff for support.

Glancing momentarily from the hunched figure to the titan and back, Gideon steeled himself and slowly circled around to get a better look at the figure and whoever might be sitting on the throne. He left the discarded banner behind where it had fallen, gripping his mace tight in both hands and keeping a good distance from the throne.

He came around, and though he still couldn't make out the hunched figure's face, he saw the archoness on the throne, sitting in her gleaming armor, her gauntleted hands gripping the knotted armrests and her face staring up at the titan with a fearful intensity. Scarlet leaked slowly from her ears over already-dried trails of blood.

"Milady!" he called as he approached, but she didn't react, her eyes locked on the smoldering titan as the cries of trapped souls mingled with the chanting of the witches, filling Gideon's mind. "Archoness Lorica!" he shouted again, taking several more steps toward her.

The hunched figure turned to face him, making Gideon stop in his tracks. It was a withered old woman, her skin sallow and spotted with age. He could only see the bottom half of her face beneath the hood, and her mouth was curled into an unnerving smile as her head slowly turned toward him.

"Another golden warrior," she said, and though her voice was small and grandmotherly, there was a hint of poison beneath the sweetness. "Have you come to save your pretty golden queen?" she asked, a wicked laugh playing on the words as they left her mouth.

Gideon swallowed hard, unable to summon a reply. The witch's smile curled further. "So many intruders into our home today," she mused with an air of wistfulness. She lifted her other hand and pointed a bony finger out at the titan in the valley. "Do you see him? The one who burns? Who stalks so purposefully south across the Valley of Wight?"

Gideon took a careful step backward, shaking his head as if the motion could make the terrible titan disappear. His grip on the haft of the mace tightened as he remembered the oath he'd sworn with Donnal and Lillian, but he hesitated, his eyes following her pointing finger toward the burning behemoth. "What... what is it?" he asked, his voice trembling.

"We do not know," she said simply. "He speaks," she added, pointing again. "Not in our world, but in yours." Gideon looked, and saw that the titan's mouth was indeed slowly moving, but it made no sound apart from the chorus of the condemned grafted onto its body. "Wither do you wander, O king of hate and flame?" she wondered aloud.

"I don't understand," Gideon managed.

"You do not need to understand," the witch said, lowering her hand to grip the staff again. "Only to fear." Her expression turned somber as she glanced back at him. "You should flee, boy," she said, "before he sees you."

Gideon's neck flushed at the idea, and he was torn between duty and abject terror. To his great shame, all he could think of in that moment was to take the archoness and flee.

"Milady!" he called again, stepping closer and reaching out to rouse her from her stupor.

"Touch her not!" the witch warned sharply, and Gideon hesitated. "The pretty golden queen is broken, you see. She must not be disturbed before she is ready." The witch's face fixed on Gideon, and although he still couldn't see her eyes beneath her hood, he felt as though he was being studied. "Oh," she said sympathetically after a moment. "You're broken, too, aren't you?"

She shuffled forward, leaning on her staff, her shabby robe sweeping the ground as she approached him. "Yes, we can feel it in you.

Broken... no golden Light for the golden warrior of the gods?" She cocked her head at him. "What a tragedy, eh, sisters?" A number of female voices whispered in agreement from beneath the hood. "Tell us your name, boy," she said.

Gideon's jaw set. He had grown up hearing all the stories of witches and knew it was never wise to treat with them. All that was visible of her hooded face was the tip of a pale, crooked nose over a ragged set of lips pulled into the semblance of a predatory smile, and he was too afraid not to answer.

"Gideon," he said after an agonized moment. "Gideon Ballad."

"Ah," the witch said knowingly, "Ballad... a song — a strong song, for a strong boy." She nodded. "But you cannot touch the Holy Light. Why?"

"How do you know that?" he asked before he could stop himself. If Sir Cormac were there, he would have cloven the witch in two already, and cast her halves off the cliff with a battlecry. Gideon knew he should do the same, but he couldn't bring himself to strike the decrepit old woman with his mace. And even if he tried, he was sure she would just summon the bloody flock to consume him, or impale him with brambles like she had the others.

The witch shrugged. "We can see the broken places in you. In all things. We can mend you, Gideon Ballad." Her voice took on a singsong cadence as she spoke, almost hypnotically, and she shuffled closer, her staff scraping along the ground. "We can fix you, and let you touch the Light...."

"You're a witch," Gideon said stupidly, feeling confused and over-whelmed by all that was happening. He realized suddenly that the chanting had ceased. He didn't know when, but the only sounds now were the wind, the occasional earth-shaking footfalls of the titan, and the muttering and whispering from somewhere inside the witch's hood.

She laughed again. "Yes, boy, we are witches," she said, and a chorus of giggling voices echoed from beneath her hood. "We are the Sisters Seidh." She lifted her head, and Gideon could finally see her eyes. They held a terrible light beneath the greyed pupils, and behind her head, within the hood, as if looking over her shoulder, were other pairs of eyes and the shadowed features of other faces. The witch smiled at him, and he recoiled, taking a step back.

"Do not be afraid, boy," she said. "We will give you what you most desire, we will help you touch the Light...." She shuffled forward again, and Gideon continued to back away, not realizing that he'd been inching toward the precipice as he had spoken with her. His foot slipped on loose rocks, and he almost tumbled over the edge before catching himself.

"You... you killed James," he said, righting himself and struggling to remember that everything that had happened was because of the very witch — or witches — here in front of him. "Lillian, everyone in the chapel...."

Gideon was surprised when the old woman's shoulders began shaking with laughter. "Ah, yes, our little trick." She looked up at him, amusement crinkling the corners of her eyes, and a shower of different laughs followed from the faces within the hood behind her own. "Your hospitalers did not like our gift, we presume?"

Gideon's jaw set firmly at the jape. "The Light couldn't heal them," he said, even though the witch was obviously well aware of that fact.

"How did we do that? That's what you want to ask, yes?" the old woman pressed, lifting her twisted staff and poking him in the chest, forcing him to fight for balance on the cliff's edge. "How did we make such grievous wounds which even the Holy Light can't heal?"

She paused, and all eyes beneath the hood turned to him expectantly.

"Yes," he finally answered through gritted teeth. He wanted to know, had to know; perhaps he could use the answer to help the others somehow.

The witch snorted. "The Light is inviolable; that's what they teach you, yes? Pure and righteous, from the gods themselves!" She clucked her tongue to a round of dissent and disapproval from the voices behind her. "Those fools know nothing of the Light. A dagger handed to a toddler."

She shook her head and sighed, then looked back up at Gideon.

"But we will fix you," she offered again, the various pairs of eyes beneath the hood all fixed on his own. "Let you touch the Light you want so badly, that you think you understand." She paused, studying his eyes. "In exchange for a simple promise."

"What?" Gideon stammered, shaking his head, unsure what to do or how to answer. "What promise?" he asked against his better judgment.

The droning blast sounded again from the titan, shaking loose rocks from the mountainside, sending them skittering down the slope and off the edge of the precipice. The powerful sound knocked Gideon off balance again, and the witch reached out a withered, claw-like hand to steady him. He recoiled at her touch but regained his footing as the sickening chorus of pained shrieks and the hiss of boiling blood and charring sinews followed.

The witch let him go and turned, shuffling back to the archoness on the twisted throne. "Your golden queen," she said, approaching her and holding up a hand as if to stroke her cheek, but pausing in the air. "She is broken, too."

Gideon scrambled away from the cliff's edge and let loose a breath. "She can wield the Holy Light," he disagreed.

"Broken not like you," the witch snapped, "but in another way. We can help her."

"Why do you want to help her?" he demanded, his voice finally regaining some strength as he watched the archoness seated upon the witch-throne, completely unaware of what was happening around her.

"He wants to know why," one of the other voices said from beneath the hood.

"Tell him, sister," another urged.

The witch turned back to Gideon. "Come close, boy," she commanded, and he reluctantly approached her. "Look," she said, and a second pair of hands reached out from her right sleeve, clutching a swatch of woven cloth. Gideon grimaced but stood his ground. "Do you see?" the witch asked, showing him the weave.

"Look — the threads, the patterns. Hers are very important, but misaligned."

"Her threads aren't right," another whisper said.

The witch held up the swatch, and Gideon looked but saw nothing but a piece of clean, bright fabric. "I don't understand," he said after a moment, unsure what was expected of him.

"He doesn't understand," one of the voices sneered.

"Idiot boy," said another.

Gideon flinched, and the witch's second pair of hands retreated, hiding the fabric back within her sleeve. "Quiet now, sisters," she said. "The boy doesn't know any better." She turned back to Gideon. "We will make her threads right again," she said. "And we will fix yours, too, if you promise us."

"Promise you what?" he asked warily, a sinking feeling in the pit of his stomach.

The witch craned her neck to look up at him, and her expression was unreadable, but the sickly green twinkle behind her eyes and those others beneath the hood made him shiver. "You must promise to stay with her," she whispered. "You must be her loyal golden knight, no matter what happens, or who should try to come between you. If you do this, we will fix your pattern, and you will become a great warrior of your Holy Light...."

"Why are you offering this?" Gideon demanded. "What do you get out of it? What do you want?"

"You must swear!" another of the voices screeched from beneath the hood.

"She is your queen," the witch said, ignoring her sister's interjection. "She will need you in the times to come. Promise."

Gideon stared into her eyes for a moment before he could bear it no longer and looked away. What was he doing, trading words with a witch? His gaze drifted over to the archoness, sitting frozen, her fingers digging into the rotted wood of the throne, her mind lost.

"What's wrong with her?" Gideon asked. "Did you do something to her?"

"She is broken," the witch repeated, a cutting anger growing in her voice. "We will fix her."

Gideon closed his eyes and took a breath. The witch was offering him what he wanted more than anything else — to be able to wield the Holy Light, as it should have been. And in return, all they asked was for him to remain near the archoness, to defend her. Where was the peril in accepting an offer like that?

Gideon opened his eyes and met the witch's gaze, staring into the sickly green glimmer. "I promise," he said.

The witch grinned wide, revealing a mouthful of rotted teeth, and somewhere inside her cloak, a different pair of hands clapped excitedly. "He promised!" one of them cried gleefully.

She turned back to the archoness. "Now, we mend," she said, and multiple pairs of hands slithered back out from her sleeves as she leaned on her staff and began picking at the archoness's armor, removing her breastplate.

"What are you doing?" Gideon asked, alarmed. The witch didn't respond, but continued to unclasp the armor until it fell away, and then she pulled open the cleft in the woman's shirt, exposing the fair, freckled skin over her heart.

Gideon blushed and looked away, but only for a moment, as his eyes were drawn back to the scene as the witch aligned many of her hands, using her fingertips to press into the archoness's skin in an intricate pattern. At the same time, another pair of hands sneaked out from the robe and worked the linen swatch, tugging violently at it, picking at individual threads and twisting the entire thing, manipulating the weave. The varied voices from within the hood began another chant as the witch herself cast her eyes up to the churning clouds above and recited some spell or incantation in a language that sounded impossible to Gideon's ears.

The archoness's eyes finally shifted from their glassy fixation on the horizon. They met the witch's grey gaze as it was lowered, but she otherwise remained frozen, as if with fear, and the old crone intoned profane words as her fingertips danced in a jerking, stabbing motion over the other woman's heart. Tears began streaming from the archoness's eyes as both women's gazes were locked, and the chanting grew louder.

Gideon watched, transfixed, as the witch's many fingers pressed into the archoness's skin, and a faint glow bloomed beneath them. Her recitation grew louder, and the look on Lorica's face was one of despair and heartbreak as tears flowed down her cheeks, and the witch's chant came to a thunderous climax, and she pressed her fingertips deep into the archoness's chest. Then the crone leaned forward and whispered something he couldn't hear into the woman's ear.

The archoness screamed, a terrible, primal sound that echoed across the valley, and Gideon stumbled backward instinctively as the archoness collapsed, slumping in the witch-hewn throne, a sheen of sweat on her brow, her eyes closed and unresponsive. The witch pulled her fingers away, revealing a pattern of dozens of perfectly round scars on the archoness's flesh, over her heart: one for each decrepit fingertip. The set of hands holding the fabric swatch also retreated back into their sleeve.

Gideon's heart pounded, and he took a breath as the witch turned to face him. "You," she said gravely, and crooked a finger at him. "Come."

He looked between the archoness and the witch. He wanted to flee, not obey, but he feared what would happen if he did. Could they actually make him able to call on the Light. Were the gods offering him one final chance to become a paladin after all? The idea was monstrous, insane: that evil witches could grant him holy power. And yet... Gideon was intoxicated by the allure of desperate hope.

He slowly obeyed, unwilling to do what he should.

"What did you do to her?" he asked fearfully.

"She is fixed," the witch said simply, as if that should suffice. "Now, as to you," she said, and beckoned him again. "Take off your silly armor and open your shirt."

Gideon felt his face flush with embarrassment, but he did as she demanded, unclasping his beaten breastplate and peeling his shirt away to reveal his bared chest. His breath came fast with trepidation as the witch raised no fewer than seven hands to his chest, the bony, crooked fingers aligning themselves in a complex pattern and hovering over his skin. A separate pair of hands produced another bit of cloth, and it looked different from that which was used for the archoness: it was dull and frayed, like sackcloth, with a single tarnished gold thread laid atop, running the length of the swatch.

The witch began her recitation again, the voices beneath the hood chanting frantically from behind her. Gideon clenched his teeth as he stared down at her many encroaching fingers and braced himself, flexing against the hideous promise of her touch. He could feel the cold of her withered flesh hovering over his skin, and his heart beat wildly as he waited for the inevitable shock and pain the archoness had experienced.

As the witch's incantation reached its peak, her fingertips touched him, and his body seized up, like he'd been struck by lightning. Every muscle in his body contracted at once, and his eyes were drawn to the witch's dimmed pupils as if compelled.

He stared into her eyes and saw things. It was dark, but he could see the shapes of his life, of those he knew, wavering and wandering before him like a play. The paths were divergent, and he stood at a crossroads. No — not at, but just beyond. One path lay before him, and the others scattered from a pace behind, and as he saw everything that could have been, he wept, and his heart was pierced not by a witch's fingers, but by an irrevocable decision already made.

In the back of his mind, through the waves of lashing grief, he heard the Sisters Seidh whisper all at once.

"Golden warrior," they said in a cacophony. "The Black Chapel beckons thee...."

CHAPTER 37

SADIA

MADAM JALILA TOOK a deep breath and sat back, the stone medallion clutched in her hand, and Dalgrim tossed the censer on the table and flopped onto his back.

"Shaper's ringing hammers!" he cursed, wiping sweat from his forehead.

"By the gods," Jalila agreed, and her eyes were wide. "I have never encountered anything like that in all my years." Her guards both tried to help her to her feet, but she slapped their hands away, and they returned reluctantly to their posts by the door.

"Is it gone?" Sadia asked, cradling her sobbing brother, and the madam frowned.

"No," she said, shaking her head vehemently. "Whatever that was, it possesses him still — but it wasn't an ifrit."

"How do you know?"

Jalila took a breath and looked across her scattered ritual items. "I've summoned spirits before, both malevolent and benign, including ifriti. But none of them were like this, with that kind of... power, or presence."

She paused, her brow furrowing, and Sadia waited anxiously for her to continue. "The ritual managed to suppress its hold on him, but I cannot say for how long. He will need a more powerful and permanent intervention, one I can not provide."

"What do I do now?" Sadia asked, feeling hopeless. "Should I take him to another healer?" Roya had claimed there were many different temples and holy places in Emra'adid, but the suggestion felt foolish even to her.

"I suppose you could," the madam said, frowning again. "But I don't think they'll be of any greater help than the jadhari was. This is beyond the capabilities of simple priests and temple clerics."

"But... who else can I go to?" Sadia demanded, desperation creeping into her voice. "There's no one else who can help us, is there?"

Madam Jalila was quiet, and Sadia felt herself breaking inside, her little brother's cries growing fainter as the madam's words echoed in her head.

"Not anyone you will find here, no," Jalila said, and Sadia's shoulders slumped as Ibrahim slowly started to calm. "Have faith — I know of a place that may be able to help him. It is not close, but if the rumors I've heard are to be believed, it will be worth the journey."

"What is it? Where?" Sadia asked hopefully.

The madam glanced at Dalgrim. "Have you heard of The Ringed City of Sagrada?"

"Sagrada?" Dalgrim asked, struggling to sit up and peer incredulously at the woman.

"Yes," Jalila answered confidently. "You've heard of it?"

"Oh, aye," the dwarf said, eyebrow cocked. "Myths and tall tales are rife about the place. But one thing's for certain — it's been locked up tight with nary a peep from within those massive walls since before I was old enough to sprout my beard."

The madam inclined her head. "True, but those myths and tall tales are relevant." She turned back to Sadia. "The city was long a famous destination of pilgrimage, renowned throughout the world for the healing and miracles that travelers could experience there."

"But it's... closed to travelers now?" Sadia asked, glancing at Dalgrim, who took a deep breath and nodded. "Why?"

Madam Jalila pursed her lips. "No one knows exactly. It is called 'The Ringed City' because of the huge walls and gates which surround and fortify the place. One day, more than a century ago, those gates shut, and no one has passed through them since. Many speculate the reason, but none know."

"Then why would we go there?" Sadia pressed, failing to understand.

"I have it on good authority that activity has been seen within the great walls," the madam said carefully.

One of Dalgrim's bushy eyebrows rose suspiciously. "Good authority, eh?"

"The coin from my emporium goes to ensuring whispers and secrets reach my ears from all over the world, my dear." Jalila crossed her legs beneath her scarlet dress and drew her shoulders back, sitting straighter. "But in any case, I have been quietly searching for a trustworthy individual to mount an expedition to investigate these claims. If the gates of Sagrada are to be reopened, well...." She smiled to herself. "That would be quite valuable information indeed."

The madam seemed lost in thought for a long moment as Sadia's leg bounced impatiently, and Dalgrim shifted on his big cushion.

"If Sagrada is alive again," Jalila finally continued, "I believe it would be your brother's best — and perhaps only — hope." She lay a hand on Sadia's knee. "It will be a long journey, my dear," she cautioned. "The Ringed City is very far, across the Salient Sea, and the lands between make for difficult travel."

Sadia looked at Jalila, then down at Ibi. The thought of traveling even farther from Qasira, from Yusuf and her sisters, terrified her; the memory of the look in Ibrahim's eyes as he struggled against the thing inside him, though, was almost too much for her to bear. "It doesn't matter," she finally said, taking a calming breath. "I have no choice. If you think this city is where Ibrahim can find a cure, I'll go."

Madam Jalila gave her a grim smile. "I admire your tenacity. And I will aid you however I may. To start," she said, glancing down at Dalgrim, "we must secure you a means of arriving to the Ringed City."

Dalgrim cocked an eyebrow at her, then shook his head vigorously. "Oh no," he said, climbing to his feet, "I'll not have any part of this madness."

"Come, come," the madam cooed, smiling sweetly. "You're always searching for your next great opportunity, aren't you?"

"Aye, and that's how I know this one stinks," the dwarf grumbled. "The *Mollysocks* will be headed back north to the Dwarven Kingdoms," he announced, dusting off his shabby robes. "I've had enough of demons, ghosties, or whatever in the blazes that thing was," he said, gesturing at Ibrahim. "'Dwarves should never leave the mountain, Dalgrim' — that's what Grandpappy Glintstone once told me, may he rest in stone, and lo and behold, I've decided he was right! Now, if you'll simply pay me for the goods I've brought you, I'll be on my way." He held out a hand to the madam, but she didn't take her eyes from his.

"My dear, please," she said, her voice dripping, "you owe me twice again what you brought on that cart today."

The dwarf seemed surprised. "Truly?" he asked, and the madam nodded, a small smile tugging at her lips. "Ach!" he said, throwing his hands up. "Put it toward my debt, then! But I'm not dragging the poor *Mollysocks* across the sea and down jungle rivers to chase phantoms in a dead city for you!"

"If you go to Sagrada, I'll wipe your debt clean."

Dalgrim waved a hand dismissively. "I'll just bring you back a hull-full of dwarven goods in a few years, once things have calmed down for me around the great desert cities." He took a step back, toward the door. "Cannae pay my debts if I'm a dead man, now can I?"

"What about your debt to this poor girl?" the madam pressed, gesturing at Sadia. "You rescued her and her brother from Qasira, yes?"

The dwarf tugged at the neck of his shabby robes. "Well, not to get too particular, but the lass paid me for passage," he corrected, and Jalila's eyes blazed.

"You charged a poor orphan girl trying to escape a city besieged by violent cultists?" she demanded, her voice like a whip.

Dalgrim's cheeks colored, and he scratched at his beard. "Well, er, I was a bit... preoccupied with other things at the time. The Qasiran city guard mistook me for someone else, you see, and—"

"Enough, Dalgrim," the woman said, interrupting him. "You began something in Qasira when you took them onboard the *Mollysocks*. Something you need to finish. I know enough about the dwarven Creed of Stone and Forge to understand that much, at least."

The dwarf barked a mirthless laugh. "Ha! The Creed also talks about dwarves making a good reputation for themselves when traveling the surface world. How's that going for me, eh?"

The woman's eyes narrowed. "I also know very well that you're a greedy little bastard, and if you're not going to do this because you've a shred of decency in you, then you'll do it for money."

Dalgrim gave her a distrustful look. "Pay me just to have it go back to buying out my debt?"

"No," the madam retorted sharply, obviously infuriated at his stubbornness. "If you take the girl to Sagrada, I'll erase your debts and pay you besides."

"It'd have to be a fortune," the dwarf scoffed, waving her off and turning to Sadia. "Listen, lass, you seem a good sort, and I wish you the best — truly. But there's no chance in any afterlife you choose that I'm having that thing aboard the *Mollysocks*," he said firmly, pointing to Ibrahim. He held her gaze for a lingering moment, and she saw a genuine compassion in his eyes before he shook his head sadly and turned to stalk toward the door.

"I'll give you a thousand gold drahm," Madam Jalila called after him, and Dalgrim froze.

He was still for a moment, considering, then shook his head. "Make it ten thousand," he said, waving her off for a second time. "It's all useless to a dead man. Find yourself some other reckless soul."

Lu came up beside Sadia and rested a hand on her shoulder. He gave her a sad smile, but turned and followed the dwarf nonetheless. Jalila's guards stepped in front of Dalgrim as he made to push through the door, but the madam signaled for them to allow him passage, and he and Lu disappeared through the doorway.

"Fret not, my dear," Jalila said as Sadia stared after the two men. "I've dealt with Dalgrim Glintstone a dozen times over, and there's a good chance he'll yet come around. Even if he doesn't, though, we'll find you another means of getting to Sagrada."

Sadia stared at the woman. "I... why are you helping us?"

"Let us be clear," Jalila said firmly, "I have been seeking someone to send to Sagrada for some time. Dalgrim is not only surprisingly capable, but also arguably mad, with the added benefit of being indebted to me." She looked wistfully at the door the dwarf had disappeared through. "I honestly never thought he'd refuse me." She took a deep breath and returned her attention to Sadia. "The fact of the matter is that I was willing to pay him to accomplish my own aims.

"But let us also be clear that I'm not a cruel woman," she added, softening her voice. "Your brother is in mortal peril, as far as I can tell, and you're willing to do anything to help him, yes?"

Ibrahim squirmed in Sadia's arms, and she looked down at him as he let out a deep breath and stretched, his eyes closed and his brow smooth. His hand fell on hers as she held him, and he grasped one of her fingers as though he was afraid she would disappear if he let go.

The last hint of resentment she'd felt toward him at the temple melted away, and she pulled him a little tighter against her.

"I chose him," Sadia said, looking back up at the madam. "I'll do whatever he needs me to."

Jalila regarded her carefully for a moment before walking over to the windows and pulling aside the thick curtains.

"Once upon a time, when I was very young, I also found myself alone," she explained, staring out onto the sunset-washed city of Emra'a-did. "Young and ignorant and without any means of fending for myself.

And then someone showed me kindness, gave me a chance." She frowned. "Sometimes, it's all a young woman needs in order to make something of herself. To become someone. It's a small thing, really, in the end. And if my coin can secure both your ends and mine, it's the least I can do."

"Thank you," Sadia whispered. She was grateful for the madam's aid, certainly, but her kindness felt colder than what she'd received from Roya at the Gentle Djinni.

"If Dalgrim doesn't take my offer, there are a few others I could turn to," Jalila mused, frowning. "They're not my first choice, but time is now precious, given your brother's state, and they will see you to Sagrada unmolested, at least. And bring me back enough news to slake my thirst."

Sadia gave an empty nod. She had no idea what the future held, and it was overwhelming and terrifying.

Jalila gave an exasperated sigh. "Now," she said, turning back to the girl. "Whoever takes you on this journey, you need to understand that your brother is in a constant state of spiritual battle, wrestling against whatever it is dwelling within him." Sadia swallowed the lump in her throat at those words. "I will send a few things with you, though, to help keep him strong." The madam drew Sadia back over to the table and her trunk.

"First of all, this talisman." She picked up the intricate, hand-shaped pendant and carefully slid the leather string necklace past Ibrahim's frail head, laying the cool stone against his bare chest. "It is a symbol called the hamsa — a protective hand, said to ward against the evil eye. Exceedingly appropriate, given the circumstances," she mused. "I wasn't sure if it would work in your brother's case, but it certainly seems to have done so. Keep it around his neck at all times.

"Also these oils — a special blend of myrrh and calamus in oil pressed from the sacred olives of Thrakia. It suppresses malevolent spiritual forces." She held out two glass phials, and Sadia took them carefully.

"You can gently rub a drop into his forehead and chest," the madam explained. "It should help to keep him lucid and alert, and it will protect him from the furious spirit that resides in him."

"Thank you," Sadia murmured, staring down at the small bottles in her hand before tucking them into the little pouch tied to her waist.

"These are not enough to fully control the forces at work, though," the madam cautioned her. "They may keep him safe for now, but they will not last forever. The sort of evil inside him hungers and grows. You must hurry, child. You must make it to Sagrada and find a cure, or...."

"Or what?" Sadia asked, fearfully.

Jalila pursed her lips and stared at Ibrahim as he drifted closer to sleep. "Or it will devour him, and consume him completely."

Sadia shuddered and gently stroked Ibi's hand as the madam looked kindly on them. "It will not come to that, dear," she assured her, though her tone didn't convey much confidence. "Not if we can help it."

Dalgrim's angry voice came muffled from the ground floor, and Jalila sighed. "Come — let's go try to persuade our stubborn little friend one last time."

She took Sadia's elbow and led her to the door, the guards falling in line behind them as the madam escorted her and her little brother downstairs.

"Listen, you half-bearded, perfumed, pompous twit!" Dalgrim's voice was shouting as they reached the balcony overlooking the emporium. "Your sister already claimed everything as payment, now tell your goonies to let me pass!"

Sadia peered over the rail at the scene unfolding below. The dwarf and Lu were just inside the door, facing off against four guards blocking their exit.

Cyrus stood nearby with his arms crossed, sneering down at Dalgrim. "Do you take me for a fool, Dwarf? You still owe Jalila a tidy little—"

"Aye!" Dalgrim barked angrily over the man. "I do take you for a damned fool! And worse besides!"

Cyrus bristled. "If Jalila was willing to release you despite your persistent debt, she would come and tell me herself! She knows better than to make such an arrangement with a lying, conniving little rat like you."

"Cyrus!" Madam Jalila's commanding voice cut through the commotion, and all the men froze and turned to look up at her. She descended the steps with her hands clasped before her, her head held high, and her expression stern.

"Yes, sister?" Cyrus replied, bowing slightly.

"You and your men are dismissed for the evening," the madam commanded. "Leave our guests to me."

Cyrus hesitated, but when Jalila shot him a scathing look, he quickly acquiesced and ordered his men away from the door. "As you wish, dear sister," he said, bowing deeply again. "Best not to keep the sultan's men waiting, anyhow...."

"Sultan's men?" Dalgrim repeated, and his eyes narrowed suspiciously. He stepped up to the wide double doors and opened one just enough to look outside, then quickly shut it again. He glanced up at Lu, who hung his head and sighed, and then over at Cyrus. "You bastard!" he roared, diving at him as the guards intervened.

"Surely you didn't think you could come and go in the city without their knowledge, did you?" the man taunted, straightening his tunic. "You're a rancid little dwarf, and you must pay for your crimes."

Dalgrim wrestled in vain against the much larger guards, trying to get at Cyrus, murder in his beady eyes.

"Oh, Cyrus, what have you done?" Jalila asked, frowning. "Off with you!" she snapped, clearly irked. "Begone!"

Her brother bowed again, grinning wickedly at Dalgrim before carrying himself proudly away from the entrance. Dalgrim stared menacingly after the man, and the guards kept a firm grip on him.

"What did you do to have the sultan's men on you?" the madam demanded, moving closer to the dwarf and staring down at him imperiously.

"Well," Dalgrim grunted as he tried to pull away from the guards' iron grip, "the *Mollysocks* was involved in an accident on the river yesterday, and some foul lies have apparently circulated that she was the cause."

"They probably looking for these, too," Lu suggested, casually lifting the string of jewelry out of Dalgrim's pocket again, and Jalila fumed.

"You just can't help yourself, can you?" she hissed. "Everywhere you go, trouble follows, but somehow you're never the one at fault."

She waved a hand, and the guards released Dalgrim. He ripped the jewelry out of Lu's hand and stuffed it back in his pocket. "Listen, Jalila," he said, looking up at the woman, "you've got a powerful influence in Emra'adid — you can make all this go away for me, I know you can."

The madam scoffed indignantly. "This is a mess of your own creation, Dalgrim. Why on earth would I sully my reputation with Sultan Hamurad to help you?"

She and Dalgrim stared at each other, and as the moment hung, something seemed to pass between them, and Dalgrim's eyes grew wide as the madam smiled triumphantly.

"Oh, no, Jalila, no, no, no!"

"Oh, yes," Madam Jalila responded confidently. "If you want my help, you'll agree to take the girl to Sagrada."

Dalgrim huffed and groused. "Well, that's just a wonderful choice you're giving me — get locked up in the sultan's dungeons or serve as your lapdog to travel halfway across the world with a demon-baby to poke the walls of a dead city!"

The madam nodded and waited patiently. They watched as the dwarf wrestled with the decision, glancing back out through the doors and tugging his beard. He looked up at Lu but found no help as the easterner stared back at him and shrugged, seeming unperturbed by either option.

"Ach, fine!" Dalgrim finally exclaimed. "I'll take the lass to Sagrada for a thousand drahm — you win!"

Madam Jalila's smile never faltered, even as she gave him a bemused look. "I think not, Dalgrim. You'll do this in exchange for my aid with the Sultan's men. Using my influence to allow you to remain a free dwarf is quite the price to pay as it is."

"Ah yes," Dalgrim answered, scratching his bald spot. "That it is, that it is. My debt then, we'll simply wipe it clean, as you said." He coughed and peeked from under one bushy eyebrow before quickly looking back down at the ground remorsefully.

Madam Jalila sighed. "You are shameless beyond imagining," she said, shaking her head in disbelief. "I thought perhaps there was a tiny part of you that might be driven to do the right thing. But you'd be willing to say or do anything for your own gain, wouldn't you?"

She turned and looked at Sadia. "Do I dare send you with the likes of Dalgrim Glintstone, my dear?" she asked. "We could find another escort for you, someone less... conniving." After a moment, it became apparent to Sadia that she was actually being asked her opinion.

Sadia looked at her little brother, then over at Dalgrim. Both he and Lu looked like scolded children, staring at their feet and shuffling uncomfortably. The madam was right: the two drunkards and their hobbled-together boat were perhaps the worst Sadia could have fallen in with. But she had, and for all their flaws, the odd pair was the only reason they'd escaped Qasira in the first place.

"When I was trying to escape the cult," she began slowly, "everyone turned me away. I was desperate, but no one would help me. Dalgrim was the only one who even bothered to listen to me." The dwarf glanced up sheepishly at her. "And even though he was fleeing the Qasiran guard anyway and took the only coin I had, he and Lu were still the ones who saved us. They didn't have to.

"So," she finished, swallowing hard and holding the woman's gaze, "I... I trust Dalgrim. I don't know why, but I do."

Jalila's flawless eyebrows rose in surprise. She considered for a moment, then looked back at the dwarf and shook her head.

"Very well," she conceded with a reluctant frown. "Dalgrim, I will take care of the Sultan's men. And erase your debts. But know this — my connections extend well beyond Emra'adid. I have associates well situated in every city on the Salient Sea, as far as the West Umbrals and even within Glinthammer beneath the Auric Bastions. If word ever reaches me that you abandoned this girl before seeing her to Sagrada, I will find you. I will track you to the farthest corner of the world, and I will have your bearded head on a platter."

The dwarf blanched. "Of course," he said, nodding vigorously. "Understood. Lu will make sure I do exactly as I say, won't you, Lu?"

The swordsman looked up and quickly flashed a reassuring smile at the madam.

Madam Jalila nodded. She took Sadia's hand, leading her past the dwarf and Lu, and pushed the door open.

The setting sun bathed the street and buildings outside in a warm, orange glow, and Sadia stepped out into the last rays of daylight. Across the flagstone street stood an orderly formation of armed guardsmen.

"Madam Jalila!" a man's voice came from the throng of soldiers. One stepped forward wearing a dark blue turban and bowed deeply. "We received a report that a wanted man had infiltrated your establishment, but I did not want to intrude on your business."

Jalila regarded him cooly. "Commander Heshram, is it not?" Sadia glanced over her shoulder and saw Dalgrim and Lu still hiding behind the door. Reza, Mariam, and her husband were all waiting a little way off with the now-empty cart Dalgrim had borrowed from Suleiman, looking at the guards with some trepidation.

"Yes, madam," the commander said, bowing again.

"It is quite unexpected that you would come to my emporium," the madam purred. "Who is it you're seeking, precisely?"

"A dwarf by the name of Dalgrim Glintstone," the commander answered. "He is sought for redress for various crimes spanning years, and we have had multiple reports of a dwarf of his description arriving in the city yesterday."

Jalila cocked her head. "I see. I trust you have evidence against him?"

"Of course, madam," Heshram answered, pulling out a sheaf of parchment. "He stands accused of causing a devastating collision on the Tajari River; the theft of valuables; chicanery; sophistry in a court of law; defamation of a number of important persons; and general villainy not otherwise specified."

Madam Jalila glanced over her shoulder at where Dalgrim was hiding, her eyes narrowed dangerously, as the commander continued. "Several merchants, captains of river vessels, and the sultan's own steward have filed grievances, and we have witnesses."

"These are very serious charges," Jalila acknowledged after clearing her throat. Sadia saw her gesture subtly behind her to Dalgrim and Lu, beckoning them forward. "Commander," she said as the pair stepped out into the sunset, carefully making their way toward the cart, "do join me within so we may discuss these charges in detail."

The commander started as he saw Dalgrim and Lu. "Madam, that's—"

"No one of consequence, I assure you," Jalila interrupted him, holding out her hand. "Come, please." The commander looked between her and the wanted men, then at his soldiers, and finally back to the madam.

He swallowed hard and nodded. "Of course, madam," he said, and Sadia marveled at Jalila's influence over him. The commander was an imposing, authoritative man, yet the madam had him wrapped around her finger. "Stand fast," he muttered to his soldiers before moving to take the woman's offered hand.

"Very good," Jalila said, and even her smile was intimidating. "I am sure we can resolve this unfortunate misunderstanding."

As she ushered the commander into her emporium, Lu laid a hand on Sadia's shoulder and nodded her toward the cart, keeping a wary eye on the loitering soldiers. Sadia caught a final, fleeting glance from Madam Jalila, and the woman gave her an elegant nod.

Sadia returned the gesture much less gracefully, and then Lu led her away from Madam Jalila's and the group of soldiers eyeing them suspiciously. Reza broke away from Heidroksimos as they neared the cart and ran up to her. "Is Ibi alright?" he asked hopefully.

"For now," Sadia answered quietly as Lu offered her a hand. He helped her and then Mariam up onto the back of the empty cart.

Reza leapt up and sat beside her as the half-giant stooped and lifted the cart by both handles and began following Dalgrim back toward the Gentle Djinni. "Does that mean we can go back to Qasira now?" the boy asked, sounding forlorn.

Sadia frowned. "Not yet, Reza. But...." She wanted to say 'soon' but couldn't. "We will." Reza gave a heavy sigh and rested his head against her arm.

CHAPTER 38

GIDEON

A LOUD, deep sound blasted Gideon awake, and he found himself on his back on the precipice, staring up at the lightning tracing the under-bellies of the clouds. He winced as he sat up and stared down at his open shirt. A dozen or more perfectly round scars were arrayed over his heart. He hesitantly touched one and shuddered at the foggy memory. Gideon scrambled to put his breastplate back on and rose to retrieve the discarded banner.

In the distance, the smoldering titan continued its slow, inexorable march, the screams of those trapped and melting upon it mercifully coming fainter than before. At the edge of the precipice, the archoness was on her knees, her holy tome laid out before her, its pages fluttering in the wind as she pored over them.

She was muttering frantically to herself as she flipped the pages of the tome madly, her gauntleted fingers trembling as she did so. "No, no, no," she kept whispering, almost like a prayer, her voice laced with desperation.

Gideon slowly approached her, still disoriented and confused about what had happened or how long he'd been unconscious. He remembered finding her on the twisted throne, and then... the witch.

As the disjoined memories returned, he glanced around fearfully, but there was no sign of the old witch anywhere. Then he remembered making a promise, and he was filled with a despair that nearly made him moan aloud. What had he done? What had he agreed to?

To protect her, he remembered vaguely, and he looked up at the archoness.

"Milady?" he asked quietly. "Are... are you alright?"

She whipped her head around to look at him, and her eyes were filled with terror, a look he'd never seen from her before. "The words..." she sputtered, her hands quaking as she held the fluttering pages down against the wind. "They're... They're not right." Her eyes had utterly lost even a trace of the powerful glow they had held since he'd met her, but they glistened wetly as she looked up at him.

The archoness stumbled to her feet and clutched Gideon by the arm. Her gauntlets dug painfully into his skin beneath his chain sleeve, and he winced. "We shouldn't have come here!" she breathed, her voice quavering as she held his gaze with wide eyes, the blood that had run from her ears staining her fair skin with dark flakes. "The Sisters, they...." She paused, looking wildly over her shoulder at the empty precipice, then up at the titan moving across the valley, dominating the skyline. "Oh, gods, no!" she wailed, her grip tightening around his arms.

Gideon grimaced, stunned at the radical shift in the woman's demeanor. He shrugged her off carefully and laid a hand on her shoulder, drawing her attention back to him. "What is that thing, milady?" he asked, glancing up at the titan as the burning heat within it slowly built in a violent orange glow beneath the blackened slag.

She took a hitching breath as tears welled in her eyes. "It's... it is inevitable," she whimpered, and as the word passed her lips, they watched the titan's smoldering inner fire reach its zenith, and a blast of boiling air, flames, and angry smoke visibly exploded out from it. There was a pause as the wall of air thundered toward them across the valley, and when it hit them, both flinched as the devastating sound and hot air crashed into them yet again.

The archoness wailed miserably and fell to her knees again, pawing at her sacred tome and fumbling her gauntleted fingers across the vellum pages. The cliff quaked beneath their feet, and Gideon looked up the mountain as the earth started shaking violently, rubble skittering and clattering down the slopes around them.

Another ear-splitting crack made him whirl around and look up the slope of the mountain they were perched on, away to their left. Gideon's stomach dropped as he watched a huge chunk of the very mountain itself break away and fall slowly down, grinding away against the slope as it plummeted toward them on its way to the valley floor far below.

Gideon rounded on the archoness, who was still bowed over her tome, mumbling frantically and sniffling through tears, as if trying to pray. "We need to go," he said urgently, trying to grab her and lift her to her feet, but she flailed her arms free, too engrossed even to look at him. "Milady, please!"

She threw him off again, violently, flipping wildly through the pages of her book, and the mountain shuddered what felt like a death throe beneath them. Across the valley and on all sides, the mountains were coming apart, huge chunks breaking and crumbling off of them and sliding down the slopes in avalanches of boulders and shale.

The ground dropped beneath their feet, and Gideon had to scramble to stay upright as the precipice shuddered and slowly started descending. He cast aside the banner of the Holy Order and grabbed the archoness with both hands to wrestle her away from the edge. Finally, she wasn't strong enough to resist him, and she just managed to snatch up her holy book as he dragged her toward the tunnel in the wall behind them, the slope growing steeper under his feet as the mountains continued to inexplicably fall apart.

The entire cliff they had been perched on was coming loose from the mountainside, slowly but surely, and as Gideon pushed into the tunnel with the archoness in tow, he prayed silently for Donnal, Sir

Cormac, and all the others, having no idea what to do but flee. The whole passage quaked around them as the precipice bearing the twisted throne collapsed away from the mountainside and plunged into the valley below. Gideon pressed on, dragging the archoness along with him while she continued to mutter and fret incoherently.

After a long moment of stumbling through the cramped, dark passage as the ground shook beneath them, Gideon caught a soft, orange glow at the tunnel's end. They pushed forward, and as they came out of the tunnel into the light, he steeled himself to be back on the precipice, still trapped in the Sisters' maddening maze.

Instead, they found themselves emerging from the side of the huge, blackened tree they had first entered, dawn cresting the horizon and splashing an orange glow across the skeletal trees of the forest. The unnatural fog that had weighed so heavily over the hill had dissipated, replaced by the natural pools of mist that dotted the early summer morning landscape.

The army of bramble monstrosities was somehow in ruins, mostly fallen apart and returned to their natural state, and were still. Gideon helped the archoness down the rough-hewn steps, and as their feet touched damp earth, she fell to her knees and laid her precious book down to open it again, seemingly obsessed. Gideon glanced around for signs of any other survivors of their company, but saw no one. The morning was eerily calm and quiet after the chaos of the collapse in the witches' realm.

"Donnal!" he called hoarsely, hoping against hope to see his friend step out from behind a tree. But there was no answer, and Donnal didn't appear. "Sir Cormac?" he called out again, less hopeful.

An angry grunt sounded from behind them, and Gideon whirled to see Battlesister Dawnhammer burst out of the crumbling hollow in the tree. She blinked against the blood-red rays of dawn, then quickly turned to help someone behind her.

Gideon ran over and watched her drag a limp body from under the arms out into the open air. A shower of dirt and debris obscured the tunnel, but after only a moment, Sir Cormac stumbled out just as the tunnel collapsed on itself, and the tree shuddered violently, a huge crack racing up the length of the blackened wood. His armor, face, and even his huge mustache were stained with blood and dirt.

The big knight scrambled back to his feet and flung himself toward the collapsed tunnel. "No!" he bellowed angrily, tearing at the wall of rotted wood and wet earth that had been shaken loose and now flooded the hollow. "The others are still in there!" he cried, and looked wildly over his shoulder. "Ballad, get over here and help me clear a path!"

Gideon started toward him but was halted as Gerda reached out and grabbed his wrist. She was kneeling beside the mangled body, desperately trying to hold a number of large, ragged wounds closed. Having discarded her steel gauntlets, her small, pale hands were stained with blood as she tried to stem the flow. She pulled him down beside her, and Gideon finally looked at the man's face.

It was Donnal. His face was pale, his lips white, and his eyes closed. Gideon fell to his knees beside his friend, shaking, unsure what to do or think.

"There's no time, Cormac!" Gerda cried, guiding Gideon's hands over another of Donnal's gaping wounds to hold it closed. Her eyes flitted up to the huge, trembling branches overhead. "The whole thing's coming down!"

Gideon tore his eyes from the gory mess of Donnal's chest to glance over at Sir Cormac, who didn't stop tearing into the wall as he looked over his shoulder, panting. "I'll not leave them behind," he growled. The knight's jaw was set, but Gideon could see the fear and despair in his eyes at the thought of leaving his recruits and fellow paladins stuck on the other side of the collapse.

Before Gerda could protest, a deep, echoing knock sounded from the massive trunk, and it shuddered, its dead wood groaning as if in agony. Then, a deafening crack split the air as one of the huge, reaching branches above broke free, shattering near the base and entering a free fall directly above them.

"Cormac!" Battlesister Dawnhammer cried desperately, still struggling valiantly to keep Donnal alive despite the certain death plummeting toward them.

Gideon laid himself over Donnal protectively as Sir Cormac roared in frustration and tore himself away from the tree, dashing toward them and tackling the archoness to drag her over to the others. As the titanic branch continued its plunge, the dead trunk began collapsing in on itself, its other limbs shearing off as it crumbled, just as the mountains in the witches' valley had.

Sir Cormac threw the archoness toward Gideon, then knelt over them all and raised his arm aloft. A brilliant, golden arc of Holy Light burst to life at his bidding, forming a protective dome over the group a heartbeat before the first plummeting branch reached them. The enormous length of wood shattered into a shower of splinters as it collided with the Light, the pieces scattering and piling up over them as the tree continued to come apart.

More and more fragments of the evil, shattered tree pounded against Sir Cormac's holy barrier, and the old man grunted and strained against the constant impacts.

"Hold!" Battlesister Gerda shouted, and she reached over to lay one small hand over his armored one, keeping the other over Donnal's most egregious wound. "Hold, Eustace," she said again, and her touch seemed to bolster him. Sir Cormac clenched his mighty jaw and roared as he held against the onslaught.

The cacophony of splitting wood and crumbling rock grew and grew as the huge, dead tree came down around them. Gideon clutched his unconscious friend to his chest, feeling his wounds continue to bleed through his fingers, powerless to do anything but cling on and hope. Finally, the crashing din of breaking branches and splintering bark slowed to a trickle, and after a long moment, Sir Cormac let his arm fall, and he slumped over, spent.

The golden barrier winked out of existence, and a shower of smaller debris rained down on them. Gideon hunched over to protect Donnal's face and wounds, then slowly shrugged a chunk of wood off his back as he lifted his head to survey the destruction around them.

A cool dawn breeze blew across the scene, sweeping away the hanging cloud of dust. Through the pile of broken limbs around them, Gideon could see that the bulk of the great, blackened trunk was gone, lying mostly in splintered chunks across the hilltop. The larger fragments had flattened many of the smaller surrounding trees, and great upheavals of earth lifted from the slopes where plunging branches had impaled the ground like hurled spears.

Gideon took a shaking breath as his eyes finally returned to Donnal, still unmoving beneath him. Gerda was simultaneously trying to hold a wound shut and cast about for any form of rag or cloth available.

"I cannae stop the bleeding," she muttered bitterly, failing to find anything other than their bare hands to stem the dark, scarlet flow.

Sir Cormac lifted his head, breathing hard, and removed his helmet to wipe the sweat from his brow, leaving a smear of muddied dust across his forehead. "They're witch-wounds, Gerda," he panted, and Gideon's heart sank.

"We have to do something!" he cried miserably, cradling Donnal's head in his lap as he watched the blood from the wounds ebb gradually slower through his own fingers.

"We brought no healers, boy," Sir Cormac said with a grunt as he lifted himself unsteadily to his feet. "And even if we had, you saw what happened in the chapel, and at the village — you know those wounds won't heal."

"But..." Gideon looked back down at Donnal's ruined body, and his vision blurred as shameful tears welled. "I can't let him die," he said, his voice quavering. "I promised."

"He fought bravely," the old paladin said, looking down on Donnal. "I found him beside one of the witch-beasts that he'd hacked to pieces before succumbing." Gideon felt the man's gauntlet rest heavily on his shoulder. "There's no shame in a death like that."

Gideon ground his teeth as he wrestled to force Donnal's wounds closed, but to no avail. Would he have to watch him die, powerless, as he had James? Their redheaded friend's pallid face loomed in Gideon's mind, the final drop of his curly head as the life left him. He never wanted to say goodbye like that again.

His vision cleared as the tears finally fell, and Sir Cormac's words broke something inside him. "No," he said defiantly through gritted teeth, and he turned his head up to look at the two paladins. "I can't wield the Light, but you can — you have to save him!"

Sir Cormac frowned, and he removed his hand from Gideon's shoulder. "No, Ballad," he said firmly, "we cannot."

"But you have to try!" Gideon demanded angrily, looking between them both. "He's a good man, and it's your duty to look after him. You can't just let him die like this when you could use the Light to heal him!"

"You forget yourself, boy," Sir Cormac growled dangerously. "None of us here swore the Oath of Weal, and we cannot—"

"Damn your oaths!" Gideon cried furiously. "You claim to serve the gods, but you'd let him die when you could save him!"

"Enough!" the old man thundered, his gauntleted fingers clinking as they closed into fists. "You dishonor your friend's sacrifice! His fate is one we'll all share someday. You can't change that."

Gideon sneered and turned to Gerda. "Please, battlesister, you can save him."

She shook her head gravely. "Listen to Sir Cormac," she said quietly, still holding her hands firm on Donnal's wounds. "You'll bid farewell to many more friends before the gods take you. Take a moment to say goodbye, lad."

Gideon despaired as he realized no help was to be had from either of them. He looked back down at Donnal, and his eyes traced over the contours of his pale face, void of the perpetual smirk he always wore. His friend's chest still moved slowly, his lips almost purple as death came to take him. After James, Gideon wasn't sure he could stand to watch another close friend go so soon. But it seemed he had no choice, so he closed his eyes and tried to steel himself to have Donnal die in his arms.

"I'm sorry," he whispered, memories of their time in training together rising unbidden and stinging the backs of his eyes. "I'm sorry, Nefteli."

We will fix you... the words of the Sisters Seidh rose in the back of his head. *We will fix your weave, let you touch the Light.*

Could it have been real? Could the witches have fulfilled their promise and made him capable of invoking the Holy Light? Gideon knew it was an insane idea, but a sudden hope surged in his chest as he began to wonder.

Taking a deep breath to steady himself, he tried to calm his mind and focus on Donnal's shallow breath and pallid, clammy skin beneath his fingers. Gideon recited a silent prayer more fervent and desperate than any he had ever uttered before, opening himself fully to the grace of the gods, entreating them to use him as a conduit for their Holy Light.

Long moments passed, and nothing happened. Gideon squeezed his eyes tighter and redoubled his focus, reciting another prayer, screaming it in his mind and furiously willing his connection to the Light.

Then, a warmth touched the top of his head, his face, and the backs of his hands as they rested on Donnal's broken form. Gideon opened his eyes, and the orange haze of dawn wasn't the only light shining down on them. A shaft of golden, Holy Light formed a wide circle around him and Donnal, and its warmth and radiance were nearly overwhelming.

He took a gasping breath as the heat of the Holy Light dried the tears on his cheeks, and he watched as the ragged wounds across his friend's body slowly began to mend, their edges working back together and knitting new flesh in their wake.

Donnal coughed, and Gideon held his breath as his eyes fluttered open, then widened as he stared up at Gideon.

"By the gods' many graces," Sir Cormac breathed, his mouth agape beneath his bloodied white mustache. A moment earlier, the big paladin had seemed ready to strike Gideon with an armored hand for his disrespect to the gods, but now he stared on in awe.

Gideon met his gaze briefly, then caught the battlesister's dour expression as she took her hands away and sat back to watch the golden pillar thrum its healing Light down onto Donnal.

Gideon looked at the illuminated area around him, shocked that it was actually happening. The Sisters Seidh had promised to mend him. And it seemed they had.

"Yes," a thrilled hiss came from beside him, and Gideon's gaze was drawn over to the archoness, who was finally looking up from her tome. "Yes," she breathed again, her eyes wide and shimmering, not with the Holy Light but with unshed tears. Her expression was manic, almost frenzied, as she studied Gideon and the pillar of Light beaming down onto him. "I see," she whispered, her voice breaking as she turned back to the fluttering pages of her holy book splayed out on the ground. "I understand...."

After a long moment, the Light faded, and Donnal coughed, taking a deep, shuddering breath. His wounds had closed, the spilled blood flowing back into his veins, and the color gradually returned to his cheeks. He looked up at Gideon and blinked, then jerked as if coming awake, holding his hands out defensively.

"It's alright," Gideon gasped, a sudden fatigue overwhelming him, and he slumped backward as Donnal cast around fearfully for a moment before realizing where he was.

"What... what happened?" he asked, looking down at his chest and prodding the areas where his wounds had been. "I was dead, wasn't I?"

Gideon couldn't answer, but Battlesister Gerda scoffed and stood. "Nearly, Crieg." She glared down at the two of them, a profound doubt and suspicion written in her broad dwarven features. "Seems your friend can invoke the Light of the gods after all," she muttered, the words sounding like an accusation.

Donnal gawked up at her, then back at Gideon, wincing as he sat up and looked him over. "Gid? How?" he asked, wide-eyed.

Gideon took a long moment to catch his breath, and could only shrug. "I prayed," he said simply, then glanced over at the archoness, who had resumed her frenzied study of the fluttering pages.

Sir Cormac shook his head and cleared his throat. "I've never seen anything like it," he said gruffly in an effort to compose himself after the awe that had struck him speechless. "In all my days, nothing."

He glanced down at the battlesister, but her frown only deepened as she looked from Gideon over to the archoness. "What's wrong with her?" she muttered, nodding toward the other woman with her chin.

Sir Cormac followed her gaze and shifted. "Are you alright, milady?" he asked, but Lorica ignored him, if she heard him at all. She was still poring over the pages in her book, whispering to herself, her eyes alight with a manic fascination.

The old paladin glanced down at Gideon. "What happened in there, Ballad?" he asked. "What's gotten into her, eh?"

Still exhausted, Gideon swallowed hard as he remembered the Sisters Seidh and their deal. He looked at the archoness and wondered what she saw in those pages. "I don't know, I... I hit my head," he lied, looking back to Sir Cormac. "I don't remember much."

Battlesister Dawnhammer glared at him distrustfully, but Sir Cormac simply nodded, an uncharacteristic weariness in the lines of his face. "Well," the old paladin said after a moment, "we'll consider all of this later. We need to gather the horses and head back to the monastery." He turned to the dwarven woman. "Try to rouse the archoness, will you?"

"Aye," the battlesister growled as he moved off to summon the horses, and her surly gaze shifted to Lorica. "I'll handle her."

She stalked toward the other woman as Sir Cormac stepped away, climbing over fallen debris toward the crest of the hill. His heavy boots crushed the brittle wreckage littering the ground around them, and a moment later, he let loose a shrill whistle that echoed out over the dawn-washed hills.

"Milady," Battlesister Dawnhammer said gruffly, laying a hand on the woman's armored shoulder.

Lorica jumped at her touch, and looked up with wild eyes from her open tome. She stared up at Gerda, trembling, her eyes shimmering with unshed tears. Her lips quivered as if she wanted to say something, but couldn't find the words. Gerda frowned down at her and tried again.

"Milady, we need to return to the monastery. The time for prayer and retrospection are not yet upon us." Her tone was firm, and the veneer of deference was slipping.

The archoness looked up at her for a long moment, then closed her mouth and nodded. She gathered up the covers of her book and snapped it shut, then took the dwarven woman's offered hand.

"Yes," she said quietly, her voice almost lost in the soft breeze and distant sounds of the horses approaching through the fog. "It is time." The archoness visibly fought to compose herself as Sir Cormac plodded back over to them, hoofbeats thundering closer up the hill behind him. "We need to go to the Sunless Citadel," she said, seeming a bit more like herself. "The archbishop must hear what we saw."

Sir Cormac and Battlesister Gerda shared a look. "What you saw, milady?" the big paladin asked carefully.

The archoness nodded. "The witches fell, but not before unleashing another evil, one I can only assume is far, far greater."

Gideon remembered the smoldering titan, heard its dreadful blast and the screams in his mind, and he shuddered.

"The witches fell?" Battlesister Dawnhammer asked skeptically. "How, milady?"

Lorica looked warmly over to Gideon. "It was a glorious battle, and Ballad struck the final blow."

All eyes turned to Gideon, who did his best not to look as surprised as everyone else.

"You kept our promise," Donnal breathed, looking his friend over in awe. "You did it. You really did it."

"Ha!" Sir Cormac shook his head as he walked over to offer each recruit a hand up. "A job well done, then," he declared, and fixed Gideon with a meaningful gaze.

Battlesister Gerda's armor clinked as she folded her arms with a scowl. "I suppose that's how you hit your head, eh?"

Gideon swallowed hard and nodded, not sure what to say. He

couldn't reveal the bargain he'd struck with the Sisters, or that as far as he knew, the witches hadn't perished at all. It was all like a fever dream, a horrible nightmare he was waiting to awaken from.

Sir Cormac hoisted him and Donnal to their feet and clapped a hand on each of their shoulders. "Let's be off then." He nodded at the horses arriving behind them, but paused to look back at the archoness. "Er, with your leave, milady."

Lorica blinked and nodded, seeming smaller and more vulnerable for a moment. Then she took a breath, reclaiming her familiar strength, and drew her shoulders back. "Yes, we will regroup at the monastery."

As Dauntless thundered up the hill, leading the surviving horses, the archoness looked toward the wreckage of the great tree; a perilous crater pierced through with massive shards of debris was all that remained.

"We've lost many," she said quietly, pensively. "But the gods saw us victorious, and the Light spared us that we may continue to serve." She looked back to them, and her expression turned stony. "For the glory of the Holy Order," she declared stoically, then strode over to her white palfrey, which shied initially at her approach.

"For the glory of the Holy Order," Sir Cormac echoed gravely, and Gerda followed after the other woman with a mutter, glaring skeptically at her back.

"You did it, mate," Donnal said as he and Gideon helped each other limp after the others. "You'll be a paladin after all. Always knew it!" His tired grin faltered. "James would be proud."

All Gideon could do was manage a silent nod, his mind racing with what the witches had done, had made him promise, and the mystery of the smoldering titan that left him deeply shaken.

Gideon struggled to haul himself up onto his skittish mare's saddle once he'd found her. He was utterly sapped of strength, whether from the terror of the Sisters' wicked realm or from having channeled the Holy Light for the first time, he couldn't say.

As the archoness led them on, Gideon brought up the rear of the survivors, and a deep terror and trepidation of seeing the titan appear magically in the valley prompted him to turn and look back at the ruins of the blackened tree as they left it behind.

There was nothing. The morning had calmed, the sun was burning away the pooled mist, and the sky was clear and free of terrors.

Donnal's stomach rumbled audibly just ahead of him, and his friend groaned. "I never thought I'd say it, but I'll be happy to get some of Brother Almin's terrible cooking again," he admitted.

Gideon gave a half-hearted nod of agreement, though the thought of the monastery conjured the image of Nefteli for him more so than food or rest.

"And to see Teli again," Donnal added, as though reading Gideon's mind. "Gods, I can't wait to see her again."

Gideon slumped further as his mare carried him carefully down the slopes and onward back to Rivenwood.

CHAPTER 39

SADIA

Sadia explained carefully to Mariam what had transpired at Jalila's as the cart bounced down the streets of Emra'adid toward Roya's caravanserai. She was careful to skirt around everything that had happened with... whatever it actually was that was dwelling inside Ibrahim; she had no idea how even to begin to explain it. Mariam listened silently to everything Sadia had to say, and she didn't pry or question her when her explanation petered off into a troubled silence.

The streets milled quietly around them as Heidroksimos dragged the cart along behind him. Dusk settled over Emra'adid, and it was answered by the lighting of hanging lanterns all throughout the city and along the winding river running through it.

Sadia's mind was alive with a thousand racing, interweaving thoughts as she idly watched the little lights spring to life throughout the darkling city, and she was overwhelmed at the idea of moving on again already. They'd just arrived at Emra'adid, and now they were to press on even further from home, from Yusuf and the girls. She was spent, emotionally and physically, and the idea of having to begin another journey was daunting.

"Sagrada!" Dalgrim grumbled loudly as he trudged along beside the cart. "What a load of old codswallop. The Ringed City's a thing of legend, and for all the wrong reasons."

Mariam looked down at him from the back of the cart, one hand resting on her large belly. "But why would your lovely friend suggest going there if it wouldn't be a help to poor Ibrahim?" she asked curiously.

"Aye, I'm sure Jalila means well enough," the dwarf groused, "but there's no doubt she's got her own designs and schemes. Nothing good will come of going to that damned city, mark my words!"

"You promised," Sadia said firmly, glaring at him, and she was surprised to see the dwarf shift uncomfortably and quickly look away from her.

"Aye, lass, that I did," he agreed bitterly. "And I'd never not keep a promise made to Jalila. More for fear of my own life than anything," he added, "but regardless — the promise will be kept. We'll leave on the morrow, I suppose." He stalked along in silence for a moment before blurting, "And I cannae take another night sleeping on the floor, so no more nightmares!" He turned and wagged a finger at Sadia and Ibrahim.

"It wasn't—" Sadia began, but she stopped herself. There was no point arguing with the stubborn old dwarf. "The madam gave me some things she said would help him. So you'll get your precious sleep."

Dalgrim's eyes narrowed, but he nodded, and they continued on.

The final few shafts light from the setting sun scattered across the underbellies of eastward-marching clouds, setting the sky ablaze above them as they finally turned into the square where the Gentle Djinni was situated. Sadia's stomach growled at the thought of a hot meal, but as soon as Roya's caravanserai came into view, Dalgrim dashed over to Heidroksimos and tugged firmly at the man's huge wrist.

"Whoa, hold on, stop!" he hissed. "Stop, you giant two-legged ox!" The half-giant glowered down at the dwarf and finally halted. Dalgrim glanced back at Sadia with wide eyes. "Aren't those your mad lads from Qasira?" he hissed, and Sadia followed his pointed finger as a deep, creeping fear slithered up from the base of her spine.

There, at the other end of the square, a group of figures wearing the bronze armor and dark orange robes of the Hierophants of the Lidless Eye had just rounded the corner. Two of them were carrying tall staffs with large, coal-filled braziers mounted at the top, casting a bright, almost violent light across the darkening square.

Between the two torch-bearers stood the tall, muscular form of the prophet, his twisted crown perched atop his clean-shaven head and the torchlight throwing dancing shadows across his bare chest. Though his arms had been wreathed in flame that day in the bazaar, they remained unmarred, free from any sign of their conflagration.

"Ow!" Reza yelped beside Sadia, and she looked down and realized she'd unintentionally dug her nails into her little brother's shoulder as the fear had taken her.

"What do we do?" she asked in a panic, vigorously rubbing Reza's shoulder as he tried to squirm away.

"Lu, ready that sword of yours," she heard Dalgrim mutter. "Big fella!" He smacked Heidroksimos's arm and gestured toward a cluster of empty merchant stalls. "Move the cart over there!" Mariam translated quietly to her husband, and Lu's hand went to the hilt of his hanging sword as they quickly moved out of the open.

Sadia leapt in fright as the loud, droning voice of the prophet boomed out over the square, and he began intoning unintelligible words as he held something aloft in his hands. The small crowd milling all stopped and stared for a moment before moving away from the cultists, leaving the square altogether. Some wore worried expressions, and others cast glances back toward the prophet over their shoulders.

"What he doing?" Lu asked, his eyes narrowed.

Dalgrim scoffed and sucked his teeth as he ducked down behind one of the empty stalls. "Ach, who knows?" he said dismissively. "A madman doing mad things." He tugged nervously at his beard. "Of all the places in this damned city, how'd they end up at Roya's?"

"I'm sorry," Mariam said hesitantly, looking between the dwarf and Sadia, "I don't understand what's happening?"

"Those are the men who tried to hurt Ibi," Sadia said, her throat dry.

Mariam frowned, her brow creased with worry, then looked up at her husband, who was hunched down awkwardly and peering out around the stall, a bemused look on his bearded face. "And you think they've come in search of him," the woman murmured, laying a hand protectively over her belly.

Sadia nodded fearfully and hugged Ibrahim's sleeping form tighter, though the child was calmer and looked more peaceful than she'd yet seen. A brief flutter of hope brightened the darkness in her heart before it was quickly snuffed out by an angry roar from the prophet, drawing everyone's attention.

The large man tossed aside whatever it was he was holding, and it splatted wetly across the flagstones of the square. "The haruspicy has faded," he growled. "I require another offering."

Sadia noticed a furtive glance pass between a number of the cultists surrounding him just as the door to the Gentle Djinni opened and Roya stepped out, her eyes widening as she beheld the strange group of men at her threshold.

She exclaimed loudly in her native tongue as she glanced down at what the prophet had discarded, then addressed the cultists directly. "What on earth is going on out here?" she demanded. "Do I need to call the city guard?"

The prophet stared down at the sturdy woman for a prolonged moment. "A thing was stolen from me," he declared, his deep voice easily carrying across the square to where Sadia huddled both her brothers close. "I seek it. The hunt has brought me here." He glanced up at the facade of the caravanserai, and his eyes narrowed. "A girl. With a child. Do you harbor them?"

Sadia's heart pounded wildly in her chest, and her eyes flicked to where Lu's hand rested on the hilt of his sword.

Roya regarded the cultist, her expression hard. "There are no children in my house," she answered. "Now, kindly leave and find some other hospitality before I summon the guards."

The prophet took a step forward, and Sadia could see the man's muscles tensing. "The haruspicy led me here," he rumbled ominously. "I will divine the truth, but you will know mercy if you aid me in the search."

"I have no idea what you're talking about," Roya answered, folding her arms in defiance, "and I want you to leave immediately."

The prophet's face fell. "One of you offer yourselves," he ordered. Sadia was confused for a moment before another cultist stepped forward and dropped to one knee in front of the prophet.

"I... I offer myself!" he declared, his voice quavering and his shoulders visibly shaking. "For the glory of Ankhatun's advent!"

"I don't like this one bit," Dalgrim muttered as they all watched, but none of them seemed to be able to look away as a palpable fear and tension grew in the square.

The prophet placed a hand on the man's shoulder. "May your offering be returned to you tenfold in the Diurnal Kingdom, faithful one," he said after a deep breath. "Rise, and remove your armor."

The man stood unsteadily and began unfastening his bronze breastplate with hands that shook violently, his chest rising and falling rapidly as he choked back fearful sobs.

"I demand you leave here at once!" Roya cried loudly, her voice shrill. She looked back over her shoulder through the door as one of her young servants stepped through. "Nasir, run and fetch the guards," she told him quietly, her words barely carrying over to Sadia and the others. "Go, quick!"

The young man dashed off, skirting around the cultists, who paid him no mind, and hurried out of the square.

"Fetch your guards," the prophet said with an audible sneer. "Fetch the sultan's army," he continued as his follower disrobed. "Gather the armies of a hundred different nations. All will perish who stand against Ankhatun's dawning."

"What madness are you speaking?" Roya demanded, no longer able to hide the tremor in her voice. She watched apprehensively as the other cultist let his armor and orange robes fall to the ground, leaving him bare aside from a simple white undergarment covering his loins.

The prophet waved a dismissive hand at her, then placed it gently against the man's face. "Faithful of the Sun," he said, his voice thrumming across the night-laden square, shadows dancing over the stark features of his face from the burning braziers carried by the cultists behind him, "your body will be returned to the world in the fullness of the Eternal Day."

"Oh, bloody hell," Dalgrim whispered.

The cultist bowed his head, and his lips moved in rapid, silent prayer. The prophet closed his eyes and bowed his own head. He inhaled deeply, and then the hand on the man's face slid down and gripped his neck, squeezing hard as every muscle in the prophet's thick arm tensed. His other hand withdrew a wicked dagger from behind his back, the inverse curve of the blade flashing in the firelight.

Sadia gasped as the hook-like blade bit into the man's belly, and she wrestled to clasp a hand over Reza's eyes to prevent him from witnessing the prophet draw the blade smoothly all the way across the width of the other man's body. The prophet lifted the man up, dragging his feet off the ground, and the wound gaped open, tiny rivulets of blood running from its clean edges. An anguished cry escaped Roya's lips as she reached out as if to help, before stopping herself.

Letting the ritual knife fall and clatter against the cobblestone, the prophet reached his free hand into the man's body as he kept him suspended in the air with the other. The squelching sound of the man's organs being drawn out of the wound was sickening, and Sadia heard Mariam silence a panicked gasp as she grasped for her husband's huge hand.

The prophet withdrew the innards and held them aloft, releasing his hold on the man's throat and letting him fall to the ground, where he moaned and wept miserably. Sadia felt Reza's body stiffen as he watched in horrified fascination from between her fingers.

The prophet worked the entrails in his hands, going through them like the pages of a book, and the cultist curled up and clutched the wound in agony as his leader drew his organs further out, tugging on them and wrenching them from his ruined abdomen.

Dalgrim's face paled as he watched the twisted spectacle, and he turned his head slowly to look at Sadia, as if he finally took seriously what she'd told him about the Hierophants in Qasira. "We have to do something about this," he grumbled, almost sounding reluctant.

"Roya sent for the city guards," Sadia said nervously. "Surely they'll—"

Dalgrim harrumphed. "The nearest barracks is down near the temple district, and it's just about this time they do the changing of the guard." He ran a hand through his hair. "Trust me, I make a point of knowing these things. The guard won't be arriving anytime soon."

"We should flee," Mariam hissed, "go to your ship and leave the city!"

Dalgrim nodded, then quickly shook his head. "I... I cannae leave Roya to deal with them." He tugged again at his beard, his brow furrowed deeply in thought. "I've an idea," he said finally. The prophet was droning on in the background, sifting through the living innards and praying in the same foreign tongue he'd used in the bazaar, over Ibrahim.

Dalgrim fished around in his pockets and finally pulled out his flask, the liquid inside sloshing audibly as he held it up. "Listen," he said to Lu, "I'll go and cause a distraction, alright? When I give you the signal, come out of the shadows and put your sword to work!"

As Dalgrim spoke, he uncorked the flask and started pouring it over himself, rubbing it into the skin of his neck, down the front of his rope, and splashing it over his beard as though he were applying a grand fragrance. The heady punch of alcohol wafted off him in a wave and burned Sadia's nostrils.

"Big man," the dwarf said, glancing up at Heidroksimos, who towered over them all even though he'd taken a knee. "You stay here and protect the women and children. But don't be afraid to wade into the fray if things get hairy, aye?"

The half-giant cocked an eyebrow and looked to his wife, who struggled to translate.

"Wait, wait," Lu said, "what signal?"

"Oh, you'll know it when it comes," Dalgrim said meaningfully, then he shook the near-empty flask next to his ear. "And one for courage," he muttered before bringing it to his lips and tipping the bottom up.

Lu watched him drink with raised eyebrows and held his hand out expectantly, but Dalgrim drained the little vessel and tossed it aside once he was done.

"Alright, you head over that way through the shadows," the dwarf said to his bodyguard, and Lu scowled and muttered to himself as he crept away, leaving the relative safety of the stalls.

"Right, lass," Dalgrim said, turning to Sadia. "If things don't go aright, you take your brothers and Mariam and her man here and scurry back to Suleiman's. You remember the way, don't you?"

Sadia blinked rapidly and squeezed Reza tighter to her to try to stop her hand from shaking. "I... I think so," she managed, wincing as the prophet's voice rose in frenzied chant, echoing across the square, and the dwarf nodded.

"Alright, then." He turned to face the cultists bathed in the lapping light of the braziers. "No one threatens my Roya," Sadia heard him mutter, and then he skulked off, skirting around the edge of the square after Lu until she could no longer see either of them in the darkness.

"We should leave, Sadia," Mariam whispered fearfully, clutching her husband with one hand and draping the other protectively over her belly. "These are very bad men."

Sadia swallowed, unsure how to answer, but the prophet's chanting rose to a shrill crescendo and then abruptly faded, drawing their attention. They all watched as he peered into the organs in his hands, sifting through them and studying them closely as the man at his feet continued to writhe in agony.

After a tense moment, the prophet lifted his head from the pile of viscera and looked at Roya. "They were here, but departed," he declared. "And they shall return."

He cast aside the intestines, and they landed wetly on the cobblestone beside the man they'd been pulled from. Roya stood frozen, her hands clasped over her mouth as her eyes darted between the prophet and the ruined man on the ground.

"So you've seen the child," the prophet said, striding smoothly up to her, "you have seen Ankhatun's stolen vessel." He stood just in front of the proprietress, towering over her, and Sadia tensed, unable to look away. "And you chose to lie to me..." he growled, letting his words hang ominously in the air.

Without taking his eyes from the woman, he gestured behind him, and the two braziers flared, the blazing firelight fully illuminating the Gentle Djinni's facade and leaving Roya hidden in the madman's hulking shadow.

"Uh-oh! I think I've pissed me britches!" Dalgrim's voice called loudly out of the stillness. A moment later, the dwarf came stumbling out of the shadows toward the caravanserai, laughing uproariously as he apparently struggled to keep his trousers up around his waist. The prophet paused, his hand outstretched, and slowly turned toward the interruption.

"Wha' a night! Wha' a night!" the dwarf continued to hoot, and the cultists all turned and watched him approach, their hands resting on the hilts of their scimitars. "I dunnae remember much, but I know it was a good one!"

Dalgrim continued stumbling right up to them as he started bellowing out a discordant song and giggling to himself. Roya peeked out from behind the prophet and gawked at the dwarf, who was making quite the show of himself.

One of the cultists glanced back at the prophet, who gave a vague nod toward Dalgrim, and as the dwarf approached, the cultist stepped forward and held his free hand out firmly, sending Dalgrim reeling back for an instant. His ability to simulate drunkenness was quite amazing, and he belched loudly, then glanced up through bleary eyes at the man who'd halted him.

"W-well, hello there, big fella," he slurred. "No need to get a-ruckus on me now!"

The prophet turned back to Roya and glared down at her. "You're expecting the thief to return," he said angrily. "When?"

Roya's lip trembled, but she kept her mouth shut tight. Dalgrim cleared his throat, then blinked half a dozen times at the cultist in his way and gasped. "Well, if it isn't me old friend Saleem! I haven't seen you in a fortnight, laddie, where've you been?"

The cultist frowned and shoved him again, but this time Dalgrim caught his wrist in one hand. "Here, I've got a present for you," he declared, then held his other hand up toward the man's face.

Sadia shrieked as a loud crack split the still night. A black cloud exploded, seemingly from the dwarf's fingertips, and engulfed the two of them for a moment. Chaos erupted in the square before Sadia could even understand what was happening as the prophet whirled away from Roya. At the same time, Lu leapt from the shadows, his blade singing as it left its scabbard and bit into the nearest cultist, splattering crimson across the brazier-lit cobblestone.

Lu's dance of blood and blade continued as the black plume rose and gradually cleared, guided off by the cool night air. The cultist who'd taken the full brunt of the explosion had fallen to his knees and was clawing at his eyes, screaming, curling wisps of smoke rising from shrapnel burnt into his face. Dalgrim stumbled back, his eyes watering and his own face streaked with black powder.

The prophet took several quick steps toward the fray, but halted himself as Lu's slender sword bit deep into the unarmored neck of one of the brazier-bearing cultists, and the man fell back, spilling glowing coals from the brazier out across the cobbled square. "No!" the prophet screamed, staring miserably down at the scattered embers.

Lu spun and slashed the back of the legs of the other man bearing a pole-mounted brazier, sending him collapsing to the ground, and the fiery bowl rang as it struck the ground and spilled its contents as well.

The blazing light that had illuminated the square faded, and Sadia had to peer closely to watch as the last remaining cultist attacked Lu, waving his scimitar wildly, only to be easily parried and then run through by the easterner's crimson-coated blade.

Reza squirmed in Sadia's arms, and some instinct made her clamp her arm firmly around him, holding him tight so he wouldn't try to dash off to help.

"Oh, Mitera!" Mariam wailed, clasping her husband's arm tightly, and the half-giant looked conflicted as to whether to help or stay and protect his wife.

In a matter of moments, though, the prophet's men were all in bloody heaps on the ground amidst the burning coals and guttering braziers, bleeding and writhing and moaning, but not yet dead.

Dalgrim vigorously rubbed at his eyes until he could keep them open, and Reza finally managed to pull free from Sadia's grasp, leaping off the cart and dashing over to Lu. She called out after him, but he ignored her.

Sadia turned in a panic to Mariam, and carefully held Ibrahim out to her without thinking. "Please," she begged. Mariam looked at her in confusion for a moment, clearly in shock, but then quickly took the child and pulled him close against her.

"What have you done?" Sadia heard the prophet scream as she chased after Reza, stumbling over the tattered hem of her dress, and she was surprised at the panic and anguish in his voice. Reza stopped beside Lu, holding his sling and a handful of rocks, but the violence had already ended. As Sadia got to him, she grabbed him in both hands and pulled him back against her, determined not to let him get away again.

Lu stared down with a cocked eyebrow, his sword held easily at his side, as the prophet mewled and whimpered, hurriedly gathering the scattered coals as best he could in an apparent attempt to preserve their embers.

He blubbered like a child as he worked, his eyes wide. "Not the darkness, no," he whined, gathering the burning coals together with his bare hands. "Great Ankhatun, let not the night swallow me, I beg you!"

CHAPTER 40

SADIA

"WHAT'S WRONG WITH HIM?" Reza asked as he stared down at the mad prophet and wriggled in vain against his sister's grasp. Lu just gave a pitiful shake of his head.

Dalgrim coughed as he patted himself down, sending little puffs of soot billowing off his robes. "Leave him to his madness. We have to get out of here." He looked over at the doorway of the Gentle Djinni. "Wait, where's Roya?" he asked with a note of concern, and no sooner had he asked than the proprietress burst back through the door and out into the square, brandishing a large iron pan in both hands and looking very ready to swing it at someone.

"Whoa!" Dalgrim called, holding his hands out. "Calm down, darling — Lu and I have everything under control." Roya met his gaze and slowly lowered the pan as Lu looked from the pile of defeated cultists to his blade, then back at Dalgrim with a frown.

"Oh, Dalgrim," Roya fretted, looking out over the carnage in the square and the prophet crawling and cradling glowing embers in his hands. "What on earth is going on?" Her eyes found Sadia. "Are these the men from Qasira?"

"Yes, and as you can see, they're not exactly in their right minds," the dwarf grumbled as he stepped carefully through the scattered coals toward Roya. "I think we should probably get out of here while he's still..." he glanced down at the terrified prophet in bewilderment, "preoccupied."

"I sent Nasim for the guards," she started to explain, but Dalgrim interrupted her.

"Aye, we heard, but my stout dwarven sensibilities are telling me to flee," he explained, walking up and taking her hand. "And any time a dwarf tells you the time's come to run, you'd do well to listen." He started off, tugging at her arm, but Roya remained rooted in place.

"No, Dalgrim," she said firmly. "It's not the first time I've had to run some ruffians away from my house, and I won't leave now, no matter how strange or awful these particular ones are."

"Roya, did you not just see this madman eviscerate that fool follower of his?" Dalgrim demanded, tugging her hand again, but she stood firm.

"I did, but I won't allow myself to be intimidated by such a vile man!"

Dalgrim huffed. "Sweetheart, you're talking nonsense—"

"Don't you 'sweetheart' me, Dalgrim Glintstone!" she snapped. "I'm the one who stayed with the Djinni, not you!" Some deep, long-held resentment bloomed like an aura around her: an anger and a sadness. "She's all I have, and I simply will not leave her."

The dwarf squirmed uncomfortably. "Ach, are you still punishing me for that?" he asked indignantly. "That was a long time ago, Roya. I thought... I thought we'd moved past it."

Roya huffed and glared down at him, her eyes smoldering angrily like the coals scattered at their feet. "You didn't just leave the Djinni, Dalgrim — you left me!"

"Is this really the right time to be talking about this?" Dalgrim sighed, throwing a wary glance down at the prophet.

"I don't care," Roya insisted. "I'm not leaving the Djinni. Let go of me, Dalgrim."

The dwarf's hand stayed on hers and pulled on her again. "I'm not leaving you here with this madman, Roya, now come along!"

"No!" she said defiantly, and planted her feet. "Let me go — now!"

Dalgrim's face fell, as did an uncomfortable silence, and the two of them stared at each other for a long moment. The quiet was broken only by the mewling prophet and the sound of Heidroksimos pulling the cart bearing his wife and Ibrahim out from behind the empty stalls to join them.

Finally, Dalgrim let Roya's hand fall from his own, and his expression turned stony. "If that's what you want." He stepped away and glanced up at his bodyguard. "Lu, tie this buffoon up, and we'll be off," he growled, gesturing to the prophet.

Lu nodded and held out his hand toward Dalgrim.

"What are you waiting for?" the dwarf demanded.

"I no have a rope," Lu said, furrowing his brows.

"What?" Dalgrim barked. "Why don't you have rope? What good are you, then?"

The easterner scowled. "Why I should have a rope?"

Dalgrim threw his hands up in frustration and launched into a tirade as Sadia dragged Reza over to the cart and forced him up onto it. The boy begrudgingly sat and folded his arms with a frustrated growl, and Sadia moved back over to Mariam to retrieve Ibrahim.

"Is everything alright?" the woman asked, gently holding the boy out. As she took him, Sadia's eyes were drawn to the prophet, who was still sitting among the scattered coals from the braziers.

He'd begun whispering to them, almost pleading with them, and she saw tears streaking down his face in the ember glow. "We need to leave," she whispered, more to herself than as an answer to Mariam.

At that moment, the sound of many booted feet marching down the avenue toward them came from outside the square. "Wonderful!" Dalgrim groused. "Here's the brave Emra'adid guard to save the bloody day." He stomped toward the others. "Best of luck to you, then, Roya!"

he growled, and climbed up onto the cart, shaking the rickety old thing beneath his heft.

Ibrahim stirred in Sadia's arms at the disturbance and whined, grimacing as he was awoken for the first time since his ordeal at Madam Jalila's. The prophet's incessant murmuring suddenly ceased, and the hairs on Sadia's neck stood on end as she looked up at him to find his eyes boring into her own, the fading embers painting shadows across his tear-stained visage.

"The vessel!" he croaked, the veins in his arms and neck distending as a fervor took him. He held his gaze on the child in Sadia's arms as he resumed his horrid chant, bellowing out the strange, indecipherable words across the square at them.

"Deepstone's fiery furnace!" Dalgrim growled in annoyance as the guardsmen finally arrived. A large group of them marched in, four abreast, carrying lanterns that threw dull light off their polished armor. "We've got a mad one here!" the dwarf called out to them, jerking his bearded chin at the prophet.

Sadia clutched Ibrahim close, unable to look away from the prophet as he focused all of his ire toward them. As he chanted, Ibi started squirming in his blanket and crying. An uncomfortable heat seeped through the blanket into Sadia's arms and chest, and she panicked as she realized what was happening.

"We have to leave!" she cried, tearing her gaze from the madman among the coals to plead with Dalgrim.

The disgruntled dwarf, however, had his beady eyes focused suspiciously on the guardsmen who'd just arrived. "Those aren't the sultan's men," he murmured, just audible over the prophet's rapid, incessant chanting. Sadia followed his gaze over to the guards, and sure enough, their breastplates gleamed bronze and bore the insignia of an angry, sun-like eye peeking over a horizon.

"Bollocks," Dalgrim grumbled as the cultists halted at the sight of their leader on his knees.

One wearing a plumed helm stepped forward. "The ship has been secured," he began, but faltered as his eyes adjusted to the dim light and he saw his bleeding, dying comrades lying on the ground. "What... what has happened?" he asked of the prophet.

Their leader, though, paid him no heed; his unnerving gaze remained fixed on Ibrahim as his voice rose in pitch and volume, whatever prayer or incantation he was reciting coming to a crescendo.

"Please!" Sadia shrieked, her voice breaking as she stumbled across the back of the cart to reach out to Heidroksimos, desperate for him to take them quickly and as far away as possible. Ibrahim was thrashing in her arms, his emaciated limbs struggling in his blanket as he cried and screamed.

"Dalgrim, what's happening?" Roya demanded, glancing nervously at the cultists and clutching her heavy pan tight.

Dalgrim didn't respond but stood very still atop the cart, as if afraid to make a move. All the while, the prophet's voice grew louder and louder. Finally, he was screaming his strange prayers, lifting two glowing coals up above his head. They smoldered in his palms, and the pain they caused flickered across his features, but still, he chanted.

The newly arrived cultists stood apprehensively, looking nearly as unnerved at the scene as Sadia felt. She heard Dalgrim curse under his breath and quickly clamber back out of the cart to jog over in Roya's direction.

"Tell him to turn the cart around!" he yelled over his shoulder at Mariam, who frantically translated to her husband, and the big man lifted the cart by the yoke and began to turn it.

Roya started inching backward uncomfortably as she realized something was amiss with the guards, and she looked to Dalgrim as he ran toward her.

Then her eyes flitted over his shoulder and met Sadia's, and despite the chaos, the older woman's lips lifted in a small smile — frightened but reassuring.

Sadia barely had time to register it before the mad prophet howled the final word of his occult prayer, forcing her eyes back down to him.

"Supplications mount upon the hating flame!" he bellowed, staring directly at her, "Thus is the command of Ankhatun!"

Sadia's stomach plummeted at hearing those unholy words repeated. His furious voice echoed over the square for a lingering moment, punctuated by Dalgrim's harried footsteps across the flagstones.

Then the prophet leapt to his feet and whirled around toward Roya, seizing her head in both hands, the coals still burning in his palms.

An evil red flame immediately engulfed her entire head, and she let out the most heart-wrenching, painful scream Sadia had ever heard. The flames traveled down, licking at her body at an unnatural pace, quickly devouring her, and the prophet screamed with her as he, too, was swallowed by the flames.

"Roya!" Dalgrim cried miserably, only halfway to her, but not breaking his short, dwarven stride. He leapt toward the inferno, brandishing a small dagger he'd pulled from some pocket, but before he made it to the flames, he was intercepted as Lu tackled him to the ground.

Sadia sobbed as Heidroksimos started jogging away with the cart in tow, and she watched Roya's flames grow and furiously pulse with some occult power. Lu leapt to his feet and started dragging Dalgrim away, following after the cart, and the dwarf fought him every step, his hoarse screams for Roya echoing across the square.

Sadia held on to her brothers tight as the prophet stepped away, and Roya's burnt husk fell away and shattered on the cobble in front of the Gentle Djinni. The prophet was once again wreathed in unholy flames, and he turned, blazing like the dawning sun, to fixate once again upon Ibrahim. "After them!" he cried, pointing, and his men dashed forward, careful to skirt around him as they gave pursuit.

Lu wrestled the devastated Dalgrim along, but they weren't fast enough to catch the cart. "You have to slow down!" Sadia called out to Heidroksimos, and the half-giant glanced over his shoulder and came to a sudden halt. Lu caught up quickly and heaved Dalgrim bodily into the back of the cart, the cultists close on their heels.

"Go, go!" Lu shouted, balancing precariously at the end of the cart, his sword held in a defensive stance. "Go to the *Mollysock!*"

Heidroksimos seemed to understand the urgency in Lu's voice intuitively, and he bolted off once again, the cart skidding and shuddering to the side as he turned left out of the square and redoubled his pace down the torchlit avenue. Sadia forced herself to look back at the pursuing pillar of flame that was the prophet, but even as terrifying as the madman was, he could not keep pace with the powerful half-giant, and as they fled further, Ibrahim calmed slightly.

Dalgrim was in a bad state, his eyes bloodshot and cheeks stained with tears. He trembled as he stared off after Roya, his mouth open in shock and his breath coming in ragged, shallow gasps.

Still in a wide stance at the back, never letting down his guard, Lu threw a quick, piteous glance over his shoulder at Dalgrim. He opened his mouth to say something, but was suddenly thrown forward as the cart came to a skidding halt. Lu fell over Dalgrim but caught himself deftly, rolling easily back up to his feet.

Heidroksimos barked something at them, and Mariam quickly asked, "Which way should he go?" Sadia looked up and saw they'd arrived at a crossing: one she didn't recognize in the dim lantern light.

"I..." she breathed, looking from Mariam to Lu, "I don't know...."

Lu's head swiveled quickly as he tried to decipher which way would take them to Suleiman's, but he looked as confused as Sadia. The sounds of shouting and rushing footsteps weren't far behind, and as Lu turned back to defend, Sadia went to one knee beside Dalgrim and put a hand on his shoulder.

"Dalgrim, which way to the *Mollysocks?*" she asked urgently, but he seemed unable to look away from the direction of the Gentle Djinni, though the place itself was already out of sight. She waited a heartbeat for him to answer, and when he didn't, she shook his shoulder as hard as she could. "Dalgrim, which way?" she cried.

Finally, the dwarf blinked, as if coming awake, and his eyes flitted over to her, then at the crossroads they were in. "Er, left," he muttered halfheartedly. "Go left." The torches of the pursuing cultists crested the hill behind them as Mariam shouted up to her husband, and he obeyed, turning on the spot and charging down the left avenue.

Sadia fell back against the rickety railing as the cart lurched forward, and she grabbed hold of Reza again. "Guide him," she yelled angrily at Dalgrim, her eyes hard. Their chance to escape teetered on a knife's edge, and she wouldn't let her compassion for Dalgrim and Roya prevent her from keeping her brothers safe.

Dalgrim looked at her with wide, bleary eyes. After a moment, he nodded and climbed shakily to his hands and knees to crawl over to the front of the cart.

The dwarf rallied and directed Heidroksimos the rest of the way without faltering. The path they took seemed far longer to Sadia, and she finally realized Dalgrim was taking a convoluted, less direct route to the hidden wharf. She kept her eyes on the road behind them as they went, and before long, there was no sign of the cultists.

Heidroksimos pulled the cart up short at the top of the narrow stair that wound down into the dank canal where Suleiman's was situated, his massive chest heaving from his inhuman exertion.

"Are they still following us?" Mariam asked nervously as she stood and laid a soothing hand on her husband's arm.

"Eh, I dunnae think so," Dalgrim mumbled, glancing back down the avenue.

Sadia stepped down from the cart, dragging Reza behind her by the hand, and started for the stairs. "We can't be sure," she said. "He found us once, he could find us again." Ibrahim, though still warm to the touch and visibly uncomfortable, had calmed the further they'd gotten from the prophet.

"Right, then," Dalgrim grumbled, climbing unsteadily off the cart. He staggered a little, and Lu caught him and helped him stand. The dwarf shrugged him off with a scowl. "Let's be rid of this awful city."

Sadia was already a dozen steps down, moving quickly but careful where she placed her feet on the slick, mossy stairs. She could hear the others following behind, but her sole focus was on getting aboard the *Mollysocks* and leaving Emra'adid and the Hierophants as far behind as possible. She wondered idly how many times she would have to flee for her life, and the thought left her feeling hollow.

Once her feet hit the sodden canal bank, she could see the *Mollysocks* bobbing gently against the wharf, and she breathed a sigh of relief. Reza complained about her grip on his wrist as she dragged him down the dilapidated wharf, but she ignored him. She'd had enough. She needed to get to Sagrada to fix Ibrahim and then finally get back to Qasira, to her sisters, to the strangely preferable normalcy of living in a cistern beneath a city that didn't even want her.

As she climbed onto the barge, she heard the bead curtains on Suleiman's shack part, and the large man himself stepped out, Dandan at his side.

"A bit late to arrive unannounced, eh, dwarf?" he grumbled down at Dalgrim. He side-eyed Heidroksimos warily as the half-giant strode up and shrugged the cart off his shoulder, letting it fall to the ground beside the shack. It let out a creaking groan as it landed in the damp soil, and one of the wheels snapped off the axle and slowly toppled.

Suleiman stared down at it for a moment and frowned. "Hmm. That'll be another twenty drahm, my friend," he mused, looking back to the dwarf.

"Aye, well, you'll have to add it to my tab," Dalgrim said, stopping beside the man and letting Heidroksimos and Mariam pass. "Listen, Suley — we've got some bad folk chasing us. Now, I led them on a little goose chase around the city, and we lost them before we headed your way, but...." He huffed in frustration. "I don't know how many of you big bastards the poor ol' *Mollysocks* can carry, but you should probably come along for a bit, just in case they manage to end up here."

Suleiman regarded him carefully. "Bad folk, eh?" he asked, teasing one end of his drooping mustache. "Not the city guard, I take it?"

"Eh, no," the dwarf answered heavily, "madmen from Qasira. But listen, Suley, they... they killed Roya." The words came thick and bitter, and Sadia watched an anguished grimace cross Dalgrim's face before he looked down at the ground.

Suleiman's dark eyebrows sunk low on his brow. "What are you saying, eh?" he demanded suspiciously, folding his big arms.

"It's true, Suley," Dalgrim insisted. "They... they burned her. Burned her alive right in front of the Djinni." His voice hitched as he said it, and Suleiman glanced at Lu, who nodded gravely.

The wharf owner's eyes widened in shock. "Roya?" he asked, bewildered. "But... why?" Then his expression hardened, and the thick muscles of his jaw flexed. "What did you do, Glintstone?"

The dwarf looked up, bristling. "It had nothing to do with me!" he raged. "It...." He glanced over at Sadia and her brothers, then sighed and met the big man's gaze again. "It doesn't matter, Suley. They killed her. And they'll kill you and Dandan both if they come this way, so get on the damned boat so I don't have to lose two friends this evening."

Suleiman frowned, and Lu stepped forward. "Dalgrim telling the truth," he said firmly. "Not his fault."

The big, turbaned man regarded both of them for a long moment as he reached down and scratched behind Dandan's floppy ears. "Roya," he said at last, "was a good woman. Emra'adid will miss her." He looked over at the *Mollysocks*, then back at the narrow stair toward the city streets. "This wharf is mine," he declared. "If your pursuers come this way," he said, reaching into the doorway of his shack and retrieving a long, heavy club wreathed in iron spikes, "Dandan and I will handle them."

"Suley," Dalgrim groaned. "These aren't the kind you want to scrap with, trust me."

Suleiman narrowed his eyes and hefted the club over his shoulder. "If they don't come this way," he continued, as if Dalgrim hadn't spoken, "perhaps we'll go on a little hunt tomorrow."

"Ach!" the dwarf growled, turning and taking a few steps before pacing back. "Just...." He let out a frustrated breath and shook his shaggy head. "Just be safe, Suley."

Dalgrim dug around in his pockets and held a fistful of his stolen jewelry out to the wharf master. "I can't stay," he said, unable to look up at the man. "I have to take the lass... elsewhere. But this should cover my debts and somewhat besides." He shook his fist insistently, and Suleiman held out his free hand to accept. Dalgrim gripped the man's hand in his, transferring the pilfered goods over, and held it. "The rest is for Roya for... for..." his voice failed him, but Suleiman nodded in understanding.

"I'll see to everything," he assured the dwarf. "Take the *Mollysocks* and go."

Dalgrim finally looked back up appreciatively and clapped his other hand on Suleiman's. "Good man, Suley," he said, coughing the weakness from his voice. Then he and Lu followed the others over to the barge.

"Wherever you're going," Suleiman called after them, staring down at the mess of glittering chains and cheap gems in his palm, "bring Dandan back something tasty, eh?"

Dalgrim held up a hand in acknowledgment, but as he climbed over the railing of his little boat, Sadia heard him mutter bitterly, "I'm never coming back to this damned city." He took the *Mollysocks'* tiller as Lu and Heidroksimos used the long poles to push the barge away from the wharf, and Reza waved sadly at Dandan as they drifted back out along the canal toward the broad Tajari River.

CHAPTER 41

SADIA

Lu hung a trio of lanterns at different points around the ship, spilling dull light around the *Mollysocks* by which to navigate the channels. Dalgrim was the most somber Sadia had ever seen him as he guided the little boat onto the big fork of the Tajari Delta, turning north to follow the current and cutting through the sparse night traffic.

Sadia sat on the deck, Ibrahim on her shoulder and Reza's head resting in her lap. She stroked Reza's hair, hoping to help him sleep, but he continued to shift uncomfortably. Ibrahim was restless, too, though no longer crying, and Sadia herself was exhausted. Her eyes felt sunken, and her lids were heavy, but she refused to rest before lulling her brothers into a gentle sleep, so she hummed quietly to them as she'd done in the cistern. Eventually, her heavy eyelids won out, and she drifted off.

SADIA WOKE SUDDENLY as the boards beneath her shifted, and she flailed her arm out in a panic to grab the rail, still too asleep to understand what was happening. She blinked her eyes and shook her head as Reza sat up wild-eyed beside her.

The deck dipped beneath them again, and Ibrahim squirmed unhappily on her shoulder at the commotion. Sadia's head finally cleared, and she looked up to see Heidroksimos striding heavily back and forth, setting the little *Mollysocks* reeling beneath him with every step, and he was shouting angrily in his foreign tongue at Dalgrim.

"Whoa, big man!" the dwarf barked, keeping one hand on the tiller as he gestured with the other. "What's he on about?" he demanded of Mariam, who was speaking anxiously to her husband, seemingly trying to calm him.

"He's upset that we're headed to sea," she explained, fretting with her hands. "We thought we were going to follow the river farther inland."

Sadia glanced around, and in the soft starlight beyond the *Mollysocks*' lanterns, she could see that they'd left the river delta and were now coasting into the open waters of what she presumed to be the Tatanqa Bay that Dalgrim had mentioned before.

"The *Mollysocks* floating downstream this entire time didn't tip him off we were headed seaward?" Dalgrim asked sarcastically.

Mariam wrung her hands. "I am sorry, we wanted to hire you to take us upriver, but with everything that happened, I think he was confused."

As they spoke, Heidroksimos continued complaining and glancing out at the silhouette of the sea, its frothy white crests marching eternally toward shore under the glow of the heavens.

"Look," Dalgrim growled impatiently, "if your man gets seasick, just tell him to lean over the railing and not make a mess on the deck, alright?"

"It's not that!" Mariam protested. "You don't understand, Thrakia is across the sea!" She was visibly upset, and it seemed to Sadia as if she were on the verge of tears.

Dalgrim cocked a bushy eyebrow. "Aye," he said slowly. "And...?"

"We're...." The woman looked miserable as she tried to explain something she clearly didn't want to share. "We're being pursued."

The dwarf gave a bitter laugh. "Well, you're in good company. Luckily for you, we're not going out into the sea — the *Mollysocks* isn't built for it. We're just following the coast west and up to Sagrada."

"It's too close," Mariam insisted, then paused and listened as her husband spoke to her, his tone severe, and she nodded, reaching out for him even as he continued pacing angrily. "He says... he says it can find him at sea," she said, her eyes misting fearfully. "Please, I can't let it find him."

Dalgrim and Lu shared a suspicious look. "Let what find him?" Dalgrim asked.

Suddenly, Heidroksimos shouted something, lifting his huge, chiseled arm and pointing behind them, back toward Emra'adid. His voice shook the deck beneath them, and all eyes turned to look.

Behind, following some distance in the wake of the *Mollysocks*, was the dark silhouette of a larger ship, its single, broad sail blotting out the stars and city lights behind it. At the prow was a bright torch or brazier, and the flickering light it cast against the billowed canvas was enough to reveal the color: an unmistakable, deep, bloody orange.

"Oh no," Sadia whispered, and Ibrahim whimpered on her shoulder.

Dalgrim squinted through the darkness. "Goldruun's blazing depths," he cursed.

The ship was gaining on them at an alarming rate, cutting through the gentle waves as banks of rowers propelled it along, and as it got closer, Sadia realized it wasn't a brazier illuminating the sale, but the mad prophet himself, still ablaze, standing at the prow, crouched as though ready to pounce.

"Bastard," Dalgrim growled furiously, letting go of the tiller and gripping the aft rail in both fists, his knuckles whitening. His dark eyes seemed almost to burn in their sockets as his jaw worked beneath his beaded beard.

"Sail, boss?" Lu asked after a tense moment, and Dalgrim finally stirred.

"Aye, let the sail out full," he said, grabbing the tiller again. "We can't outrun them, but we can buy some time." He turned and beckoned to Reza. "Get over here and take the tiller, lad!" he bellowed, and Reza leapt to his feet instantly, shrugging out of Sadia's grip and running over to the stern.

Dalgrim took the boy's hand and guided it to the tiller. "Just keep her steady," he instructed quickly. "That star up there, you see it? Just keep the tip of the mast there lined up with it." He clapped Reza's shoulder and then stalked toward his cabin.

"Can you do something to make us go faster?" Sadia asked, standing and following him as Ibrahim grew increasingly fitful in her arms. "Like you did before?"

Dalgrim threw her a dark look. "I'm afraid not, lass. Tonight, we're fighting, not fleeing."

Sadia stopped short in disbelief. "You saw what he did," she insisted as the dwarf ripped aside the shabby curtain across the cabin doorway. "We can't fight him!"

"Oh, I saw," he agreed. "And I'm going to make him pay for it." The inside of the cabin was dark, and Sadia could only make out vague shapes in the shadows.

"Big man, come here!" Dalgrim barked, waving Heidroksimos over, and the half-giant frowned and approached, his heavy footfalls forcing Sadia to reach out for the rail to steady herself as the *Mollysocks* bounced beneath her. "Grab that, there," he told the big Thrakian, pointing. "No, this one, here!"

Dalgrim turned to Sadia as Heidroksimos started hauling something heavy out onto the deck, grabbing her upper arm and forcing her a few steps toward the prow. "Take the wee one — and the pregnant one," he added, taking Mariam's hand and transferring it over to Sadia, "and hunker down on the other side of the cabin."

"Please," she cried, panicking as the larger ship cut through the waves toward them at an alarming pace, "I can't let him take Ibrahim!"

"He won't," the dwarf growled, and turned to face her, a wild look in his eyes. "I've a plan," he breathed raggedly. "Just get to the prow and stay down. Keep your head below the rail. Now, go!" He gave her a shove and turned back to Heidroksimos.

Sadia hesitated, and Mariam led her by the hand to the front of the *Mollysocks*. "Come," the woman urged, her voice shaking. "He is right — we need to get out of the way." Sadia followed her under the low canopy slung between the prow and the cabin.

As Mariam carefully lowered herself down, her hand protectively on her belly, Sadia glanced back at Reza, dutifully holding the tiller straight, his face scrunched up in concentration. Behind him, the huge sail loomed as the ship bore down on them, and the prophet's flaming form was clearly visible, down to the manic look in his eyes.

Sadia bit her lip and deliberated for only a moment before making up her mind.

"Here," she said, passing the baby to Mariam.

"What?" the woman asked, surprised, but taking Ibrahim carefully into her arms.

"Keep him safe," Sadia said, grinding her teeth against the fear in her heart. "I have to go to Reza."

Mariam's eyes widened, and she leaned to look around the corner of the cabin. "Sadia, no," she protested, "you should stay here!"

Sadia quickly wrestled the vial of blessed oil out of her little belt pouch as she bent over to ensure the hamsa medallion was still secure around Ibrahim's neck. "Rub this into his skin," she told Mariam. "It will help protect him."

"Protect him from what?" the woman demanded.

Sadia didn't answer, but straightened and looked her squarely in the eyes. "Promise me you'll keep him safe," she insisted, and the fear and desperation she felt must have been clear because Mariam nodded reluctantly.

Sadia took a deep breath to steel her nerves and turned, but Mariam's hand clamped around her wrist, halting her. "Mariam, I have to—"

"Listen!" the woman said sharply, meeting her with a hard gaze.

"Listen to me — my Heidroksimos is very dangerous when the fervor of battle takes him. Keep yourself and your brother out of his way, do you understand?"

The look on the woman's face made Sadia pause, but she swallowed hard and nodded.

"I'll watch Ibrahim, then," she said, releasing her strong grip.

Sadia took a step backward, then turned and ran to Reza. He looked up at her as she got to him, holding the tiller in both hands, his brow creased as he concentrated on his task. Off the back end of the *Mollysocks*, the cultist's ship was nearly on top of them, and a dozen or more of the armored men were standing ready to board.

The approaching vessel maintained its speed as it adjusted course slightly to come up alongside them, and the rowers on the near side drew in their oars to allow the ships to close. Lu stood ready on that side, his blade drawn and ready to strike, while Heidroksimos stood like a pillar, his powerful arms held at his sides, eyeing the men on the other ship with violent intent.

Dalgrim was draped over a pile of odds and ends spilling out of the cabin, tossing an occasional item out over his shoulder, clearly looking for something. "Aha!" he cried, and kicked his short legs, sliding off the pile and landing back on the deck. He turned around, holding a blocky crossbow in both hands, a handful of bolts grasped between his teeth.

He grinned in satisfaction and set the device down, working the crank quickly to draw the string back.

Sadia moved over to him as the other ship started pulling around and flanking them. "What's your plan exactly?" she asked, gripping the railing behind her with one hand, her eyes locked on the prophet.

Dalgrim grunted as the bowstring nocked, and he pulled the bolts from his mouth. "Right — when I give the signal, your brother there is going to pull that tiller hard to the left. As hard as you can, eh, lad?"

Reza blinked at him, then nodded vigorously, his eyes wide.

"And then what?" Sadia pressed. The cultists on the other ship readied their scimitars, the keen edges glinting in the overwhelming firelight.

"Then we escape out to sea," Dalgrim explained confidently. "But first, I'm going to take my crossbow here...."

The other ship's prow overtook them, and Sadia shivered under the prophet's insane gaze. "Yes?"

"And I'm going to shoot that bastard in the face," he finished, affixing a bolt to the crossbow and lifting the complex apparatus to his shoulder. The dwarf took a breath and held it as he lined up a shot, following the flaming form perched on the other bow, and Sadia's own breath caught as the moment stretched.

Finally, the crossbow fired, and the sudden thwack of the bolt releasing made Sadia jump. The bolt shot across the narrow gap, missing the prophet entirely and whistling well past him into the dark sea beyond.

"Bollocks," Dalgrim growled, then started rapidly cranking his weapon again. "Now, lad, now!" he called to Reza, and Sadia turned to see her brother frozen in place for a moment, looking petrified. Then he pulled on the tiller with all his might — but in the wrong direction.

The *Mollysocks*, though not a speedy vessel, was surprisingly nimble, and the forward left shoulder of her deck veered hard into the oncoming ship, sending a violent shudder through the hull and throwing everyone aboard off their feet.

Sadia's grip on the railing was all that saved her from falling overboard, and she scrambled to recover as a sheet of seawater spilled over onto the deck before sliding back off as the barge ground against the timber of the other ship.

"What in blazes?" Dalgrim cried angrily, chasing after his scattered crossbow bolts on all fours. "The other way, lad! The other way!" he bellowed, and Reza threw all his weight into tugging the tiller back the other way, blushing furiously.

Sadia followed the railing over to him as fast as she could and added her strength to his. "What happened?" she asked.

"I couldn't remember my right and left!" he cried in a panic, and the two of them hauled the tiller around as far as it would go.

The *Mollysocks* careened back to the right, and the hull of the cultists' ship groaned and splintered as the sharp edge of the barge's prow pulled free. But it was too late; half a dozen cultists in tarnished bronze armor successfully made the leap onto the deck of the *Mollysocks*.

Two of them charged straight at Sadia and Reza, but were intercepted by Lu, whose blade cut an arc just in front of them, forcing them to stop short. One of them stumbled backward, and his boot rolled on a stray crossbow bolt, sending him sprawling onto his back.

Lu pounced on him and drove his sword through the man's throat, and at the same time, Heidroksimos battled the others all on his own. He lifted one man and hurled him into the sea before his comrades could even react, and then the rest were upon him.

Their blades flashed and danced, and Sadia's eyes couldn't follow the furious battle.

She heard Dalgrim shout, "Straighten her out, lass!" The dwarf had his crossbow loaded up once more and loosed a bolt at one of the men assailing Heidroksimos, and this time, it landed true, punching through the eyeball-styled sun icon emblazoned on the man's breastplate. "And hold her steady!"

Sadia helped Reza straighten the tiller out again and glanced over her shoulder at the ship behind, which was struggling to maneuver after them. The wind was not on their side, however, and the sail above snapped as it was tugged forward and back, and the *Mollysocks* slowed to a crawl as it cut across the undulating waves.

In that moment, Sadia realized she knew nothing about sailing or how to correct the barge's trajectory. She looked in a panic to Reza as the cultist's ship came around and started gaining once again. "What do we do?" she asked shrilly.

Her brother looked around, at a loss. "I don't know!"

"Let out that line!" Dalgrim yelled across to them, pointing.

"I'll do it!" Reza dashed over to the spot the dwarf had indicated and started wrestling with the rope where it was tied off on the rail. Sadia held the tiller in both hands, feeling useless as she watched the men fighting and the prophet's vessel cutting hard around to intercept them.

"Deliver me Ankhatun's vessel!" the voice of the prophet roared from across the waves. "Bring me the child or be consumed by his righteous fury!"

Sadia's eyes widened, and her heart pounded in her chest. She whirled at a grunt from Reza to see the rope go slack, allowing the crossbeam beneath the sail to swivel until it caught the wind again. The *Mollysocks* lurched forward and started gaining speed, tilting and dipping as she rode the crests and troughs out to sea.

"Lookout!" Dalgrim cried as another trio of soldiers came swinging across the water on ropes. Lu ducked and rolled as the cultists landed deftly, their blades flashing, then leapt to engage them.

Three more armored Heirophants on the other ship started reeling in the ropes to cross over as well. Heidroksimos saw it and growled, planting his massive foot into the soldier charging him, sending the man flying off the *Mollysocks*. Then he ran toward the edge of the deck and leapt, flying an inhuman distance across the water toward the other ship and intercepting a cultist swinging on one of the ropes.

The force with which he launched himself sent the barge reeling under Sadia's feet yet again, and she heard him crash onto the prophet's ship just as the other two cultists swung over.

Lu was quickly surrounded, and his sword danced wildly around him to deflect the combined assault. Dalgrim fired another bolt, but it glanced off his target's helmet, and he cursed and cast the weapon aside. He jogged over to her and took the tiller, pulling it to guide the *Mollysocks* further away from the encroaching vessel.

"That was your plan?" Sadia demanded angrily as Lu dispatched one of the remaining cultists onboard.

Screams sounded from the other vessel, and she and Dalgrim both turned to see Heidroksimos wreaking havoc among the cultists, tossing them like sacks of grain out into the sea and crushing others in his hands or beneath his feet.

"It was a fine plan!" Dalgrim retorted, glancing back at the

Mollysocks' sail and guiding her slightly to the right. "Besides, big man seems to be handling things over there."

Sadia gripped the railing as she watched the prophet, still wreathed in mystical flames, leap from the prow and attack the half-giant. Heidroksimos lifted one of the long oars against its lock, snapping it in half and swinging the splintered end at the madman. The prophet ducked beneath the blow and lunged forward, throwing his flaming fists against the man's naked chest, and Heidroksimos stumbled backward with a grunt.

"Hmm," Dalgrim mused, squinting over his shoulder. "Maybe he's not doing so well."

As the two ships slowly drew closer despite Dalgrim's best efforts to steer the *Mollysocks* away, the half-giant tried to hold his own, but the prophet was simply too fast and nimble. His fiery fists flew and struck again and again, and soon, the big Thrakian's skin was scorched and blistered, and his face bore a furious grimace.

On the *Mollysocks*, Lu was beginning to sweat beneath his round reed hat; being outnumbered for so long was proving to be a greater challenge than Sadia had yet seen him meet. He sunk to one knee, his blade held out defensively in both hands while two cultists rained down blows, trying to break him. A sharp, fleshy crack sounded as a fast projectile hit one of the cultists in the throat, and he recoiled backward, dropping his scimitar and clawing in agony at his neck.

Sadia looked over to see Reza unfold his sling and load another stone, his tongue sticking out as he took aim and set his makeshift weapon whirling over his head, ready to deliver another little missile.

"Heidroksimos!" Mariam's shrill scream cut through the wind, the waves, and the din of combat, and Sadia froze in terror.

The pregnant woman fell to the deck from behind the cabin, clutching Ibrahim to her as an armored cultist stood over her, shouting and trying to wrench the baby from her grasp. She resisted, and he hit her in the face. Still, Mariam would not let Ibrahim go, shielding him beneath her, and the cultist drew his blade and held it aloft.

Before anyone could do anything, her husband's deafening roar thundered across the gap. Sadia turned and saw the gigantic man barrel through the prophet's whirling flames, knocking him aside, then race to the prow and launch himself out over the water toward his wife's assailant.

As he sailed through the air, swirling storm clouds roiled to life above him, lightning tracing through the darkness. A brilliant, arcing white light coalesced in his fist, and it grew into a hissing, furious lightning bolt. Sadia's hair drifted upward, and she stared in awe as the air took on a powerful charge.

Heidroksimos drew his arm back and hurled the blinding white spear with all his terrifying strength.

The air around the *Mollysocks* exploded, and Sadia was knocked back against the railing as a peel of thunder rang out. By the time she recovered, the cultist who had assaulted Mariam had vanished, and the deck where he had stood was black and smoldering with an ember glow. Heidroksimos landed in the water beside the barge and instantly burst out, hauling himself up and rushing to his wife.

"What in blazes?" Dalgrim cried in bewilderment as he staggered back to his feet and wiggled his fingers in his ears. Lu and the last remaining cultist had both been bowled over by the lightning blast and were wrestling on the deck, scrambling for their weapons.

Heidroksimos knelt beside Mariam, but Sadia couldn't see past him to know whether she was alright. "Ibi," she breathed, but the sound of creaking timber coming from beside them forced her to look away and up at the cultists' ship as it closed on the *Mollysocks*.

"Damn it all," Dalgrim growled, taking Sadia's hand and placing it on the tiller. "Hold her steady," the dwarf ordered, "and wait for my command — we're going to try that trick again. But this time, we'll make it work."

Sadia fought to steady herself and wrestled with the tiller as the dwarf marched back over to his cabin, past Lu and the cultist, grabbing Reza and dragging the boy along on his way.

Lu finally managed to flip the cultist over and wrap one arm under the man's chin. The cultist's eyes went wide, and he clawed at the arm strangling him, but Lu held him tight until, finally, the man stopped moving. Sadia didn't know if he was dead or unconscious, and she didn't feel guilty for hoping it was the former.

Lu panted as he reached for his sword where it had fallen to the deck, but before he could retrieve it, the sound of wind-whipped flames came from overhead, and the prophet's bare, flaming feet slammed into the deck beside him. The madman kicked Lu hard in the midsection, sending him rolling and tumbling across the deck of the *Mollysocks*, right off the edge and into the sea.

He turned on Sadia, towering over her, the heat from his dark flames singeing the ends of her hair. "I know you," he seethed, the fire licking at his skin pulsing. "I could not see it at first, but now I understand." Sadia winced against the heat as she leaned back, fighting to maintain her grip on the tiller.

Behind the prophet, Reza was helping Dalgrim pull something huge and heavy out of the cabin. The dwarf tugged hard, then danced backward, moving Reza out of harm's way as the strange iron vase fell over and bounced heavily on the deck.

Sadia looked past them, hoping Heidroksimos would intervene, but the half-giant was cradling Mariam in his arms, paying no heed to what was happening behind him.

The prophet stooped, bringing his flame-wreathed face closer to hers, and she cried out as she felt the skin on her face start to blister.

"You are the avatar of Naharia, the harlot moon," the prophet whispered, the words burning her ears, and she clenched her eyes shut, trying to lean as far back as she could. "The mother of the nightfall. The Diurnal Kingdom cannot be ushered in while you and your vile progeny persist. Now..." he stood back to his full height and loomed over her, the frenzy of his flames quickening, "give unto me Ankhatun's vessel."

"No!" she cried defiantly, her voice hoarse from the dry, oppressive heat. "You can't have him!"

The prophet fumed before her, and Sadia was sure that her hands turned to ash, just like poor Roya, but somehow she managed to hold the tiller tight, even as it started blackening to cinder in her grasp from the heat of the evil flames.

"Now, lassie!" Dalgrim's voice hollered from beyond the prophet, and she chanced a look through the flames to see him sitting atop the iron jar, its gaping, open mouth pointed directly at her. "And take cover!"

Sadia screamed in pain and fear and pulled the tiller as hard as she could, then threw herself onto the deck to scramble away.

The prophet turned to face Dalgrim as the barge swerved beneath them, kicking its aft back at the other ship once again. As the iron jar rolled beneath the dwarf, he steadied it with his feet, and the imposing madman swayed with the motion of the little barge until it righted itself.

Then he trained his blazing eyes on the dwarf and lifted an arm to point menacingly. "Pyre thyself on Ankhatun's righteous—"

The iron vase between Dalgrim's legs bucked, and a massive ball of flaming iron shot out the end of it. The concussive force left Sadia deaf, and she watched the prophet disappear as the hellish projectile tore through him, carrying his fiery form off the back of the *Mollysocks* before slamming into the side of the cultist's vessel.

The larger ship now behind them listed dangerously from the impact and was engulfed in billowing black smoke as the timber of its hull exploded, sending a shower of splinters raining down over the surrounding waters.

The *Mollysocks* glided away on the wind as the ship behind her rolled back over, and water poured through the hole in her hull. Sadia watched in shock as the handful of remaining cultists on board panicked and fought the flames uselessly while their ship proceeded to sink.

Dalgrim lifted himself from where he'd been bucked off the big iron thing and went to the aft rail. "That was for Roya, you bastard!" he roared at the inky black waves that had swallowed the prophet. "May your twisted soul forever rot alongside your bloated corpse," he muttered, and spat into the sea.

Reza ran over to Sadia and knelt beside her. "Are you alright?" he asked, helping her to her feet.

Sadia looked down at her hands. Her skin was tight and hot, and she could feel the blisters swelling across them, but she gave him a tight-lipped smile and nodded. "Ibrahim," she said, and Reza took her arm and helped her over to the bow.

"Help!" a cry came from the darkness beyond the ship, and they stopped to look. "I'm not good swimmer!" Lu's voice called miserably.

Dalgrim waved Sadia and Reza on. "I'll fetch him," he said, stooping to take up a coil of rope from the pile of refuse in front of the cabin.

Heidroksimos knelt silently beside his wife, holding her in both arms. As Sadia and Reza approached, his head snapped around, and he snarled, but relaxed when he saw it was them.

Mariam's lip was split, blood trickling down her chin, and her ankle and the end of her dress were burnt and singed, but otherwise, she looked unharmed. She cradled Ibrahim in her arms, and Sadia fell to her knees to take him from her.

"He's alright," Mariam assured her.

Sadia adjusted the blanket around Ibrahim's face and found him calm once again. His skin was anointed with the sacred oil, and he was no longer hot to the touch. "Thank you," she said to Mariam, and the woman gave a weak smile, then winced and placed her hands on the swell of her belly.

"Are you alright?" Reza asked nervously.

"I fell," Mariam answered uncertainly. "It's not good for a woman in my condition to fall. But I think all is well, for now." She reached up and laid a hand against her husband's bearded cheek. "My love," she said gently.

Heidroksimos leaned into her hand as stared down at her, and Sadia couldn't help noticing the guilty expression on his face.

Sadia stood and led Reza away, leaving the married couple to have a moment alone. They walked back to the stern where Dalgrim was helping Lu haul himself out of the sea and back onto the deck.

"Evildoers?" Lu asked, breathing hard and looking around for his sword.

"No more evildoers, Lu," Sadia answered softly.

In the distance, the prophet's ship burned as it sank, its main mast snapping and toppling into the sea. After a few lingering moments, the last of the flames were doused as Tatanqa Bay claimed the shattered vessel.

"Well," the dwarf grumbled as the eastern swordsman collapsed on the deck, panting and dripping. "I'd say a drink is in order, eh?"

"Yes, please," Lu groaned, and Dalgrim went to the cabin, returning with a bottle of amber-colored liquor.

"This is the good stuff," he insisted, uncorking it and taking a swig before passing it over to Lu. He looked at Sadia and winced when he saw the state of her arms and face. "Ach, lass," he sighed, walking over and taking her hand carefully in his to inspect it. "Come, I've something for this in my cabin."

Reza took Ibrahim from her and sat down against the rail while Sadia allowed Dalgrim to lead her. The dwarf kicked a path through the paraphernalia scattered across the deck, then started rummaging through a wall-mounted cabinet filled with jars and vials.

"Did you see what Heidroksimos did?" she asked quietly after a moment.

Dalgrim paused and glanced at her. "Aye, I saw it. I don't know what it was I saw, but I saw it." He plucked a jar from the shelf, unscrewed it to take a sniff, scowled, and placed it back. "There's something about those two they've not told us," he muttered. "But we'll deal with that another day."

Sadia nodded and looked away, out toward the sea. The ringing in her ears had finally ceased, and the nighttime waters seemed almost impossibly serene after the battle they had just waged.

"You did well, lass," Dalgrim said, pulling her attention back to him.

She shook her head, surprised at the comment. "I didn't do anything. I was too afraid to do anything useful."

"No," he said firmly, stopping to look meaningfully at her. "Everything you're doing for that wee one, it's...." He paused, his jaw working underneath his bristly black beard. "Your dedication to fixing whatever it is that's wrong with him — it's admirable. And it moved Roya."

He blinked rapidly when her name passed his lips. "She's... she was a good woman, mark my words, but a hard one, too, and she never suffered fools gladly. She liked you. Saw something special in you — I could tell."

He chuckled, but his humor flirted dangerously with a panicked sorrow. "She doesn't send just anyone to her people at Vaharabajra, you know." Sadia smiled sadly, and the dwarf took a deep breath. "You're a good lass, is what I'm saying, and a brave one... and Roya saw it, too."

He exhaled, staring past her for a moment — then, as if catching himself, turned back to the shelf and pulled another jar down to inspect it. His words touched her, humbled her, but she didn't know how to respond.

"Ah, here it is," he declared, holding up a little clay jar. "Arnica oil. An old apothecary friend told me once it's good for burns." He held it out, and she took it in both hands, afraid the stiffness in her fingers would cause her to drop it otherwise.

"Thank you," she said, and Dalgrim patted her arm and moved past her through the door. "I'm sorry," Sadia blurted, and he stopped to look at her. "About Roya," she finished, guilty tears stinging behind her eyes. "If I hadn't found you in Qasira, then—"

"Stop," he interrupted, holding up a hand and gritting his teeth. His eyes shone in the lanternlight as they looked up into hers. "You did nothing wrong by Roya. I did." He turned his head up toward the starry sky and waited until his voice wasn't weak. "I left her twenty years ago, you know. And then again tonight." He closed his eyes. "I loved her, I did," he whispered, like a prayer. "Truly."

The orange glow of the lanterns reflected off the trail of silent tears that ran down into his beard, and Sadia wiped carefully at her burnt cheeks as she wept with him. He was quiet for a long moment, and when he finally looked back at her, he was composed.

"I'm not a good man, Sadia," he confessed. "Jalila's right about that. A swindler, a thief, a hundred rotten things besides. But I tell you this," he said, and he placed a hand on her shoulder. "I'll get you and your brothers to Sagrada, and if whatever we find there can't help him, I'll get you to the next place. I'll see this through with you to the end. For Roya."

Sadia's tears flowed freely as she threw her arms around him, and he hugged her back. "I promise you," he repeated, and she believed the conviction in his voice. She clung to him as her tears fell, and he let her, patting her back and comforting her until she was calm.

"Thank you, Dalgrim," she managed tearfully as she finally released him.

He nodded and offered a sad, tired smile. "Go put that ointment on, aye? And get some sleep." He gave her shoulder a comforting squeeze, then started back toward the tiller.

Sadia returned to her brothers, both of whom were already asleep on the deck, Reza curled on his side with Ibrahim held protectively against his chest. She knelt and dabbed the salve onto her burns, the cool oil providing a small but instantaneous relief. Once her hands and face were covered, she lay down beside the boys and draped her arm over both of them.

She was exhausted, and the gentle rocking of the boat, the soft lapping of the waves against the hull, and the distant cry of seabirds quickly lulled her to sleep as Dalgrim steered the limping *Mollysocks* back toward the coast.

ONLY MOMENTS after closing her eyes — or so it felt — a voice from the stern woke her.

"Why'd you do it, you stupid bastard?" the voice asked miserably. Sadia lifted her head, struggling to open her eyes. Two of the lanterns had flickered out, and the sky beyond was still blanketed with stars.

The only lantern still lit dangled from a pole at the back end of the

Mollysocks, and in the dim light, she could see Dalgrim collapsed against the aft rail, one hand up on the wreckage of the tiller as he half-heartedly guided the ship and the other still wrapped around the empty liquor bottle. Lu was passed out nearby, and the dwarf was weeping and muttering to himself.

"Why'd you let go of her hand?" he whimpered quietly, his eyes red and swollen. "Why'd I let go of her hand?"

Sadia stirred, the fog of sleep clearing, but Reza and Ibrahim still slumbered peacefully, so she didn't move. Instead, she lay her head back down, fighting tears of her own as she listened to Dalgrim weep, and she prayed silently to Naharia and Vamudri both for Roya, a woman who had hardly known her, but whose kindness had been greater than any Sadia had ever known.

EPILOGUE

GIDEON

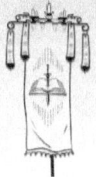

"HE DOESN'T HAVE A CHOICE," Battlesister Gerda argued vehemently as she stalked back and forth before the chapel altar. "You saw what he did — a miracle, perhaps, but if he can invoke the Light to heal, his choice of oath has already been made."

She halted and turned to look up defiantly at Sir Cormac as Gideon watched quietly from his pew nearby, awaiting his fate. Donnal sat beside him, snoring softly and slumped against Nefteli on his other side. The archoness had pushed their pace back to the monastery, and after a full report to Bishop Delwyn and a meal at the mess, they had gathered in the chapel, apparently so Gideon could choose his oath and swear it.

"He hasn't chosen yet, Gerda," Sir Cormac protested, leaning his heavy frame against the wall as he watched his dwarven comrade pace restlessly. "I don't know that we can force Weal on him simply because he used the Light to heal in a desperate moment."

The battlesister turned on her heel to glare up at him, and Gideon was surprised to see the old man shift uncomfortably under her gaze.

She glanced aside at Gideon and growled. "A private word, Cormac." The dwarven woman's boots clanked off down the aisle toward the vestibule, and the big paladin followed after her, leaving the handful of remaining recruits in the quiet chapel.

Gideon sighed, unsure exactly what was happening or what his future held. After a moment, Nefteli disentangled herself from Donnal's somnolescent form and came over to sit down beside Gideon.

She took a seat quietly, and he could feel an uncharacteristic unease from her. He looked up at her, but she kept her dark eyes on the floor and said nothing. After a long pause, she finally spoke. "I prayed for you," she said, her voice breaking. "For all of you."

Her hand found his and gripped it tightly as two small tears rolled down her proud cheeks. Staring down at her dark fingers intertwined with his, his heart stopped for a concerning moment.

"We lost so many," she lamented, lifting her head to search the relief of the pantheon carved into the wall above the altar. "It feels like my prayers were in vain, yet...." She finally looked at him, and the votive candles around the chapel glimmered in her eyes. "You did it, Gideon. You saved Donnal." Her grip tightened, and he squeezed her back.

"I was terrified," he admitted quietly. "I couldn't... I couldn't let him die." Unbidden tears of his own welled in his eyes, and he quickly blinked them away. "Not after James."

She nodded, and her voice quavered. "I'm sorry about James," she said earnestly. "And everyone we lost. I can't even imagine...." She trailed off and shook her head. After another moment of silence, she frowned and looked at him again. "How did you do it? How did you save him? I thought you couldn't channel the Holy Light."

Gideon took a breath and held it. He couldn't tell her about the witches. The archoness had claimed them vanquished, but Gideon hadn't witnessed any such thing. Instead, he had made them a promise, and he bore the burning scar of their fingerprints on his chest. And because of his promise, presumably, he summoned the Light of the gods. It made no sense, but it sounded like heresy, that much he was sure.

"Battlesister Dawnhammer called it a miracle," he finally said with a shrug. "I don't know how I did it. Desperation, maybe." He glanced over at Donnal, who had slunk further down, snoring softly. "I just couldn't let him die."

Nefteli nodded and followed his gaze, and Gideon watched her expression soften as she studied Donnal's sleeping face. "Thank you," she whispered. "He means so much to me... you both do."

Her words were kind, loving, but they made his heart sink. "We kept our promise to you," he said, forcing a smirk. "I just wish everyone else could have made it, too."

He wanted to tell her how much it had hurt to watch James die, to see Lillian be deceived and throw herself from the cliff. He wanted to tell her about the king of hate and flame, the Sisters Seidh, all of it... but he couldn't. He simply didn't know how.

Loud metal footsteps sounded across the marble floor behind them, and Nefteli quickly let go of his hand as they turned to look back. The sudden clangor roused Donnal, too, and he snorted awake, hauling himself up straight in the pew and looking confused.

Archoness Lorica strode purposefully down the aisle toward the altar, Battlesister Gerda and Sir Cormac in tow, Bishop Delwyn toddling after on his staff.

"Rise, Gideon Ballad," she called, her voice ringing off the walls as she approached. "The time has come to choose your oath and swear it."

Gideon rose swiftly to his feet and stood at attention as she reached the altar and turned to face them. She no longer exuded the frenzied fascination she had in the aftermath on the hill, but instead had regained her steely composure, and he felt the weight of her gaze like a heavy yoke.

The archoness looked from him to the dwarf and the old paladin. "I understand there is some disagreement about his right to choose an oath," she prompted.

The battlesister grimaced and threw her large red braids behind her with a toss of her head. "Aye, milady," she answered grimly. "The lad invoked the Holy Light and healed his comrade. And further, he healed him of the infamous witch-wounds, which none of our other healers could treat. You saw it yourself. I believe that proves his value as a healer, and therefore, he should swear the Oath of Weal, as all our hospitalers must."

Sir Cormac nodded, but then spoke up. "That he did, milady, but the choice of oath is a privilege granted to all who pass their trials."

"He didn't pass the trials," Gerda countered, glaring up at Sir Cormac.

The big man stared down at his diminutive comrade, his fluffy white eyebrows furrowed. "His trial was far more dire than any we've ever imposed on our recruits here at the monastery."

"But he did not prove capable of invoking the Light when tested," the dwarven woman growled, "when the choice of oath is granted."

"Enough," Archoness Lorica's voice cut through the argument. Silence fell across the chapel, and Gideon stood awkwardly by, his fate at the mercy of her decision. The woman's eyes bored into his as she considered, and then she nodded once. "Come and kneel," she instructed, and he did as he was ordered.

Gideon swallowed hard as he approached, finding it hard to believe the intimidating archoness was the same woman who had wept and mewled on the witches' hill. His knees ached as they met the hard marble steps of the altar, and he bowed his head. He waited a long moment in uncomfortable silence until the hairs on his neck stood on end as he wondered if she expected him to say something.

Finally, she spoke. "Which oath would you choose, Ballad?" the archoness asked, and he was surprised at the gentleness of her tone.

Gideon lifted his head and blinked at her, then glanced over at Nefteli, who watched him intently. He took a breath. "I want to be a paladin, milady," he confessed, his voice thick with desperation. "I want to wield the Light as a warrior."

The archoness looked down on him for a long moment, her eyes shrewd and discerning.

"The battlesister is wise, Gideon," she finally said, quietly. "You have proven to be a gifted healer. The Oath of Weal is yours — the choice made by the gods themselves."

His heart sank at her words, and he hung his head, his blond tresses hiding his shame and disappointment. He looked up again as she touched his shoulder.

"Have faith," she said, her golden eyes glowing eerily in the low light of evening. Her hand drifted down to his chest, and the witches' scars there burned as her gauntleted fingers grazed over them and lingered as if she knew exactly where they were beneath his shirt.

Her eyes flashed. "Swear you, Gideon Ballad," she began, her powerful voice carrying easily throughout the chapel, "to serve as an agent of the gods' will, as either the executor of their vengeance, or the instrument of their mercy, and in all matters to be a shield against the evils that plague this world, from this moment until you draw your final breath?"

Gideon's heart was torn in two. "I swear it," he breathed, readying himself for the next part of the oath.

The archoness nodded solemnly. "And which oath will you claim and keep? Weal or Woe?" Her golden eyes blazed down on him, and his scars burned beneath her touch. "I... I claim the Oath... of Weal," he said, forcing the words from his mouth. He wanted to weep as he said it, as his dream slipped away yet again.

"And will you keep it jealously?" she prompted after a moment.

Gideon stared back up at her, and her expression flickered as she seemed to recognize the fury behind his eyes. "I will," he answered in a rasp.

She held his gaze for a lingering moment before removing her hand from his chest. "Rise, then, Gideon Ballad — son of the Holy Order. Invoke the Holy Light to heal the wounds of the world, and never to inflict them. Go forth and walk the paths of the just and righteous until you meet St. Thylessia at the brink of eternity."

Gideon grit his teeth as he climbed to his feet and turned to face the others. Donnal gave a cheer, beaming from his seat in the pew, but

Nefteli's face was pained. Sir Cormac and the battlesister both looked on solemnly, and the bishop merely leaned wearily on his staff, his expression tired.

It wasn't the oath he would have chosen, but as they filtered out of the chapel, Gideon steeled himself. In the morning, they would ride for the Sunless Citadel, and from there, he had no idea where the Church Merciful would take him. His only consolation was the hope that perhaps he could now stay with Nefteli, whatever distant corner of the world they might be sent to.

As the cool evening air kissed his skin, though, Gideon's heart was heavy, and he stared at the distant western mountains, remembering the smoldering titan, and the fear and pain its presence had inspired in him. The memory frightened him, and as his friends guided him off to the barracks for a well-earned rest, he couldn't shake the specter of an uncertain future: one he feared was haunted by the choices he himself had made.

APPENDIX A
IMPORTANT PERSONS

Sadia al-Yetim

Fatherless, from no family. An orphan of no renown or consequence, considered abandoned by the gods of day and night. And yet, when a child was in danger, she alone moved to help, despite her own misgivings.

"Mother Naharia, spare not your love from the fatherless, but by living according to your own loving and gentle ways, may we earn the strength to walk the path laid before us. Lead our hearts to patience, our hands to charity, and our words to kindness."

— The nightly prayer of Sadia al-Yetim. Once overheard in a crowded bazaar, she likely misremembered and recites a prayer of her own creation, perhaps more fervent than the original.

Reza al-Yetim

Bold and fearless likely to his own detriment, the young orphan was left to die by whoever sired him, but loved him not. He bears the title of al-Yetim with pride, and though it was Sadia who found and cared for him, Reza is convinced that it is she who needs him, and he is fiercely protective of the girl who made him her family.

"Reza al-Yetim, slayer of giant rats and conquerer of the Qasiran alleyways, at your service!"

— The means by which young Reza would often introduce himself, if able to do so before his older siblings managed to stop him.

The Prophet of the Lidless Eye

His name unknown even to himself, the young boy learned from apostate astrologers of the one true god, Ankhatun, whose watchful eye rose each day only to close each night, leaving the world to the cold of night. The boy came to believe that if Ankhatun never closed his eye, perhaps the world could be rid of the vile dark that haunted him so.

The apostates taught a young boy how to divine hidden knowledge through haruspicy, and by that profane art, he discovered a banished god to seal away the night.

But that god's aims were his own.

Dalgrim Glintstone

A Gilded Dwarf who left the Auric Bastions in shame to seek his fortune elsewhere. His trusty barge, the *Mollysocks*, has known a dozen different names and carried the ambitious dwarf the length of the Tajari River, from the Land of a Thousand Waters to Emra'adid and all along the coast of the Salient Sea.

"Wanted for larceny against the nobility of Estwyn's Loch. Known to use the alias Hamfist Gemworthy. Fond of craven tricks and ploys. Exercise caution during apprehension."

— Warrant from the West Umbrals, one of many similar posted in cities throughout the north and south alike.

Lu Song

An errant swordsman from the Empire of Xibang who fell in with Dalgrim to escape his own blade. He often dreams of the night he earned his exile, but has found the merciful embrace of wine and liquor can help keep such nightmares at bay.

"Upon grandfather's blade, I swear never to return to Xibang unless to carry out my vengeance. I pray your Soul has found rightful honor among the Celestial Court. I am sorry."

— Lu Song the swordsman before boarding the ship that would bear him west on his exile.

Suleiman the Fat

Suleiman's wharf is the entrance to wealthy Emra'adid for thieves, miscreants, swindlers, and charlatans. The wise ones always bring a treat for Dandan.

A dilapidated old shack sits on the city's maze of canals, the only place Emra'adid's bright sun never touches. There, Suleiman learned to harden his heart, though some still see in him a hint of the nobility and honor for which his father was known.

Roya Maramasi

Hailing from Maramasa, Roya's mother married a trader from Emra'adid, who loved his wife and daughters very much. Both succumbed to illness when Roya was still quite young, and she chose to be bold and leave all she'd known behind, venturing to her father's homeland and hoping for something entirely new.

Full of joy and hope, Roya opened the Gentle Djinni caravanserai with her betrothed. When he left, her heart never recovered.

MARIAM OF ITHAKOS

A devout follower of Hyphaestia, goddess of mercy. The lovely young Mariam, daughter of a renowned shipwright, fell in love with a man who was destined for a glorious death. Now she carries his child, and she will do anything to protect her husband.

Reviled by her people, Mariam seeks atonement for her great sin; she simply could not let Heidroksimos suffer any longer.

HEIDROKSIMOS OF ITHAKOS

A man of enormous size and strength; all he knew was violence, but that changed when Mariam freed him.

"Conqueror of Ahegion, favored of the gods."
— Inscription upon a statue of Heidroksimos in Ithakos, quickly demolished following his betrayal.

Madam Jalila

Jalila learned early the value of making friends, even — if not especially — with the less savory denizens of wealthy Emra'adid. A life of poverty had been thrust upon her, but the young woman never let her hunger die; when her charm and biting intellect couldn't yield the results she needed, Jalila never shied from employing violence and deception to get what she felt was meant to be hers.

"I am no angel, Dalgrim, but that woman does things no lady should ever do to get what she wants. When she smiles, I see only the cold gaze of a stalking serpent."

— *Roya Maramasi, sharing her unsolicited opinion of Dalgrim's most frequent employer.*

Gideon Ballad

From youth, he dreamt of becoming a paladin. Days of hard work fishing in his father's small boat were payment, he decided, for the honor and glory he would achieve. Gideon's understanding of the Holy Light, however, was naive and hopeful — far-flung from the truth of the matter. His time at the monastery left him unsure of his place in the world, and a mote of anger seeded his heart.

"He was meant to be the best of us, the purest and the strongest. Even his damned hair is golden! I should have seen it earlier."
— *Donnal Crieg, best friend of Gideon Ballad.*

DONNAL CRIEG

Inarguably affable, and somewhat-less-arguably competent, the handsome lad from Morningdew left his little village to fulfill a duty his father never did. His first foray into danger after completing his trials left him shaken, but the unflappable youth remained unbroken, and he built a wall in his mind to keep his pain behind, so that he could still be the gregarious youth his friends needed him to be.

"What do you make of Crieg?" Sir Cormac asked.

Battlesister Dawnhammer scowled. *"He doesn't take anything seriously — a bad habit for any soldier."*

"Perhaps, but there's something in him, Gerda," the old paladin stressed. *"Something special."*

NEFTELI HENUTEP

When the Serpent Kings seized control of Akhum, enslaving those who did not escape, they never imagined the wrath they'd earned from one young girl who would go on to become a healer in the Holy Order, the most prestigious organization in the country where her people sought refuge.

"Cruelty and foul designs turn the steadfast and loving nature of the righteous to abject wroth."

— *Traditional proverb from the Annals of the Pharaohs.*

Battlesister Gerda Dawnhammer

Gerda hails from the Irondelves, the dwarven city built beneath the West Umbrals. After helping to conquer the cave giants, she felt called to the surface lands, where she fought alongside a young paladin named Eustace, who eventually convinced her to join the Holy Order.

"Mogrim Dawnhammer was a terror, known to sow chaos and fear among his foes. He had a hammer smithed that was worthy of his name, wrought from steel and secret gold that shimmered in the torchlit mines. Alas, Mogrim was bested the day of the hammer's first battle — crushed beneath a blind cave giant's stony foot. His golden hammer fell beside him in the midst of the horde. His daughter was the only one fierce enough to retrieve it."

— Dalgrim Glintstone, recalling a tragic tale to a group of guests during the Gentle Djinni's heyday.

Sir Eustace Cormac

A towering man and a terror on the battlefield, his allies are often surprised by the warmth and strength that he can exude. Eustace has an undying fondness for his compatriot, Gerda Dawnhammer, and the two of them have managed to stay side-by-side for many years, all the way to an unlikely posting at a monastery in Rivenwood — a strange reprieve from the violence the Church Militant typically demands of them.

From the mountains to the sea, few haven't heard the name of Eustace Cormac, the paladin who survived half a dozen crusades, who crushes his foes by blade and by Light, and who would give his life for any innocent soul who needed him.

James Byrne

With no other choice, James left home to offer himself to the Holy Order, and though jovial and unserious by nature, he was at first afraid. While he presumed nothing more awaited him than a quick and painful death, the boy was struck by the magnitude of faith he encountered and the miracles he witnessed, and he began to take the oath seriously.

"I swear I'll come back to you once I pass the trials, Sarah. And you, too, Mercy. And you, Ginny."

— James Byrne to three young ladies who came to the hamlet's edge to wave him a teary goodbye as he set out for Rivenwood.

ARCHONESS LORICA

Long removed from her childhood on the Seashell Isles, Lorica — the Fifth Archon — ascended from her role as a paladin and was entrusted by the gods themselves with an incomparable connection to and strength in the Holy Light. She is known among her peers for her drive and intensity, but in the recesses of her divinely-touched psyche, she wrestles with the nature and truth of the Light.

"Cantus, Antiphon, Hymnus, Chorus, Lorica, Anthem, Dirge: the seven archons shall be the epitome of faith, strength in the Light, and devotion to the gods and to the Holy Order."

— An excerpt from the Encyclical of St. Oronos, penned at the founding of the Holy Order and expounding upon the nature and necessity of paragons of the faith.

BISHOP FRANCIS DELWYN

The Churches Militant and Merciful were split hundreds of years ago when the saints were given the Holy Light. Ever since then, the divinely appointed archbishop delegates to bishops beneath him to shepherd the flock. Delwyn was a promising young priest, dedicated and devout, and was elevated to the status of Bishop of the Holy 3rd Regiment of the Church Militant. Unfortunately, he proved an inept leader, and after a brief but disastrous campaign against the Twilight Elves, he subsequently sought a more peaceful post overseeing trainees. Delwyn has guided the faithful of Rivenwood Monastery for many years.

"Rivenwood Forest is an idyllic setting for a monastery, and the grounds are truly beautiful. In speaking to the residents of nearby villages and hamlets, I have understood there to be whispers of dark forces hiding in the woods, although I'm given to dismiss these as the superstitions of folk in need of the beneficence of the Holy Light."

— Letter from the young Bishop Delwyn to his mother upon assuming authority over Rivenwood Monastery.

APPENDIX B
IMPORTANT PLACES

QASIRA

One of the emirates — wealthy city-states dotting the Great Nahridi Desert — Qasira sits primly on the Tajari River where it bends northward to run to the sea. Known for its spices, impressive temple district, and a baleful emphasis on lineage and ancestry that defines one's place in society, Qasira is an oasis amid the hostile desert for weary travelers — as long as they behave themselves.

Emir al-Muhariq loved his son. But when he was seduced by profane prophecy, the fear that gripped him forced his hand to what had previously been unimaginable.

EMRA'ADID

The Jewel of the Tatanqa, Emra'adid is the gateway between the nations of the south and the northern kingdoms through which all goods and travelers must pass. Situated on the Tajari River delta, the city is home to folk from all over the world who came and resettled, making it a center of many different cultures all living under the rule of his majesty, the glorious sultan.

"The sultan might sit a gilded throne, but everyone knows Jalila is the one you make sure never to cross."
— Suleiman the Fat, explaining how Emra'adid works to a young, newly-arrived pickpocket at his secret wharf.

WEST UMBRIA

The Kingdom of West Umbria is an expansive stretch of land that runs between the oceanside West Umbral Mountains and the eastern Salient Sea, and comprises fertile farmlands, peaceful forests, and various baronies and duchies, all sworn to the Umber King, who rules from the cliffside citadel known as Dusk's Vigil.

Shadows are said to harbor evil intentions from coming to light; the peaks of the West Umbrals tower high and cast a long shadow over the land.

XIBANG

Far to the east, across the Barrier Sea, lies the great Empire of Xibang, yet mysterious to the lands around the Salient Sea. While few westerners ever make the perilous journey to the east, those who do speak of warring kingdoms, celestial dragons, towering palaces, and sprawling, ancient cities.

In a sacred glade, nestled in the shadow of Mount Baohu, stands one of the Gates of Heaven. There, an immortal guardian challenges any foolish enough to approach. Those who cannot answer his question nourish the glade with their blood.

— A passage from historical records of Xibang, composed by the great scribe Zhao Hengshi

---

THE DWARVEN KINGDOMS

Known collectively as 'the Dwarven Kingdoms', ancient underground realms such as Glinthammer, Emberforge, and the Irondelves have rich, storied histories. In truth, they are sometimes more different from one another than even from the humans who often dwell on the lands above them. The scale and wealth of such dwarven kingdoms is legendary, as is the infamous pride of the dwarves, and they are known to make powerful, though reluctant, allies.

When the world was young, the Stonefather awoke and gathered up the earth to form into mountains. He had nine sons, and each went their own way and built their own kingdom, some of which are now said to be lost.

MARAMASA

The timeless city of Maramasa sits in the fertile Dira Valley, built up along their sacred river. Ancient stone temples and palaces rise above the lush canopy, and the learned jadhari use magic from the gods to keep the horrors of the surrounding jungles at bay.

"Beloved Vamudri, the Blossom Vine, showers sacred Maramasa in her protective tears; she weeps for her sons and daughters, the sick and the suffering. The magic of the rain and of the rushing Dira have guarded the city for a thousand generations, and will again for a thousand more."

— *Raja Gama, after the miraculous death of his wife.*

AKHUM

South from the Salient Sea, the River Kheferu runs to the land of Akhum, cutting its way through a deep and narrow canyon. It opens upon a lush oasis where the secluded kingdom sits among a sea of rolling dunes, nestling fertile fields in the shadows of its impressive architecture: pyramids and palaces, statues and obelisks, which legends say the gods of the land themselves erected.

On the night the Serpent Kings revealed themselves and seized power, the Grand Pyramid turned black, and most of those who were not corrupted were enslaved.

Thrakia

Thrakia is a land embroiled in seemingly endless war as its many city-states vie for supremacy over each other. The gods demand that a king be chosen to ascend as a new deity, and so strength, valor, and ingenuity are highly prized among the people of the scattered archipelago. Wars are waged amongst brothers and cousins on land and at sea as the mightiest warriors enjoy great adulation and renown in pursuit of the greatest purpose set forth by Thrakia's pantheon: victory.

"Hear, O Thrakia, the Edicts of Oridion:

First Edict: Let no man flee the battle or disgrace himself in surrender.

...

Fifth Edict: Let none betray the trust of his people or abandon another in need."

— Excerpt from the Edicts of the Gods, the moral instructions given to the First Fathers of Thrakia.

SAGRADA

Once a destination for pilgrimages by people all over the world, the once-holy city closed its towering gates centuries ago, and the impenetrable rings of the city walls have prevented any from so much as peering within Sagrada since that time. It endures in story and a few living memories as a place of healing, where the gods of every religion and the spirits of nature cooperated to bring healing to the ill, the wounded, and the desperate. The world has been inarguably darker since the shutting of those mighty gates.

"None have passed those gates since that day, neither in nor out, though some who venture too close to the walls claim to hear the ceaseless weeping of the Queen in Crimson, who was the one to seal the city off all those years ago."

— *Tall tale from one of the greybeards in the West Umbrian village of Wintry*

---

www.ingramcontent.com/pod-product-compliance
Lightning Source LLC
Chambersburg PA
CBHW051519250626
47156CB00001B/152